T3-BEA-562

MONTGOMERY COLLEGE LIBRARY
ROCKVILLE CAMPUS

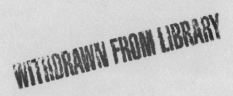
WITHDRAWN FROM LIBRARY

YTMU08J YMAJ MOTOVIMHZAW

THE NOVELS OF
VIRGINIA WOOLF
From Beginning
to End

THE NOVELS OF

VIRGINIA WOOLF

From Beginning to End

By MITCHELL A. LEASKA

The John Jay Press
The City University of New York
1977

Copyright © 1977 Mitchell A. Leaska
Afterword copyright © 1977 John Lehmann

All rights reserved. Published in the United States by The John Jay Press, 444 West 56th Street, New York, New York 10019.

Sections of this book originally appeared in different versions in *Virginia Woolf Quarterly, Virginia Woolf's Lighthouse,* and *Bulletin of The New York Public Library.*

Excerpts from the works of Virginia Woolf and from *Virginia Woolf: A Biography* by Quentin Bell are reprinted by permission of Harcourt Brace Jovanovich, Inc.; copyright, 1920, by George H. Doran and Company; copyright, 1948, 1950, 1953, 1954, 1955, 1959, by Leonard Woolf; copyright, 1922, 1925, 1927, 1931, 1937, 1948, by Harcourt Brace Jovanovich, Inc.; copyright © 1972 by Quentin Bell; copyright © 1976 by Quentin Bell and Angelica Garnett.

FIRST EDITION

Library of Congress Cataloging in Publication Data

Leaska, Mitchell Alexander.
    The novels of Virginia Woolf.

    Bibliography: p.
    Includes index.
    1. Woolf, Virginia Stephen, 1882-1941—Criticism
and interpretation.   I. Title.
PR6045.072Z773   823'.9'12   77-5012
ISBN 0-89444-005-5

Manufactured in the United States of America
Designed by Marilan Lund

Show me some green
And I'll grant you a season
Give me a twig
And I'll weave you a sky

Hand me a *no*
And I'll plant you a reason
Raise me a *yes*
And I'll bury an *I*

Charles Philbrick
1922-1971

To whom this book is dedicated

A Note on the Author

Mitchell A. Leaska was graduated from Brown University and earned his Ph.D. from New York University. He was Lecturer in English at Brooklyn College of The City University of New York and has been teaching at New York University since 1966. He is author of *The Voice of Tragedy* (1963), *Virginia Woolf's Lighthouse: A Study in Critical Method* (1970), and edited *The Pargiters* by Virginia Woolf, the Novel-Essay Portion of *The Years* (1977).

Contents

Preface — xi

Introduction — 3

The Voyage Out, 1915 — 12

Night and Day, 1919 — 39

Jacob's Room, 1922 — 62

Mrs. Dalloway, 1925 — 85

To the Lighthouse, 1927 — 118

The Waves, 1931 — 159

The Years, 1937 — 190

Afterword, by John Lehmann — 237

Bibliography — 243

Index — 257

Acknowledgements

First I should like to thank the Author's Literary Estate, The Hogarth Press Ltd., and Harcourt Brace Jovanovich, Inc. for granting me permission to quote from Virginia Woolf's works. I am indebted to the Henry W. and Albert A. Berg Collection, The New York Public Library, Astor, Lenox and Tilden Foundations for access to the holograph manuscripts of Virginia Woolf's novels and for allowing me to include unpublished portions of them in this book. Thanks are also extended to those critics and publishers from whose works brief quotations appear in this text and are acknowledged in the footnotes.

My personal debts are few in number but difficult of recompense. I am grateful to Quentin Bell not only for his vigorous support of my earlier work, but also for his unwavering encouragement throughout the growth of this book; to John Lehmann for our long hours of conversation from which I always emerged enlightened and further challenged; to Louise DeSalvo for her penetrating responses to each of these chapters in their various drafts; to Harry Segessman for guiding the manuscript through press with ease and efficiency; to Lola L. Szladits, Curator of the Berg Collection, both for guarding with grace the greatest single collection of Virginia Woolf's manuscripts and more especially for giving so generously of her impeccable scholarship; and finally to my former teacher, Louise M. Rosenblatt, whose finest lesson I have, throughout the writing of this book, borne in mind constantly: namely, to consider, in any transaction with a literary text, the role of the reader.

New York University   M.A.L.
January 25, 1977

Preface

The chapters which follow are the extension of an earlier book published here and in England under the title, *Virginia Woolf's Lighthouse: A Study in Critical Method.* The critical method developed in
that book, fully explained in Chapter 2, in its most basic outline,
consists of separating and analyzing the voices—the multiple perspectives—and then re-assembling the text in an effort to reach some
defensible interpretation of the relationships among the novel's principal *personae.* The method was applied to five of the seven novels
discussed in this study with rigorous consistency and felicitous consequences. The two exceptions were *Jacob's Room* and *The Years.*
Because of the experimental nature of *Jacob's Room,* the analytical
apparatus had to be adjusted somewhat to accommodate for the
novel's extraordinarily unique design.

The Years presented a different kind of problem. Virginia Woolf
intended the work originally as a "novel of fact," a "novel-essay";
but she changed her plan after writing approximately one-quarter of
the book. The change of plan—something that had never happened
in any of her other novels, and appears to have passed unnoticed
even by Leonard Woolf—forced Mrs. Woolf into the strange and
difficult position of attempting to fuse fact and fiction within the
same creative universe of *The Years.* The fusion, in so far as she suc-
ceeded in achieving it, created a confusion of artistic aim which resulted, in published form, in a kind of aesthetic confession of a
thinly-veiled autobiographical order. That is to say, the published
version of *The Years* is a curious, but highly polished, amalgamation
of artistry, artifact, and artist's life. Therefore, in order to provide
the reader with as full an account of this novel as possible, it was
necessary to incorporate into the text of the chapter on *The Years*
some discussion of its origin and evolution, as well as to draw upon
biographical sources for critical illumination—a practice which I
have, in the main, restricted to footnotes in the discussions of her
other novels.

These preliminary remarks aside, my interest was and remains
centered on the novels of Virginia Woolf. To have subtitled this book

"From Beginning to End," I am aware, carries with it the implication that I have written a work possibly more comprehensive than it may seem. However, to have included a discussion of the short fiction, the biographies, the essays, and the articles would have been to scatter the reader's attention and perhaps blur the focus; it would have led him down endless by-paths of critical inquiry (however valuable) rather than kept him staunchly on the highroad of Virginia Woolf's novels—the most sustained and the most strenuous of her artistic achievements.

The omission of *Orlando*—that daring and witty adventure into androgyny—could easily, though not quite reasonably, be explained away by reminding the reader that Mrs. Woolf herself called it *"A Biography."* But more to the point, although *Orlando* may be read on several levels for meaning, its scope, direction, and texture are aesthetically so different from the novels themselves, that to have included a discussion of that brilliant but incongruous piece of phantasy between these covers would have been tantamount to committing a violation of literary kinship.

The decision to omit *Between the Acts* was by far the most delicate and difficult to make. For the novel was published on 17 July 1941, a little under four months after Virginia Woolf's suicide. We know now, from new available sources, how seriously ill Mrs. Woolf was in the early months of 1941, when she asked John Lehmann (at the time, Leonard Woolf's partner at The Hogarth Press) to read her typescript of the novel and to cast the deciding vote as to whether it should be published. Before his telegram and subsequent letter of praise reached her, however, Mrs. Woolf had already decided, as she explained in her last note to him, "that I can't publish that novel as it stands—it's too silly and trivial." She said further that she would "revise it and see if I can pull it together" for publication by the autumn of that year. (John Lehmann, *In My Own Time,* Boston: Little Brown and Co., 1969, p. 292.)

There is more in this letter to John Lehmann and a great deal more to the story behind *Between the Acts* than this brief narrative indicates. Anyone who has examined the Woolf papers, however, knows that even when a novel was in the galley- or page-proof stage of production, Mrs. Woolf frequently made very substantial changes in the text. We know also how prone she was seriously to underestimate herself as a writer, just after finishing a novel. So that if she herself considered this beautiful and profound novel "silly and trivial" in March 1941, it would require quite some critical clairvoyance to predict what it might have become had she lived through the spring and summer of 1941 and revised it to conform with her artistic intention.

To adopt anything more than the most speculative and tentative stance in approaching a posthumously published novel upon which its author has *not* passed final approval, seems to me to tamper with certain ethical principles which are at variance with the unwritten codes of critical responsibility. For that reason, I considered it neither my right nor my privilege to comment on *Between The Acts* in this book. From a critic's point of view, *The Novels of Virginia Woolf: From Beginning to End* must properly begin with *The Voyage Out* and ethically end with *The Years*.

THE NOVELS OF VIRGINIA WOOLF

VIRGINIA WOOLF

From Beginning
to End

Introduction

In 1932 the first two books about Virginia Woolf were published: Winifred Holtby's *Virginia Woolf,* London (Wishart) and Floris Delattre's *Le Roman Psychologique de Virginia Woolf,* Paris (J. Vrin). In the next thirty years, a mere dozen substantial studies appeared. Since 1970, however, many gallons of ink, tons of paper, and miles of typewriter ribbon have been put to the service of analyzing, explicating, and describing the work of Mrs. Woolf. The exact reason, or reasons, for this eruption of interest is better left to the more distant vision of future literary historians. Certainly since this volume adds more weight to the already groaning shelf of recent material, some sort of justification seems necessary. And the best reason for having made this study can be found in an essay by Virginia Woolf herself in which she wrote: ". . . one element remains constant in all novels, and that is the human element; they are about people, they excite in us feelings that people excite in us in real life."[1]

Some excellent scholarship has been brought to many of her novels, and much impressive insight has illuminated their pages. But a great deal of the best criticism begins at a point quite *beyond* the fundamental and challenging consideration of human beings and their relationships. One need only glance at the bibliography in any recent book about Virginia Woolf to see titles heavy with such words and phrases as "philosophy," "artistic vision," "impressionism," "expressionism," "concepts of time," "time and duration," "sensibility," "social consciousness," and "mythic elements." Of course these refer to important matters, and inevitably they find their way into any serious study of her work.

But if her novels "are about people"—as of course all novels are—then it is with her people that we must begin: a close and careful concern with what they think and say, how they perceive the world in which they find themselves, how they behave by themselves, how they act and react to others. The people of the novels must be examined first before we move on to the more philosophic matters in

---

1. "Phases of Fiction," *The Bookman,* April, May, and June 1929; reprinted in *Granite and Rainbow,* New York and London: Harcourt Brace Jovanovich, A Harvest Book, 1975, p. 141.

the high chambers of Mrs. Woolf's subtle and complex art. Our concerns, in other words, are basic ones. Why, for example, does Rachel Vinrace dream of bestiality and confinement after being kissed by an older man? What motivates Katherine Hilbery to study mathematics at night in hiding? Why does Jacob Flanders's mother hold up his shoes to Bonamy at one novel's end? What do dogs and trees mean to Septimus Warren Smith? What is behind all Mr. Ramsay's despotic behavior and Mrs. Ramsay's self-sacrifice? What do the square and oblong mean to Rhoda? Why does Eleanor Pargiter want to evade the question of her father's adultery?

Each novel poses one of these questions which may appear embarrassingly naive, but an attempt to answer any one question, one soon discovers, requires taking into account the whole fabric of that single novel. That is to say, Virginia Woolf is a very close and difficult writer, and one does not have easy access to her fictitious people. They are created cumulatively, obliquely; through nuance and innuendo. They are created by a questing, willful intelligence. And to see them in all their depth and complexity very often requires our closest attention to such seemingly negligible details as a character's nervous stammer, the braced posture of fear, the stray but eloquently incongruous thought, the fastidiously-placed slip of the tongue, the novel or poem or play he picks up to read. These and countless other details are not extraneous and are never decorative. They all attach fiercely to some idea of what life and living feel like at some particular time and place to a person of some particular spiritual constitution, and all of these details the reader must catch, sense, and assemble into some implicit pattern of meaning.

Some critics have done this with remarkable skill, but much of what they say is based upon the *product* of their understanding of the novel. They have caught the nuance, identified a relation, felt the emotional curvatures, untangled the skein, and reassembled the threads. Very often, however, instead of telling us *how* they have arrived at a meaning, they have too quickly ascended to those sun-blazed regions where metaphysical speculation has its sovereignty, where in special cases quite new and quite unreadable critical language has had to be invented, where theoretical formulation becomes so solipsistic that no one—if he has had the good fortune to follow the line of argument—would dare to contradict, let alone question, the authority of those pronouncements.

This book is happily not addressed to those experts. Its humbler concern has been to show those who are reading Mrs. Woolf for the first time *how* one arrives at a reasonable meaning of the novels; what the reading *process* involves for the particular reader who (presumptuous as it may seem) is at the moment writing this particular sentence. In no sense, then, should these chapters—each a separate unit in itself—be construed as an attempt to "correct" or even to amplify any of the works which make up the critical canon to date. Rather, they should be seen as simply another path of approach, another effort at entering into and discovering what Mrs. Woolf's imaginary worlds are about by attending primarily to her fictional people—how as human beings of her imagination, they all sum up. So that even when the benign light of understanding refuses to illuminate their relations with one another, we may dimly perceive their relation to the great natural timepiece of life and death.

The reading of any novel is a far more complicated business than many realize, and to read one of Virginia Woolf's novels is almost certainly an art of considerable difficulty. It is an art, which when mastered, yields its enduring rewards in having stretched the imagination, quickened feeling, and heightened perception. For we are engaged in a transaction with an extraordinarily saturated mind and are often faced with that strangely beautiful yet even more strangely unexplainable and unscripted hieroglyphic of feeling which will not reveal itself fully even with the most patient and persistent probing.

No one except that very rare individual of consciously cultivated literary *hauteur* can deny the complexity of the Woolf novels. How many notes blacken the white margins of the book as we, the common readers, sit under the glare of a lamp? How many premature interpretations we make alone as we read, only later to realize that they are reckless brouhaha? How many sudden flashes light up our minds as we turn the pages in the quiet of our rooms? And yet, *paradoxically,* even as we are sounding the lilt of this word or that phrase, catching the image in high flight, linking this character's thought with another's impression, everything for the moment seems thoroughly right, is in perfect harmony or in perfect counterpoint; everything so seamless, stable, in its appropriate place.

But—and here is where the paradox comes in—we are rarely at ease, seldom in that complacent, dropsical mood we so often lapse into when reading, say, a novel by Dickens or Trollope. *But why?* So the question lifts its broad and immensely furrowed brow. Why are we not at ease? Where is the source of that tension which makes the mind's eye nervously flutter and pinches the ganglia of understanding into uncomfortable apprehensiveness? Part of the answer may be that we have been put in possession of some complex feeling which very nearly approaches raw sensation, something nameless and voiceless. We may have been given a vast and potent stimulus which does not live where simplicity and logic have their sanctuary, but rather lodges in those deep rich precincts of the mind where the darkest charters of human survival are kept.

We need only randomly thumb through the five or six volumes of the published essays to discover how long and how persistent was Virginia Woolf's belief that the most fecund reservoir of a writer's imagination was to be found in the unconscious mind. In a 1919 essay, she wrote that **Defoe** "seems to have taken his characters so deeply into his mind that he lived them without exactly knowing how; and, like all unconscious artists, he leaves more gold in his work than his own generation was able to bring to the surface."[2] In 1928, she wrote of Thomas Hardy's novels that "there is always about them a little blur of unconsciousness, that halo of freshness and margin of the unexpected which often produce the most profound sense of satisfaction. It is as if Hardy himself were not quite aware of what he did, as if his consciousness [his mind] held more than he could produce, and he left it for his readers to make out his full meaning and to supplement it from their own experience."[3] In a paper read to The Women's Service League in 1931, we hear her again insisting "that a novelist's chief desire is to be as unconscious as possible. He wants to induce in himself a state of perpetual lethargy. He wants life to proceed with the utmost quiet and regularity. He wants to see the same faces, to read the same books, to do the same things day after day, month after month, while he is writing, so that nothing may

2. *The Common Reader: First Series,* New York: Harcourt, Brace and World, Inc., A Harvest Book, 1955, p. 94; London: The Hogarth Press (Tenth Impression), 1962, p. 127.

3. *The Common Reader: Second Series,* New York: Harcourt, Brace and Co., A Harvest Book, 1956, p. 225; London: The Hogarth Press (Eighth Impression), 1965, p. 248.

break the illusion in which he is living—so that nothing may disturb or disquiet the mysterious nosings about, feelings round, darts, dashes and sudden discoveries of that very shy and illusive spirit, the imagination . . . . I want you to imagine me writing a novel in a state of trance."[4] In a 1933 essay about the novels of Turgenev, she wrote that "Turgenev is among those who hold that the right expression . . . is not to be had by observation, but comes from the depths unconsciously."[5] In a broadcast delivered in April 1937, discussing the writer's use of words, Mrs. Woolf said emphatically that "words, like ourselves, in order to live at their ease, need privacy. Undoubtedly they like us to think and they like us to feel, before we use them; but they also like us to pause; to become unconscious. Our unconsciousness is their privacy; our darkness is their light . . . ."[6] In a paper read to the Workers' Educational Association in May 1940, Mrs. Woolf said: "Unconsciousness, which means presumably that the under-mind works at top speed while the upper-mind drowses, is a state we all know. We all have experience of the work done by unconsciousness in our daily lives. You have had a crowded day, let us suppose, sightseeing in London. Could you say what you had seen and done when you came back? Was it not all a blur, a confusion? But after what seemed a rest, a chance to turn aside and look at something different, the sights and sounds and sayings that had been of most interest to you swam to the surface, apparently of their own accord; and remained in memory; what was unimportant sank into forgetfulness. So it is with the writer. After a hard day's work, trudging round, seeing all he can, feeling all he can, taking in the book of his mind innumerable notes, the writer becomes—if he can—unconscious. In fact, his under-mind works at top speed while his upper-mind drowses. Then, after a pause, the veil lifts; and there is the thing—the thing he wants to write about—simplified, composed. Do we strain Wordsworth's famous saying about emotion recollected in tranquillity when we infer that by tranquillity he meant

4. "Professions for Women," *The Death of the Moth and Other Essays,* New York and London: Harcourt Brace Jovanovich, A Harvest Book, 1974, pp. 239-40.

5. *The Captain's Death Bed and Other Essays,* New York: Harcourt Brace Jovanovich, A Harvest Book, 1950, p. 55.

6. *The Death of the Moth,* pp. 206-207.

that the writer needs to become unconscious before he can create?''[7]

With such evidence of Virginia Woolf's preoccupation with the unconscious, one might be misled into believing that she had simply to get herself into a kind of trance, and a novel—whole, autonomous, composed—would float effortlessly to the surface. That was certainly not the case. Anyone who has examined the holograph and typescript versions of each novel knows immediately that laborious and exhausting revisions followed the first, most essential, creative act of writing out the novel from beginning to end. A careful examination of the first drafts, especially, shows that by saying "the veil lifts; and there is the thing—the thing he wants to write about . . . ," Mrs. Woolf meant that only when the imagination, the "under-mind," was given free rein would the very complex emotional sub-structure of the book emerge; which after considerable rewriting and rearranging would eventually carry the weight of the finished novel—accurately tuned, perfectly accented, fully shaped. But what was always of uppermost importance to her was that those emotions, often incompatible and in feral combat with each other, of the overheated "under-mind" be somehow brought out into the open and reconciled with each other in a single line of vision. So that "the 'book itself'" as she wrote, "is not form which you see, but emotion which you feel."[8]

In a fictitious letter to one Reverend William Cole in 1932, Mrs. Woolf, in a severely critical mood, complained to him: "You write and write, ramblingly, listlessly, like a person who is trying to bring himself to say the thing that will explain to himself what is wrong with himself."[9] The statement has a peculiar angle in it because of its underlying assumption that if one could successfully explain to himself what was wrong with himself, then the writing would be compressed, direct, spirited; he would be able to say "the thing" without diffusion and dispersion, but with fixity, stability—and *unity.* Mrs. Woolf wrote in an essay on E.M. Forster, "if there is one

---

7. *The Moment and Other Essays,* New York and London: Harcourt Brace Jovanovich, A Harvest Book, 1974, p. 134; London: The Hogarth Press (Uniform Edition), 1952, pp. 109-110.

8. *The Moment and Other Essays,* New York and London, p. 160; London, p. 130.

9. *The Death of the Moth,* p. 79.

gift more essential to a novelist than another it is the power of combination—the single vision."[10]

But the essential "power of combination" implies a deep and fundamental separateness that one experiences in life itself. It implies a disequilibrium in one's personal being which compels the artistic sensibility to achieve a balance of those contrasts and cleavages in life which cloud the individual consciousness with a sense that he is out of step with the world, that there is indeed something "wrong with himself" which needs to be explained. For with every rift in the human being, with every division in the mind, considerable tension is inevitably generated, and the width of the division invariably determines the nature and strength of that tension. As Virginia Woolf said more than four decades ago, "few poets and novelists are capable of that high degree of tension which gives us reality."[11]

If, however, we are to interpret her use of the word *reality* to mean gaining access to the undifferentiated matrix of that inner world where opposing forces are vibrant with life; to mean recognizing, without being overwhelmed by, the contents of that sequestered realm of half-light and mystery; to mean effecting a union between those warring forces, and bringing order out of chaos, then we are able to understand what she means by *tension* which, although it has the power to disfigure and impoverish the ordinary human being, is the very food and drink of the creative mind. It is that tension between the outer and inner worlds which the novelist must tolerate to a very large degree in an effort to pacify, or at least moderate, opposing forces by bringing their discordant fragments together in a truce of amity. Apparently the Reverend William Cole was unable to moderate those discordant fragments, thereby causing him to "write and write" without discovering what was "wrong with himself."

But whatever was wrong with the good Reverend, it may be hazarded, is also wrong with us—and was wrong with Virginia Woolf. For despite what may appear an inflated comparison, we *do* indeed all have private inner worlds which, except in very rare instances, "are, to varying degrees, at odds with the external world; and the contents of these inner worlds and the tensions engendered

10. *The Death of the Moth*, p. 166.

11. *The Death of the Moth*, p. 197.

by them have much in common."[12] Novelists in general, and Virginia Woolf in particular, however, have used these tensions to reach resolutions of them through a progression of creative efforts to self-understanding and temporary self-acceptance. We need only look at the sequence of her novels to see the pieces of a very large mosaic which externalized a rich and powerful phantasy life: Rachel Vinrace, motherless, and doomed to a mysterious death when marriage raised its head and lowered Rachel's; Katherine Hilbery trying to connect the world of abstraction and solitude to the world of companionship with independence; Jacob Flanders, fatherless, and flattened by an overpowering mother; Clarissa Dalloway and Septimus Warren Smith, both bent on death, grappling with problems of love and guilt, sanity and insanity.

It is not necessary to abstract and oversimplify the novels to see what Virginia Woolf meant in 1920 when she observed that in Henry James's letters no explicit mention is ever made of his books, and yet the thought of his work is never for a moment absent from his mind: "All refers to his writing; all points in to that preoccupation. But so far as actual statement goes the books might have sprung as silently . . . as daffodils in spring. No notice is taken of their birth. Nor does it matter to him what people say. Their remarks are probably wide of the point, or . . . uttered in unavoidable ignorance of the fact that *each book is a step onward in a gradual process of evolution, the plan of which is known only to the author himself.*"[13] Not until the final volume of Leon Edel's monumental life of Henry James appeared in 1972, could we know with what uncanny accuracy Mrs. Woolf wrote. But the real point is that she was perhaps thinking not so much of Henry James as of the "process of evolution" she herself would be undergoing in the next twenty years of her creative life. If the process of evolution meant growth, then that growth could only occur by the increasing consciousness not only of the disharmonies which blemished her own inner life, but also of their relationship to the outer world. As she tunnelled her way into the deeper defiles of her past, she grew increasingly aware that the untapped ore of her own being had an ingredient common to others: a common struggle of life

12. Anthony Storr, *The Dynamics of Creation,* New York: Atheneum, 1972, pp. 236-37.

13. *The Death of the Moth,* p. 148. Italics are mine.

in the common pursuit of living.

Mrs. Woolf might have been speaking of herself when she said in 1919 that Defoe's work "is founded upon the knowledge of what is most persistent, though not most seductive, in human nature."[14] She might have said, not of Jane Austen, but of herself that "Whatever she writes is finished and turned and set in its relation, not to the parsonage but to the universe."[15]

Beyond her great technical virtuosity and towering command of the language, there is something profoundly compelling about Virginia Woolf. Not only could she descend into those deep caverns where undisturbed memory stores the dissonances and impurities of love and loss, hatred and sorrow, but she could blaze new paths of reconciliation and integration, and bring those oddities of the mind to the surface, making them acceptable for *us* to face and to assimilate with a stern sense of encounter and resolution. She had the poet's gift and the novelist's power to make us believe in her people by investing them with a quality beyond the personal—something primary and common to us all. The authority and authenticity of her writing rest in her ability to surmount the vexations which strafed her own private universe and to connect them to the civilized discontents and frail burdens each of us bears in simply being human.

14. *The Common Reader: First Series,* New York, p. 97; London, p. 131.

15. *The Common Reader: First Series,* New York, p. 140; London, p. 171.

The Voyage Out

The Voyage Out was Virginia Woolf's first novel. It is a strange, difficult, and still unpopular book. Compared with the aesthetically finished works she produced as a mature novelist, it is somewhat uneven, and her technique sometimes obvious. However, compared with the works of a less able writer, this first published volume is an extraordinary display of a bristling mind enunciating a carefully structured, multi-levelled, image of life.

In the novel are all the principal themes which were to appear repeatedly in her later works as well as the many technical singularities and stylistic habits which became increasingly refined with time. It is curious, then, that *The Voyage Out* has received very little critical attention, aside from studies of her complete works. For it provides us with a glimpse of a major creative sensibility grappling with masses of complex and elusive material. It also provides us with a literary specimen which augured the mastery Mrs. Woolf was ultimately to achieve as a novelist.

Among the comments made during the minor critical flutter the novel aroused at the time of its publication in England and later in America, Constance M. Rourke identified the novel's center by writing, more than four decades ago, what is transparently evident today:

It is the fact of human relationships which first and always seems to engage Mrs. Woolf . . . . She is constantly aware that anything like complete understanding between people is rare and transitory, but she always knows that the establishment of such understanding is the perpetual human concern . . . . What she cares about is entirely the train of the impulse to create relationships, the lapses back, the substitutions, the sterile recessions; and she has her clear sense . . . of how they all sum up.[1]

"The impulse to create relationships" was indeed Virginia Woolf's high concern; and it is precisely with *how* she created these relationships in her fiction that our own exploration should begin. And "how they all sum up," to use another of Miss Rourke's

1. *The New Republic,* 5 May 1920.

phrases, places us in closer range to the novel's thematic design and guiding authority.[2]

In its barest outline, the story is about Rachel Vinrace, a twenty-four-year-old girl, who, after sailing on her father's ship (ironically called *Euphrosyne*)[3] with her aunt and uncle, Helen and Ridley Ambrose, departs with them for a vacation on an island off the coast of South America. Helen Ambrose is determined to educate her niece to the larger life of experience and wisdom. Under Helen's tutelage on the island, Rachel meets and becomes attached to Terence Hewet. After an expedition inland with some other tourists, she gets a headache, develops a fever, becomes delirious, intermittently comatose, and finally dies. Life goes on. The story ends.

This outline is merely the story; it is not the plot as E.M. Forster defines it,[4] because there is no apparent element of cause and effect, without which the story is not only illogical but also meaningless. And while life may be illogical, a novel may not. To disregard the principle of causality is to disregard, among other things, why Helen assumes the responsibility for her niece's education, what in Rachel and Terence generates their mutual attraction, or why Rachel's dying is the proper conclusion of the book. To ignore these questions is surely to limit and to diminish one's experience of all that the novel offers. For if we begin to trace the progress of each principal character's thoughts and utterances, the deeper and stronger heartbeats of human beings interacting with one another begin to emerge, and with them, the shape and meaning of the novel.

We meet Helen Ambrose for the first time with her husband on their way to the ship. "It was only by scorning all she met that she kept herself from tears . . ." (9;2)[5]. Virginia Woolf has drawn a quick

2. The method by which Mrs. Woolf creates her characters cumulatively while simultaneously defining their relationships is demonstrated in Mitchell A. Leaska, *Virginia Woolf's Lighthouse: A Study in Critical Method,* London: The Hogarth Press and New York: Columbia University Press, 1970, Chs. III and IV.

3. Joy, one of the three Graces in classical mythology.

4. *Aspects of the Novel,* New York: Harcourt Brace and Co., A Harvest Book, 1927, p. 86.

5. The unitalicized page number in parentheses following each quotation refers to the first American paperback edition published by Harcourt, Brace and World, 1969; the italicized number refers to The Hogarth Press edition (Eighth Impression), 1965.

sharp line to begin a complex portrait; her making Mrs. Ambrose need to scorn people to hold her emotions in check tells us a good deal about Helen's private chemistry. For that detail can be read as our first clue to a personality characterized by a heavily veiled and highly controlled aggressiveness.

On board ship, Mrs. Ambrose observes Rachel critically:

Her face was weak rather than decided, saved from insipidity by the large enquiring eyes; denied beauty . . . by the lack of colour and definite outline. Moreover, a hesitation in speaking, or rather a tendency to use the wrong words, made her seem more than normally incompetent for her years (20; *14-15*).

Having depreciated her hostess, Helen concludes that "Women of her own age usually boring her, she supposed that girls would be worse . . . that she would be vacillating, emotional . . ." (20;*15*). And further, "Rachel was an unlicked girl, no doubt prolific of confidences, the very first of which would be: 'You see, I don't get on with my father'" (23;*18*). Chapter I ends with this bold though partial sketch of Helen Ambrose.

The next chapter begins with Helen's reflections on Rachel's father, Willoughby Vinrace: "She suspected him of nameless atrocities with regard to his daughter, as indeed she always suspected him of bullying his wife" (24;*20*). As we have learned from her observations of Rachel, we recognize Helen's unfortunate inability to see anyone in his more redeeming aspects; and this negativity signals the presence of at least two other ingredients in her make-up which will later manifest themselves. First, when she is not in command, as she cannot be on Willoughby's ship, the constraint she feels takes the shape of resentment: "Rachel seemed to get on very well with her father—much better, Helen thought, than she ought to—" (33;*30*). Second, when her will to power is frustrated, she fancies the agent of her frustration as being victimized: ". . . she considered Rachel aesthetically; lying unprotected she looked somehow like a victim dropped from the claws of a bird, but considered as a young woman of twenty-four, the sight gave rise to reflections" (37;*35-36*). Those "reflections" lead Helen logically to the notion that this unprotected "victim" will need her protection and her guidance. She will take charge of Rachel and make her into someone new—and someone *dependent* upon her.

When the Dalloways appear and Rachel befriends Clarissa, Helen "seeing Rachel arm-in-arm with a comparative stranger, looking excited, was amused, but at the same time slightly irritated" (61;*66*). Later, Helen, sensing Rachel's attraction to Dalloway, studies her niece after the Dalloways have disembarked:

Rachel's obvious langour and listlessness made her an easy prey, and indeed Helen had devised a kind of trap. That something had happened she now felt pretty certain; moreover, she had come to think that they had been strangers long enough; she wished to know what the girl was like, partly of course *because Rachel showed no disposition to be known* (79;*88*).[6]

In these few lines, we recognize a rather militant energy about to gauge its strength; for Helen must now assert herself if she is to succeed in separating Rachel from her father in order to manage her niece's life: "'Tell me what happened,' said Helen. She had to keep her lips from twitching as she listened to Rachel's story" (80;*89*). But the twitching lips as she hears of Rachel's brief encounter bespeak a more profound condition, unassimilated and unresolved; they are a dramatization of the present state of her marriage, of her sense of loneliness, of her need to nourish herself through the experiences of others.

The portrait begins to enlarge as we see Helen more sympathetically when she decides that "she would very much like to show her niece . . . how to live, or as she put it, how to be a reasonable person" (83;*94*). But to one so vigorously gubernatorial, Helen's decision becomes synonymous with determination: she will have Rachel to herself "even if she had to promise a complete course of instruction in the feminine graces." Her determination, however, is frosted with a curious blend of triumph and mockery, for "She could not help laughing at the notion of it—Rachel a Tory hostess!—and marvelling as she left him [Willoughby] at the astonishing ignorance of a father" (86;*98*).

Part of Mrs. Woolf's success in creating Helen Ambrose is in the ironic tension produced by leaving the character wholly unaware of her own motives. Having established herself as Rachel's mentor, Helen writes in a letter:

6. In any of the quoted matter here and throughout the chapter, unless otherwise specified, the italics are mine.

It's an odd fate that has put me in charge of a girl . . . considering that I have never got on well with women . . . . However, I must retract some of the things that I said against them. If they were properly educated I don't see why they shouldn't be much the same as men—as satisfactory I mean . . . (96;*109-110*).

As readers, we know that the changes occurring in Rachel are largely the result of Helen's doing, and yet "Mrs. Ambrose would have been the first to disclaim any influence, or indeed any belief that to influence was within her power" (124;*143*). It is precisely because of this blind spot that Mrs. Ambrose can manipulate her charge so blamelessly and so effortlessly. Her relationship to Rachel is, as she says, "'like having a puppy in the house . . .'" (145;*169*).

Her association with St. John Hirst brings into clearer relief two other manifestations symptomatic of her forcefulness. The first is her need to squelch open expressions of sentimentality, because they threaten her into compliance, a feeling which to her is tantamount to imprisonment. The second is the need to see herself in the elevated position of one who pities the downtrodden and gives advice from managerial altitudes. For example, Hirst, having just confessed some personal things about himself to Helen, ends by praising her "exceptionally nice nature." However,

If Hirst had looked at her . . . he would have seen Helen blush, partly with pleasure, partly with the impulse of affection towards the young man who had seemed, and would seem again, so ugly and so limited. She pitied him, for she suspected that he suffered, and she was interested in him, for many of the things he said seemed to her true; she admired the morality of youth, and yet she felt imprisoned (206;*244*).

Minutes later, Hirst asks Helen to make a decision for him that will determine his future career:

"Leave Cambridge and go to the Bar," she said. He pressed her for reasons. "I think you'd enjoy London more," she said. It did not seem a very subtle reason, but she appeared to think it sufficient. She looked at him against the background of flowering magnolia. There was something curious in the sight. Perhaps it was that the heavy wax-like flowers were so smooth and inarticulate, and his face . . . was so worried and garrulous (208-209;*246-47*).

Her offhand decision about something so important, together with the unflattering juxtaposition of magnolia blossom and Hirst's distorted face, have an implicit eloquence. Having won his confidence and affection, Helen can be unthinking about him, even careless. Put another way: when her influence over him is secure, her interest in him dwindles.

The relationship which develops between Helen and her niece as Rachel begins to blossom is also significant. It calls to mind Anna Freud's account of the governess who invested great effort in getting her pupil to succeed, and then rejected him when he did. "It [success] made the pupil an independent being who could no longer be identified with her own life. The hostile feelings toward him arose from envy; she could not help grudging him the success which she herself had never attained."[7] The incident at the dance suggests something like that of the governess's reaction: Helen looks at Rachel and sees that she was

flushed and looked very happy, and Helen was struck by the fact that in this mood she was certainly more attractive than the generality of young women. She had never noticed it so clearly before.

"Enjoying yourself?" she asked. . . .

"Miss Vinrace . . . has just made a confession; she'd no idea that dances could be so delightful."

"Yes!" Rachel exclaimed. "I've changed my view of life completely!"

"You don't say so!" Helen mocked. They passed on (163;*191*).

The emotional links being forged between Rachel and Hewet have a deeper effect on Helen:

Helen and Rachel had become very silent. Having detected . . . a secret, and judging that Rachel meant to keep it from her, Mrs. Ambrose respected it carefully, but from that cause, though unintentionally, a curious atmosphere of reserve grew up between them. . . . Always calm and unemotional in her judgments, Mrs. Ambrose was now inclined to be pessimistic. She was not severe upon individuals so much as incredulous of the kindness of destiny, fate, what happens in the long run, and apt to insist that this was generally adverse to people in proportion as they deserved well. Even this theory she was ready to discard in favor of one which made chaos triumphant, things happening for no reason at all, and every one groping about in illusion and ignorance. With *a certain pleasure* she developed these views to her niece. . . . How did she know that at this very moment both her children were not lying dead, crushed by motor omnibuses? (221;*269*)

7. *Psychoanalysis for Teachers and Parents,* trans. Barbara Low, Boston: Beacon Press, 1935, pp. 108-109.

How fully Virginia Woolf understands Helen Ambrose, especially the consequences of that sense of loss which thwarts her drive to power: her desperate, unconscious effort to poison the atmosphere with irrationality and gloom and death; her inclination to feel victimized and defeated, and hopelessly to want to massacre all that is, or could be, happy and flourishing. Whatever satisfaction in life or in love Helen Ambrose may have been denied must also be denied to others, particularly to Rachel whose increasing independence deprives Helen of her most cherished substitute for real satisfaction: transitory fulfillment through others.

As Rachel strives to grow, Helen increasingly withdraws into herself. And Mrs. Woolf adds her final strokes to the portrait of an incompatibly riven personality. On the expedition,

> Mrs. Ambrose looked and listened obediently enough, but inwardly she was prey to an uneasy mood not readily to be ascribed to any one cause. . . . She did not like to feel herself the victim of unclassified emotions (277;*340*).

That now Mrs. Ambrose is "prey" and "victim" is the surest index of the inner havoc which causes one to fear one's own emotions, particularly "unclassified emotions"; for these are largely undefined, and how they will express themselves is largely unpredictable. Helen is therefore at the mercy of unknown emotions, and her victimization is difficult for her to tolerate. Threatened, she makes a deliberate effort to rechannel her attention: "Her mind . . . *occupied* itself with anxieties for Ridley, for her children, for far-off things, such as old age and poverty and death" (278;*340*). Some of these may appear morbid subjects with which to "occupy" the mind, but to Helen they are at least identifiable and consequently less perilous than feelings which are undefined.

Her phantasies are also worth noticing, because they contain a peculiar mixture of violence and protectiveness. As she ponders the "delicate flesh of men and women," her mental excursion leads her to "A falling branch, a foot that slips, and the earth has crushed them or the water drowned them. Thus thinking, she kept her eyes anxiously fixed upon the lovers, as if by doing so she could protect them from their fate" (286;*349-50*). The counterpoise of the lovers to human frailty and death is particularly rich in implication; Rachel, Terence, and their attachment to one another have put Helen in this lugubrious state of imagining disasters, yet it is they whom she wants to protect. What could be more expressive of one who sees herself as unvanquishable and omnipotent?

But the price exacted for Helen's self-idealization is very dear, because the image's sustenance comes not from within, but from without. Mrs. Ambrose is paradoxically at Rachel's mercy, and her *élan vital* collapses without the external nourishment Rachel can provide by remaining attached to her alone. For as Mrs. Woolf tells us: "Rachel had passed beyond her guardianship. A voice might reach her [Rachel's] ears, but never again would it carry as far as it had . . . she felt strangely old and depressed" (287;*351*). If this isolation is what living felt like to Helen, we begin to see that her estranged figure too might be a very large part of Hewet's unwritten book about "the things people don't say."

St. John Hirst, ugly and limited, is a checkerboard of militance and compliance. That he manages somehow to place the blame on others for his own limitations suggests that his use of blame prevents him from punishing himself for those very deficiencies which are the source of his pain. But more important, it says something about the adjustments he has made in a world which to him is populated by unconditionally hostile human beings. Living in such an *ambience* of menace quite naturally makes it necessary for him always to exert control over other people, for fear that (as he imagines) they will tear him to shreds; and the means of control most amenable to Hirst is to make others feel under obligation to him.

When Hirst is faced with what he recognizes to be real strength, however, he feels—in so far as he is able—an attraction. because in strength there is the possibility of protection. He looks at Helen and is "attracted to her by the sound of her laugh. She was laughing at Miss Allan . . . . He liked the look of her immensely . . . her largeness and simplicity, which made her stand out from the rest like a great stone woman, and he passed on in a gentler mood" (135;*157*).

At the dance, after Rachel has suffered one of Hirst's verbal attacks, Hewet tries to comfort her by saying that there is " 'a great deal more in him than's ever been got at. He wants some one to laugh at him. . .' " (157;*184*). In Hewet's simple utterance, we discover the primary mechanism by which Hirst's contempt for himself is reversed and projected onto someone else. His motivation is simple: if people laugh at him, then he has legitimate cause to abuse them in return. Moreover he has satisfied the need for punishment which he feels he deserves for being inadequate; at the same time, it is punishment far less painful than that which he would inflict upon himself. For, any abuse coming from someone else and interpreted as punishment, has the curious energy to transform itself into a kind of expiation, which in Hirst's case, frees him to make further assaults on others in the name of self-defense. His behavior is therefore a manifestation of his attempt to resolve the turmoil generated by his limitations, and simultaneously to satisfy the implacable inner demands of self-protective power.

His response to Helen Ambrose is particularly illuminating. "Directly Helen was left alone for a minute she was joined by St. John Hirst, who had been watching for an opportunity"(160;*187*). He manages to separate her from the crowd and begins to register his disgust: " 'The whole thing makes me sick . . . Consider the minds of those people—their feelings' " (160;*188*); he then articulates his own endowments, in obvious self-defense: " 'And of course I am—immensely clever,' said Hirst. 'I'm infinitely cleverer than Hewet. It's quite possible . . . that I'm going to be one of the people who really matter . . . though one can't expect one's family to see it,' he added bitterly" (161;*188-89*). From that immodest preamble, Hirst launches into an elaborately detailed history of his life, speaking of "matters which are generally only alluded to between men and women when doctors are present, or in the shadow of death" (162;*190*). He concludes by saying " 'So there's no reason whatever for all this mystery!' " (163;*191*) What "this mystery" is requires little imagination, when later Hirst says to Hewet, " 'What I abhor most of all . . . is the female breast. Imagine being Venning and having to get into bed with Susan!' " (184;*216*) His exchange with Helen shows clearly that he sees in her a spiritual mother, a protectress. Further, by divulging facts of his life which required a hushed voice, he has made a claim on Helen, a claim which, stripped of its emotional gauze, says: "I have confessed things to you that are very personal. Because you have listened, you are now under obligation to me never to betray my confidence or to do anything to harm me." Through this kind of subtle manoeuvre, Hirst can feel his indignation as something right, and he can righteously wield his intellectual prowess like a cudgel: " 'If you're clever it's always taken for granted that you're completely without sympathy, understanding, affection—all the things that really matter. Oh, you Christians! You're the most conceited, patronising, hypocritical set of old humbugs in the kingdom!' " (202;*239*)

But when such pugnacity comes from deep feelings of inferiority, the toll demanded is impoverishing, because so much else in him is usurped by the energy required to feed his pervasive envy and smoldering bitterness. As he eloquently says to Helen: " 'Of course I am, disgustingly bitter, and it's a beastly thing to be. But the worst of me is that I'm so envious. I envy every one. I can't endure people who do things better than I do—perfectly absurd things too—waiters balancing piles of plates—even Arthur, because Susan's in love with him. I want people to like me, and they don't' " (206;*243*).

Another characterizing trait in Hirst is his tendency to blur, even confuse, causal connections between the consequence of his behavior and its relation to his personal difficulties. "He was never happy," for example.

He saw too clearly the little vices and deceits and flaws of life, and seeing them, it seemed to him honest to take notice of them. That was the reason, no doubt, why people generally disliked him, and complained that he was heartless and bitter. Certainly they never told him the things he wanted to be told, that he was nice and kind, and that they liked him. But it was true that half the sharp things he said about them were said because he was unhappy or hurt himself (311;*381*).

What on the surface appears to have a cause-and-effect relationship, of course, does not: the connections linking his original unhappiness, his derogatory habit, the aversion it arouses, the flattery he is consequently denied, the unhappiness it reinforces—all are at best logically circular, self-perpetuating, and inevitably self-intensifying. We as readers may see how obvious these connections are, but Hirst himself is blind to them. Recognizing Hirst's muddled thinking, we should not be surprised that "His feelings about Terence and Rachel were so complicated that he had never yet been able to bring himself to say that he was glad that they were going to be married" (312;*381*). Nor is it a surprise during Rachel's illness to find him in such a state of helplessness and isolation that something as senseless and unrelated as "The appearance of one light after another in the town" beneath them was capable of producing "in Hirst a repetition of his terrible and disgusting desire to break down and sob" (351;*429*).

That he should consider venting his feelings as something "terrible and disgusting" aligns Hirst closely with Helen who feels victimized by "unclassified emotions." To both the principle of mastery is prominent, and losing control of the expression of feeling is as terrifying to one as the inability to compartmentalize an emotion is threatening to the other. Finally, Hirst's need to be the sacrificial master-mind in every public situation aligns him, in a pseudo-complementary way, to the compliant, affection-giving Hewet, regardless of whatever else their friendship may have yielded.

And what are we to say about Terence Hewet, this apparently prosperous young man who for some reason falls so quickly in love with Rachel? Who, despite all appearances of his appeasing and conciliatory nature, thinks that

relations between different people were so unsatisfactory, so fragmentary, so hazardous, and words so dangerous that the instinct to sympathise with another human being was an instinct to be examined carefully and probably crushed (194;*229*)?

Beneath Hewet's extremely deceptive surface simplicity there is hazard and danger. His relationship to women and how it meshes with the general pattern of his life are ill-defined, for we are told that

Although they [Hewet and Hirst] had known each other for three years Hirst had never yet heard the true story of Hewet's loves. In general conversation it was taken for granted that there were many, but in private the subject was allowed to lapse. The fact that he had money enough to do no work, and that he had left Cambridge after two terms owing to a difference with the authorities, and had then travelled and drifted, made his life strange in many points where his friends' lives were much of a piece (108;*124*).

As singularly general as this passage may read, several striking conclusions may be gleaned from it. First, Hewet's "loves" are probably questionable, precisely because he wishes publicly to give the impression that there were many; and if there were "many," one wonders what compulsion drove him to seek out so much unassorted and transitory affection. Moreover, Hewet's feeling capable of loving so many people implies a need to suppress such things as striving for ambitious goals or expressing any assertiveness, for ambition and assertion tend to hamper unconditional or affectionate acquiescence. And it is in this aimless suppression that we understand Hewet's difficulty with authority, his inhibition to work toward a worthwhile goal, his directionless drifting. Stated differently, he is deficient in maturity; by which is meant, he lacks the ability to control the direction of his life and to assume full responsibility for the choices he makes.

There is something of the awkward boy in him, a kind of uncomfortable diffidence, which comes into sharper focus as his portrait enlarges. On the picnic when he and Rachel accidentally discover two of his guests in love play, "Hewet felt uncomfortably shy" (140;*163*); a moment later, after Rachel expresses her sadness for the newly-engaged couple, he replies: " 'Just because they're in love,' . . . 'Yes,' he added after a moment's consideration, 'there's something horribly pathetic about it, I agree' " (141;*164*).

As his feeling for Rachel grows, numerous contradictions emerge and suggest a deep-seated ambivalence within him. For example, when Hirst has just monopolized Rachel's attention and Hewet is exasperated, "He rose, took his hat and dashed out of doors" (239;*292*); and "Everything he saw was distasteful to him" (240;*293*). Thinking that Hirst has taken Rachel from him, Hewet becomes violently jealous, but interestingly does absolutely nothing to prevent it.

To trace Hewet's thoughts here is important because we see played out before us the way in which so compliant an individual deals with a situation requiring strong and spontaneous assertion—something alien to his *conscious* attitudes. First he wonders how a union between Rachel and Hirst would affect him, and he asks, " '. . .am I in love with her?' " Yes, he was in love with her, but he "checked himself by asking whether he wanted to marry her? That was the real problem . . . and it was necessary that he should make up his mind. He instantly decided that he did not want to marry any one." He then has two unpleasant phantasies of married life, "and even more so was the third picture, of husband and wife and friend. . . ." After conjuring up several other domestic scenes, he concludes that married people were always "walled up in a warm firelit room.

When, on the other hand, he began to think of unmarried people, he saw them active in an unlimited world" (241;*294-95*).

Avoidance then is the way Hewet copes with life. He wants to be intimate, which on his terms means that he wants also to be free and active to seek out limitless affection from all directions and in all quantities. This is the way of life for one who is uncertain of himself. It is no curiosity, then, that he spends his time drifting about, accumulating "loves," however short-lived, whether real or imaginary. The most salient feature of his existence is that it makes very few lasting demands on him, chief of which is the demand to make the mature effort to keep alive for a lifetime the trust and good will of a wife.

Unsure of himself and unsure of Rachel, the affectionate, unassertive Hewet feels threatened with desertion; and the subjective logic of his inner life dictates that he must discover some way to win Rachel, thereby relieving himself of the fear of any future rejection. Thus on the expedition, he braces himself for the conquest; he "saw that the time had come as it was fated to come, but although he realized this he was completely calm and master of himself" (269;*330*). The love scene follows; and later in their walk out of the woods, he loses his way:

> At first Terence was certain of his way, but as they walked he became doubtful. They had to stop to consider, and then to return and start once more, for although he was certain of the direction of the river he was not certain of striking the point where they had left the others. Rachel followed him, stopping where he stopped, turning where he turned, ignorant of the way, ignorant why he stopped or why he turned (272;*333*).

Whether or not we interpret this passage symbolically as Hewet's losing his *emotional direction* after the impact of committing himself to Rachel, the phrasing attests unequivocally that Rachel, in declaring her love for him, has yielded to his leadership; and in that sense, both literally and poetically, she is being fatefully led by a lost leader.[8]

In his meeting with her on the following day, Hewet's "confession" leads us directly to the major premise of his internal world as

---

8. We have to assume that during this scene, Hewet asks Rachel to marry him because it is only mentioned later as a *fait accompli.*

well as to his most efficacious means of emotional insurance:

"Do you love me?" Terence asked . . . . She murmured inarticulately, ending, "And you?"

"Yes, yes," he replied; but there were so many things to be said . . . . It was difficult, frightening even, oddly embarrassing. . . .

"Now I'm going to begin at the beginning," he said resolutely. "I'm going to tell you what I ought to have told you before. In the first place, I've never been in love with other women, but I've had other women. Then I've great faults. I'm very lazy, I'm moody—" He resisted, in spite of her exclamation, "You've got to know the worst of me. I'm lustful, I'm overcome by a sense of futility—incompetence. I ought never to have asked you to marry me, I expect . . . . All that's been bad in me, the things I've put up with—the second best—" (280-81;*343-44*).

A field of contrasting emotional forces is being established, and on it we catch the ray of an ill-fated star. For Hewet is laboring under some complex need to give Rachel an unsolicited account of his dark side. That by itself is not uncommon, but the peculiar tone of his speech has the quality of rehearsed self-deprecation, as though his "confession" carries with it for Rachel, half privilege, the other half penalty. Beneath its benign manifest content, are the malignant inaudible claims: "If you accept me now, flawed as I am, remember that I have warned you. Whatever freedoms I take or future claims I make, I am entitled to; and you will never desert me."

When he reads the conclusion of his novel about an unhappily married man who returns out of duty to his negligent wife, we come upon the most telling statement of how Hewet sees the relationship between a man and a woman:

"They were different. Perhaps in the far future, when generations of men had struggled and failed as he must now struggle and fail, woman would be, indeed, what she now made a pretence of being—the friend and companion—not the enemy and parasite of man" (297;*364*).

It is only when we see what Rachel might have meant to Hewet that we will perhaps understand why over her deathbed he says, " 'No two people have ever been so happy as we have been. No one has ever loved as we have loved' " (343;*431*).[9]

---

9. The first of these two sentences is almost identical to the one which concluded Mrs. Woolf's suicide note to her husband. See Leonard Woolf, *The Journey Not the Arrival Matters,* New York: Harcourt, Brace and World, 1969, p. 94.

We meet Rachel for the first time on her father's ship "waiting for her uncle and aunt nervously . . . . She looked forward to seeing them as civilised people generally look forward to the first sight of civilised people, as though they were of the nature of approaching physical discomfort . . . . She was already unnaturally braced to receive them" (14;*7*). Her waiting "nervously," her sense of people connected with "physical discomfort," her being "unnaturally braced"—inconspicuous though they may seem—are important clues to some profound disturbance here. Rachel is someone who finds human associations an enormous strain and who is disproportionately anxious at the prospect of acting as hostess.

Mrs. Woolf wastes no time in giving us additional details: Rachel is an only child; her mother died when she was eleven; she was raised by two spinster aunts whose feelings for the girl are vapid at best: " 'But you know I care for you . . . because you're your mother's daughter, if for no other reason, and there *are* plenty of other reasons. . .' " (36;*34*).[10] These details begin to explain why Rachel finds people a fearful source of tension; and implied in her fear is the vital need to keep an emotional distance between herself and others, as well as to numb to a large extent her own feelings: "To feel anything strongly was to create an abyss between oneself and others who feel strongly perhaps but differently. It was far better to play the piano and forget all the rest" (36;*35-36*). Thus music becomes one of the safeguards and comforts in her solitary world, but she has another more reliable means of protecting herself from people; and that is, *through phantasy,* to abstract them:

Let these odd men and women . . . be symbols—featureless, but dignified, symbols of age, of youth, of motherhood, of learning, and beautiful often as people upon the stage are beautiful (37;*35*).

Her symbolic transformation of others not only keeps human beings at a distance, but also to a degree denies them their very existence. When we consider the way these details of her life constellate, we are not surprised at her spontaneous reply to Clarissa Dalloway's inquiry about the prospect of marriage, that " 'No. I shall never marry'. . .'" (60;*64*).

---

10. The italics are Virginia Woolf's.

One telling incident occurs early in the book when Richard Dallo-way, in a moment of temptation, suddenly embraces and kisses Rachel. She falls back in her chair "with tremendous beats of the heart, each of which sent black waves across her eyes," (76;*84*) with chilled and trembling body and a tumult of emotion amounting to physical pain. That the kiss of an older man should produce such an excessive and visceral reaction raises some questions as to its cause: Is it Virtue in distress? Has she never been kissed before? Has her detachment been violated? Has sensuality a forbidden meaning to her?

Through dramatic sequencing, Mrs. Woolf gives a vivid hint as to the cause of the reaction in the dream Rachel has that very night:

. . . she was walking down a long tunnel, which grew so narrow by degrees that she could touch the damp bricks on either side. At length the tunnel opened and became a vault; she found herself trapped in it, bricks meeting her wherever she turned, alone with a little deformed man who squatted on the floor gibbering, with long nails. His face was pitted and like the face of an animal. The wall behind him oozed with damp, which collected into drops and slid down. Still and cold as death she lay, not daring to move. . . .

Mrs. Woolf is describing a sequential dream of terror, confinement, frustration, ugliness, and bestiality; and we only see how closely its overt content is linked with sexuality when we follow Rachel's phantasy immediately after waking:

She felt herself pursued . . . . A voice moaned for her; eyes desired her. All night long barbarian men harrassed the ship; they came scuffling down the passages, and stopped to snuffle at her door (77;*86*).

The dream and the phantasy are quoted in full, first, because a paraphrase would destroy the almost identical linguistic correspon-dence the dream has to parts of Rachel's delirium in the final chapters of the novel when her death is being both foreshadowed and symbolically enacted; and second, because the animal face in the dream and the barbarian men in the phantasy call to mind the bestial countenances of the bewitched travellers in Milton's *Comus,* which Hewet is reading to Rachel at the onset of her illness (Ch. XXV). The significance of these references to the novel's meaning will be developed later. But first, a more definite picture of the pressures and currents within Rachel's globe of consciousness is needed.

Out of her cautiously hemmed-in life emerges one of Rachel's most crucial needs—the need for privacy. But it is a very peculiar kind of privacy overlaid with contradictory elements of self-sufficiency, self-protection, and defiance. Her room at the Ambrose villa, for instance, becomes a place where "she could play, read, think, defy the world, a fortress as well as a sanctuary"; it was "an enchanted place, where the poets sang and things fell into their right proportions" (123;*142*). The sanctuary must also serve as fortress, because people exert so much strain on her. At the dance, for example, she has an unpleasant encounter with Hirst. After he leaves, Rachel looks around, feeling herself "surrounded by the faces of strangers all hostile to her, with hooked noses and sneering indifferent eyes." Again she feels endangered, and the consequence of that feeling is a phantasy as assertive as it is extravagant:

She would be a Persian princess far from civilisation, riding her horse upon the mountains alone, and making her women sing to her in the evening, far from all this, from the strife and men and women—(155;*181*).

Her mental manoeuvre is another means by which Rachel struggles with situations which produce so much anxiety; it is figuratively her instrument of self-preservation.

Closely connected with Rachel's need for privacy is the necessity to avoid attachments which put her imagined freedom in imaginary jeopardy. Hewet's determination to know Rachel, for example, arouses in her an irritation caused by a fear of confinement:

Why did he make these demands on her? Why did he sit so near and keep his eye on her? No, she would not consent to be pinned down by any second person in the whole world . . . . "I like walking alone, and knowing I don't matter a damn to anybody . . . I like the freedom of it. . . (215).[11]

In this final utterance, knowing that it will hurt Hewet to hear it, Rachel flings her inaccessibility at him. In a masterful stroke, Mrs. Woolf further explores their feelings to expose another essential tendency in Rachel which might otherwise remain obscure. Rachel asks Hewet about his novel, and he answers in a way which makes her think that he has forgotten her actual self entirely; and

11. The Hogarth Press text differs from the American edition cited. But notice: ". . . she would not . . . be pinned down by any *second* person. . . ." For who is the *first* person pinning her down? Her father? Helen Ambrose?

She was instantly depressed. As he talked of writing he had become suddenly impersonal. He might never care for any one; all that desire to know her and get at her, which she had felt pressing on her almost painfully, had completely vanished (216).[12]

It is apparent not only that she is projecting onto Hewet her own earlier feeling of estrangement, but also that she is enunciating her need to remain independent while simultaneously wishing to hold his interest and affection. Here we find in Rachel that strange compound of detachment and subtly concealed superiority—freighted with fear. For what she is essentially saying is: "Give me affection, but please understand how difficult it is for me to return it. Continue your interest in me, but don't interfere. My freedom must remain inviolate."

So urgent is the need to maintain the security of her isolation, that her very feeling-self is choked off almost to numbness. She cannot, in fact, even *name* her emotion for Hewet; that too is denied its existence:

What had happened to her she did not know. Her mind was very much in the condition of the racing water to which Helen compared it. She wanted to see Terence; she was perpetually wishing to see him when he was not there; it was an agony to miss seeing him, but she never asked herself what this force driving through her life arose from (222;*271*).

Later, she is still unable to define her feeling:

Although these moods were directly or indirectly caused by the presence of Terence or the thought of him, she never said to herself that she was in love with him, or considered what was to happen if she continued to feel such things . . . (223;*272*).

To attribute her blindness to inexperience would be to misread one of the most important characteristics of her buried life. Not to recognize her *inability* to experience the strong and binding emotion of love would be to misunderstand the devastation ultimately wrought when Rachel submits to Hewet and permits him to trespass the boundaries of her lonely freedom with his declaration of love and proposal of marriage.

Reference here is being made to the second scene between Rachel and Hewet on the expedition up the Amazon. After the party has

---

12. Here too the British text differs slightly from the American.

been put ashore, the couple somehow get separated from the rest, and Rachel becomes conscious of a feeling which she supposes is happiness. The passage is the strangest—and has received the least comment—of any in Virginia Woolf's fiction:

Voices crying behind them never reached through the waters in which they were now sunk. The repetition of Hewet's name in short, dissevered syllables was to them the crack of a dry branch or the laughter of a bird. The grasses and breezes sounding and murmuring all round them, they never noticed that the swishing of the grasses grew louder and louder, and did not cease with the lapse of the breeze. A hand dropped abrupt as iron on Rachel's shoulder; it might have been a bolt from heaven. She fell beneath it, and the grass whipped across her eyes and filled her mouth and ears. Through the waving stems she saw a figure, large and shapeless against the sky. Helen was upon her. Rolled this way and that, now seeing only forests of green, and now the high blue heaven, she was speechless and almost without sense. At last she lay still, all the grasses shaken round her and before her by her panting. Over her loomed two great heads, the head of a man and a woman, of Terence and Helen.

Both were flushed, both laughing, and the lips were moving; they came together and kissed in the air above her. Broken fragments of speech came down to her on the ground. She thought she heard them speak of love and then of marriage. Raising herself and sitting up, she too realised Helen's soft body, the strong and hospitable arms, and happiness swelling and breaking in one vast wave. When this fell away, and the grasses once more lay low and the sky became horizontal, and the earth rolled out flat on each side, and the trees stood upright, she was the first to perceive a little row of human figures standing patiently in the distance. For the moment she could not remember who they were (283-84;*346-47*).

This remarkable passage can be read both literally and metaphorically. In the literal sense, it has the quality of discontinuity common to hallucination; it also makes Helen's rough physical handling of Rachel both bizarre and monstrous. Metaphorically, the passage is a highly elliptical transcription of Rachel's *actual or imagined* initiation into womanhood. But whichever the case may be, one characteristic of the passage remains salient: the images suggest erotic turbulence, a swirling mixture of sensuality and violence.

If, metaphorically, the events described actually occurred, Rachel's phantasies are significant because Helen's image is evoked and made to participate; and this means that in phantasy, Helen—the more "qualified" woman—is relegated the role which situationally belongs to Rachel. If the passage is a description filtered purely through Rachel's altered consciousness, the situation appears uncertain and ominous; that Helen's kissing Hewet and talking of love and marriage make Rachel a passive observer rather than an active participant; and that only by sheer effort does Rachel become part of this triangle in which Helen's body alone is experienced (no mention is made of Hewet's body).[13] In this context, Rachel's earlier exclamation, " '. . . men are brutes! I hate men!' " (82;*92*) assumes another dimension. We understand more readily why she "seemed to be able to cut herself adrift from him [Hewet] and to pass away to unknown places where she had no need of him" (302;*370*).

Rachel's ability to become detached from a threatening closeness is, in effect, her only means of self-protection, even survival. It is therefore essential for her to feel that "although she was going to marry him and to live with him . . . and to be so close to him, she was *independent* of him; and she was *independent* of everything else" (315;*386*). By the end of the novel, we know that no sacrifice was too great to safeguard her tragically helpless independence, with all its watery solitude.

The onset of Rachel's headache and the development of her illness are important to the novel's final integration. Hewet is reading *Comus* aloud, and Rachel experiences "curious trains of thoughts suggested by words such as 'curb' and 'Locrine' and 'Brute,' which brought unpleasant sights before her eyes, independently of their meaning" (327;*399*). The virgin Sabrina is being called to break the spell which the debauching Comus has cast on the Lady of Milton's masque. We recall too that according to Geoffrey of Monmouth, Sabrina [hafren] is the illegitimate daughter of Locrine and Estrildis [essyllt]. Locrine, the son of Brute, despite his promise to marry Gwendolyn [guendoloena], "was inflamed with love" for Estrildis who gives birth to Sabrina. After Locrine's death, Gwendolyn, whom Milton calls Sabrina's "stepdame," in a fit of rage, orders Estrildis and Sabrina "to be taken and drowned in the river" (*Historia Regum Britanniae*, 1136[?]).[14]

---

13. Rachel's almost child-like pleasure in feeling Helen's body reminds one of her feeling in a brief scene with Evelyn Murgatroyd: "She put her hand on Rachel's knee . . . . Rachel felt much as Terence had felt that Evelyn was too close to her, and that there was something exciting in this closeness, although it was also disagreeable" (249;*304-305*).

14. This reading is based on presumably the most authentic translation of the *Historia* by Acton Griscom, M.A., *The Historia Regum Britanniae of Geoffrey of Monmouth, with*

We may only speculate on what implications this poem has for Rachel, or what private meanings she may attach to the invocation of Sabrina, who is "sitting/Under the glassy, cool, translucent wave." However, it is precisely at this passage in the poem, and in this scene in the novel, that Rachel's head begins to ache. So that we need to examine what is found in the dilirium which follows and the way in which certain elements of that delirium function to connect not only with the Severn stream (Sabrina's abode) but also with the dream material which followed Richard Dalloway's kiss. For example, Rachel's nurse who was playing cards while tending her becomes the sinister woman holding the cards of destiny "only now in a tunnel under a river. . ."; and within seconds, Rachel shut her eyes

and found herself walking through a tunnel under the Thames, where there were little deformed women sitting in archways playing cards, while the bricks of which the wall was made oozed with damp, which collected into drops and slid down the wall. But the little women became Helen and Nurse McInnis . . . (331;*404-405*).

That the little deformed man in the damp oozing tunnel of the dream is now replaced by little deformed women in an identical tunnel is of special interest because the erotic bestiality of the dream is now linked with the female deformity of Rachel's delirium; and in both instances Rachel feels total helplessness. Moreover, that Helen becomes one of the deformed women assumes significance when we recall that it was Helen and Hewet who were kissing in the expedition scene.

The inferences to be drawn from these connections enlarge considerably when we learn that for Rachel, during her periods of consciousness, all

sights were something of an effort, but the sight of Terence was the greatest effort, because he forced her to join mind to body in the desire to remember *something*. She did not wish to remember; it troubled her when people tried to disturb her loneliness. . .(347;*424*).

Contributions to the Study of Its Place in Early British History, London, New York, and Toronto: Longmans, Green and Co., 1929, pp. 254-256. There are some variations to the story. According to Spenser, for example, Gwendolyn slays Estrildis and drowns Sabrina (*The Faerie Queen,* Bk. II, Cant. X, 19). In Swinburne's tragedy of 1887, called *Locrine,* Sabrina throws herself into the river after her parents' death (Act V, Scene ii). And in the 1595 play of unknown authorship, *The Lamentable Tragedie of Locrine, the eldest sonne of Kinge Brutus,* Sabrina's first attempt to take her life is unsuccessful through lack of courage, but she later commits suicide by drowning herself (Act V, Scene vi).

Throughout this part of the novel, the material having the strongest resonance concerns Rachel's escape under water from her hallucinatory torturers:

At last the faces went further away; she fell into a deep pool of sticky water, which eventually closed over her head. She saw nothing and heard nothing but a faint booming sound, which was the sound of the sea rolling over her head. While all her tormentors thought she was dead, she was not dead, but curled up at the bottom of the sea (341;*416*).

The importance of this passage is in Mrs. Woolf's keeping in the foreground Rachel's connection with the virgin Sabrina and her drowning at the hand of the overpowering stepmother, Gwendolyn. This connection may be part of the reason why for Rachel, "Helen's form stooping to raise her in bed appeared of gigantic size," and why that form "came down upon her like a ceiling falling" (347;*423*). But whether we agree or not, we must recognize that this illusion of being overwhelmed, though not necessarily for us, has for Rachel the unrelenting starkness of reality itself.

Having explored the novel's most fully-realized characters, how do we interpret their relations so as to arrive at some reasonable organization of the work? The question is not an easy one, and E.M. Forster's description of *The Voyage Out* as "vague and universal"[15] is of little critical assistance. Why is it vague? How is it universal? It is true that Mrs. Woolf does not tell us everything, just as life does not; we are forced to piece the material of this novel—much of it given through implication and gleaned through inference—together into a whole.

Whatever conclusions we reach, however, must necessarily center on Rachel's fate in the book; and her death demands our closest attention. Those critics who have ignored it have generally been forced to interpret the book on the airless heights of abstraction. Those who have dealt with Rachel's death have assumed that it was caused by a tropical fever or a local fever or vegetables not properly washed or, as one critic put it, "a microorganism . . . proliferating"[16] in Rachel's bloodstream. However, because the cause of her death is

15. Recorded by Virginia Woolf in her *Diary,* 6 November 1919.

16. Bernard Blackstone, *Virginia Woolf: A Commentary,* New York: Harcourt, Brace and Co., 1949, p. 30.

intentionally made ambiguous, its occurrence assumes an aura of tragic pointlessness; and this is no small part of Mrs. Woolf's plan. As another critic points out: "The temptation . . . arises to explain the natural occurrences affecting human beings in the terms of rational understanding of civilized society, i.e. to give a reasonable explanation for Rachel's dying."[17]

To give a "reasonable explanation" for her death, however, is by no means the same as giving a *cause* for that death. And this is exactly what Mrs. Woolf has consciously avoided doing. The question arises: Would a sentence, even a word or two, attributing Rachel's fever to some lethal agent have damaged the novel's design? The answer, of course, is no. More than anything else, such an addition would have reinforced the theme of the tragic meaninglessness of Rachel's death; it would have added substance to Holtby's thesis that Mrs. Woolf "sets life against death as though thus to discern more clearly what it means"[18] and to Guiguet's statement that the whole novel expresses "—a conception of the universe and of existence."[19] Most important, it would have limited our interpretation and fixed it on these lofty planes.

The author, however, names no proliferating organism, specifies no unwashed vegetables; and we are at liberty to speculate on why we are not able "to give a reasonable explanation for Rachel's dying." For this statement suggests that the novel can be read on a different plane—a plane on which rationality has no meaning, where contradictory forces flourish and haunt the crepuscular regions of dream and delirium.

These regions are difficult in criticism: they are full of screens, deceptions, and pitfalls. Yet a critic must dare to tread these grounds, provided he analyzes with objectivity and maintains constant vigilance for new and contradictory material. The task becomes extremely arduous with a work as long as *The Voyage Out,* because with the interactions as complex as they are, the associational

---

17. Josephine O'Brien Schaefer, *The Three-Fold Nature of Reality in the Novels of Virginia Woolf,* The Hague, London, Paris: Mouton & Co., 1965, p. 43.

18. Winifred Holtby, *Virginia Woolf,* London: Wishart & Co., 1932, p. 61.

19. Jean Guiguet, *Virginia Woolf and Her Works,* trans. Jean Stewart, New York: Harcourt, Brace and World, Inc., 1965, p. 206.

demands of the text are as enormous as the juxtapositional effects are evasive. Moreover, when we read a novel which moves forward through indirection, much of its latent meaning, embedded in the language and imagery, can only be uncovered in a manner which is strictly inductive and largely conjectural.

With these considerations in mind, it was possible to proceed on the critical axiom that everything in the published work is relevant in one way or another; that is, *everything is there not by chance, but by choice*—choices emanating from Virginia Woolf's mental fabric, whose threads were spun sometimes from consciousness, more often from the darker precincts.

Two of the most illuminating illustrations of choice, found in the Holograph and Typescripts of *The Voyage Out,* are the two places where Mrs. Woolf altered the text to such a great extent, that they represent in one case the choice to obscure the meaning of a scene; and in the second, to insinuate, through poetic allusion, a larger meaning. The first scene is that of Rachel and Hewet on the expedition; the second is the scene in which Rachel's headache begins.

The expedition scene in the Holograph (dated 21 December 1912) reads as follows:

Before Mr. Flushing could do more than protest, Helen was off, sweeping over the ground at a considerable pace. The figures continuing to retreat, she broke into a run, shouting Rachel's name in the midst of great panting. Rachel heard at last; looked round, saw the figure of her aunt a hundred yards away, and at once took to her heels. Terence stopped and waited for her. But she swept past him . . . pulling handfuls of grass and casting them at Rachel's back, abusing her roundly as she did so with the remnants of her breath. Rachel turned incautiously to look, caught her foot in a twist of grass and fell headlong. Helen was upon her. Too breathless to scold, she spent her rage in rolling the helpless body hither and thither, holding both wrists in one firm grasp, and stuffing eyes, ears, nose, and mouth with the feathery seeds of the grass. Finally she laid her flat on the ground, her arms out on either side of her, her hat off, her hair down. "Own yourself beaten!" she gasped. "Beg my pardon!" Lying thus flat, Rachel saw Helen's head pendent over her, very large against the sky. A second head loomed above it, "Help! Terence!" she cried. "No!" he exclaimed, when Helen was for driving him away. "I've a right to protect her. We're going to be married."

For the next two seconds they rolled indiscriminately in a bundle, imparting handfuls of grass together with attempted kisses. Separating at last, and trying to tidy her hair, Helen managed to exclaim between her pants, "Yesterday! I guessed it!"

In the Earlier Typescript (undated) the scene begins in much the same way, with Helen pursuing Rachel:

Suddenly Rachel stopped and opened her arms so that Helen rushed into them and tumbled her over on the ground. "Oh Helen, Helen!" she could hear Rachel gasping as she rolled her, "Don't! For God sake! Stop! I'll tell you a secret! I'm going—to—be—married!" Helen paused with one hand upon Rachel's throat holding her head down among the grasses. "You think I didn't know that!" she cried. For some seconds she did nothing but roll Rachel over and over, knocking her down when she tried to get up; stuffing grass into her mouth; finally laying her flat upon the ground, her arms out on either side of her, her hat off, her hair down.

"Own yourself beaten," she panted. "Beg my pardon, and say that you worship me!"

Rachel saw Helen's head pendent over her, very large against the sky. "I love Terence better!" she exclaimed.

The Later Typescript (undated) is changed again to the Holograph version, with the exception of one sentence: "For the next two seconds they rolled indiscriminately in a bundle, imparting handfuls of grass together with gestures which under other conditions might have been described as kisses." We have only to reread the published text—both the American edition (283-84) and the British (347)—to see how drastic the changes are both in the material and in the angle of perspective, and to realize how obscure the published version became as a result of the alterations.

The scene in which Rachel's headache begins also underwent extensive change. The Holograph begins directly with:

"There is a gentle nymph not far from hence,
That with moist curb sways the smooth Severn stream.
Sabrina is her name, a virgin pure;
Whilom she was the daughter of Locrine,
That had the sceptre from his father Brute."
Terence's voice was pleasant enough; but nevertheless her head ached.

The Earlier Typescript eliminates this material and begins:

Next morning a very strange thing happened. Rachel woke up suddenly and felt as if she had been dried by fire. She was wide awake, but instead of being white and cheerful the wall opposite her stared; and the movement of the blind as if filled with air and dragged slowly out trailing the cord behind it seemed to her terrifying like the movement of a strange animal. She shut her eyes, and the pulses in her head beat so strongly that each thump seemed to tread upon a nerve. She turned from side to side opening her eyes now and then in the hope that this time the room would look as usual . . . . She got out of bed and stood upright supporting herself by the brass ball at the end of the bedstead which cold at first soon became hot in her palm. The pain in her head and limbs proved that it would be far more intolerable to stand and walk than to lie in bed, so that she lay down and accepted the idea that she was ill.

The Later Typescript is almost identical to the Holograph, and in the published version (Ch. XXV), the lines from Milton are again introduced, but now they are preceded by a brief description of the day's intense heat.

The significance of these alterations in the course of the novel's growth is considerable, because they provide us with a vivid glimpse of Virginia Woolf's mind at work in the *unguarded act of creation*. When we examine the revisions of the expedition scene, it becomes clear that the enormous difference between the published text and the Holograph creates a disquieting ambiguity; that is, when we read the published text literally, the quality is so hallucinatory that we are encouraged to interpret the material as fragments of Rachel's distorting consciousness. When we read it figuratively as a scene of physical intimacy, the nature of the image fragments again appear as products of phantasy. In both instances, because the material is being filtered to us as Rachel alone experiences it, we are forced unto a plane which is at least one remove from reality. It is through the clarity of the Holograph that we see the obscurity of the finished product insisted upon.

The scene of Rachel's headache onset is a different matter. In both the revised and the published versions, there is no question that Rachel is ill. That Mrs. Woolf chose to introduce again the *Comus* material in the finished text, however, obliquely enlarges the meaning of the illness through the implications of the virgin Sabrina, her death at the order of an enraged and jealous stepmother, and the spellbound Lady whose virtue is imperilled. If we add to these what we already know of Rachel—her sheltered past, her detachment which she calls "freedom," her curious relationship to her father, her imperfect identification with Helen as a woman and her ambivalence toward her as mentor and substitute-mother, her confused relationship to Hewet for whom she feels intermittent love and confinement, her unconscious feelings of sexuality and its association to violence and bestiality—an extremely complex constellation of contradictory and emotional cross-currents emerges.

Her commitment to marry Hewet, who is neither sufficiently mature himself nor emotionally resourceful enough to "look after" her, coupled with Helen's obvious withdrawal after the marriage proposal, leave Rachel helplessly overwhelmed and destined to a life, which for her, is potentially filled with recrudescent uncertainty. Her only recourse then, on a level far below awareness, is to protect herself; and protection in Rachel's sequestered world is synonymous with withdrawal.

But her withdrawal is extreme: ror the mysterious principle of psychic alchemy dictates how the fires will burn in the crucible of her fevered mind before the transformation is complete. Thus, her death is consciously unresisted, unconsciously sought: *it is a self-willed death.* For just as one escapes a life, too threatening to tolerate, through periods of unconsciousness or insanity, so too can one withdraw from life, assured of greater permanence, through death.

We are never told whether she was sacrificial hostess to lethal microorganisms. We do know, however, from Rachel's thoughts and phantasies, and especially from her dream and delirium, the breadth of her innocence, the depth of her isolation, and the intensity of her fears. With that knowledge, Rachel's death becomes all the more moving and the laws governing human nature all the more unrelenting. Even as Hewet's grief has the resonance of Heathcliff's at the death of Catherine Earnshaw, there echoes in the final chapter the despair of Cowper's "we perished, each alone," because we know that in her dying, Rachel was "beneath a rougher sea/And whelmed in deeper gulfs than he."

Night and Day

The very pen that moved so haltingly across the long pages of *The Voyage Out* was raised again to write *Night and Day*. For the two novels, in the deepest substructions of feeling, are corollary to each other: on different levels of civilized existence, they tell almost the same story. What makes the second novel appear different from its predecessor is its London setting with tea gatherings and drawing-rooms, its codes of conventional behavior and social stricture. The characters are cast in a world unlike that of *The Voyage Out,* where in the primitive wilds of the island off the coast of South America, elemental feelings are quickened and the rude blasts of passion wreak their destructive forfeitures. But the difference is only a surface one. What remains the same in *Night and Day* is its central figure, Katherine Hilbery, who is much like Rachel Vinrace, but is four years older, more experienced, and more aloof.

The central issue in *Night and Day* is love and marriage: what they are; what they mean; what the relationship is between them. Around that center revolves a whole galaxy of polarities: fact and phantasy, reality and illusion, freedom and bondage, order and chaos. However, that Katherine, unlike her prototype, is still alive at the novel's end indicates a shift in Virginia Woolf's view of human relations: she no longer views polarities as "either/or" choices but senses them now as existing side by side. Her title, *Night and Day,* is therefore a fitting one indeed for a novel of compromise in its strictest sense, of adjustment to differences by mutual concession. As a result the book is not a drawing-room comedy as some readers have called it; but rather a series of subtle explorations into the nature of love, the conditions of marriage, the mystery of human beings, and the opaque lines which separate the real from the illusory.

We get to know the major characters of this limited universe gradually, just as they get to know themselves and those whose lives brush against their own. It is a slow and intricate process, but as we move through the tortuous paths of alternatives and indecisions, we catch brilliant glimpses of thought and feeling which enlarge the meaning of human intercourse and define more clearly the range of its laws.

The initial sketch of Katherine Hilbery is a provocative one. We see her first pouring out tea, with perhaps "a fifth part of her mind"(9;*1*)[1] occupied with what she is doing. On this occasion she first meets Ralph Denham, with a "rather malicious determination not to help this young man, in whose upright and resolute bearing she detected something hostile to her surroundings . . ."(14;*6*). We learn that as the grand-daughter of the famous poet, Richard Alardyce, Katherine's conception of life is bounded by the names of past literary giants whose ghostly glory "intruded too much upon the present, and dwarfed it too consistently, to be altogether encouraging to one forced to make her experiment in living when the great age was dead"(39;*33*). She has worked for ten years with her romantic mother in a vain attempt to produce a biography of the great poet; and because so much of her "time was spent in imagination with the dead . . ." (39;*34*), she "sometimes . . . felt . . . it was necessary for her very existence that she should free herself from the past. . . ." However, we may wonder why, when she is not working among the ranks of the dead, "life . . . proved to be of an utterly thin and inferior composition"; or why, unlike her loquacious mother, she "was inclined to be silent; she shrank from expressing herself even in talk . . ." (43;*38*). For taciturnity is not a prerequisite to the writing of biography.

The suspense is not prolonged, for we soon learn that Katherine is oddly given to daydreams of "taming . . . wild ponies upon the American prairies, or the conduct of a vast ship in a hurricane round a black promontory of rock. . . ." Stranger still, "she would rather have confessed her wildest dreams of hurricane and prairie than the fact that, upstairs, alone in her room, she rose early . . . or sat up late at night to . . . work at mathematics. No force on earth would have made her confess that." The reason is that to Katherine "mathematics were directly opposed to literature," and when we discover how much to Katherine Mrs. Hilbery represents "the confusion, agitation, and vagueness of the finest prose" (45-46;*40*), we understand why "Her mother was the last person she wished to resemble, much though she admired her" (46;*41*). When we interpret the emotional content of these thoughts, it becomes clear that

---

1. The unitalicized page number in parentheses following each quotation refers to the first American paperback edition published by Harcourt Brace Jovanovich, Inc., 1973; the italicized number refers to The Hogarth Press edition (Eighth Impression), 1966.

Katherine prefers the exactness and impartiality of figures *precisely* because they are the opposite of all that her mother represents to her.

Katherine's detachment at the tea table, her immersion in the past, her daydreams, her fondness for the lifeless symbols of mathematics —all together suggest a kind of effortless separation from people and from the present. Even this early in the novel, she seems to be a picture of aloofness and emotional inertia; she appears to be someone who, from the periphery, observes rather than takes part in life.

The extent of her aloneness is insinuated in a scene in Mary Datchet's rooms. At a social gathering the two young ladies are getting acquainted. Mary laughs at Katherine's calling her Miss Datchet:

"Mary, then, Mary, Mary, Mary."
So saying, Katherine drew back the curtain in order, perhaps, to conceal the momentary flush of pleasure which is caused by coming perceptibly nearer to another person (60:56).

To conceal the momentary flush of pleasure. Here is our clue to seeing the hidden side of Katherine. What may seem on the surface a reaction of shyness is a deception; for to conceal the pleasure of coming nearer another person has a double implication. On the one hand, Katherine's pleasure in human contact indicates that despite her aloofness and detachment, she feels the *need* of other people; on the other hand, that she needs to hide her pleasure indicates her inability or unwillingness to communicate that agreeable sensation to another human being. In Katherine, then, we have in an encapsulated form *the need of contact in conflict with the need of distance.*

These opposing needs explain to a large extent Katherine's peculiar relationships with Rodney and Denham, her extravagant phantasies, and her pleasure in the unpopulated world of abstract symbols. At one point, for example, when Katherine is pondering her future with Rodney, she wishes that "no one in the whole world would think of her." It then occurs to her that in their married life together, eventually "She would come to feel a humorous sort of tenderness for him, a zealous care for his susceptibilities, and, after all, she considered, thinking of her father and mother, what is love?" Conspicuously absent in Katherine's thought, however, is what Rodney might give her in return; we guess that he might give her very little. In the phantasy which follows, we see that in her never having known love, she has built an image of love and marriage which is wildly romantic—complete with "waters that drop with resounding thunder" and a "magnanimous hero, riding a great horse by the shore of the sea" (106-107;*107-108*). Waking from her daydream, she considers a loveless marriage, realizes the futility of her imaginary flights, "and went back to her mathematics . . ." (108;*108*).

Of course Rodney cannot give her anything that could compare with the exotic turbulence of her phantasy; but as far as Katherine was concerned, "He gave her peace, in which she could think of things that were far removed from what they talked about. Even now, when he sat within a yard of her, how easily her mind ranged hither and thither!" Life with Rodney would be one in which "she held a pile of books in her hand, scientific books, and books about mathematics and astronomy which she had mastered"(138;*141*). What Katherine calls "peace" then is actually freedom to live in a phantasmal world "where feelings were liberated from the constraint which the real world puts upon them . . ." (141;*145*). So that we can appreciate her saying, "I want to work out something in figures—something that hasn't got to do with human beings" (195;*203*). Remembering her prior thought that "the process of awakenment [from phantasy] was always marked by *resignation* and a kind of *stoical acceptance* of facts" (141;*145*),[2] we can understand why earlier she needed to conceal her pleasure of a close human contact.

Clearly, Katherine finds people a terrible strain; she is able only to establish ties with a certain kind of person: one who will not intrude upon the joys of her daydream world, who will not depend upon her for reassurance or make excessive demands of any kind. Unfortunately, William Rodney does not understand Katherine's need for privacy; and his lack of perception is the reason why Katherine ultimately cannot marry him.

Her Christmas visit at the Otways reveals other facets of Katherine which reflect her inner world. Rodney is present, making a nuisance of himself at every turn with his plucking jealousy, injured vanity, childish insecurity, his concern for outward appearance—all of this acting as an abrading irritant to Katherine. He is so submerged in his own incoherent yearnings that he fails to see how dangerously close

2. The italics are mine, unless otherwise specified.

he comes to treading on the forbidden ground of her freedom; how so much of his tiresome presence prevents her from slipping off into her private world. The closer he tries to get, the more defiantly she resists him. Her waking life may be one of "resignation" and "stoical acceptance," but that resigned stoicism is possible only when she can escape to that other narcotizing world of dream for peace and emotional refreshment. However, since Rodney keeps her chained to the world of fact by his persistent clutching and clinging, Katherine has no choice but to free herself of him. She escapes by breaking off their engagement and admitting that she does not love him—and never did.

The strangest part of their disengagement occurs when Katherine, watching Rodney brush dead leaves from his coat,

. . . flinched, seeing in that action the gesture of a lonely man.
"William," she said, "I will marry you. I will try to make you happy."
(247;*259*)

Her sudden renewed willingness to marry him after seeing his loneliness tells us a good deal about her. Although the marriage for Katherine would be loveless at best, she can at least feel pity for Rodney, which is an even more reasonable emotional substitute for love. Because pity is a one-way feeling, it diminishes the need to comply with those greater expectations of love; and it leaves her sense of freedom intact—a necessary condition for any relationship she might have. Implied in that condition, moreover, is the idea that Katherine can keep all of her joys, fears, and sorrows to herself while having the benefit of Rodney's company.

Just how much she needs someone's *unintrusive* companionship is brought out in a subsequent scene in Rodney's rooms. Katherine is with him; and after dinner, Rodney, in a fit of peevishness brought on by her seeming indifference to him, resumes his letter to Cassandra. He wants to hurt Katherine by pretending to ignore her:

He wrote on, without raising his eyes. She would have spoken, but could not bring herself to ask him for signs of affection which she had no right to claim. The conviction that he was thus strange to her filled her with despondency, and illustrated quite beyond doubt the infinite loneliness of human beings. She had never felt the truth of this so strongly before. She looked away into the fire; it seemed to her that even physically they were now scarcely within speaking distance; and spiritually there was certainly no human being with whom she could claim comradeship; no dream that satisfied her as she was used to be satisfied; nothing remained in whose reality she could believe, save those abstract ideas—figures, laws, stars, facts, which she could hardly hold to for lack of knowledge and a kind of shame (284;*299*).

The poignancy of the scene comes as much from Katherine's isolation as from Rodney's inability to fathom its depth and to understand how profound are the seams of her vulnerability, how menacing to her sense of self is his unwillingness to give her some assurance, however inadequate it may be, of his affection.

The sequence of the scene brings up still another, more subtle, facet of Katherine's make-up. His ignoring her has hurt, and her withdrawing to contemplate the loneliness of human beings makes her appear oblivious to everything around her. That attitude of remoteness has foiled Rodney's wish for some demonstration of bewildered emotion; and at once reft of grace, "the exasperating sense of his own impotency returned to him." With it also returns the thought that "he could never do without her good opinion" (284-85;*300*). Interpreting her protective withdrawal as *insouciance,* Rodney elevates her again to an exalted height; and seeing her thus, he can appeal to her for help—especially in the matter of his match with Cassandra. In Katherine's abstracted state, "His obvious wish to explain something puzzled her, interested her, and neutralized the wound to her vanity" (287;*302*). So begins their discussion of what romance is and what it is not. When Katherine agrees that neither felt it for the other, she realizes that now having openly acknowledged it "revealed possibilities which opened a prospect of a new relationship altogether" (288;*303*). In it Katherine will be Rodney's helper, his restorer of confidence: someone to calm him during his little tempests of doubt and confusion. In that role, she assumes all the responsibility which should properly be his: "'I wish to do whatever you tell me to do,' he said. 'I put myself entirely in your hands, Katherine.'" It is therefore Katherine who must plant in him the idea that he is "'or might be, in love with Cassandra? . . .'" He agrees—with head bowed. In their "new relationship," then, she must, she soon discovers, also be his procuress! Again, with her "stoical acceptance of facts" and after "a moment of surprising anguish, she summoned her courage to tell him how she wished only that she might help him . . .'' (290-91;*306-307*). It is small wonder that his last words in the scene are: '' 'Katherine, I worship you'. . .'' (291;*307*). Rodney has not seen Katherine's ''moment of surprising anguish'' quickly wrenched into an intense need to remain serenely detached; and missing it, under the steamy cloud of his own urgency, he has misinterpreted her offer as a kind of miraculous inner strength, great enough to be venerated.

To be worshipped, to be idolized, however, is very different from being loved. It is the price Katherine must pay to maintain her independence. We only see how much self-denial is involved when later she arranges for Cassandra to make a visit to London. It is a plan which delights Rodney, who ''took her hand and pressed it, not in thanks so much as in an ecstasy of comradeship.'' Katherine knows however that '' 'He's already gone . . . far away—he thinks of me no more' '' (327;*345*).

Her match-making, however, has within it an ingredient of power not unlike that associated with self-sacrifice or martyrdom—the kind of power which inspires both awe and worship. Although the dark provenance of her need to sacrifice remains obscure, we dimly sense that Katherine's pursuit of freedom and her need to avoid the friction of human contact have been unconsciously rationalized in her own mind in such a way as to make her behavior appear superior—as though it were an outer show of some inner devotional flame. Thus, her efficiency in running the household (a refuge from the world, with only her father and mother to deal with), her stoic determination in the hopeless task of completing the biography (a refusal to pursue some large ambition of her own), her reticence in society (an unwillingness or inability to immerse herself in the ''menacing'' atmosphere of others), and her secret pleasure in abstract science (a substitute for and denial of deeper human passions). Little wonder then that ''It was in her loneliness that Katherine was unreserved'' (336;*355*).

These details of a lonely existence may seem disparaging of Katherine, but they are intended only to emphasize how flattened the contours of her life have become in her quest for freedom and independence; and to provide a background for unravelling her peculiar attraction to Denham—and his even more peculiar attraction to her.

The impression one gets of Ralph Denham in the early pages of the novel is neither a simple nor a sympathetic one. He is scornful, arrogant, and domineering. At their first meeting when Katherine shows him some relics of her family—one of the most distinguished in England—he promptly derides them to her annoyance. "He was amused and gratified to find that he had the power to annoy his oblivious, supercilious hostess, if he could not impress her; though he would have preferred to impress her" (18;*10*). Minutes later, after leaving the Hilbery house with a sharp slam of the door, he thinks that "if he had had Mr. and Mrs. or Miss Hilbery out here he would have made them, somehow, feel his superiority, for he was chafed by the memory of halting awkward sentences which had failed to give . . . a hint of his force" (23;*16*). He continues, still in thought,

"She'll do. . . . Yes, Katherine Hilbery'll do. . . . I'll take Katherine Hilbery" (24;*17*).

All her attributes which in her presence "he had been determined not to feel, now possessed him wholly," and he imagines changing her physical appearance for a "particular purpose." But "His most daring liberty was taken with her mind, which . . . he desired to be exalted and infallible, and of such independence that it was only in the case of Ralph Denham that it swerved from its high, swift flight, but where he was concerned . . . she finally swooped from her eminence to crown him with her approval. . . . Katherine Hilbery would do; she would do for weeks, perhaps for months" (24-25;*17-18*).

In these few lines, Ralph Denham emerges vividly as a man who is uncommonly aware of the value of his new "possession," as one who harbors a rapacious and confused sort of discontent. He annoys, because he cannot impress; others should feel his force, because he is weakened by awkwardness; he must possess someone of quality, because he needs to be bolstered. More specifically, he is a man of such ambivalence that he experiences himself alternately as two different people—the exalted man, inflated with scorn and pride, and the worthless man, choked with inferiority and envy.

We need only to look at his room to see the perfect setting for the worthless man: "There was a look of meanness and shabbiness in the furniture and curtains, and nowhere any sign of luxury or even of a cultivated taste, unless the cheap classics in the book-case were a sign of an effort in that direction"(26;*19*). Here, paradoxically, is where the masterful Denham lives with an old crippled bird for companionship. Even these wretched surroundings, however, can be taken to serve a counterfeit purpose; for they bespeak their occupant to be a model of self-sacrifice, who denies himself in order to keep his family alive, to keep a roof over their heads, to educate his brothers—in short, one who is their only salvation. But all of this is fraudulent in spirit. For as Denham himself says later: " 'I wanted to be the saviour of my family. . . . I wanted them to get on in the world. That was a lie, of course—a kind of self-glorification, too . . .' " (222;*232*).

Here precisely is the focus of Denham's life: an endless quest for glory—whether in reality or in imagination. Just how his quest manifests itself can be seen in most of what he thinks, says, and does; and it tells us a good deal about the one Denham who works as a solicitor in reality and the other Denham who lives on giddy heights in phantasy. Moreover, it is a life he is proud of: "a life rigidly divided into the hours of work and those of dreams; the two lived side by side without harming each other."

His relentless striving for power in his office explains why Denham was not "altogether popular" with his co-workers, for he was "too positive . . . as to what was right and what wrong, too proud of his self-control. . . ." His "rather ostentatious efficiency" was annoying. "Indeed, he appeared to be rather a hard and self-sufficient young man, with . . . manners that were uncompromisingly abrupt, who was consumed with a desire to get on in the world . . ." (127-28;*130*). With so passionate a need to overcome any obstacle to glory, it is not "astonishingly odd" (as Mary Datchet thought) that he spent Monday, Wednesday, and Saturday each week learning about the breeding of bulldogs; or having "a collection of wild flowers found near London"; or visiting weekly "old Miss Trotter at Ealing, who was an authority upon the science of Heraldry . . ." (128-29;*131*). These time-consuming pursuits raise him above and blot out the shabby conditions of his actual life. They help him to identify with the wealthy, the cultivated, and the crested families of England.

Denham's drive toward personal aggrandizement also shows itself in his attitude toward people. In one short scene, Rodney and Denham begin to talk about Rodney's play. Denham, knowing that he is expected to ask to see the manuscript, hesitates for a moment, because "He [Rodney] seemed very much at Denham's mercy, and Denham could not help liking him, partly on that account" (74;*71*). While Rodney gets the manuscript, Denham casually takes from a book-case a handsome edition of Sir Thomas Browne and reads it for some time, to Rodney's great satisfaction. Two days later, Denham receives in the mail the very volume he had admired. However, "From sheer laziness he returned no thanks . . ." (76;*73*). If we translate "sheer laziness" to "utter disregard for other people's feelings," we are closer to the mark, because it is Denham's "disregard" which is unperiphrastically expressive of his callousness toward anyone who is, or can be, of no use to him.

His treatment of Mary Datchet is also callous. During his visit to her family's house, we learn that he felt drawn to her more in the country "because she was more independent of him than in London, and seemed to be attached firmly to a world where he had no place at all" (188;*195*). She is attractive now, because her independence makes no hindering claims on him. At their meal together in the village, we begin to see how totally blind he is to her love for him and consequently how selfishly he regards her. Without yet having told Mary anything about his feeling for Katherine, he sits happily across the table from her and suddenly—almost casually—decides "that he would ask Mary to marry him" (228;*239*). He checks himself, however, and as their talk becomes increasingly serious, it dawns on him that she loves him, "and although he had quite made up his mind to ask her to marry him, the certainty that she loved him seemed to change the situation so completely that he could not do it" (230-31;*241*). We can understand why he will not ask her, because his certainty of her love has brought Ralph's divergent selves into violent, intolerable conflict with each other: "At one moment he exulted in the thought that Mary loved him; at the next, it seemed that he was without feeling for her; her love was repulsive to him. Now he felt urged to marry her at once; now to disappear and never see her again" (231;*242*). His indecisiveness is the unedited testimony of that *ordinary* Denham wanting the lifelong companionship of a sensible, hard-working human being like Mary Datchet in formidable combat with the *grandiose* Denham needing to materialize his imaginary godlike image by conquering the unordinary Katherine

Hilbery with whose family's fortune and fame his own signature can become linked.

There is more to it than that, however. When he finally does offer marriage and Mary refuses on the grounds of the proposal's insincerity, **Denham frankly admits that " 'I never said I loved you'. . . ."** In his reasoning which follows, we get an illuminating glimpse of his subjective logic:

"I believe I care for you more genuinely than nine men out of ten care for the women they're in love with. It's only a story one makes up in one's mind about another person, and one knows all the time it isn't true. Of course one knows; why, one's always taking care not to destroy the illusion. One takes care not to see them too often, or to be alone with them for too long together. It's a pleasant illusion, but if you're thinking of the risks of marriage, it seems to me that the risk of marrying a person you're in love with is something colossal" (252-53;*265*).

What strikes deepest is the word *risk*—used twice. For if we annex to it *taking care not to destroy the illusion,* Denham's premise for marriage then becomes two-fold: first, that there must be no risk of destroying his illusion of his companion; and second, that there must be no risk of his companion's illusion of him being destroyed.

If the marriage is to be a safe one, it must rest upon this chilly premise of preserving phantasy-figures; it is a foundation upon which real intimacy takes on a very different meaning. Mary, down-to-earth and full-blooded as she is, understandably cannot possibly fulfill Denham's requirement of allowing him to live half his life in those glorified dreams in which "he figured in noble and romantic parts. . ." (127;*129*).

There is someone who would suit his need perfectly, and that some-one of course is Katherine Hilbery. From their first meeting, Ralph has made of her such a phantom pleasure and such a glorified possession that when he went to her, he had to shake himself awake "in order to prevent too painful a collision between what he dreamt of her and what she was" (146;*150*). That he requires a companion who is also given to phantasy largely explains his attraction to Katherine. She has the added "quality" of a lofty, dream-like indifference to everything around her; and it is her indifference which inspires him to the wildest of mental excursions: "It would be easy, Ralph thought, to worship one so far re-moved . . . easy to submit recklessly to her, without thought of future pain" (147;*151*). Notice again, however, that it is not love for one within his orbit of feeling that would be easy for him; it is *worship for one so far removed.*

To follow Katherine and Ralph when they are with each other is as difficult as following four total strangers trying mightily to establish some semblance of fellowship. The scene in which Ralph first tries to communicate to Katherine his feeling for her is a crucial one; for it illustrates profoundly the double lives each of them lives and unveils as well their unconscious manoeuvres—in a kind of cerebral fencing—to settle somehow the dual urges which separate them on the one hand, and unite them on the other.

They are by the river, and Ralph—the grand Denham—thinks that he must "question her . . . severely . . . and make them both, once and for all, either justify her dominance or renounce it" (296;*312*). If she is to him the stronger, he will "recklessly submit to her," but if she is not, then his mastery over her is certain. However, as he is as unsure of himself as he is of her, he must start somewhere if he is somehow to get his emotional ledgers straight; and so begins by saying: " 'I've made you my standard ever since I saw you. I've dreamt about you; I've thought of nothing but you; you represent to me the only reality in the world.' " But his strained voice made his words "appear as if he addressed some person who was not the woman beside him, but someone far away" (297;*313*). We know of course that he is addressing the phantom Katherine. The real Katherine, however, recalls Mary's words—" 'Ralph Denham is in love with you' "—and she rebukes him for dishonesty. Ralph, shaken back to reality, replies: " 'I'm not telling you that I'm in love with you. I'm not in love with you' " (298;*314*).

When Katherine asks him to explain himself, he replies: " '. . .I've come to believe that we're in some sort of agreement; that we're after something together; that we see something. . .' " (299;*315*). He then proceeds to an orderly and detailed recital of his present situation and future prospects, to which Katherine is only partly listening; for "She was feeling happier than she had felt in her life. If Denham could have seen how visibly books of algebraic symbols, pages all speckled with dots and dashes and twisted bars, came before her eyes. . . [and then] looking up through a telescope at white shadow-cleft discs which were other worlds, until she felt herself possessed of two bodies, one walking by the river with Denham, the other . . . above the scum of vapours that was covering the visible world."

There it is! Her happiness: her algebraic figures, her soaring above the "scum" of the world. And while Katherine is not aware of the cause of her happiness—for "she was not free; she was not alone; she was still bound to earth by a million fibres. . ."—we know that it is caused by Denham, who "certainly did not hinder any flight she might choose to make, whether in the direction of the sky or of her home. . ." (300-301;*317*).

Free of the restraints of having one "in love" with her, Katherine can live the double life of body bound to earth and mind adrift in the ethers of space. More succinctly: she has the pleasure of Denham's physical companionship without relinquishing the cerebral independence of a dreamer. In a word, she has the familiar "solitude without loneliness." We discern too why only a Denham—so much resembling her in his double vision of life—can give her this happiness. For in asking whether "the Katherine whom he loved [was] the same as the real Katherine," we see how jarring for him the difference must be "between the voice of one's dreams and the voice that comes from the object of one's dreams!" (302-303;*319*) Here is the unique basis for their mutual attraction: *each is essentially free of the other.*

Their revelation to one another has, however, been only a partial one, one not yet sufficient to effect any real agreement. At their meeting in Kew Gardens, the terms of their compromise will be made. In that scene we observe an extremely supple exploration of feeling in the sequential interplay of their thoughts and utterances. During their stroll Katherine owns that she "can't endure living with other people. An occasional man with a beard is interesting; he's detached; he lets me go my way, and we know we shall never meet again. Therefore, we are perfectly sincere. . . ." When Denham contradicts her, she reflects, "How arbitrary, hot-tempered and imperious he was!" A mental enumeration is made of all his bad points, "And yet she liked him" (334-35;*354*).

Denham, on his side, is trying stoutly to discover her weak point and "was ashamed of his savage wish to hurt her, and yet it was not for the sake of hurting her, who was beyond his shafts, but in order to mortify his own incredibly reckless impulse of abandonment . . . . He seemed to see that beneath the quiet surface of her manner . . . there was a spirit which she reserved or repressed for some season[3]

3. In the American edition "reason" appears instead of "season."

either of loneliness or . . .—of love" and decides that "it was in her loneliness that Katherine was unreserved" (335-36;*355*). The sequence of his thoughts becomes complicated by the two selves of Denham now in friction with each other. The humble Ralph wishes to hurt his exalted object, thereby curbing his own recklessness while the imperious Ralph, not wishing really to hurt her, wants merely to weaken her sufficiently to keep his own grand self-image from collapsing under the force of her spirit.

But if she was "beyond his shafts," how can he resolve these opposing urges? For Denham, the solution is in highlighting Katherine's loneliness, for this perception of her by no means diminishes her value. Indeed he feels enlarged by it, because "he might be the one to share her loneliness, the mere hint of which made his heart beat faster and his brain spin" (336;*356*). In Ralph's double vision, if the real Katherine is lonely, she needs him. That need, according to Ralph's distorted logic, directly confirms the fictitious values he has unduly appropriated to himself. Consequently, in thinking that he can share her loneliness, he believes, somewhat perversely, that he can also share her status, the social rank he so desperately wants.

It is on the potent coil of this phantasmal spring that Denham can now assert the conditions upon which their relationship is to rest. His first condition is that of perfect sincerity; he is convinced that "there are cases in which perfect sincerity is possible—cases where there's no relationship, though the people live together, if you like, where each is free, where there's no obligation upon either side" (337;*356-57*). Having laid down the foundation for friendship, he proceeds to elaborate its terms:

> "In the first place, such a friendship must be unemotional," he laid it down emphatically. "At least, on both sides it must be understood that if either chooses to fall in love, he or she does so entirely at his own risk. Neither is under any obligation to the other. They must be at liberty to break or to alter at any moment. They must be able to say whatever they wish to say. All this must be understood" (337;*357*).

These are the terms Ralph offers. These are the terms Katherine accepts. Having thought of all the difficulties—even a "definite catastrophe"—into which such a friendship might plunge them, Katherine knew that "Surely if any one could take care of himself, Ralph Denham could; he had told her that he did not love her"

(338;*358*). (Interestingly, this is what Katherine heard. What Ralph actually said was that he was not "in love" with her.)

Although the terms of their relationship may have an almost brutal impersonal authority, if we remember that "anything that hinted of love . . . alarmed her" and that almost everything about Ralph suggests his feeling unlovable, then the impersonality of their "contract" makes perfect sense. For each of them is so inhibited in human contact that the need to protect oneself—the need to protect the dream each lives with—is understandably powerful. In other words, because each has made so large an emotional investment in an illusion, only on such terms as proposed by Ralph, can a "safe" relationship between them be established.

We discover indirectly, however, that it is Ralph who first "violates" one term of their agreement in saying aloud to himself, " 'I love her' " and a moment later " 'I'm *in* love with you!' " (386;*409*) The placement of his utterances is significant because of all that has transpired since their meeting in Kew Gardens. Earlier, when Katherine and Ralph were visiting the zoo, Ralph refused Katherine's coin to buy food for the bears. She asks him why. But

He refused to tell her. He could not explain to her that he was offering up consciously all his happiness to her, and wished, absurdly enough, to pour every possession he had upon the blazing pyre, even his silver and gold. He wished to keep this distance between them—the distance which separates the devotee from the image in the shrine (368;*390*).

Aside from the humorous equation of "all his happiness . . . [his] every possession" to the shilling he has actually paid, the distance he wishes to keep between them is what calls attention to itself. Soon the "devotee" is going to put his enshrined "image" to the acid test: it would be

. . . a daring plan, by which the ghost of Katherine could be more effectually exorcised than by mere abstinence. He would ask her to come home with him to tea. He would force her through the mill of family life; he would place her in a light unsparing and revealing. His family would find nothing to admire in her, and she, he felt certain, would despise them all, and this, too, would help him. He felt himself becoming more and more merciless towards her. By such courageous measures any one, he thought, could end the absurd passions which were the cause of so much pain and waste (371;*394*).

Katherine then must be subjected to his family, the shabbiness of the house, the babble of children, because he was "determined that no folly should remain when this experience was over" (376;*399*).

What he is testing, of course, is Katherine's strength to ward off disillusionment; for her maintaining the phantasy is above all what matters to Denham. But despite Katherine's initial misery at the encounter, soon she is happily caught up in the swirl of the Denham household; and she has triumphed. After Ralph confesses his reason for asking her home and admits his defeat, Katherine attempts to correct his impressions and to subdue his phantasies, but she is unsuccessful:

> "You come and see me among flowers and pictures, and think me mysterious, romantic, and all the rest of it. Being yourself very inexperienced and very emotional, you go home and invent a story about me, and now you can't separate me from the person you've imagined me to be. You call that, I suppose, being in love; as a matter of fact, it's being in delusion. All romantic people are the same," she added (381;*404*).

Katherine cannot fathom the importance of Ralph's "being in delusion"; she cannot fully understand how vital it is for him to keep her exalted and enshrined and illusory. If she did, she would realize that her accepting him is interpreted in Ralph's imaginary world as confirmation of his fictitious self—the self whose source of energy must be Katherine if the grand image of Ralph Denham is to remain mobilized.

Katherine begins to accept Ralph, and soon she loves him. She is not "in love" with him, as she says to Cassandra, " 'But I love him,' said Katherine" (403;*427*). She knows that her real self will always be secondary to the dream of her which Ralph cherishes. She also knows that their lives, at most, can only run parallel to one another, never converging. And yet her love is genuine. How are we to interpret this strange relationship? What can Ralph give her that in her present circumstances she does not, or could not, have?

These questions cannot be resolved squarely, because Virginia Woolf's method of indirection requires that *apparent* logical connections between events be omitted; and without causes and effects, we are left with huge ambiguous valleys of complex feeling which must somehow be understood and assimilated. Many connections seem either to originate or to cluster around some obscure link between the anchored life Katherine leads with her parents and the life adrift she experiences with Ralph.

Mrs. Hilbery plays a very large part of the daily ritual at Cheyne Walk, and from the very beginning, Virginia Woolf gives us hint after hint that Katherine's romantic mother, despite her ineluctable charm and vivacious loquacity, is a compulsive ensemble of considerable sharpness, determination, and strength. Having identified herself with a great and glorious past, Mrs. Hilbery is not at all troubled by how much she dwarfs those around her, particularly Katherine. Nor does she trouble herself with the fact that she has wasted some ten years of her daughter's life on a biography that will never be finished. It comes as no surprise that Katherine, minimized by the splendor of another century and used (along with her father) as "a rich background for her mother's more striking qualities" (45;*39*), should feel despondent and emotionally wizened. Nor is it surprising that during one of her futile mornings of biographical labor, "Katherine looked at her mother. . . .[and] had

suddenly become very angry, with a rage which their relationship made silent, and therefore doubly powerful and critical. She felt all the unfairness of the claim which her mother tacitly made to her time and sympathy, and what Mrs. Hilbery took, Katherine thought bitterly, she wasted (115-16;*117*).

However, acknowledging that "her mother must be protected from pain," Katherine is chained to a woman who, with the greatest of ease, makes all kinds of claims on others, in her multi-colored forms of self-interest. It is clear then why Mrs. Hilbery does not want to see her daughter married:[4] she would lose too vital an object of utility and support. But Katherine, having for a mother someone "beautifully adapted for life in another planet" (44;*39*) is, like Rachel Vinrace, essentially motherless.

Mr. Hilbery also occupies a central, though much less dramatized, role in Katherine's domestic life. We sense from the start that he is a resigned and powerless man, given only to the day-to-day commonplaces imposed by custom and social consciousness. Together with

---

4. " 'But, Katherine,' Mrs. Hilbery continued. . . 'though, Heaven knows,. I don't want to see you married. . .' " (103;*103*).

Katherine, he functions as a prop for his wife's histrionic effusions. Throughout the novel he remains sensitively neglected, oddly obscured. Only in its closing pages do we get some startling flashes of his relationship to Katherine. When he tries to reproach his daughter for her part in the liaison between Cassandra and Rodney:

Somehow his faith in her stability and sense was queerly shaken. He no longer felt that he could ultimately entrust her with the whole conduct of her own affairs after a superficial show of directing them. He felt, for the first time in many years, responsible for her (468;*496*).

Later, while waiting for Mrs. Hilbery to return, "he counted lugubriously the number of hours that he would have to spend in a position of detestable authority *alone with his daughter*" (478;*506*).

These passages by themselves could easily go unnoticed were it not for one of his later thoughts, when he attempts to fathom Katherine's relationship to Denham. They are all at tea, and Mr. Hilbery is gazing at Ralph:

He respected the young man; he was a very able young man; he was likely to get his own way. He could, he thought, looking at his still and very dignified head, understand Katherine's preference, and, as he thought this, he was surprised by a pang of acute jealousy. She might have married Rodney without causing him a twinge. This man she loved . . . . An extraordinary confusion of emotion was beginning to get the better of him. . .(499-500;*529*).

A moment later, Katherine, waking from a reverie, announces blankly:

"We're engaged," . . . looking straight at her father. He was taken aback by the directness of the statement; he exclaimed as if an unexpected blow had struck him. Had he loved her to see her swept away by this torrent, to have her taken from him by this uncontrollable force, to stand by helpless, ignored? Oh, how he loved her! How he loved her! (500;*529-30*)[5]

Without looking again at his daughter, Mr. Hilbery comments to Denham and strides from the room,

leaving in the minds of the women a sense, half of awe, half of amusement, at the extravagant, inconsiderate, uncivilized male, outraged somehow and gone bellowing to his lair with a roar which still sometimes reverberates in the most polished of drawing-rooms. Then Katherine, looking at the shut door, looked down again, to hide her tears (500;*530*).

---

5. Exactly to whom the "he" refers in "Oh, how *he* loved her!" is not clear. From what precedes, we cannot be certain whether the "he" refers to Denham or to Mr. Hilbery.

Mr. Hilbery's shock, his wrench of jealousy, Katherine's tears—all that has remained subterranean throughout the novel—rise to the surface and assume a heightened significance, because they suggest a relation between daughter and father which has at its core a powerful component of *emotional incest*. Katherine and Mr. Hilbery are to each other, not so much daughter and father as wife and husband in their emotional alignments. Finally Katherine's willingness to assume the burden of running the house and acting toward her mother protectively, and indeed maternally, begin to make sense.

Katherine has been assigned the role of wife; she has been given the authority; she has assumed the responsibility. Her acceptance of that role, however, has sharply curtailed her emotional education; and she is not at all prepared, now at the age of twenty-seven or twenty-eight, for the relatedness between a man and a woman which marriage involves. In consequence, Katherine is tethered to a mother and father who assure her status and material privilege, but provide sparse means for emotional growth. Her wish for freedom then can be interpreted as her dimly-conscious urge to be free of her family.

Against this family background Katherine's love for Ralph is made understandable. Because he is in love with her image, she has the advantage and the comfort of his living presence and simultaneously the freedom to soar to the lifeless realm of symbols and planets and stars. Such a relationship is expressive of her deep-seated ambivalence to both dependency *and* freedom. It is the kind of union which William Rodney could never have with Katherine, nor Mary Datchet (for different reasons) with Ralph. We may call it a love relationship, or we may call it by another name. But in some large way, the feelings Katherine and Ralph bear for each other are not so much the love for each other's person, as they are the love of the freedom to "make-believe" which each provides the other—the large freedom to drift to one's own airy sanctums. It is a paradoxical sort of shared solitude.

To watch the pair at very close range is to speculate on what their lives will be like, married or not, in the months ahead. Sitting across the table from her, Ralph looks at Katherine and reflects that "there was something distant and abstract about her which exalted him and chilled him at the same time." When he declares that he doesn't know her and never has, she replies: "'Yet perhaps you know me better than any one else' . . ." (421;*446*) and continues, "'but you can't think how I'm divided—how I'm at my ease with you, and how I'm bewildered. The unreality—the dark . . . when you look at me, not seeing me, and I don't see you either. . . . But I do see . . . heaps of things, only not you' " (421-22;*447*). Watching Ralph's exaltation struggling against chill and Katherine's ease struggling against bewilderment, we are witnessing two Ralphs and two Katherines engaged in the valiant effort to prevent the real from sullying the illusory.

After Katherine at last confesses her love to Ralph, we see the most acute form of their phantasmal excursions, something that has become so persistent as to be "christened their 'lapses'":

Ralph expressed vehemently . . . the conviction that he only loved her shadow and cared nothing for her reality. If the lapse was on her side it took the form of gradual detachment until she became completely absorbed in her own thoughts, which carried her away with such intensity that she sharply resented any recall to her companion's side. It was useless to assert that these trances were always originated by Ralph himself, however little in their later stages they had to do with him. The fact remained that she had no need of him and was very loath to be reminded of him. How then, could they be in love? (473;*501*)

Katherine tries to explain to her mother that in her relation to Ralph, it was

"as if something came to an end suddenly—gave out—faded—an illusion—as if when we think we're in love we make it up—we imagine what doesn't exist. That's why it's impossible that we should ever marry. Always to be finding the other an illusion, and going off and forgetting about them, never to be certain that you cared, or that he wasn't caring for someone not you at all . . ." (484;*512-13*).

One can hear rumbling beneath Katherine's words the confusion and turmoil engendered by her grim fear of marriage, a fear masking and muting the greater, more primordial, fear of loss.

Overwhelmed as she has been by her mother and silently manacled to her father, she is not prepared to deal with a man and the prospect of marriage as an emotionally mature woman might. But as long as she remains under the roof in Cheyne Walk, she has at least the advantage of being Miss Katherine Hilbery of Chelsea. With Denham, however, she cannot be sure of what she might become should his illusion of her suddenly deteriorate. Her uncertainty is further complicated: while she knows already what Ralph's phantasies are, up to this point he has been denied the privilege of knowing where her mind wanders during her "lapses." Would he approve if he knew? Would it totally destroy his illusion of her to know that she works problems in mathematics? Would he be scandalized at something so "unfeminine" in her?[6] Katherine cannot know.

Virginia Woolf, however, has subtly introduced an incident of great importance in the Kew Gardens scene where Katherine forgot her purse containing a "certain paper." That "certain paper," we discover almost two hundred pages later, is similar to those which fall from her hand the morning Ralph unexpectedly appears at her door. Her papers are crowded with mathematical formulations. She permits him to see them, for now it is Ralph's turn to discover the *other* Katherine:

> She blushed very deeply; but as she did not move or attempt to hide her face she had the appearance of someone disarmed of all defences. . . . The moment of exposure had been exquisitely painful. . . . She had now to get used to the fact that some one shared her loneliness. The bewilderment was half shame and half the prelude to profound rejoicing. Nor was she unconscious that on the surface the whole thing must appear of the utmost absurdity. She looked to see whether Ralph smiled, but found his gaze fixed on her with such gravity that she turned to the belief that she had committed no sacrilege but enriched herself, perhaps immeasurably, perhaps eternally (492;*521-22*).

Ralph has discovered her secret self. She has passed the supreme test. His image of her has not been disturbed; and we understand her relief.

One obstacle remains in the testing, however. Ralph must know if Katherine understands the meaning of his "little dot" surrounded by flames, for

6. There are at least three direct references in the text to Katherine's masculine traits. It is probably not by mere chance that twice she is referred to as Shakespeare's Rosiland, the young princess of *As You Like It,* who disguised as a man, plays out the better part of the comedy feigning bold manliness—and, incidentally, in the end marries Orlando. This is not to imply that Katherine is by any means a manly woman, but merely to point out that Mrs. Woolf's alluding to Rosiland suggests that she, like other great writers before her, saw the possibility of both the masculine and the feminine co-existing within the same individual. We find elsewhere: "Where Katherine was simple, Cassandra was complex; where Katherine was solid and direct, Cassandra was vague and evasive. In short, they represented very well the manly and the womanly sides of the feminine nature. . ." (341;*362*).

somehow to him it conveyed not only Katherine herself but all those states of mind which had clustered round her since he first saw her pouring out tea on a Sunday afternoon. It represented by its circumference of smudges surrounding a central blot all that encircling glow which for him surrounded, inexplicably, so many of the objects of life, softening their sharp outline, so that he could see certain streets, books, and situations wearing a halo almost perceptible to the physical eye (493;*522*).

Katherine does understand: "'Yes, the world looks something like that to me too.'" His joy is profound. A mystical kind of union between them has at last been established, for "they shared the same sense of the impending future, vast, mysterious, infinitely stored with undeveloped shapes which each would unwrap for the other to behold . . ." (493;*523*). Ultimately, in their alikeness each can preserve his own separateness without feeling too much isolation.

In his essay, "The Early Novels of Virginia Woolf," E.M. Forster wrote: "It is easy for a novelist to describe what a character thinks of. . . . But to convey the actual process of thinking is a creative feat, and I know of no one except Virginia Woolf who has accomplished it."[7] *To convey the actual process of thinking.* That is a luminous phrase. For the extent to which the novel succeeds is the extent to which we are able to feel that process, experience the intimacy the author has made possible between the reader and her imagined people. The greater our intimacy, the more fully we perceive the complexity of the personalities encountered, and the more vibrant for us become the problems and vagaries of marriage and love and solitude with which each character struggles.

One of Virginia Woolf's earliest critics said that by the end of *Night and Day,* "the dream world became identified with reality, the night changed into day, the union was complete, a union not so much of a man with a woman, as of a man with himself, a woman with herself."[8] Penetrating as it is, the statement needs to be slightly altered. Night has not changed into day in any real or figurative sense. What has taken place, however, with Katherine's and Ralph's mutual discoveries of each other, has been their acceptance of the idea that the life of night, Illusion, and the life of day, Reality, *co-exist.* Which life predominates depends upon where one is at any

7. *Abinger Harvest,* New York: Harcourt Brace and Co., 1936, p. 113.

8. Winifred Holtby, *Virginia Woolf,* London: Wishart & Co., 1932, p. 93.

given moment in one's own sovereign world. Accepting the co-existence of illusion and reality, Ralph and Katherine can now individually accept the duality—and the fissure—each recognizes in his own life. Only with this acceptance can Katherine willingly relinquish the deadening security of her family and embrace the freedom to continue, less encumbered, to live her double life. For it is she who asks why there should be

this perpetual disparity between the thought and the action, between the life of solitude and the life of society, this astonishing precipice on one side of which the soul was active and in broad daylight, on the other side of which it was contemplative and dark as night? Was it not possible to step from one to the other, erect, and without essential change? (338-39;*358-59*)

She is certain that with Ralph the answer would be Yes.

Night and Day does not end on the blissful and boisterous note of everyone's living happily ever after. Instead, we close the book with the sense that the real work of living is going to begin. For how secure can one feel about one's partner, when each cherishes his own sacred regions? adores his private idols? Yet now Katherine has at least the company of one similar to her in inclination; so that now she also has someone with whom to share her loneliness.

In accepting themselves as they are, they are also able to accept each other. There is a union. But whether that union is ever to be made legal through marriage, we do not know. Nor is it important. The spirit of camaraderie is beyond the shadow of law. In the end, we know that between Katherine and Ralph a bond of friendship has been established—one founded on adjustment and independence, compromise and freedom. And as in real life, it will be in a perpetual state of renewal. For as Byron once wrote in his *Hours of Idleness,* "Friendship is Love without his wings."

Jacob's Room

If, as some serious readers maintain, Virginia Woolf meant us to supply at least as much as she suggests in *Jacob's Room,* then the serious critic is in serious trouble. For the implication is that the text becomes a different novel for each reader; and that from personal reservoirs of memory, experience, and feeling, a reader may furnish the otherwise lifeless page with whatever he pleases; that the book becomes a massive Rorschach test, a series of stimuli with no response controls. If one reading of a book is as valid as any other reading, then all literary criticism is futile. Anyone who has read *The Voyage Out* or *Night and Day,* however, realizes that although variant readings are possible, indeed encouraged, there are defined limits built into the texts which restrict the individual fancy. There is no reason to suppose then that in *Jacob's Room,* her third novel, Mrs. Woolf should have chosen to indulge her readers with what at first glance appears to be a kind of literary free-for-all.

Regardless of whatever defects it may have—and there appear on close reading to be very few—*Jacob's Room* has the unmistakable imprint of original and fastidious design, full of collisions, interruptions, and concussions; but it is a design of carefully counter-poised pictures, sounds, and rhythms. The pictures are sometimes cosmic, sometimes microscopic. The sounds sometimes boom like rockets and clang like cymbals; sometimes they are sighings and murmurings so soft as to be almost inaudible to the human ear. The rhythms either throb powerfully or are just barely perceptible. We are approaching a prose novel which depends heavily upon the techniques of poetry where meanings linger long after the sounds of the page have died down, and the dust of memory has settled.

One must ask whether Mrs. Woolf felt sure enough of herself to communicate emotional sequences with sufficient force to make themselves felt; or whether the reader, prepared for a prose piece, is baffled and bewildered by the poetry and fails to experience anything but some desperate hieroglyphic of vivid and monumental confusion.

One early critic saw the scheme of the novel as the children's pencil-game of connecting numbered points with lines until a picture emerged: ". . . the thrill was to see the picture taking shape and guess what it might turn out to be. In something like the same way *Jacob's Room* presents you with a set of not obviously related points—incidents, thoughts, feelings, conversational snatches, flecks of foam on the streams of consciousness; and all the time as you read, the pencil of your mind is guided from point to point, drawing in the significant lines so that the pattern emerges, and at the end you are left with a picture of Jacob Flanders, somewhat impressionistic but an unmistakable likeness."[1]

The analogy is apt except for two things. First, there are no spatially pre-patterned points in the reading process: we read in time, from word to word, from line to line; and second, the "unmistakable likeness" implies that we are in possession of some premeditated picture of Jacob with which to compare the success or failure of the finished product. Since neither is the case, it seems preferable to think of the reader's re-creation of the text as a person at work with an *unmarked* embroidery frame: the needle breaks through the fabric's surface, makes a stitch or two, then disappears below the surface; the thread has a particular color, weight, and texture—and since we are dealing with words, it has also a particular sound and accent. The first needle and thread remain below the frame; then a second appears, makes its stitch, and vanishes. If we multiply the process by any number of different strands, emerging, stitching, and disappearing, we get an idea of the reader's task until the frame is filled. We get also some notion of how difficult his task is while reading when we realize that the total re-creation must be held in memory.

The sequence of the various threads—those concentrated moments of feeling—determines the sequence of the reader's emotional evocations. But the way in which those moments are laid side by side determines the quality and intensity of the feelings evoked. Thus, it is in Virginia Woolf's ordering and juxtapositioning of the stimuli that she controls the reader's range of response, both in his head and in his heart; that she models her meaning with an infinite variety of image and accent, angle and outline; until all the strands are seen together in one majestic picture, complete, and in full light.

1. R.L. Chambers, *The Novels of Virginia Woolf,* London: Oliver & Boyd, 1947, p. 29.

There is very little of explicit cause and effect in the novel. The hasty abstract provided below[2] gives only a vague notion of what the book is about and only a slight glimmer of what kind of person Jacob is. Yet the novel is well-populated, and Jacob is at its center. Is it true, as Mrs. Woolf twice says, that "It is no use trying to sum people up. One must follow hints, not exactly what is said, nor yet entirely what is done" (31,154;*29,153*)?[3] If the novel is not exactly concerned with what people say or do, then the hints that we are asked to follow must be in the novel's sequential and juxtapositional pattern. The hint is neither in "Utterance One" or "Action One" nor in "Utterance Two" or "Action Two," but rather in where the utterances and actions are placed in relation to one another; for the positioning of the material affects the reader in a way that he experiences *beyond* the printed page something half heard and dimly perceived, but unmistakably implied by the relationships among the fictional ingredients.

A careful look at the opening pages of *Jacob's Room* will give an idea of the method Mrs. Woolf was to perfect in her next novel. (Here the attempt is only to simulate what a reader might feel when coming to the book for the first time.) We meet Betty Flanders by reading through her eyes the words she is writing: "So of course, there was nothing for it but to leave." But leave what? We are not told. Her eyes fill and look up; and we too look up to see through her tear-filled eyes a bay quivering, a lighthouse wobbling. The tears are winked away, and the optical distortion is corrected. Now we look again at her page and see that the "blot had spread." "'. . . nothing for it but to leave,' she read." Why repeat the line? Why the tears?

2. Outwardly, the novel is built on a sequence of scenes during the various times and stages of Jacob Flanders's life. We see him first as a child on holiday with his mother and brothers (I), then as a boy collecting butterflies in Scarborough (II); we follow him through his Cambridge days (III), and another holiday at Cornwall with his friend, Timmy Durrant (IV); then we are given a sketch of his life in London (V), his meeting Florinda (VI); and a party at the Durrant's (VII); then follows his (unspecified) job in London and his brief affair with Florinda (VIII); his relationship with Bonamy, a visit to a brothel, and his afternoon at the British Museum (IX); his meeting Fanny Elmer and her infatuation with him (X); then, from his brief Bohemian stretch in Paris (XI), we follow him to Italy and then to Greece where he falls in love with Mrs. Sandra Wentworth Williams (XII); his return to England which is about to become engaged in war (XIII); and finally his death (presumably) in combat (XIV).

3. The unitalicized page numbers in parentheses following each quotation refer to the American paperback edition published by Harcourt, Brace and World, 1960; the italicized numbers refer to The Hogarth Press edition (Tenth Impression), 1965.

Again we are not told. But having been placed behind Betty Flanders's eyes, we are too close to her not to sense some vague knot of sadness in a woman we know nothing about.

In the next two paragraphs, we discover parenthetically that she has sons called Jacob and Archer; and that the month is September. We wait for her to finish whatever it is she is writing and find a perambulator mentioned. So there is another child somewhere, we guess.

The fifth paragraph begins: "Such were Betty Flanders's letters to Captain Barfoot—many-paged, tear-stained." But who is Captain Barfoot? Her husband? Would a husband be addressed by rank? No. Then what is her relationship to him? And why that curious name, Barfoot? For one thinks of clubfoot; swollen foot; Oedipus. And "Seabrook is dead." Is Seabrook then her husband? Still, we are left in the dark.

But Mrs. Woolf swiftly turns the clock back: "Tears made all the dahlias in her garden undulate in red waves. . . ." Betty Flanders is recalling her house in Scarborough while still on the sand in Cornwall—with tears of the present now flowing and connecting with tears of the past; and the thought draws in Mrs. Jarvis, the rector's wife, who looked upon widows as "lonely, unprotected, poor creatures." Then, finally, we read the omniscient statement: "Mrs. Flanders had been a widow for these two years."

If we pause for a moment and consider how much we have been jostled about in time and space, how much we have had to guess about the people named and their relations, and how much has been omitted, we begin to realize what Virginia Woolf meant when she asked her readers to "follow hints." For she has placed us in the present, given us a strand or two of information, locked us into a particular consciousness in a particular state of feeling, and has forced us to speculate on the origin of that feeling. She has essentially reversed conventional narrative form by giving us an effect before indicating its cause. And while we are following hints, attempting to fathom causes in the past, we are simultaneously moved forward in fictional time.

Eleven paragraphs further, we are with Jacob, climbing a rock; and "a small boy has to stretch his legs far apart, and indeed feel rather heroic, before he gets to the top" where in a hollow of water he finds a crab: " 'Oh, a huge crab,' Jacob murmured" as the crab "begins his journey on weakly legs. . . ." But the crab is not huge: it is Jacob who is small; so that he sees, as we are made to see from his angle of vision, the creature in relative proportion. We and Jacob also see an "enormous man and woman" lying on the beach. Through his child-like exaggeration we sense how extreme his terror must be when he runs from them toward a "large black woman" screaming "Nanny! Nanny!" only to be confronted by a large black rock—and himself lost.

Because we are, for the moment, resident in Jacob's consciousness, we feel all the immediacy of his terror. We also understand how quickly his terror can vanish when his childish curiosity is caught by a "whole skull—a cow's skull, a skull, perhaps, with teeth in it." However, the grown-up world of Mrs. Flanders intervenes to scold Jacob, to let him and us know it is a sheep's skull. She then sweeps her sons off to their lodging house, with Jacob still clutching the sheep's jaw which he has managed somehow to rescue.

Those sections selected from the first chapter deal specifically with Mrs. Flanders and Jacob and demonstrate Mrs. Woolf's cumulative method of creating character through her handling of narrative viewpoint. Other threads are however interspersed throughout the chapter which give metaphorical hints of causes and effects. They are hints which urge the reader to speculate on Jacob's fate in the novel. The threads referred to are those juxtapositions which have a strange, almost unanalyzable, fixity. On one of the opening pages, for example, Steele, the painter, pleased with an effect in his picture, looked up "and saw to his horror a cloud over the bay." Directly following this: "Mrs. Flanders rose, slapped her coat this way and that. . . ." Now the logical reader will think that if Steele saw the cloud, Mrs. Flanders also saw it and is rising to leave. Perfectly true. But the two sentences, placed side by side so casually, with no apparent connection, suggest something else: when clouds appear, the sun is blocked, and the wind rises. Here, however, instead of the wind rising, Betty Flanders rises, "slapping her coat this way and that," just as the wind might. The juxtaposition, then, is invested with an almost subliminal suggestion of the natural force of the woman—a force which on that very night will assume the strength of hurricane gales.

After Mrs. Flanders rises, Virginia Woolf moves us to Jacob, climbing the rock, and here a quite intricate sequence begins. Jacob, a small boy with small legs, captures a crab journeying on "weakly legs"; suddenly he sees the "enormous man and woman" and flees in terror towards a rock which he thinks is Nanny. Lost and miserable, he discovers a skull, and curiosity consoles him. Caught by his mother, he is able only stealthily to retrieve the sheep's jawbone from the skull. On their way to the lodging house, Mrs. Flanders tells her sons the cheerless story of a man who lost his eye in a gunpowder explosion, "aware . . . in the depths of her mind of some buried discomfort." On the sand, not far from the enormous man and woman, "not far from the lovers lay the old sheep's skull without its jaw" and "sea holly would grow through its eye-sockets."

The juxtaposition of the skull's eye-sockets and a man's lost eye offers a faint foreshadowing. More evocative, however, is the placement of the skull beside the lovers, with its jawbone in Jacob's hands; because separated as they are, neither part is able to function: the eyeless skull beside the lovers[4] cannot hold its grip; and the toothed jawbone in Jacob's possession cannot bite. In a sense, the tension of the scene and the painter's horror at seeing the cloud are justified; for during the night the winds rise, and there is a hurricane at sea. Indoors Mrs. Flanders and Rebecca, with the children in bed, plot "the eternal conspiracy of hush and clean bottles," as if all motherhood were in conspiratorial alliance. While the wind is hurling and tearing and leaping across the coast, "Jacob lay asleep, fast asleep, profoundly unconscious. The sheep's jaw with the big yellow teeth in it lay at his feet." But in the rain outside, in its half-filled bucket, the "crab slowly circled round the bottom, trying with its weakly legs to climb the steep side; trying again and falling back, and trying again and again."

Throughout the first chapter, numerous seemingly irrelevant and trifling details collect, pile up, and fall into a pattern of implicit relevance. Their sequence and their infallible arrangement, together with the ebb and flow of repeated phrasal connections, have a prophetic solemnity and a cumulative poetic force of great sadness

---

4. The eyeless skull links with a later scene—dim, inconclusive, somehow connecting: ". . . Fanny's idea of Jacob was more statuesque, and eyeless["I"-less?] than ever" (170;*170*).

and helplessness. We think of the sheep's jaw and wonder what Jacob's grip on life will be, as he lies so profoundly asleep. We recall the weakly legs of the helpless crab and are reminded of the legs of the little boy; and we wonder how firm Jacob's stand in life will be, how sure his footing, how successful his ascent to self-realization in the stormy years still unlived.

It is no accident that Mrs. Flanders's words open the novel; and that with her in attendance, the novel ends. Although her words are few and widely scattered, her shadowy presence is somehow felt on almost every page. Part of the reason may be that when she does occupy our attention, what she says or does is rendered with such force and determination. Of all the characters, she alone seems to know best her own mind and is least likely to be swayed and knocked by others. But we are left with some doubts about her; and it is a tribute to Virginia Woolf's method that she can portray Betty Flanders with such prosaic vividness while leaving her motives so inscrutable and so concealed.

Her relationship to Captain Barfoot, for example, is not at all clear from her "many-paged, tear-stained" letters to him or from the Captain's attentions which "flooded her eyes for no reason that any one could see perhaps three times a day." We learn early in the book that she is a handsome widow of about forty-five, has a great deal of physical energy, is so attractive to men that "wives tugged their husbands' arms" (15;*13*) when they passed her, and that her dead husband, Seabrook, was a useless man who had "run a little wild" (16;*14*). Part of this description may explain why Betty Flanders is attractive to Barfoot, lame and missing two fingers, a man with "something military in his approach" (26;*24*); a man whose marriage to an invalid wife has gone dry. It does not explain, however, why Betty Flanders is attracted to Barfoot whom she has known for more than twenty years.

Mrs. Woolf, however, has given us sufficient hints to follow. For when Barfoot arrives on his usual Wednesday visit, Mrs. Flanders enters the room out of breath, flinging a window open, straightening a cover, picking up a book "*as if* she were very confident, very fond of the Captain, and [*as if* she were] a great many years younger than he was. Indeed, in her blue apron she did not look more than thirty-five. He was well over fifty" (28;*27*).[5] It is in her feeling so much younger (and therefore dependent) than the Captain that Betty Flanders, we may fairly guess, derives her greatest pleasure. In her girlish excitement and reliance on him together with his austere and rigid manliness, we sense a relationship not so much as that between a man and a woman as between a *father* and a *daughter;* and for Mrs. Flanders, whose marriage seems not to have yielded much satisfaction, the feeling is genuine enough.

Another, darker, less sympathetic, side to Betty Flanders, however, emerges when we consider her relationship to Mr. Floyd, a clergyman, eight years her junior. Having, in his spare hours, taught her sons Latin for three years, Floyd, in all his clerical innocence, suddenly declares his love for her and proposes marriage. As she read Floyd's declaration, "Up and down went her breast. Seabrook came vividly before her" (20;*18*). And a moment later: " 'How could I think of marriage!' she said to herself bitterly. . . . She had always disliked red hair in men, she thought, thinking of Mr. Floyd's appearance. . . ." Thus her note of refusal "was such a motherly, respectful, inconsequent, regretful letter that he kept it for many years" (21;*19*).[6]

She had always disliked red hair in men. Can Mrs. Flanders's *first* reason for refusing Floyd have been so superficial? It is probably not, but it speaks volumes. That the proposal immediately evokes Seabrook's memory obliquely suggests that Betty Flanders has had her bout with marriage and sex. She has her Captain Barfoot to depend upon; to feel secure with; to be sexually unencumbered by. She has her three sons as living testimony of her womanhood and motherhood. Consequently, all the young Floyds in the world (red-haired or not) mean little to her. Them, she can use, later refuse, perhaps even abuse.

That little rhyme of judgment may seem harsh, but Virginia Woolf insists upon it. When Mr. Floyd is preparing to leave, for example,

5. Italics are mine, here and throughout the chapter, unless otherwise noted.

6. In the first Holograph Notebook of *Jacob's Room,* one finds Betty Flanders's first reaction to Floyd's proposal to be: "It was, probably, that the idea of copulation had now become infinitely remote from her" followed by "And I've always disliked red hair in men. . . ." The quotation is given only because it sheds light on the deeper foundation of her affection for Captain Barfoot, with all its *conscious* filial chasteness.

he asks the boys to choose any of his possessions as a remembrance of him; and the youngest son selects a kitten. Some years later, Mrs. Flanders, stroking the now aged cat, remarks: "'Poor old Topaz' . . . and she smiled, thinking how she had had him gelded, and how she did not like red hair in men" (22-23;*20*). Surely, the juxtaposition speaks for itself? But if this is Betty Flanders as woman and as mother, then what can we expect Jacob Flanders to become both as man and as son?

Very little of Jacob comes to us filtered through his own consciousness. He is presented to us largely through the distorted impressions and distorting perspectives of the people who inhabit his world. It is not true, however, that Jacob is just a nebulous figure, a name, which we search for in vain and never find. Despite Mrs. Woolf's assertion that "It is no use trying to sum people up," her nimble pen is at work incessantly and insistently, here with a nudge, there with a push, urging us on to follow her hints; for the novel abounds in hints of all kinds. The real task is not only to recognize one when we are pushed toward it, but to interpret in in a way that will give lustre to everything that has come before it and shine ahead on all that is to follow.

But the book is so compact, so compressed with hints, that it is difficult to know where to begin to follow those twists and turns which will enable us to see the finer features of Jacob emerge from the plethora of small details and slight touches. Perhaps if we look first at the women in his life, a veil or two might be lifted. We might wonder, for example, about his relation to his mother when we discover Jacob, aged nineteen, a student at Cambridge, "feeling the pocket where he kept his [mother's] letters," or keeping in his room there "a photograph of his mother" (38-39;*36-37*). And then there is Clara Durrant in the scene by the grapevine, where Jacob is speaking quite matter-of-factly, while Clara is wildly imagining him as a lover: "'You're too good—too good,' she thought, thinking of Jacob, thinking that he must not say that he loved her. No, no, no" (63;*61*). There is of course no clue whatever that Jacob is thinking of declaring his love; and only later, after his Cambridge days, do we find that he had in his room "the black wooden box where he kept his mother's letters . . . and a note or two [from Clara] with the

Cornish postmark. The lid shut upon the truth" (70;*69*).⁷ We can only speculate on that truth later when we find that "of all women, Jacob honoured her [Clara] most" (123;*122*). Is it Clara's innocence that Jacob *honoured*—instead of loving her? Is it her purity, her inviolability, to which Jacob is sufficiently attracted to keep her notes beside his mother's letters in his black box? We cannot be sure. But it seems a fair guess, especially when we consider his relations with other women—less anchored women of more relaxed virtue.

Jacob's relationship to Florinda reveals a part of him to us. A brainless prostitute swearing to chastity, Florinda has her attractions for Jacob; and their "comradeship [was] all spirited on her side, protective on his . . ." (78;*77*). Returning to his room one evening, Jacob, looking at Florinda, reflects that "Beauty goes hand in hand with stupidity." A hint is dropped that a sudden physical urge is aroused in him, but despite his essay on the defence of indecency, "Jacob doubted whether he liked it in the raw." Suddenly he wished to return to "male society, cloistered rooms, and the works of the classics . . ."; but it is too late, because

Then Florinda laid her hand upon his knee.

After all, it was none of her fault. But the thought saddened him. . . .

Any excuse, though, serves a stupid woman. He told her that his head ached.

But when she looked at him, dumbly, half-guessing, half-understanding, apologizing perhaps . . . then he knew that [male society] cloisters and classics are no use whatever. The problem is insoluble (82;*81*).

In this brief but eloquent scene, we have the boldest expression thus far of Jacob's "insoluble" problem: because to him the sexual act is indecent, carnal desires are met with contrary blasts of blame. As a result he is profoundly ambivalent towards women. When physical intimacy threatens, he wishes to return to male society and solitude. However, his need of reversion is useless, because he is, as we shall later discover, also ambivalent towards men. In short, at this stage in his life, Jacob is unable consciously to turn either to a woman or to a man with any degree of assurance or guarantee of acceptance.

7. In the first Holograph Notebook, we find ". . . the black wooden box where he kept his mother's letter, his old flannel trousers, & a great many photographs of [*young men*]. He was disappointed but on the whole more puzzled than disappointed. Anyhow the lid shut upon the truth." Italicized words within brackets indicate that the matter was deleted in Holograph.

Time passes. Jacob is employed. Mrs. Flanders's letters continue. Virginia Woolf again insists, now by negative suggestion, that the reader feel the indomitable pressure of his mother upon Jacob's adult life:

Meanwhile, poor Betty Flanders's letter . . . lay on the hall table—poor Betty Flanders writing her son's name . . . as mothers do . . . suggesting how mothers down at Scarborough scribble over the fire . . . and can never, never say . . . Don't go with bad women, do be a good boy; wear your thick shirts; and come back, come back, come back to me (90;*89*).

The letter remains on the hall table that evening when the bedroom door is shut with Jacob and Florinda behind it:

But if the pale blue envelope . . . had the feelings of a mother, the heart was torn by the little creak, the sudden stir. Behind the door was the obscene thing, the alarming presence, and terror would come over her as at death, or the birth of a child. Better, perhaps, burst in and face it than sit in the antechamber listening to the little creak, the sudden stir, for her heart was swollen, and pain threaded it. My son, my son—such would be her cry uttered to hide her vision of him stretched with Florinda. . . . And the fault lay with Florinda. Indeed, when the door opened and the couple came out, Mrs. Flanders would have flounced upon her . . . (92;*90-91*).

"Poor Betty Flanders," however, need not have flounced upon Florinda, nor even have worried very much about her young son. For Jacob is already half emasculated and quite strangled by his mother. Thus he can satisfy his physical hunger only with prostitutes— whether with Florinda now in his room or later with Laurette in a brothel. Prostitutes do not represent the inviolable mystery of a mother, nor do they represent the untouchable purity of a Clara. So that if sex to Jacob is indecent, and if the body urges him on to indecency, then Jacob must consider himself to be bad. And what could be more appropriate for a "bad" boy than to lay with a "bad" woman?

But Jacob is not aware of this, for he is not a cerebral man. Mrs. Woolf too often reminds us that his ability to attract lay not in the powers of his mind but in the sinews of his physicality. Indeed, he is so incredibly naive that he thinks "these little prostitutes, staring in the fire, taking out a powder-puff, decorating lips at an inch of looking-glass . . . have an inviolable fidelity" only to see Florinda "turning up Greek Street upon another man's arm" (94;*93*). And so another rent is torn in the membrane of his tender masculinity—and outraged vanity.

No, Mrs. Flanders need not worry about her son's having any enduring relations with women. For in addition to what we already know, we discover that he is terrified of women who are vehement in their feeling. Fanny Elmer, for example, on first meeting him, becomes infatuated with Jacob, imagines living with him, and soon tries to attract his attention by playfully dropping her glove. When Jacob, unconscious of the manoeuvre, quite innocently returns the glove to her, "she started angrily. For never was there a more irrational passion. And Jacob was afraid of her for the moment—so violent, so dangerous is it when young women stand rigid; grasp the barrier; fall in love" (118;*117*).

Of all Jacob's fragile amours, it is his romance in Greece with Mrs. Sandra Wentworth Williams which sends his rockets soaring and flaring. Again, his body attracts this aging but beautiful coquette. Once her roving eyes have fixed upon Jacob, it takes only a little while for Sandra, with the help of her resigned and vestigial husband, to draw Jacob to her lure. Within a day, having declined the Williams's invitation to accompany them to Corinth, Jacob resolves to go to Athens alone, only now "with this hook dragging in his side" (147;*146*). Several days later, lying in bed, he is thinking about the problems of civilization which the ancient Greeks had solved so remarkably, when "the hook gave a great tug in his side . . . and he turned over with a desperate sort of tumble, remembering Sandra Wentworth Williams with whom he was in love" (150;*149*).

This passage is somewhat misleading, because it hints that the hook is symbolic of his love for Mrs. Williams. And although the woman has certainly baited him, it seems unlikely that Jacob at this stage would think of his new romance as some painful instrument dragging at his side, because his attachment has in no way yet been bruised or frustrated. The hook is, however, *associated* with Sandra Williams, for she has that peculiar combination of vigor, sadness, age, and beauty which is very enticing to Jacob. As they climb a hill, he thinks how

Mrs. Williams said things straight out. He was surprised by his own knowledge of the rules of behaviour; how much more can be said than one thought; how open one can be with a woman; and how little he had known himself before (146;*146*).

Mrs. Williams's intoxicants are working their magic, but what Jacob does not soberly recognize is the similarity of Sandra's alluring qualities to those of his mother. So that quite unconsciously, Jacob, aged twenty-six, responds to Sandra Williams as an adolescent might to a maternal mistress, and we may safely assume that the tugging he feels is from the hook on a line held by Mrs. Flanders far off in Scarborough. Thus, however well the ancient Greeks solved at least one problem of civilization—namely, the Oedipal complication—we must all agree with Jacob that "their solution is no help to us" (149;*149*).

Later meeting the Williamses in Athens, Jacob is whisked off by Sandra who suggests that they go to the Acropolis at night. Beneath the sound of their talk, we learn that "He had in him the seeds of extreme disillusionment, which would come to him from women in middle life. Perhaps if one strove hard enough to reach the top of the hill it need not come to him—this disillusionment from women in middle life" (159;*158*). The passage begins to swarm with meaning when we realize that "women in middle life" refers not only to Sandra Williams, but to Betty Flanders as well.

During their romantic ascent, Virginia Woolf introduces what appears to be a subtle digression to get Mrs. Flanders into the foreground. Somewhere in the darkness of their climb to the Acropolis, Jacob gives Sandra a book of Donne's poems: "'Here. Will you keep this?'" he asks.

Now the agitation of the air uncovered a racing star. *Now* it was dark. *Now* one after another lights were extinguished. *Now* great towns—Paris—Constantinople—London—were black with strewn rock. . . . The English sky is softer, milkier than the Eastern. Something gentle has passed into it from the grass-rounded hills, something damp. The salt gale blew in at Betty Flanders's bedroom window, and the widow lady, raising herself . . . sighed like one who realizes, but would fain ward off a little longer—oh, a little longer!—the oppression of eternity.
But to return to Jacob and Sandra (160;*159-60*).

We need not return to Jacob and Sandra, because we have really not left them. Mrs. Woolf has only blocked our view of them and whatever it is they are doing. She has stopped mechanical time with the "Now" which begins each of the four opening sentences. She moves us in space to England, introduces several sensuous nature images, and lowers us into the oppressive bedroom of Mrs. Flanders who is hoping against nature to prevent what seems inevitable. And eclipsed as this passage may be, the simultaneity achieved technically not only suggests a time correspondence between the couple's presumed love-making and Mrs. Flanders's terrible loneliness, but also forces us to connect the *fertile* presence of the determined Sandra Williams to the *haunting* presence of the equally determined Betty Flanders. The "promiscuous" mother and the "virgin" mother are now in deadly combat.

In a final master stroke, Mrs. Woolf, by leaving us uncertain as to whether Jacob and Sandra reached their actual or metaphoric destination, poetically transfigures the journey into a pilgrimage of considerably heightened significance:

As for reaching the Acropolis who shall say that we ever do it, or that when Jacob woke next morning he found anything hard and durable to keep for ever? Still, he went with them to Constantinople (161;*160*).

If Jacob did not wake the next morning to find anything "hard and durable"—and the sentence, "*Still,* he went with them. . . ." tells us that *he did not*—then Jacob has not symbolically reached the top of that hill which would prevent "this disillusionment from women in middle life."

Whatever else we may wish to say of Jacob, one thing is clear: his relationships with women are both immature and unsatisfactory. Clara, in her purity, can only be honored; Florinda, robbing him of his virginity, drenches him with humiliation; Fanny is so passionate that she terrifies him; Sandra, a safely married seductress, lures him only for an escapade. In each instance, Jacob is either defeated or self-defeating; and when we remember Mrs. Flanders's shadow hovering over him at each step in his life, we feel more painfully the wounding tugs of the hook metaphorically embedded in his side.

When Jacob senses defeat from the women he attracts, he seeks refuge in "male society," and Timmy Durrant, one of his earliest friends, is a member of that refuge. The scene of their sailing together to the Scilly Isles contains some passages which are streaked with innuendo. We discover that the boys had quarrelled for some unstated reason connected with opening a "tin of beef, with

Shakespeare on board''; and for some unstated reason, Jacob begins to sulk. Just prior to this, we are told that Timmy, in full command of the boat, was a sight that "would have moved a woman. Jacob, of course, was no woman. The sight of Timmy Durrant was no sight for him, nothing to set against the sky and worship; far from it. They had quarrelled" (47;*45*). Later, Timmy, too busy with scientific observations to remember the quarrel, interrupts Jacob's sulkiness with a question; and immediately "Jacob began to unbutton his clothes and sat naked, save for his shirt, intending, apparently, to bathe" (48;*46*). One wonders why Virginia Woolf inserts "apparently" into the sentence. For what other reason than bathing would Jacob take off his clothes? And why is his nakedness mentioned three times in two pages? What does it add to the scene? How does it relate to his gloominess? When he plunges into the sea, gulps water, gasps, and must be towed by a rope and hauled on board, we begin to reason that at last Jacob has found a way to become once more, in his distress, the focus of attraction. Seeing Jacob as a naked center of attraction, we recognize the operation of a narcissistic device of attention-getting.[8] For whatever Jacob may lack in mind, he has always been assured by women that he compensates for that lack with his physique.

There is more to it than that, however; and Mrs. Woolf seems to want to persuade us of a deeper relation between Jacob and Timmy. We feel that persuasive pressure in a brief exchange between Jacob and Mrs. Durrant:

"I want to hear about your voyage," said Mrs. Durrant.
"Yes," he said.
"Twenty years ago we did the same thing."
"Yes," he said. She looked at him sharply.
"He is extraordinarily awkward," she thought, noticing how he fingered his socks. "Yet so distinguished-looking."
"In those days. . ." she resumed, and told him how they had sailed. . . "my husband, who knew a good deal about sailing, for he kept a yacht before we married". . . (61;*60*).

---

8. Mrs. Woolf was to write something similar in spirit in *Orlando,* (New York: Harcourt, Brace and Co., 1928, p. 155): "For nothing . . . is more heavenly than to resist and to yield; to yield and to resist. Surely it throws the spirit into such a rapture that nothing else can. So that I'm not sure . . . that I won't throw myself overboard, for the mere pleasure of being rescued by a blue-jacket after all."

The friendship between Jacob and Timmy in no way parallels the relationship between Mr. and Mrs. Durrant, yet the comparison of husband and wife to two young men is another instance of Mrs. Woolf's method of obliquely and shrewdly inserting a hint at the idea into her narrative.

The relationship between Jacob and Bonamy, however, is flashed upon us with more glaring boldness. Although Bonamy's name has been mentioned before, it is not until the brief scene with Jacob in Bonamy's room that we begin to sense the nature of their friendship. Through the housekeeper we learn of their fight over a broken coffee-pot:

> . . .there were Sanders [Flanders] and Bonamy like two bulls of Bashan driving each other up and down, making such a racket, and all them chairs in the way. They never noticed her. She felt motherly towards them . . . . And Bonamy, all his hair touzled and his tie flying, broke off, and pushed Sanders into the arm-chair, and said Mr. Sanders had smashed the coffee-pot and he was teaching Mr. Sanders—(102;*101*)

The passage reads as if the broken pot were merely an excuse for wrestling, for prolonged physical contact; and in that tossing light we see what is meant by the housekeeper's remark: " 'Women'—she thought, and wondered what Sanders and her gentleman did in *that* line. . ." (102;*100-101*).[9]

Only later in an exchange among Mrs. Durrant's guests are we given a fluent explanation of Bonamy himself: "And that is the very reason . . . why she [Clara] attracts Dick Bonamy . . . . Now *he's* a dark horse if you like. And there these gossips would suddenly pause. Obviously they meant to hint at his peculiar disposition—long rumoured among them."[10]

> "But sometimes it is precisely a woman like Clara that men of that temperament need . . ." Miss Julia Eliot would hint (154;*154*).

The hints continue:

> "He [Jacob] doesn't overwork himself anyhow."
> "His friends are very fond of him."
> "Dick Bonamy, you mean?"
> "No, I didn't mean that. It's evidently the other way with Jacob. He is

9. The emphasis is Virginia Woolf's.

10. The emphasis is Virginia Woolf's.

precisely the young man to fall headlong in love and repent it for the rest of his life" (155;*154*).

Again Virginia Woolf is saying one thing and suggesting another. It is not Bonamy but Jacob who feels strongly for Clara Durrant; and if "men of that temperament" need a woman like Clara, then it is really Jacob to whom reference is ironically being made.

The scene between the two young men after Jacob's return from Greece heavily accents the homosexual weight of their friendship:

"The height of the season," said Bonamy.

He was sarcastic because of Clara Durrant; because Jacob had come back from Greece very brown and lean . . . because Jacob was silent.

"He has not said a word to show that he is glad to see me," thought Bonamy bitterly.

A moment later:

"Very urbane," Jacob brought out.

"Urbane" on the lips of Jacob had mysteriously all the shapeliness of a character which Bonamy thought daily more sublime, devastating, terrific than ever, though he was still, and perhaps would be for ever, barbaric, obscure.

The exchange continues:

"The height of civilization," said Jacob.

He was fond of using Latin words.

Magnanimity, virtue—such words when Jacob used them in talk with Bonamy meant that he took control of the situation; that Bonamy would play round him like an affectionate spaniel; and that (as likely as not) they would end rolling on the floor.

"And Greece?" said Bonamy. "The Parthenon and all that?"

"There's none of this European mysticism," said Jacob.

"It's the atmosphere, I suppose," said Bonamy. "And you went to Constantinople?"

"Yes," said Jacob.

Bonamy paused, moved a pebble; then darted in with the rapidity and certainty of a lizard's tongue.

"You are in love!" he exclaimed.

Jacob blushed.

The sharpest of knives never cut so deep (164-65;*163-64*).

From these lines, there can be no doubt that Bonamy "who was fonder of Jacob than any one in the world" and "who couldn't love a woman" (140;*139*)—is erotically bound to Jacob. But the extent to which Jacob is receptive to Bonamy's homosexual feelings is left entirely to the liveliness of our own imaginations.

Mrs. Woolf does however insert at least two seemingly extraneous scenes—and very little in Woolf is "extraneous"—which suggest that Jacob, although perhaps not quite homophilic himself, most assuredly enjoys attracting men who are themselves so inclined. Consider, first, the scene in the British Museum when "a pudding-faced man pushed a note towards Jacob, and Jacob, leaning back in his chair, began an uneasy murmured conversation, and they went off together . . . . Jacob came back only in time to return his books" (107;*106*). The second is in the hotel in Greece where the waiter "Aristotle, a dirty man, carnivorously interested in the body of the only guest now occupying the only arm-chair, came into the room ostentatiously, put something down, put something straight, and saw Jacob was still there" (138;*137*).

It is no coincidence that Mrs. Woolf puts into Jacob's hands, later that evening after the British Museum, a copy of the *Phaedrus* to read. Nor is it a coincidence that several pages later Mrs. Woolf has Jacob alone at night with his chess board: he "raised the white queen from her square; then put her down again in the same spot. He filled his pipe; ruminated; moved two pawns; advanced the white knight; then ruminated with one finger upon the bishop. Now Fanny Elmer passed beneath the window" (114;*114*). This passage captures the symbolic parallel between Jacob's hesitation in dealing with the queen (the female who will not budge) and the ease with which he moves the knight (the male he can manoeuvre). Comparing Jacob's masculine gesture of filling his pipe with Fanny Elmer's proximity, we have something reminiscent of an earlier scene at a dance with Florinda:

Jacob could not dance. He stood against the wall smoking a pipe.
"We think," said two dancers. . ."that you are the most beautiful man we have ever seen."
So they wreathed his head with paper flowers. Then somebody brought out a white and gilt chair and made him sit on it . . . . Then Florinda got upon his knee and hid her face in his waistcoat. With one hand he held her; with the other, his pipe (75;*74*).

With one hand he held her; with the other, his pipe. Here is that expansive image forcefully assuring us of Jacob's private and primitive narcissism which balances the feminine with one hand and the masculine with the other. Stated negatively, it is the symbolic picture of an ambivalent man with both hands tied.

Shortly after Virginia Woolf arrived at an idea of a new form for the new novel which was to become *Jacob's Room,* she recorded in her *Diary* on 26 January 1920: "but conceive (?) *Mark on the Wall, K*[ew]. *G*[ardens]., and *Unwritten Novel* taking hands and dancing in unity. What that unity shall be I have yet to discover; the theme is a blank to me; but I see immense possibilities in the form I hit upon more or less by chance two weeks ago. I suppose the danger is the damned egotistical self. . . ."

The reader of *Kew Gardens* quickly realizes that the world is being conveyed to him primarily from a snail's point of view; so that he receives a series of impressions which simulate the random organization of almost pure observation and non-differentiating perception. As four couples pass the flower bed, the reader catches fragments of speech and thought which fracture time and space. The fragments, however, provide just enough of the familiar to give the semblance of reality. It was precisely this fracturing of temporal and spatial relations that Mrs. Woolf experimented so imaginatively with in writing *Jacob's Room.*

In *The Mark on the Wall,* she demonstrated a technique of recording the stream of impressions which intrude themselves upon the mind. With the "mark on the wall" as her point of departure, Mrs. Woolf traces the immediate associations which color and enhance each other while simultaneously calling forth new ones into play. The cerebral excursion triggered off by the external object proceeds by shuttling back and forth between a hazy past and a shimmering present; and the effect is that of expanding an ordinary moment into a psychological moment of much greater stretch and height and depth. It was the freedom of association with its concomitant effect of time expansion, which were to become part of Mrs. Woolf's technical repertoire for *Jacob's Room.*

It was *An Unwritten Novel,* however, which left its deepest impress in *Jacob's Room;* for it accents most eloquently that as single human units of life, how little we are able to see below the surface: how restricted we are in our knowledge of others near to us; how little we know of the thought behind the human face; of the meaning in the folded hands; of the reason for the stifled sigh—and how scalding the disappointment is when we discover the mistakes we make when we try to fathom anyone beyond our solitary selves, however much one has said and however much more one has left unsaid. "But something," wrote Virginia Woolf, "is always impelling one to hum vibrating . . . at the mouth of the cavern of mystery, endowing Jacob Flanders with all sorts of qualities he had not at all . . . what remains is mostly a matter of guess work. Yet over him we hang vibrating" (73;72).

Critics who have hung vibrating over Jacob have had a good deal to say about him, but they have had generally more to say about the complexities and confusions of Mrs. Woolf's experiment. It is true on a superficial level that part of the novel's meaning is in its reminding us that we live in odd corners, clutching a piece of looking-glass into which we gaze, seeing not our own reflection but the image bestowed upon us by those people who linger in the significant orbit of our private lives. But the question remains: What does that looking-glass reflect of Jacob? For surely, Mrs. Woolf, so delicate an analyst of human relations, would not have written a novel of one hundred and seventy pages merely to prove her point that "it is no use trying to sum up people." Nor would very much be gained by agreeing with those critics who insist that Mrs. Woolf was incapable of creating characters. Despite the unhesitating procession of disconnected thought and often unanalyzable image, despite the measured pageant of luminous moments placed perpendicular to horizontal and trivial incidents, despite the continual shifting in time and space, the reader, if determined to follow the novel's disquieting obliquities, does indeed get a substantial picture of Jacob as well as a sense of the emotional contours of his inner life. And what finally emerges is not what E.M. Forster so positively described Jacob as—"The solid figure of a young man."[11]

What does emerge is a disturbed young man, weighed down by many vague pressures only hinted at, which we must discover some-

---

11. "The Early Novels of Virginia Woolf," *Abinger Harvest,* New York: Harcourt, Brace and Co., 1936, p. 109.

how through misty clouds of association. His relations with women are neither mature nor fulfilling: they are heavy with defeat. Nor are his relations with men wholly satisfactory: the emotionally dislocated need in Jacob's narcissism with Timmy Durrant (who is really the "solid figure of a young man") develops with time and becomes hardened and habitual in his relationship with Bonamy. For in that alliance—restricting as it is, psychologically and socially—the "extra-ordinarily awkward . . . yet so distinguished looking" Jacob is glorified in the longing eyes of his homosexual companion, Bonamy; and in that reflecting mirror Jacob can feel idolized, "monolithic—oh, very beautiful!—like a British Admiral. . ." (165;*164*). In a word, Jacob *needs* Bonamy, because he makes Jacob feel that he indeed possesses all those exalted qualities which, as Mrs. Woolf often enough reminds us, he indeed lacks.

It is no accident of memory that two entire paragraphs of the concluding one-page chapter appear *verbatim* earlier in the text:

Listless is the air in an empty room, just swelling the curtain; the flowers in the jar shift. One fibre in the wicker arm-chair creaks, though no one sits there (39;*37*).

This passage appears first in a description of Jacob's room in Cambridge, where among other things is "a photograph of his mother." One is immediately struck by the ghostly creaking of the empty arm-chair, as if so early in Jacob's life, death already haunts his room. The second passage reads:

The rooms are shapely, the ceilings high; over the doorway a rose, or a ram's skull, is carved in the wood. The eighteenth century has its distinction. Even the panels, painted in raspberry-coloured paint, have their distinction. . . (70;*69*).

This room in London, besides its furniture from Cambridge, has now in addition: "the black wooden box where he kept his mother's letters . . . . The lid shut upon the truth." Also in this room now are Bonamy and Jacob together.

When these two passages appear together on the final page of the novel, the first co-positioning of mother (photograph) and death (creaking chair) compared to the second of mother (letters) and Bonamy (homosexuality) suddenly assume a new configuration of vastly heightened semantic resonance. For clearly the final confrontation of Mrs. Flanders and Bonamy in the empty room of Jacob, now dead, has the connecting force of a union curiously potent with consequence; for it implies a fatally-charged circuit of motherhood, homosexuality, and death.

But there is more to ponder on this final page. Just as Virginia Woolf in *The Voyage Out* hinted that the death of the motherless Rachel was caused by tropical fever, here she conveniently provides us with a "war" to take the life of the fatherless Jacob. Although some direct, and many more indirect, references are made to war, *Jacob's Room* is not, as Mrs. Woolf's first biographer would have us believe, a "war novel."[12] If it were simply that, too many images which intersect and echo throughout the work would become derelict experimental exercises in poetic ambiguity, and everything that has led to Jacob's death would appear random and senseless. Mrs. Woolf does, however, provide us with a backdrop of battlefield; but although the distant concussion of war may lend the novel a certain poetic amplitude, it does not satisfy its deeply-worked pattern of meaning. And here one must be cautious, for it is generally agreed that works which tend to move away from prose statement cannot, in criticism, be explicated systematically, because poetry is schematic; it has its provenance in a vast indefinite nimbus of faint idea and fugitive image, not readily susceptible to the rigid finality of critical pronouncement. Can we, then, make a critical pronouncement about the novel's last two lines:

"What am I to do with these, Mr. Bonamy?"
She held out a pair of Jacob's old shoes.

Why of all things would Virginia Woolf end the book with a pair of "old shoes"? What possible bearing can they have on all that has preceded these lines? We need only glance back over the book, however, to see that "old shoes" are indeed linked in numerous and subtle ways with names and objects having to do with feet. At the novel's beginning Captain Barfoot is introduced as the lame gentleman so dear to Betty Flanders. His wife, Ellen Barfoot, is an invalid; and there is Seabrook, dead, "who had gone out . . . and refused to

---

12. Aileen Pippett, *The Moth and the Star: A Biography of Virginia Woolf,* Boston and Toronto: Little, Brown and Co., 1955, p. 158.

change his boots" (16;*14*). When Jacob chooses as his farewell gift from Mr. Floyd "the works of Byron in one volume," we are reminded that Byron himself limped because of a clubfoot. Later in Cambridge we learn that Jacob's "slippers were incredibly shabby, like boats burnt to the water's rim" (39;*37*). Still later in London, we discover that Jacob cannot dance, cannot manage his feet socially.

It is not necessary to extend the references to feet to realize how closely interwoven this image is in the novel and how its contexts continue to proliferate. What seems strangely most to impress itself on the reader's memory occurs in the first chapter when the child Jacob is climbing the rock, and "a small boy has to stretch his legs far apart, and indeed to feel rather heroic, before he gets to the top," where he discovers the crab on "weakly legs."

For we reach the end of the first chapter with the little crab "trying with its weakly legs to climb the steep side; trying again and falling back, and trying again and again." And we reach the end of the novel with Mrs. Flanders holding Jacob's old shoes. If we recall her thought of Seabrook's death as being somehow connected with his refusing to change his boots, we begin to sense a misty constellation of elements taking shape: the widowed Mrs. Flanders, possessive of her son, holding his old shoes to Bonamy whose homosexual attachment to her son is unknown to her produces a very uncanny effect. In that elliptical but eloquent final gesture is the embodiment of the idea that metaphorically, Jacob's legs, throughout his life, have never been strong; his footing has never been secure. Like the little crab of his childhood, his ascent to adulthood and real emotional freedom has failed; his effort to grow beyond himself into an adult world has, from the beginning of Jacob's life, been hopelessly denuded of grace.

Mrs. Dalloway

"For there she was." So ends Virginia Woolf's fourth novel; and upon these four words rests the full weight of its meaning. Exactly how we interpret them depends upon how we have read all the preceding pages; whether we have caught in this novel's seamless world of psychology and doubt the minute signals strewn everywhere, the small half visible evasions and turns which have the shaping power of invention and suggestion; whether we have heard those near inaudible sounds and repetitions of word and phrase which collect and build an edifice of feeling so infallibly arranged and welded together; whether we have glimpsed the shadow play of consciousness and motive so abysmal with ambiguity and possibility as to make critical commentary appear to reside in some ablative region on the far side of language.

"As the publishers frankly say," wrote the reviewer, D.R., "'This novel does not belong to the multitude.' The Galsworthy refinement will not always be understood, nor are all readers proficient in the difficult gymnastic of jumping in and out of other people's skins. But it is a book which will be highly praised by the sensitive minority."[1] Joseph Wood Krutch who interpreted the novel through Clarissa, who to him "seems to assure those who come near her that life, even though it have neither harmony nor meaning, may yet be lived with a certain comeliness if one does not ask too much of it; and thus Mrs. Woolf reinvestigates a very old sort of loveliness."[2] Another reviewer found a "resentfulness" in Clarissa, "some paucity of spiritual graces, or rather some positive hideousness." Having admired Mrs. Woolf's prose and compared her with her contemporaries, he returns to the novel through Clarissa: her impressions, her memories, "the events which are initiated remotely and engineered almost to touching distance of the impervious Clarissa, capture in a definitive matrix the drift of thought and feeling in a period, the point of view of a class, and seem

1. *The Independent,* 20 June 1925.

2. "The Stream of Consciousness," *The Nation,* 3 June 1925.

almost to indicate the strength and weakness of an entire civilization."[3]

Some of the entries Virginia Woolf made in her *Diary* during the revision of *Mrs. Dalloway* lead us to suspect that she knew many of her reviewers would not understand the intricacy of her design and would miss the connections between Clarissa and Septimus. She was right. Probably because she thought her readers would not understand its design, she wrote a preface to the novel when it was to be reprinted in 1928. In it she provided an important clue to the novel's form and meaning:

To tell the reader anything that his own imagination and insight have not already discovered would need not a page or two of preface but a volume or two of autobiography. . . . Of *Mrs. Dalloway* then one can only bring to light at the moment a few scraps, of little importance or none perhaps; as that in the first version Septimus, who later is intended to be her double, had no existence; and that Mrs. Dalloway was originally to kill herself or perhaps merely to die at the end of the party.[4]

This statement quite naturally generated a whirlwind of new readings of the novel, but the question of *how* Septimus is Clarissa's double has remained a stony and stubborn riddle. As Keith Hollingworth wrote: "The clue, nevertheless, remains a puzzle in itself: when the differences between Septimus and Clarissa bulk larger than the likenesses, how can he be her double?"[5] The answer to that is not easy, but to get at part of it requires our understanding something of Mrs. Woolf's method[6] in order to see how the *personae* are aligned in relation to one another.

It may seem strange that Mrs. Woolf herself was unaware of her method until 30 August 1923 when she was writing *Mrs. Dalloway,* then called *The Hours.* On that day she recorded in her *Diary:* "I should say a good deal about *The Hours* and my discovery: how I dig out beautiful caves behind my characters: I think that gives exactly

3. John W. Crawford, *The New York Times Book Review,* 10 May 1925.

4. "Introduction," *Mrs. Dalloway,* New York: Modern Library, 1928, p. vi.

5. "Freud and the Riddle of *Mrs. Dalloway,*" *Studies in Honor of John Wilcox,* A. Dayle Wallace and Woodburn O. Ross, eds. Detroit: Wayne State University Press, 1958, p. 240.

6. See Edward A. Hungerford, "'My Tunnelling Process': The Method of 'Mrs. Dalloway'," *Modern Fiction Studies* (Summer 1957), pp. 164-67.

what I want; humanity, humour, depth. The idea is that the caves shall connect and each comes to daylight at the present moment.'' Approximately six weeks later, on 15 October, she wrote: ''It took me a year's groping to discover what I call my tunnelling process, by which I tell the past by instalments, as I have need of it. This is my prime discovery so far; and the fact that I've been so long finding it proves, I think, how false Percy Lubbock's doctrine is—that you can do this sort of thing consciously.''

The importance of unconsciousness in writing was long known to Mrs. Woolf. She wrote in her 1919 essay on Defoe that ''like all unconscious artists, he leaves more gold in his work than his own generation was able to bring to the surface.''[7] And she was to say some years later that ''a novelist's chief desire is to be as unconscious as possible. . . . so that nothing may disturb or disquiet the mysterious nosings about, feelings round . . . of that very shy and illusive spirit, the imagination.''[8] That the ''tunnelling'' was occurring without Mrs. Woolf's being conscious of it implies that those ''mysterious nosings about'' were in reality deep penetrations; so that the ''very shy and illusive spirit'' was free to make associations which defied logical order and explicit statement. For rational order would merely burlesque meaning, and clarity would deform the springs of feeling. This means that if we as readers are to discover the buried gold of her novel, we too must plumb those interpsychic ''caves'' and connect them in such a way that they will illuminate the dark interiors where the elusive substance of each character's sequestered life is first felt and then ultimately revealed.

On the novel's first page we are introduced to Clarissa, making preparations for the party she is to give on that evening in June 1923; and quite incidentally, two details are provided by a friend watching Clarissa wait to cross a London street. There was ''a touch of the bird about her . . . though over fifty, and grown very white since her illness'' (4;*6*).[9]

7. *The Common Reader: First Series,* New York: Harcourt, Brace and World, Inc., A Harvest Book, 1955, p. 94; London: The Hogarth Press (Tenth Impression), 1962, p. 127.

8. *The Death of the Moth and Other Essays,* New York and London: Harcourt Brace Jovanovich, A Harvest Book, 1974, p. 239.

9. The unitalicized page number in parentheses following each quotation refers to the first

Given her age and a hint of her physical condition, we are placed in Clarissa's consciousness and allowed to follow the play of her thoughts. The name of Peter Walsh is mentioned, and we learn of a romance between them at Bourton. Clarissa had refused to marry him because "in marriage a little licence, a little independence there must be between people living together day in day out in the same house; which Richard gave her. . . . But with Peter everything had to be shared; everything gone into. And it was intolerable . . ."(10;*10*).

Clarissa's need for freedom and independence is clear enough, but it becomes complicated when other irreconcilable feelings are introduced. "She felt very young" and "at the same time unspeakably aged. She sliced like a knife through everything; at the same time was outside, looking on" (11;*10*). These polarities are so extreme that they suggest a connection with the thoughts immediately following: "She had a perpetual sense . . . of being out, far out and alone; she always had the feeling that it was very, very dangerous to live even one day" (11;*10-11*).

These simultaneous yet opposing feelings, her sense of aloneness, of life's being a dangerous business, all begin to vibrate with meaning when they are considered in relation to her "party consciousness."[10] It becomes increasingly apparent that Clarissa's gatherings are a means by which she measures her own worth: they are her opportunity for gaining the approval and admiration of others; and she knows that "half the time she did things not simply, not for themselves; but to make people think this or that; perfect idiocy she knew . . ." (13-14;*12*). That she continues to give parties to bolster her own sense of self, however, bespeaks a profound dissatisfaction with herself; a feeling so deeply rooted that she *wishes to be someone other than Clarissa Dalloway:* "She would have been . . . dark like **Lady Bexborough. . . . She would have been, like Lady Bexborough, slow and stately; rather large; interested in politics like a man. . . ."** The extremity of her dissatisfaction becomes clear

---

American paperback edition published by Harcourt, Brace and World, Inc., 1964; the italicized number refers to The Hogarth Press (Chatto and Windus) edition (Twelfth Impression), 1968.

10. See Frank Baldanza, "Clarissa Dalloway's 'Party Consciousness'," *Modern Fiction Studies* (February 1956), pp. 24-30.

when she thinks, "But often now this body she wore . . . this body, with all its capacities, seemed nothing—nothing at all" (14;*13*). How more succinctly to convey an alienation from what one feels to be one's physical value.

The extent to which these feelings threaten self-annihilation is hinted at in a seemingly random memory Clarissa has during her morning hour on Bond Street: "She remembered once throwing a shilling into the Serpentine" (12;*11*). That memory only becomes significant many hours and some two hundred pages later, when she learns of Septimus's suicide. Re-living his death in her imagination, Clarissa thinks: "She had once thrown a shilling into the Serpentine, never anything more. But he had flung it away" (280;*202*). A subtle one to be sure, but a connection exists between Septimus's fatal plunge and Clarissa's fear of and simultaneous urge toward death. We do not sense her morbidity until considerably later when we have assimilated enough of her impressions to grasp Mrs. Woolf's method of conveying Clarissa's personality piece by piece. Only then do we begin to see in this sane but very depressed character a whole galaxy of conscious manoeuvres which are in essence unconscious attempts to resist the devastating demands of an impoverished self-esteem.

The whole phrasing of Clarissa's life appears to be an effort toward order and peace; it is a valiant attempt to overcome human weakness and folly. She needs to make her home perfect, to make her social position glitter—to become an ideal human being. To idealize oneself, however, is to impose severe and crippling restrictions on one's spontaneous and natural ebb and flow. Hatred, for example, must be choked off because it fades her glowing image. So that Clarissa's contempt for Doris Kilman becomes that "brutal monster," as she calls it: "never to be content quite, or quite secure, for at any moment the brute would be stirring, this hatred, which, especially since her illness, had the power to make her feel scraped . . . gave her physical pain, and made all pleasure in beauty, in friendship, in being well, in being loved . . . rock, quiver, and bend as if indeed there were a monster grubbing at the roots, as if the whole panoply of content were nothing but self love! this hatred!" (17;*15*) Hatred of course is a natural emotion, but it is not natural for Clarissa. What we have here then is an ideal, a phantom, self inflicting merciless punishment on the real, the suffering, Clarissa.

The incident involving the mysterious motor car with its blinds drawn is another instance of the way Clarissa dramatizes the inexorable logic of her divided inner life. No one at the scene knows who is in the car, but "It was probably the Queen, thought Mrs. Dalloway . . . the Queen. And for a second *she wore a look of extreme dignity . . .*" (23-24;*19-20*).[11] As the car passes by, Clarissa thinks of the "candelabras, glittering stars, breasts stiff with oak leaves . . . the gentlemen of England, that night in Buckingham Palace. And Clarissa, *too,* gave a party. *She stiffened a little;* so she would stand at the top of her stairs" (25;*20*).

Considering her private terrors and torments and noting the way she exalts herself in phantasy—equating herself with the highest of English royalty, vying at party-giving with the Queen—we realize how vital it is for Clarissa to protect herself from self-destruction by assuming a mask as glorified as the need for it is intense. Again, however, we must remind ourselves that the idealized queen-like hostess is not the real Mrs. Dalloway.

How her tendency toward self-inflation is triggered off in her personal relations is aptly demonstrated in the scene with Peter Walsh, who appears unexpectedly after living for years in India. Early in the meeting the mind of each is occupied with thoughts of their past romance at Bourton; and they are alternately critical and reminiscent. Finally, at Clarissa's bidding, Peter mentions presumably what he came to her for: "'I'm in love'. . . . 'In love,' he repeated, now speaking rather dryly to Clarissa Dalloway; 'in love with a girl from India.' He deposited his garland. Clarissa could make what she would of it" (66-67;*50*). For Clarissa the shock of the news and the terrible sense of loss cause an instantaneous tempest of hatred to burst forth: "That he at his age should be sucked under in his little bow-tie by that monster! And there's no flesh on his neck; his hands are red; and he's six months older than I am! her eyes flashed back to her; but in her heart she felt, all the same, he is in love. . . . But the indomitable egotism which for ever rides down the hosts opposed to it . . . this indomitable egotism charged her cheeks with colour. . . . He was in love! Not with her. With some younger woman, of course" (67;*50-51*). The emotional sequence is important: hatred ["monster"], anger, envy, loss, and finally injured pride.

11. The italics are mine throughout the chapter unless otherwise specified.

In a sense, Clarissa has been punctured and deflated. Now something must happen. Something must be immediately mobilized to restore her—and to diminish Peter. Consequently, a chain of disparagements of him and his past builds up in her mind: ". . . it was his silly unconventionality, his weakness; his lack of the ghost of a notion what anyone else was feeling that annoyed her, had always annoyed her; and now at his age, how silly!" Her disdain is somehow communicated to Peter: "I know all that . . . I know what I'm up against . . . and then to his utter surprise, suddenly . . . he burst into tears; wept; wept without the least shame, sitting on the sofa, the tears running down his cheeks" (69;*52*).

What follows his eruption is illuminating, because just as his admission of love for another woman sparks in her a rush of pain and fury, so too does her reaction to his weeping eloquently reveal the emotional dynamics of her divided self:

And Clarissa had leant forward, taken his hand, drawn him to her, kissed him—actually felt his face on hers before she could down the brandishing of silver flashing—plumes like pampas grass in a tropic gale in her breast, which, subsiding, left her holding his hand, patting his knee and, feeling as she sat back extraordinarily at her ease with him and light-hearted, all in a clap it came over her, If I had married him, this gaiety would have been mine all day! (69-70;*52*)

Peter's tears have suddenly made Clarissa motherly, with a kiss and a pat on the knee; *his* deflation in her presence has been an act of obeisance for the suffering he has caused her. It elevates and enlarges Clarissa as a loved, admired, and needed figure. In her maternal role of comforting this "naughty boy" for loving another woman, her pain has eased, her confidence has been renewed, her feeling of loss and rejection is diminished. Now she can sit back "extraordinarily at her ease with him and light-hearted. . . ." Clarissa has triumphed, certainly. But this "gaiety" that would have been hers all day had she married Peter, makes her triumph by no means a vindictive one. The fact that simply being at ease and feeling light-hearted are "gaiety" to Clarissa is a sensitive index as well as a poignant statement of how lonely and unhappy her life must be. Only she knows that "It was all over for her"; and later: "He [Richard] has left me; I am alone for ever. . ." (70;*52-53*). So that when we see through this dense crisscross of feelings the elegant and aloof Clarissa disparaging others, assembling lofty personages, having to say, "Here is *my* Elizabeth,"

⌈being outwardly the mark of perfection, we must understand her self-
glorifications as a protective device, a kind of mental analgesic to
assuage her depressive uncertainty, frustration, and sense of impov-
erishment.⌋ As in the scene with Peter, when the idealized Clarissa
fails—even temporarily—the real Clarissa is in mortal danger.

Has Mrs. Woolf, we might ask, provided us with any clues as to
how or why Clarissa Dalloway has come to be what she is? There is
only one brief passage which points indirectly to an important piece
of past history; and it runs as follows:

> "I often wish I'd got on better with your father," he [Peter] said.
> "But he never liked any one who—our friends," said Clarissa; and could
> have bitten her tongue for thus reminding Peter that he had wanted to
> marry her (62;*47*).[12]

As soon as we read the sentence directly as, "My father never liked
any one who wanted to marry me," we may fairly guess why earlier
Clarissa thought that "narrower and narrower would her bed be"
(45-46;*35*).

The reverie immediately following her words requires extremely
close attention, because it throws light on a series of elements which
constitute a central preoccupation of Clarissa Dalloway, aged fifty-
one. Her reverie, moreover, insinuates a connection with her feelings
of futility and isolation:

> The candle was half burnt down and she read deep in Baron Marbot's
> *Memoirs*. She had read late at night of the retreat from Moscow. For the
> House sat so long that Richard insisted, after her illness, that she must sleep
> undisturbed. And really she preferred to read of the retreat from Moscow.
> He knew it. So the room was an attic; the bed narrow; and lying there
> reading, for she slept badly, she could not dispel a virginity preserved
> through childbirth which clung to her like a sheet. Lovely in girlhood,
> suddenly there came a moment—for example on the river beneath the
> woods at Clieveden—when, through some contraction of this cold spirit,
> she had *failed*[13] him. And then at Constantinople, and again and again. She

---

12. This is strikingly reminiscent of the bond between Rachel Vinrace and her father, and the
even more startling attachment between Katherine and Mr. Hilbery; and if we reverse the
sexes, the same holds true for the relationship between Jacob Flanders and his mother. That is
to say, in each novel thus far, Mrs. Woolf has introduced an unnaturally powerful bond either
between father and daughter or between mother and son.

13. Mrs. Woolf's use of the verb *fail* is a very curious choice in the present context, because
sexually, it is the man who "fails" his partner through impotence. Even a frigid woman may
refuse her man or may "fake" the act, but there is no failing him. A woman's conditioning
may be such that she is unable to participate genuinely in the act of sexual intercourse; and if
so, she has failed herself. But that failure is emotional, not physical.

could see what she lacked. It was not beauty; it was not mind. It was something central which permeated; something warm which broke up surfaces and rippled the cold contact of man and woman, or of women together. For *that*[14] she could dimly perceive. She resented it, had a scruple picked up Heaven knows where, or, as she felt, sent by Nature (who is invariably wise); yet she could not resist sometimes yielding to the charm of a woman, not a girl, of a woman confessing, as to her they often did, some scrape, some folly. And whether it was pity, or their beauty, or that she was older, or some accident—like a faint scent, or a violin next door (so strange is the power of sounds at certain moments), she did undoubtedly then feel what men felt (46-47;*35-36*).

Examining the passage sequentially, we are struck first with Clarissa's attraction to the violence of personal heroism and glory written full in the *Memoirs* of General Marcelin de Marbot. Her attraction in itself is provocative. But its more fundamental significance is in the thought it triggers off: of the "virginity preserved through childbirth" which she could not dispel; and that, in turn, makes her conscious of her frigidity, of her having "failed" her husband at Clieveden, at Constantinople, and repeatedly thereafter. Her train of thought from Marbot (with all its implied masculinity), to virginity, and then to frigidity is worth tracing, because it leads us directly to her admitting her being unable sometimes to resist "yielding to the charm of a woman. . . ." And her attraction to a woman brings us back full circle to her attraction to, perhaps identification with, Marbot's manliness: because when Clarissa yields to a woman, "she did undoubtedly then feel what men felt." Significantly, the conditions of her attraction are such that she must hold the position of power and dominance. If the women are in need, Clarissa yields because she is needed; if a woman has beauty, she yields through a narcissistic urge to win her; if a woman is younger, she yields because she has both age and experience to help her and to guide her.

This partial reading will seem less shocking if we examine the passage which directly follows this reverie; it is a passage which contains the most thinly disguised and highly erotic writing to be found in any of Mrs. Woolf's published fiction:

. . . she did undoubtedly then feel what men felt. Only for a moment; but it was enough. It was a sudden revelation, a tinge like a blush which one tried to check and then, as it spread, one yielded to its expansion, and rushed to

14. The emphasis is Virginia Woolf's.

the farthest verge and there quivered and felt the world come closer, swollen with some astonishing significance, some pressure of rapture, which split its thin skin and gushed and poured with an extraordinary alleviation over the cracks and sores! Then, for that moment, she had seen an illumination; a match burning in a crocus; an inner meaning almost expressed. But the close withdrew; the hard softened. It was over—the moment. Against such moments (with women too) there contrasted (as she laid her hat down) the bed and Baron Marbot and the candle half-burnt (47;*36-37*).

Even the most literal reader will not fail to sense in the passage a poetic transcripton of erotic activity. But more important, the passage is expressive of a profound confusion in Clarissa's sexual identity. That is, it cannot be read with any degree of certainty as to where exactly Clarissa sees herself in the sexual action. There are, however, at least three different possibilities: first, following as it does the thought that she could feel "what men felt," we see Clarissa in a masculine role experiencing "the moment" with a woman; second, the shift of the pronoun to "one" (in the clause, "one yielded to its expansion"), now places Clarissa as the woman in a heterosexual position; third, the parenthesis, "(with women too)," repeats as it were the entire passage, but now exclusively in homo-sexual terms. There pervades also in this "moment" of "rapture" a hint of violence ("swollen," "pressure," "split") mixed in with the erotic. But for Clarissa this is the "moment." Observe further that "Against such moments . . . there contrasted . . . the [ever-narrowing] bed and [the terrifically masculine] Baron Marbot and the candle half-burnt [of her solitary sleepless nights]."

The ambiguity of the passage should not be seen as a failure in Mrs. Woolf's artistry, but rather as an intricate mosaic of thoughts, feelings, and memories in the mind of a woman to whom sexuality is both a cause of ambivalence and a source of confusion. For it leads Clarissa to "—this question of love . . . this falling in love with women. Take Sally Seton; her relation in the old days with Sally Seton. Had not that, after all, been love?" (48;*37*)

The question is important because it uncovers so much about that single June day in Clarissa's life. As she recalls the summer of her eighteenth year, with Sally Seton under the same roof at Bourton, she remembers "going downstairs, and feeling as she crossed the hall 'if it were now to die 'twere now to be most happy.' That was her feeling—Othello's feeling, and she felt it, she was convinced, as strongly as Shakespeare meant Othello to feel it, all because she was coming down to dinner in a white frock to meet Sally Seton!'' (51;*39*) Some two hundred pages and many fictional hours later in the novel, Clarissa ponders Septimus's death and asks: "But this young man who killed himself—had he plunged holding his treasure? 'If it were now to die, 'twere now to be most happy,' she had said that to herself once, coming down in white'' (281;*202-203*).

Her memory of Bourton is obvious enough, but the word "treasure'' pressed directly beside the quotation from *Othello* sounds a peculiar chord whose fuller harmony can only be heard if we remember that on that evening at Bourton, "Sally stopped; picked a flower; kissed her on the lips.'' For Clarissa that gesture of love must indeed have been her "treasure'.''; for now in reverie, some thirty-three years later, that kiss still echoes in her mind as "the most exquisite moment of her whole life. . .'' (52;*40*). And as she thinks back of Peter Walsh's wanting to marry her, she recalls "how impossible it was ever to make up her mind—and why did I make up my mind—not to marry him? she wondered that awful summer?'' (61-62;*47*) We as readers can make a connection that Clarissa cannot: for when we juxtapose Clarissa's love for Sally against her father's not liking anyone who wanted to marry her, we understand why she refused to marry Walsh and why for her it was "that awful summer.''

The splintering effects of a tacitly possessive father, the frustration of a genuine love, the need to refuse a man who would force her to share everything—all this we may speculate has weakened Clarissa's emotional axis and split her in two. One part of her lives in helpless, enforced isolation; while the other lives in an armory of protective self-glorification; and both parts are at once contradictory and mutually intensifying. Understanding her duality, we can be sympathetic towards Clarissa when an "old bald-looking cushion in the middle of her sofa'' (57;*44*) threatens her sense of grandness; and when later, having calmed herself, she is grateful "to her servants for helping her to be what she wanted, gentle, generous-hearted'' (58;*44*). We can appreciate the fragmentation of her buried life and the almost paralyzing strain on her to achieve somehow a precarious balance of all the warring forces inside her. Sensing the full pattern of her sorrow and discontent, we know, as does she, that

That was her self when some effort, some call on her to be her self, drew the parts together, she alone knew how different, how incompatible and composed so for the world only into one centre, one diamond, one woman who sat in her drawing-room and made a meeting-point, a radiancy no doubt in some dull lives, a refuge for the lonely to come to, perhaps; she had helped young people, who were grateful to her; had tried to be the same always, never showing a sign of all the other sides of her—faults, jealousies, vanities, suspicions. . .'' (55;*42*).

It would be difficult to describe with greater honesty or at a finer pitch the real Clarissa cutting into that diamond a sparkling image which is so essential to her staying alive in her private world of disappointment and solitude.

The first impression of Peter Walsh is one of a passive, ineffectual, and self-defeating man. Before meeting him on the page, we learn from Clarissa that "he had married a woman met on a boat going to India! Never would she forget all that! . ,. . And she wasted her pity. For he was quite happy, he assured her—perfectly happy, though he had never done a thing that they talked of; his whole life had been a failure" (10-11;*10*).

When he first appears at Clarissa's, he thinks critically:

Here she is mending her dress; mending her dress as usual . . . here she's been sitting all the time I've been in India; mending her dress; playing about; going to parties; running to the House and back and all that, he thought, growing more and more irritated, more and more agitated. . . (61;*46*).

Yet he wants to tell Clarissa of his new love, the wife of a Major in the Indian Army: "Shall I tell her . . . or not? He would like to make a clean breast of it all. But she was too cold . . . sewing, with her scissors; Daisy would look ordinary beside Clarissa. And she would think me a failure, which I am in their sense. . . . Oh yes, he had no doubt about that; he was a failure, compared with all this—the inlaid table . . . the chair covers and the old valuable English tinted prints—he was a failure!" (64-65;*49*). Sitting beside her, "His powers chafed and tossed in him. He assembled from different quarters all sorts of things; praise; his career at Oxford; his marriage, which she knew nothing whatever about; how he had loved; and altogether done his job" (66;*50*). With his "powers" thus assembled, he describes his Daisy: "'A married woman, unfortunately. . . . She has

. . . two small children; a boy and a girl; and I have come over to see my lawyers about the divorce.' There they are! he thought. Do what you like with them, Clarissa! There they are!'' (67-68;*51*) Moments later he is in tears, being patted and comforted by Clarissa!

This disorderly procession of thoughts and utterances on the surface appears to be a straightforward expression of someone emotionally muddled. However, it is really a deceptive mask which Peter himself is not conscious of wearing. If we make certain connections, a coherent system of his motives begins to emerge. For one thing, Peter Walsh's persistent need to share implies an inability or unwillingness to do or enjoy anything by himself and consequently explains his indiscriminate and unsuccessful marriage to "a woman met on a boat. . . ." That inability also hints at a predominantly negative self-regard: he is weak and worthless; therefore, in order to do anything, he needs someone stronger; and to enjoy anything, he needs someone more worthy.

Just how battered his self-esteem is becomes obvious in the scene at Bourton when Richard Dalloway appears and wins Clarissa from Peter: "And all the time, he knew perfectly well, Dalloway was falling in love with her; she was falling in love with Dalloway; *but it didn't seem to matter.* . . . He said to himself as they were getting into the boat, 'She will marry that man,' dully, *without any resentment*; but it was an obvious thing. Dalloway would marry Clarissa. . . . *He deserved to have her*'' (94-95;*70*). Here is the clearest ring of Peter's sense of insignificance. For when one has so low a self-estimate, one is not afforded the luxury of so ambitious a passion as jealousy. In his passivity, moreover, Peter has essentially encouraged a situation which insures his failure. As he admits, "he was absurd. His demands upon Clarissa . . . were absurd. He asked impossible things. He made terrible scenes. She would have accepted him still, perhaps, if he had been less absurd" (95;*70*). Rejection and failure, however, are essential to Peter, especially when he has manoeuvred a situation in which another person must reject Peter and then assume the responsibility for his failure; that is, when he can actively thrust onto someone else his own sense of nothingness, Peter can then passively remain the innocent victim. With or without the outside agent, however, his inclination toward self-defeat becomes a recurrent pattern and explains why "he had never done a thing they had talked of,'' why at his age his choice of partner should be a young married woman with two children, and why he should return to Clarissa "to make a clean breast of it all.''

To make a clean breast of it all is the most significant phrase in the whole sequence. For Peter has come as a penitent to Clarissa; and his "confessing" his new prospect of marriage to her has multiple levels of function, most or all of which he is probably unaware. His news of Daisy acts as a spark which ignites in Clarissa an urge to punish him; this she does by wordlessly communicating to him the futility of his marital prospect, which causes the flood of tears. On another level, by his "confession" he encourages Clarissa to force him into effacing himself; and when he does, he rouses her suddenly into becoming dominant, expansive, maternal; and that in turn provides him with the opportunity to act as a child would who is suddenly disburdened of guilt and then accepted back lovingly by its "mother" despite its faults and failures. On still another level, his shameless self-humiliation can be read, simply, as a fierce though indirect plea for affection and security. Seeing how these levels overlap and interlock, we understand how attractive each is to the other in this role of mother and child. For that is the role each has assumed.

Defeat for Peter has another important function. It is the surest *justification* for his constant appeals 'for love, understanding, forgiveness, and help. So long as he is life's pawn and pushed mercilessly from one humiliating defeat to another, he has no qualm, for example, "At fifty-three . . . to come and ask them [Whitbread and Dalloway] to put him into some secretary's office, to find him some usher's job teaching little boys Latin, at the beck and call of some mandarin in an office. . ." (112;*83*). Nor can he "understand why Clarissa couldn't simply find them a lodging and be nice to Daisy; introduce her" (240;*174*).

Earlier we had a glimpse of something seemingly contradictory in Peter's annoyance at finding Clarissa mending her dress; he seems to feel that for the past five years she *should have expected* him to return at any moment from India. The annoyance, however, points to still another of his mental habits; namely, the tendency to confuse something he would like with something he considers to be his due: Why was not Clarissa expecting his unexpected visit? By the same subjective logic, his identifying with the downtrodden, someone "at the beck and call of some mandarin," enables him to make claims freely on other people, because he feels entitled to those claims, whether they are reasonable or not.

These privileges to which he feels entitled, however, exist only in his own mind; and the result is a kind of overt self-deception. His making claims on others is fundamentally his way of subordinating while simultaneously chaining himself to people and living parasitically off them. He says himself: "yet nobody of course was more dependent upon others . . . it had been his undoing" (240-41;*174*). And his undoing is caused precisely by the almost diseased quality of that dependency; that is, the greater his appeal to others, the greater the possibility of disappointment; the greater the frustration of disappointment, the greater the need to appeal, and accordingly the more stringent the claims. The process is self-intensifying and tends increasingly to separate him from others. In the end it means extreme isolation.

The depth of his aloneness is conveyed dramatically in his walk through Trafalgar Square where he spies an attractive young woman unknown to him. He follows her through a section of London.[15] In his phantasy, she "shed veil after veil, until she became the very woman he had always had in mind. . ." (79;*59*); and he follows her, fancying himself "a romantic buccaneer, careless of all these damned proprieties. . ." (80;*60*) until she turns down a street and disappears into a house. "Well, I've had my fun; I've had it, he thought. . . . And it was smashed to atoms—his fun, for it was half made up, as he knew very well; invented, this escapade with the girl; made up, as one makes up the better part of life. . . . all this one could never share—it smashed to atoms" (81;*61*).

Phantom pleasure of course cannot be shared, and much of Peter's life appears to be a mute testament of his solitary phantasies. How much self-minimizing must be required to feel incapable of experiencing real pleasure; how great a sense of unworthiness to feel successful pursuits a taboo; and how vital is the mechanism of failure to feel free, to have escaped the "old nurse waving at the wrong window." Such are the peculiar constituents of a man with a brittle

---

15. It is significant that the scene directly follows his visit to Clarissa from whom "He had escaped! was utterly free. . . . feeling like a child who runs out of doors, and sees, as he runs, his old nurse waving at the wrong window" (78;*59*).

emotional architecture held together by rivets of anger and fear.

Such also is the vision of a man for whom "Nothing exists outside us except a state of mind . . . a desire for solace, for relief, for something outside these miserable pigmies, these feeble, these ugly, these craven men and women" (85;*63-64*). For these are Peter's thoughts just before he falls asleep in Regent's Park. And Mrs. Woolf suggests the extent of his solitude in a poetic passage about a solitary traveller—a passage which correlates objectively to the affective experience during Peter's dream of Bourton. The traveller is in quest of his conception of womanhood, "this figure made of sky and branches. . ." who will "shower down from her magnificent hands compassion, comprehension, absolution . . . who will, with a toss of her head, mount me on her streamers and let me blow to nothingness with the rest" (86-87;*64*). The great figure, however, becomes poetically transformed into an elderly woman in search of "a lost son . . . a rider destroyed . . . the mother whose sons have been killed in the battles of the world." Another transformation takes place as the solitary traveller advances; she becomes the "outline of the landlady . . . an adorable emblem which only the recollection of cold human contacts forbids us to embrace" (87;*65*).

It would be difficult to explicate the passage on any literal level of meaning; but in tracing its feeling sense, we can locate metaphoric ingredients which somehow connect womanhood and motherhood to uncertainty, to ambivalence, to death, to thwarted hopes, and finally to loneliness; and all of these, in a close and subtle way, have some connection with Peter's rejection at Bourton and possibly all the subsequent failures in the life of this "lost son," this "rider destroyed."

When he awakes, his words are: " 'The death of the soul' " (88;*65*).[16] He is expressing a brand of fatalism, and how it operates in Peter's relations with women in general and to Clarissa in particular is worth noticing. Several fragments of what he is thinking will take us below the surface of what appears to be merely a random train of thought. Having just received Clarissa's note, he wonders what life would have been like had they married: "But it would not have been

---

16. There are possibly subtler connections: Peter's leaving Clarissa, his feeling childlike and free, the nurse waving from the wrong window, his phantom escapade; and their relation to what directly follows the solitary traveller passage: the elderly nurse over *a sleeping baby* as well as beside *a sleeping Peter.*

a success. . . . The other thing, after all, came so much more natural-ly" (236;*171*). Then he thinks of his mediocre accomplishments, his crankiness, and reflects that "it was odd that *he* should have had . . . a contented look; a look of having reserves. It was this that made him attractive to women who liked the sense that he was not altogether manly" (237;*171-72*). This thought is followed by the notion of his susceptibility to women, especially girls, but "only up to a point. She said something—no, no; he saw through that. He wouldn't stand that—no, no." He then acknowledges that "He was a man. But not the sort of man one had to respect. . ." (237;*172*); he is not like Daisy's husband, Major Simmons. The comparison leads him to con-template his prospective marriage to Daisy, this "dark, adorably pretty girl" who "would give him everything! . . . everything he wanted!" (238;*172*) There is, however, a sudden change of heart: "Well indeed he had got himself into a mess at his age." He then reflects on Mrs. Burgess's idea that his absence "might serve to make Daisy reconsider. . ." (238;*173*), that "it might be happier . . . that she should forget him. . ."; because "when Daisy asked him, as she would, for a kiss, a scene, [he] fail[ed] to come up to the scratch. . ." (240;*174*). We also discover that he liked "above all women's society . . . their faithfulness and audacity and greatness in loving which though it had its drawbacks seemed to him . . . so admirable . . . and yet he could not come up to the scratch, being always apt to see round things (Clarissa had sapped something in him permanently), and to tire very easily of mute devotion and to want variety in love, though it would make him furious if Daisy loved anybody else, furious! for he was jealous, uncontrollably jealous by temperament. He suffered tortures! But where was his knife. . ." (241;*174-75*).

Most of the latent content of his thoughts begins to emerge when we observe their sequence. His thought that marriage would have failed with Clarissa, for example, leads almost directly to the idea that he was attractive to women who liked his being "not altogether manly." Buried in this juxtaposition is the insinuation that the rela-tionship between him and Clarissa is not based on the normally understood attraction between a man and a woman. Exactly what their relation is becomes apparent when we consider both his *not* requiring respect and his *limited* susceptibility to girls: the former has in it an element of self-devaluation, and the latter suggests the presence of confusion and insecurity which are components of a pseudo-masculine assertiveness. Protection and assurance are what Peter wants in his relations with women, and these are largely what he finds in Clarissa. So that with a minimized masculine self-image, his attraction to someone as masterful and at times maternal as Clarissa is potent indeed, but it is a non-sexual and generally self-subordinating attraction.

The bond between him and Daisy is of a very different order. Her youth and her attraction to him satisfy his vanity, and her already being a wife and mother means that a future with her has potential failure built into it. Therefore, the threat of meeting the demands of a mature relationship is diminished for him. Nevertheless, he does think that perhaps "Daisy might reconsider." If we remember that she will give him everything, including "mute devotion," despite his inability to "come up to the scratch," we realize that her love for him cannot provide him with any real assurance of the self-value which he desperately lacks. It is therefore understandable that he needs "variety in love"; for each new conquest temporarily narcotizes his permanent sense of worthlessness. The tortures he would suffer if Daisy were unfaithful should not be interpreted as jealousy so much as the pain of rejection: her infidelity would further crush his counterfeit image as a man. For above all, his masculinity is too fragile to be niggled with.

This network of seemingly contradictory forces in Peter has its most resilient fibers in the bond between him and Clarissa. Just as he finds security in someone he thinks is as strong and superior as Clarissa; so Clarissa, to gratify her own private yearnings, cherishes Peter for his weakness and dependency. Although it is not the attraction between a man and a woman in the usual physical or psychological sense of the word, the attraction is a mutual, even if perhaps not a wholesome, one.

From what has been said of Peter, one might expect to find a great seething hostility locked up in him; for one cannot contain such submerged feelings of self-contempt, dependency, and frustration without generating some very acute need for rebellion. However, nowhere in the novel does he erupt in anger or violence;[17] and none

17. Psychologists tell us that the difference between fear and anger is a very fine one: when one is in a predicament one cannot handle, the experience is fear; but as soon as one finds he can cope with the situation, the fear immediately becomes anger. (The various contexts in which Peter handles his pocket knife very beautifully illustrate the difference.)

takes place because Peter is psychologically ineffectual as a combatant. For him, any urge towards overt aggression must be quickly blocked and smothered.

Mrs. Woolf, however, has been careful to indicate that the urge is in him by alerting us indirectly to Peter's conspicuous attachment to his pocket knife. The different contexts in which the knife appears in the novel clearly indicates its significance to him. In his morning visit to Clarissa, for example: "She's looking at me, he thought, a sudden embarrassment coming over him. . . . Putting his hand in his pocket, he took out a large pocket-knife and half opened the blade" (60;*46*). As they converse, he ponders his failure and the luxury he mistakenly interprets Clarissa's life to be, and thinks: "And this has been going on all the time! . . . week after week; Clarissa's life; while I—he thought; and at once everything seemed to radiate from him; journeys; rides; quarrels; adventures; bridge parties; love affairs; work; work, work! and he took out his knife quite openly . . . and clenched his fist upon it" (65;*49*). The knife appears again in the "made up" escapade with the young woman he is about to follow: "Straightening himself and stealthily fingering his pocket-knife he started after her to follow this woman, this excitement. . ." (79;*59*). Later in the day he thinks how furious he would be if Daisy loved anyone else, "for he was jealous, uncontrollably jealous by temperament. He suffered tortures! But where was his knife . . ." (241;*175*). Finally, that evening before he enters Clarissa's house to be at her party, it comes over him that "The body must contract now, entering the house . . . the soul must brave itself to endure. He opened the big blade of his pocket-knife" (250;*181*).

If we examine these five instances consecutively in their respective contexts, we discover that the knife—whether as an instrument of offense or defense in Peter's conceptual armory—is psychologically functional for him in several ways. First, its association with his feelings for Clarissa who "had sapped something in him permanently" transforms it into a blade designed for castration. Second, when it appears in juxtaposition to the waste and failure of his life, it becomes a device for self-destruction. Third, it is a substitute for sexual aggression in his phantasy with the unknown young woman, a violent means of stoutly denying his impotence. Fourth, when he imagines Daisy's infidelity to him, it becomes an implement of punishment for rupturing the thin skin of his injured and questionable pride. Lastly, it is a defensive weapon in Clarissa's world, a society which lessens and threatens him. The knife is thus a constant companion for a man who knows that "The soul must brave itself to endure."[18]

So that tied hand and foot in his pervasive sense of worthlessness and fear, Peter Walsh, not surprisingly, shares with Clarissa—although for different reasons—the feeling that "As we are a doomed race, chained to a sinking ship . . . let us, at any rate, do our part . . . decorate the dungeon with flowers and air-cushions; be as decent as we possibly can" (117;*86-87*). With or without his knife, such is the power of hopelessness in this really solitary traveller.

The cumulative picture we get of Septimus Warren Smith is one of extreme sensitivity, heavily weighted with self-recrimination and strangely mixed with flights of delusory grandeur. These impressions of him, however, are only symptoms of an inner malaise which ultimately explains his behavior and links him in the profoundest way to Clarissa Dalloway.

We meet him for the first time when the car with its mysterious personage is passing. He is "about thirty, pale-faced, beak-nosed . . . with hazel eyes which had that look of apprehension in them. . . ." At that instant, for no apparent reason, he thinks that "The world has raised its whip; where will it all descend?" (20;*17*) As the car with the drawn blinds moves down the street filled with traffic and onlookers, Septimus becomes suddenly filled with terror: "this gradual drawing together of everything to one centre before his eyes, as if some horror had come almost to the surface and was about to burst into flames, terrified him. The world . . . threatened to burst into flames. It is I who am blocking the way. . . . Was he not being looked at and pointed at; was he not weighted there . . . for a purpose? But for what purpose?" (21;*18*)

For what purpose, indeed! His reaction is so obviously irrational that we may reasonably ask more than just that: Who is he to think

18. Erwin Steinberg, on the basis of Freud's dream interpretations, calls the knife a phallic symbol. But that, it seems to me, tells us very little unless we know what significance the phallus has for Peter. Without that knowledge, we are left simply with a verbal symbol translated into a dream symbol—and nothing more. See "Freudian Symbolism and Communication," *Literature and Psychology,* April 1953, pp. 2-5.

that he is causing the congestion? What grand image prompts him to feel stared at, pointed at? What is there about the car's "drawn blinds" and on them the "curious pattern like a tree" to trigger his terror, to threaten his world with flames? And what is this "horror" which "had come almost to the surface"? We cannot answer. Too little information is given; but there is something in the arrangement of the elements to suggest that Septimus's self-accusatory feelings, his panic, and his fear connect in some remote and wordless way to the drawn blinds of the car. We are lead to suspect, moreover, that buried deep in him are feelings of guilt so overwhelming that dread of exposure prompts him to say to his wife, " 'I will kill myself' " (22;*18*).

A contradictory tendency, however, complicates the picture of Septimus. Despite his apparent sense of guilt, he regards himself in a strikingly Messianic way: he is "the greatest of mankind, Septimus, lately taken from life to death, the Lord who came to renew society . . . the scapegoat, the eternal sufferer. . ." (37;*29*). The compound of guilt and godliness in him is laden with implications. If Septimus feels himself to be a godhead, one can fairly assume that he feels in possession of a super-morality which makes him superior to ordinary mortals, makes him their "Lord." But at the same time, and more important, it would follow that whatever guilt he experiences must originate in something he has done which he feels to be a violation of his society's code of morality. Consequently, the more superior he feels, the more moral he must be, and hence the more susceptible to morality's violation; and the more extreme the morality, the greater and more severe the guilt experienced when a violation is thought to have been committed.

But these are merely *effects* we see in Septimus. If we look for the *causes* of those feelings which so brutalize him, we need to begin by examining his relation to Lucrezia, because it is with her that his moral scars throb most with pain. There is a scene, for example, in which he is on the sofa, and Rezia is holding his hand "to prevent him from falling down, down, he cried, into the flames!" (100;*74*) He is suddenly seized with terror when he notices her wedding ring gone. " 'My hand has grown so thin,' she said. 'I have put it in my purse,'. . . ." But he drops her hand. "Their marriage was over . . . the rope was cut; he mounted; he was free, as it was decreed that he,

Septimus, the lord of men, should be free; alone (since his wife had thrown away her wedding ring; since she had left him). . ." (101;*75*).

Only later does his feeling abandoned by Rezia become significant. We learn that "he became engaged one evening when the panic was on him—that he could not feel" (131;*96*). We learn further that he became engaged after the war—in which his friend, Evans, was killed—after finding himself in an Italian rooming-house where the owner's daughters made hats. It is here that he discovered in the night "these sudden thunderclaps of fear. He could not feel"; and it was here among the sisters, that he felt protected: "he was assured of safety; he had a refuge. But he could not sit there all night." So, "He asked Lucrezia to marry him. . ." (131;*96-97*). If this circumstance was the basis of their marriage, it is understandable that feelings of guilt should haunt him, that his "crimes" should shake their fingers "in the early hours of the morning at the prostrate body which lay realising its degradation; how he had married his wife without loving her; had lied to her; seduced her. . . ."

Again we need to remember that this is a *secondary effect:* it is the *result* of an act committed out of panic. When we search for the cause of the panic, something more fundamental emerges which, like an awful arcanum, is solemnly chained to "the sin for which human nature had condemned him to death; that he did not feel. He had not cared when Evans was killed. . ." (137;*101*). Septimus reminds us so many times that "he could not feel" that readers have tended to see *that* as his crime. However, not being able to feel, in itself, is not a crime: it is a consequence for which somewhere a cause must exist. Because his inability to feel is unequivocally connected with Evans's death, our question at once becomes: What was the relation between Evans and Septimus that the death of one should cause a psychic paralysis in the other?

Mrs. Woolf insinuates Septimus's feeling for his officer, Evans, through a very intricate pattern of metaphoric relations and syllogistic repetitions; so that each repeated and related word gains from the one preceding it and adds pressure of meaning to the one following it. Recall that Septimus is struck by panic when the mysterious car passes, the drawn blinds of which had on them "a curious pattern like a *tree*" (21;*18*). Later in Regent's Park talking to himself, Septimus says: "Men must not cut down *trees*. . . . No one kills from hatred" (35;*28*). Then "A sparrow perched on the *railing* opposite chirped Septimus, Septimus, four or five times over and went on drawing its notes out, to *sing* freshly and piercingly in *Greek* words how there is no *crime* . . . they *sang* . . . in *Greek* words, from *trees* in the meadow of life. . ." (36;*28*). Rezia, his wife, interrupts his reverie by suggesting they go, but another trickle of memory comes through a torn seam of his past: "He *sang*. Evans answered from behind the *tree*. The dead were in *Thessaly,* Evans *sang,* among the orchids. There they waited till the war was over, and now the dead, now Evans himself—'For God's sake don't come!' . . . But the *branches* parted. A man in grey was actually walking towards them. It was Evans! . . . I must tell the whole world, Septimus cried. . ." (105;*78*). Rezia reminds him of the time, because they have a doctor's appointment. " 'I will tell you the time,' said Septimus . . . very drowsily, smiling mysteriously. . . . As he sat smiling at the dead man [Peter Walsh!] in the grey suit the quarter struck. . ." (106;*79*). The connections between panic and trees, between trees and Evans, and between Evans and Greece need no elaboration: they clearly link panic in Septimus to a loss which aggravates profound longing.

Interwoven in the fabric of Septimus's mind, however, is another thread which we can follow. The clues attending it are subtler and the implications more resonant than those attending his terror. With the scene still in Regent's Park, Septimus stares ahead where "White things were assembling behind the *railings* opposite. But he dared not look. Evans was behind the *railings*!" (36;*28*) Within view from his park bench were "*dogs busy* with the *railings, busy with each other*. . ." (39;*30*).[19] Later, in a moment of extreme excitement, he thinks: "The supreme *secret* must be told to the Cabinet; first that *trees* are alive; next there is no *crime*; next *love, universal love,* he muttered, gasping, trembling. . . . No *crime; love;* he repeated . . . when a Skye *terrier* snuffed his trousers and he started in an agony of *fear*. It was turning into a *man*! He could not watch it happen! It was horrible, terrible to see a *dog* become a *man*! . . . Why could he see . . . into the future, when *dogs* will become *men*?" (102;*75-76*) Then we learn that Septimus was among the first to volunteer in the war,

19. If we remember that Mrs. Filmer's area *railings* figure into Septimus's suicide, then, through displacement, implied here once more is Mrs. Woolf's unholy trinity of animality [dogs], sexuality ["busy with each other"], and death [railings].

and it was in the trenches where

> he developed *manliness*; he was promoted; he drew the attention, indeed the affection of his officer, Evans by name. *It was a case of two dogs* playing on a hearthrug; one worrying a paper screw, snarling, snapping, giving a pinch, now and then, at the old dog's ear; the other lying somnolent, blinking at the fire, raising a paw, turning and growling good-temperedly. They had to be together, share with each other, fight with each other, quarrel with each other. But when Evans (Rezia who had only seen him once called him "a quiet man," a sturdy red-haired man, undemonstrative in the company of women), when Evans was killed . . . Septimus, far from showing any emotion or recognising that here was the end of a friendship, congratulated himself upon feeling very little and very reasonably (130;*95-96*).

The imaginative evolution of dogs to men, the relationship of Septimus and Evans being a "case of two dogs," the co-positioning of "love" and "crime" are allusions to homosexuality too obvious to be ignored. Whether or not the homosexuality was physically expressed is not recorded in the text and is of no consequence. What is important is that the love Septimus felt for Evans was so powerful that he could not acknowledge the stark fact of their permanent separation. For Septimus, the truth of Evans's death, had to be pushed from consciousness, had to be buried deep to be made tolerable. The immediate arrest of pain, however, exacted its toll very dearly in Septimus through a sudden numbness of feeling and a subsequent loss of sanity.

That is only part of it, however. With Evans's death, what might otherwise have lain dormant begins to awaken in Septimus: the dim consciousness of his love for Evans suddenly becomes criminal: a deviation from "normality" and therefore a transgression of society's moral code. So that it is the actual loss, followed by the immediate insurgence of guilt, which allow Septimus, on the one hand, to congratulate himself for "feeling very little and very reasonably," and, on the other hand, to feel tortured that "he could not feel"—so great is the fear of being crushed by a society whose stability he thinks he has threatened by the "crime" of his homosexuality. Because of everything that he has done or felt, nothing in the future that he might do, to him, can have the imprimatur of society.

In this dim but steady light, his madness becomes a fugitive and uncertain flight from a world of human beings who "have neither kindness, nor faith, nor charity. . ." who "hunt in packs. Their packs scour the desert and vanish screaming into the wilderness. They desert the fallen" (139;*99*). Because he feels himself a prey, he needs Rezia's protective hand (not her love) "to prevent him from falling down, down . . . into the flames!" where he sees "faces laughing at him, calling him horrible disgusting names. . ." (100;*74*). And to Septimus, this is why to Shakespeare—in whom he reads his own sexual ambivalence—"Love between man and woman was repulsive. . . . The business of copulation was filth. . . ."

Rezia, for all her loving and caring, however, does not understand her husband; she does not understand the phantasmagoric depth of his guilt or the special quality of his suffering. Consequently, in her innocence, she unwittingly imposes still another horror on the thin-blown edges of his tormented mind: "she must have children. . . . But she must have a boy. She must have a son like Septimus, she said" (134;*99*). "She was very lonely. . . . She cried for the first time since they were married." "His wife was crying, and he felt nothing; only each time she sobbed . . . he descended another step into the pit." Precisely at this point, Septimus sees his wife—his only refuge—unknowingly turn against him in wanting a child. It is as though the ravaged citadel of his manhood were under assault, and he is forced to surrender: "now other people must help him. People must be sent for. He gave in" (136;*100*). The help appears in the form of Dr. Holmes, a coarse and blundering man who cannot possibly understand Septimus's delicate moral bondage.

Thus Septimus feels entirely cut off, condemned, alone. It was at this time—six weeks *before* the day of Clarissa's party—that "the great revelation took place. A voice spoke from behind the screen.[20] Evans was speaking. The dead were with him. 'Evans, Evans!' he cried" (140;*103*). By the time Septimus visits Sir William Bradshaw (on the actual day of Clarissa's party), Evans has appeared before him on several occasions. His only hope for relief is to get out into the open what he considers his crime, for as he himself says: " 'Communication is health. . .' " (141;*103-104*).[21]

In the interview with Bradshaw, Septimus thinks: "In the War

20. The "screen" which appears repeatedly until his suicide is inconspicuously linked with the "drawn blinds" of the passing car, where we witness his terror for the first time.

21. The fuller meaning of Septimus's thought, " 'Communication is health . . .' ", becomes

itself he had failed" (145;*106*). His "failure," however, is a sexual
and therefore a moral one: it is his physical disgust for women
coupled with his love for Evans; and *that* he must communicate to
the doctor:

> He had committed an appalling crime and had been condemned to death
> by human nature.
> "I have—I have," he began, "committed a crime—"
> "He has done nothing wrong whatever," Rezia assured the doctor
> (145;*107*).

Again Rezia has acted innocently but destructively: she has put up
the screen, drawn the blinds, as it were, and blocked her husband
from confessing (and herself from seeing) what he feels he *must* confess if he is to live. Septimus makes another attempt:

> But what if he confessed? If he communicated? Would they let him off
> then, his torturers?
> "I—I—" he stammered.
> But what was his crime? He could not remember it.
> "Yes?" Sir William encouraged him. (But it was growing late.)
> Love, trees, there is no crime—what was his message?
> He could not remember it.
> "I—I—" Septimus stammered (149-50;*109*).

In his second attempt to communicate, his own mental censor has
been called into action. The interview has failed.

That afternoon in their rooms several recurrent ideas and images
begin to connect in such a way as to suggest the dusky emotional
atmosphere in which his suicide is to take place. Rezia is thinking that
Septimus lately would suddenly become excited, wave his hands, and
cry out "that he knew the truth! He knew everything! That man, his
friend who was killed, Evans, had come. . . . He was singing behind
the *screen*" (212;*154*) or "he would lie listening until suddenly he
would cry that he was falling down, down into the *flames*!"
(213;*155*). Septimus then looks at Rezia and wonders "what was
frightening or disgusting in her as she sat there in broad daylight,
sewing?" (216;*157*) Some minutes later, a little girl delivering the

---

apparent if we turn to Mrs. Woolf's essay on Montaigne in which she wrote: "Communication
is health; communication is truth; communication is happiness. To share is our duty; to go
down boldly and bring to light those *hidden thoughts which are the most diseased.* . . ." *The
Common Reader: First Series,* New York: Harcourt, Brace and World, Inc., A Harvest Book,
1955, p. 66; London: The Hogarth Press (Tenth Impression), 1962, p. 93.

evening paper appears; Rezia kisses the child, gives her sweets, laughs and plays with her, as Septimus watches his childless wife thus happily engaged. Suddenly, "He was very tired. He was very happy. He would sleep. He shut his eyes" (219;*159*) but the rest is only momentary, for "He started up in terror. What did he see? The plate of *bananas* on the *sideboard*. Nobody was there. . . . That was it: to be alone forever. That was the doom [his marriage proposal to Rezia] pronounced in Milan . . . to be alone forever. He was alone with the *sideboard* and the *bananas*. He was alone, exposed on this bleak eminence. . . . As for the visions, the faces, the voices of the dead, where were they? There was the *screen* in front of him. . . . Where he had once seen mountains . . . faces . . . beauty, there was a *screen*. 'Evans!' he cried. There was no answer . . . the *screen*, the *coal-scuttle*, the *sideboard* remained to him. Let him then face the *screen*, the *coal-scuttle*,[22] and the *sideboard* . . . but Rezia burst into the room chattering" (220;*159-60*).

When we examine this final sequence against the preceding one—his fear of falling into the flames, his wife's happiness with the child, his terror of having been abandoned—his seeing his marriage as doomed becomes an almost pre-ordained culmination, according to the laws which govern his deranged, inner logic. There is, however, more to understand in this sequence. The three objects Septimus sees in the room become invested with subliminal, transfiguring powers which endow them with a transparency through which we sense a far deeper meaning and significance. For Mrs. Woolf has created a highly evasive kind of associational magic through her choice of objects that Septimus sees in his terror: the sideboard (and the bananas), the coal-scuttle, and the screen. All of these objects, by their juxtaposition, are somehow associated with

---

22. Septimus's preoccupation with *flames* and *fire* throughout the novel are more than mere ravings of a madman; the same holds true for his facing the *coal-scuttle*. If we remember Mrs. Woolf's subtle parenthesis, "('Septimus, do put down your book,' said Rezia, gently shutting the *Inferno*)" (133;*98*), then we realize that he is concerned with the transforming, punitive fires of Hell. But more important, his curious name *Septimus* (seven) now assumes an informing function. For his reading the *Inferno*, through some rhetorical magnetism has the force to suggest that his name is linked with the Seventh Circle, the *septimus circle*, of the Inferno where punishment is meted out to those guilty of violence and brutality. In the First Round of Circle Seven, those engaged in *war* are tormented [Septimus and Evans]; in the Second Round, those guilty of *violence against themselves* [Septimus's suicide]; and in the Third Round, those having committed *crimes against* God, *Nature*, and Art [Septimus's homosexual love for Evans; in Canto XIV, *Sodomites* are specifically singled out].

Evans; they function no longer as mental pictures but, through their repetition, as metaphoric displacements of increasing semantic potency. The *sideboard* becomes for Septimus the solid substance of the real world; it is something as touchable and stable as Evans had been to him. (Symbolists in psychology will want to interpret bananas as phallic, and with very good reason.) The *coal-scuttle* loses its ordinariness and becomes transfigured into that container of fuel which feeds the ravaging furnaces of Hell where Septimus must suffer punishment for his guilt. The *screen,* just as the car's drawn blinds which caused his panic, dematerializes and becomes that psychic barrier which blocks and conceals from consciousness his real feelings for Evans, feelings which must be brought to light and kept conscious. Now, Septimus—this time alone—is courageously prepared to face them; but again, Rezia innocently bursts in at that crucial moment of imminent self-realization.

Unable to divest himself of his nameless guilt, unconsciously devastated by the loss of Evans, victimized by Bradshaw and now overpowered by Holmes, with nowhere to siphon his impotent rage, Septimus's last frantic moments are freighted with horror and hate. We believe that "He did not want to die. Life was good. The sun hot. Only human beings—what did *they* want?" (226;*164*)[23]

With Holmes's final intrusion, Septimus has no recourse. All the violence has reversed itself and has turned inward. But the "screen" between him and his officer has not been removed. Society has not purged him of his love for Evans, has not "cured" him of his feeling for another man. In his death, that love remains vaulted and unvoiced. So that in his defiant leap to oblivion, he has, as Clarissa wished, "plunged holding his treasure."

Even a hasty perusal of all that has been written about *Mrs. Dalloway* will underscore the importance of understanding the relationship between Clarissa and Septimus as a necessary condition to resolving the novel's meaning. Much of the criticism points out the different orders of similarity shared by the two characters: their bird-like appearance; their emotional intensity; Clarissa's tendency to identify with exalted personages, Septimus's Messianic urge; her

23. Italics are Virginia Woolf's.

dependence upon Richard for stability, his dependence upon Rezia for protection; the shared content of their consciousness in the "Fear no more. . ." line from *Cymbeline*; Clarissa's fascination with the Napoleonic hero, Marbot, Septimus's emotional link with the war. These are, however, more or less obvious correspondences which connect the two.

One parallel which has received the least critical attention is Clarissa's and Septimus's attitudes towards their marriage. In neither union does there appear to be any profound relatedness. More explicitly, in both marriages, the condition of the union is one of cohabitation founded on need rather than on love. For Clarissa, the world Richard offers her is one of silver, servants, society; it is a fortress against all the outside reminders of her personal sense of insufficiency. More important, her world of privacy and freedom is a situation of solitude without much loneliness. Marriage for Septimus was the result of panic; a desperate union in which Rezia offers him safety and protection; a refuge from all the private demons populating his morbid imagination; thus, "he married his wife without loving her." In other words, one lonely sane woman and one even lonelier insane man have used marriage to retreat from a world which for them lours with risk and punishment, on the one hand; and to ease the sentence of solitary confinement, on the other. So that if they have perverted marriage to that purpose, the consequence is not only frigidity for Clarissa and impotence for Septimus, but also a farrago of guilt for their deficiency in one sanctum of the marital bond.

If Clarissa and Septimus have failed as marriage partners in one important way, it is not because they have mistakenly chosen marriage as a refuge, for that choice is a consequence. They are failures because of what prompted them to withdraw initially to seek such a refuge. Here the matter begins to ramify in subtle and complex ways. If we remind ourselves that Clarissa refused to marry Peter because with him, "everything had to be shared; everything gone into," then we realize that it was her love for Sally Seton that she could not share, a feeling she has kept alive in memory throughout her married life with Richard.[24] As a married woman, however, the price she pays

24. As Clarissa thinks of Septimus's death, some important thoughts are inconspicuously juxtaposed: "She had schemed; she had pilfered. She was never wholly admirable. . . . And once she had walked on the terrace at Bourton. It was due to Richard; she had never been so

for that love is "an emptiness about the heart of life; an attic room," where "Narrower and narrower would her bed be." The sequence of her thoughts about Bradshaw's profession reveals further the enormity of that price: "For think what cases came before him—people in the uttermost depths of *despair*; people on the verge of *insanity; husbands and wives*" (278;*200*). Consequently, the guilt she may feel for sexually denying her husband has a source, an origin of which she is aware. Whether Clarissa accepts her love for Sally as an unnatural emotion or as a moral violation will have no fatal consequences, because she is conscious of her feeling. And conscious of it, Clarissa can manage it, assimilate it, and allow it to become a part of her natural being.

With Septimus, however, it is a different matter; and so too are the consequences. The guilt he feels for having married out of panic and for being unable to father a child are secondary effects. The primary effect is his inability to "feel" after the death of Evans, a psychic paralysis[25] resulting from a loss so great as to be consciously unendurable. The primary cause of these effects is the love which Septimus once felt for Evans, a love which he feels to be a trespass of an accepted social order. In blind obedience to some personal edict, then, Septimus suppresses the emotional significance of Evans from memory. Despite Evans's appearing repeatedly in phantasy, Septimus cannot make the connection between his earlier feelings and the man who is their object. So that with Evans now dead, what Septimus once felt becomes a dark menacing stain, an act of crime. The feeling for Evans and the memory of him are so alien to one another that they cannot be brought to consciousness for assimilation. Just as panic seized him at the mysterious car's drawn blinds, so too in the panic of recollection the invisible "screen" is thrown up between himself and his friend each time the language of Eros

---

happy" (282). That she should include in her self-accusations the reference to the terrace at Bourton [Sally's kiss] is clear enough. But what immediately follows is extremely significant; for the happiness which Richard has given her, in her mind, translates into something like this: "Despite all my failings and faults—even my love for another woman—you, Richard, have accepted me, have not questioned or meddled, have not required much of me as a woman. In a word, you have been my mainstay. Without you I should have been dead long ago." The Hogarth edition reads somewhat differently: "And once she had walked on the terrace at Bourton. Odd, incredible; she had never been so happy" (*203*).

25. Nowhere in the novel is there any evidence that Septimus's psychological state is the result of shell shock, as many critics have claimed.

attempts to communicate with the cells of memory. As a result, Septimus remains rigid with confusion—and radiant with misery.

If, as Tolstoi said, "All that a man has felt remains with him in memory. We all live by memories,"[26] then what do we say of Septimus in whose last moments vital feelings are still untouched by memory, life-saving connections are still unmade? For it is precisely in his incompleteness that Septimus, Clarissa's double, is *simultaneously her opposite.*

On one side, we recognize in Septimus a personal sense of social violation so exaggerated and a moral conditioning so brittle that his love for another man must remain frozen in a well of feeling where devastation is wrought though guilt, hate, insanity, and finally suicide. Clarissa, on the other side, beneath her varnish of perfection, acknowledges her love for another woman and lives with it. The old submerged experience of Sally Seton has gained ascendency in the dim waters of memory, and consequently in consciousness. Therefore, whatever she must do now to maintain a precarious and artifical harmony within, and however delicate the scales of her life may be, she survives, even if she must live predominantly in the remembrance of a past.

Her identification with Septimus after his death, in the most theosophic sense, thus becomes a private act of communion: his "sin" is also hers; but Septimus, "Lord of men," dies in order that Clarissa may live. The ritual of his sacrifice for her takes place in the little room where she goes to re-live his actual death and to reflect on the thing that really mattered, "a thing, wreathed about with chatter, defaced, obscured in her own life, let drop every day in corruption, lies, chatter. *This* he had preserved" (280;*202*). If by "This" she means the integrity of one's love for another—whether it be homophilic or not—then we understand why Septimus's suicide "was her disaster—her disgrace" (282;*203*). But in the psychological sense, in her identification with Septimus, Clarissa has transferred onto another's shoulders an ancient burden of guilt which has been almost too much for her to bear; so that in Septimus's death, she becomes

26. A. B. Goldenveizer, *Talks with Tolstoi,* p. 137. It is worth noting that Virginia Woolf together with S. S. Koteliansky translated this book which The Hogarth Press published in 1923, the year Mrs. Woolf was deep in the writing of *Mrs. Dalloway.*

the spectator of her own tragedy.

But there is the hint of a far deeper identification taking place in this little room. Thinking that she has "done with the triumphs of youth," Clarissa walks to the window, parts the curtains, and

in the room opposite the old lady stared straight at her! . . . She was going to bed, in the room opposite. It was fascinating to watch her, moving about, that old lady, crossing the room. . . . It was fascinating, with people still laughing and shouting in the drawing-room, to watch that old woman, quite quietly, going to bed. She pulled the blind now. The clock began striking. The young man had killed himself; but she did not pity him; with the clock striking the hour . . . she did not pity him, with all this going on. There! the old lady had put out her light! The whole house was dark now with this going on, she repeated, and the words came to her, Fear no more the heat of the sun. She must go back to them. But what an extraordinary night! She felt somehow very like him—the young man who had killed himself (283;*204*).

In this hushed and shrouded little scene something like a transformation occurs in Clarissa—a final sanative movement forward to meet her self. She hears of the death, re-lives it, feels remorse as she recalls Bourton, remembers her love for Sally,[27] sees Septimus's death as her disgrace, watches the old lady, is uplifted, thinks again of Septimus, and prepares to rejoin her guests.

That Septimus's death, in Clarissa's mind, has become absolution for a love which has made her inadequate in her marriage has its own discordant sound. What curiously echoes throughout the scene, however, is the meaning behind her brooding fascination with the old woman and her solitary bed-time preparations. Feeling now purged as she does, her life has been renewed, and a veil of serenity descends upon her. She seems to see, in the room across the way, the nameless, voiceless old lady symbolically enacting a part which Clarissa will play in the years approaching. Calmly, now, she accepts old age and the idea of death; for through Septimus, she too has preserved her "treasure." Having kept what finally mattered, she is released; she is relieved. Now she can bear the loneliness of her isolation and cling to the memory of her love—but in the private vault of a remembered past, so sequestered that the world should never know, could never

27. The memory of Sally is displaced by: ". . . had he plunged holding his treasure? 'If it were now to die, 'twere now to be most happy,' she·had said to herself once, coming down in white" (281;*202-203*).

understand, and would never accept.

One is strangely reminded of remote parallels in Tolstoi's *Anna Karenina*. In her grand passion for Vronsky, Anna has run counter to her society's laws, just as she has failed morally in her responsibility to her husband and to her son. Her social disorientation, her guilt, and finally her despair make death by suicide inevitable. So too with Septimus. His love for Evans, his throttling of feeling, his marrying for the wrong reason, his inability to give Rezia a child—together assemble into what Septimus believes to be his moral violation of a social order whose laws now refuse to ratify his life. In consequence, his guilt, his rage, his anguish, and finally his suicide—that ultimate defiance of a society he *feels* both severed from and victimized by.

In contrast to Anna Karenina, however, is Konstanin Levin. Although he is a good father and a faithful husband, his obsession with suicide becomes so overwhelming that "he hid the cord that he might not be tempted to hang himself, and was afraid to go out with his gun for fear of shooting himself. But Levin did not shoot himself, and he did not hang himself; he went on living."[28] He went on living because he faced his dilemma and came to terms with it. So too with Clarissa. By refusing to deny her deficiency in marriage, by acknowledging her deceptions, by admitting in private and safeguarding in memory her love for another woman, Clarissa is prepared to go on living, even if ever more inwardly.

Thus the novel's last line, "For there she was," suggests a stately image of selfhood—poised, radiant, symmetric. But it carries also the fuller suggestion of a *new* Clarissa: one just emerged from perilous depths, chastened, finally at one with herself, more fully conscious, and perhaps more enduring. So that in the end, this is the Clarissa whom neither Peter nor Sally nor Richard will ever know as we know her, we who have seen "flash after flash" illuminating the "caves" connecting Clarissa and Septimus, "in the primeval darkness where light has never visited them before."[29]

28. Trans., Constance Garnett, New York: The Modern Library, (n.d.), p. 918.

29. Virginia Woolf, "Pictures," *The Moment and Other Essays,* New York and London: Harcourt Brace Jovanovich, A Harvest Book, 1974, p. 175; London: The Hogarth Press (Uniform Edition), 1952, p. 141.

To the Lighthouse

In *A Writer's Diary*, Virginia Woolf's fifth novel was mentioned for the first time on 14 May 1925. "This is going to be fairly short; to have father's character done complete in it; and mother's; and St. Ives; and childhood. . . . But the centre is father's character, sitting in a boat, reciting We perished, each alone, while he crushes a dying mackerel." Exactly how long the book had been "incubating" in her mind is not possible to determine. The remarkable thing about this statement is that it was written in 1925, when Mrs. Woolf was 43 years old; and the novel she was about to write would be drawn from the tangled skeins of memory reaching back to a year not later than 1895, when her mother died—with Virginia Stephen herself aged thirteen. The book was to be built from blocks hewn from a past at least thirty years old, from that mausoleum of memory where voices have lost their edge, where tapers flicker and dim, and the heavy powders of waste are thick.

To the Lighthouse, generally considered Mrs. Woolf's finest novel, stands as confirmation of her mastery of a complex and disciplined form. In it she was able to present, within severely circumscribed limits of time, a wide range and multiplicity of experience by careful and constant movements in and out of the minds of her characters. With the sureness of a mature artist, she selected out of the flux and chaos of appearances particular thoughts, sensations, and impressions; and arranged them so as to render a fabric of experience which conformed to her own singular and penetrating vision.

The general shape of the novel is not in the least complicated. It is composed of three parts of unequal length of which the first and longest section, "The Window," covers the better part of a day. In it are introduced all the principal characters as well as the central issue: whether or not an expedition to the Lighthouse will take place on the next day. The second and shortest section, "Time Passes," is a poetic interlude which marks the passage of ten years, and parenthetically includes the deaths of several members of the family. The third section, "The Lighthouse," covers the early hours of the morning on which the trip to the Lighthouse, suggested ten years earlier, is made.

But this simple abstract of the text is pure deception. It does not, can not, begin to suggest the novel's strangely haunted atmosphere of doubt, of pain, of despair—of interrogation. For Mrs. Woolf was concerned with exploring the estrangements and confusions of human relationships, the complexities of describing what "living" feels like. In her explorations she had once more to abandon those methods by which the conventional novel arrested and sustained interest, and in their place to create moments of consciousness, the arrangement of which would enlarge the moments already experienced as well as those yet to come—in short, to create deliberately an order in which the multiple contents of consciousness would, at any particular moment, light up the past and anticipate the future. She did not wish to "describe *what* we have all seen so that it becomes a sequence" (Neville's words in *The Waves*) but wanted to describe *how* her people have experienced what they have seen, and *how* to their individual personalities these experiences stand in relation to one another and to some central idea. It is from this concern that she achieved a unity of design which crowns her triumph in *To the Lighthouse*.

In an essay which appeared soon after the novel was published, Mrs. Woolf wrote: "For in order that the light of personality may shine through, facts must be manipulated; some must be brightened; others shaded; yet, in the process, they must never lose their integrity. And it is obvious that it is easier to obey these precepts by considering that the true life of your subject shows itself in action which is evident rather than in that inner life of thought and emotion which meanders darkly and obscurely through the hidden channels of the soul."[1] However, if we examine the way in which she created her characters, we find that contrary to what she wrote, she did indeed follow that meandering "inner life of thought and emotion" at times to its darkest and most obscure corners. In two or three direct strokes of the pen, we begin to get a rough outline of Mrs. Ramsay's inner life, for example, as she talks to her young son in the novel's opening

1. "The New Biography," *New York Herald Tribune*, 30 October 1927; reprinted in *Granite and Rainbow*, New York and London: Harcourt Brace Jovanovich, A Harvest Book, 1975, p. 150.

line, and later in her reaction to her husband. When Mr. Ramsay contradicts her forecast for the next day, he appears, *in her mind,* to be "grinning sarcastically . . . disillusioning his son and casting ridicule" (10;*12*)[2] upon her. She senses his pride in the accuracy of his judgment but knows that "What he said was true. It was always true. He was incapable of untruth; never tampered with a fact; never altered a disagreeable word to suit the pleasure or convenience of any mortal being, least of all his own children . . ." (10-11;*13*).

With impressive economy, Mrs. Woolf has given us in less than three pages a small but vivid picture of Mrs. Ramsay's relationship to her son and to her husband as well as some indication of the woman's emotional state. A little further on we are also given some idea of her generosity towards the Lighthouse keeper, her sympathy for his isolation, and in general her desire to comfort those less fortunate mortals needing her bounty.

Throughout these opening pages we are easily persuaded to sympathize with Mrs. Ramsay, because she represents the maternal compassion and charity we value. We tend to feel averse to Mr. Ramsay (and to Tansley) for having contradicted and upset the person who has won us over. Our attachment increases when we glimpse a few details of her appearance and discover her thoughts: "When she looked in the glass and saw her hair grey, her cheek sunk, at fifty, she thought possibly she might have managed things better—her husband; money; his books. But for her own part she would never for a single second regret her decision, evade difficulties, or slur over duties" (14;*16*). The tinge of her self-pity is over-shadowed by our admiration for this paradigm of selflessness.

Her trip to town with Tansley, however, introduces a new ambiguous possibility and perhaps a slight dislocation of our judgment. Before departing with this young man whom she had earlier thought odious, she stops to ask Carmichael if she can get him anything. But he wants nothing. As if prompted by her sense of uselessness to Carmichael, she confides his past to Tansley, telling him of Carmichael's early and unsuccessful marriage, the poverty, the hardship, the gradual decay—possibly aware that this confidence

---

2. The unitalicized page number in parentheses following each quotation refers to the first American paperback edition published by Harcourt, Brace and World, 1964; the italicized number refers to The Hogarth Press edition (Fourteenth Impression), 1967.

will flatter Tansley and make him feel important. But in the midst of this, she suddenly notices a circus bill and, momentarily forgetting Carmichael, suggests that they all go to the circus. Having given Tansley, by her suggestion, an opportunity to bewail his own history of poverty and hardship, she reflects that she "saw now why going to the circus had knocked him off his perch, poor little man, and why he came out, instantly, with all that about his father and mother and brothers and sisters. . . . What he would have liked, she supposed, would have been to say that he had gone not to the circus but to Ibsen with the Ramsays. He was an awful prig—oh yes, an insufferable bore" (22;*24-25*). This passage, read even out of context, indicates none of the kindness and charity we have been led to expect from Mrs. Ramsay. Indeed her thoughts seem heavily weighted with condescension and antipathy.

And here Virginia Woolf begins to enlarge our image of Mrs. Ramsay by applying some sharply identifying strokes to her portrait of the woman. When her husband, for example, rebukes her for questioning his judgment about the weather, she ponders his callousness:

> To pursue truth with such astonishing lack of consideration for other people's feelings, to rend the thin veils of civilisation so wantonly, so brutally, was to her so horrible an outrage of human decency that, without replying, dazed and blinded, she bent her head as if to let the pelt of jagged hail, the drench of dirty water, bespatter her unrebuked. . . .
> She was quite ready to take his word for it, she said. Only then they need not cut sandwiches—that was all. They came to her, naturally, since she was a woman, all day long with this and that; one wanting this; another that; the children were growing; she often felt she was nothing but a sponge sopped full of human emotions. Then he said, Damn you. He said, It must rain. He said, It won't rain; and instantly a Heaven of security opened before her. There was nobody she reverenced more. She was not good enough to tie his shoe strings, she felt (51;*54-55*).

Her reaction to his heedlessness of others' feelings is appropriate enough, as is her idea that she is a sponge saturated with human emotions. What is curious, however, is the end of her reflection: her feeling "not good enough to tie his shoe strings," because her next thought begins a steady progression towards a very contradictory tendency in her personality. Knowing that her husband is ashamed of his outburst, she imagines his wanting to be "warmed and soothed,

to have his senses restored to him, his barrenness made fertile . . .''
(59;*62*). At that moment, a disagreeable sensation comes over her, a
sudden physical fatigue the genesis of which is too distasteful to put
into words: and it is precisely her feeling of *superiority* over Mr.
Ramsay:

> . . . she did not like, even for a second, to feel finer than her husband;
> and further, could not bear being entirely sure, when she spoke to him,
> of the truth of what she said. Universities and people wanting him, lec-
> tures and books and their being of the highest importance—all that she
> did not doubt for a moment; but it was their relation, and his coming to
> her like that, openly, so that any one could see, that discomposed her; for
> then people said he depended on her, when they must know that of the two
> he was infinitely the more important, and what she gave the world, in
> comparison with what he gave, negligible (61-62;*65*).

How significant it is that Mrs. Ramsay, with all her self-sacrificing
and goodness, even her tendency to put herself down, should
suddenly dwell on her husband's inferiority to her! should be
reminded of his financial inadequacy, and to suspect that his last
book "was not quite his best." These thoughts reinforce her deepest,
unrecognized need to feel her success and his failure. Just how
disturbing that idea is to her, we shall discover when this fundamental rift in her being begins to reveal itself in other ways.

As we begin to be aware of Mrs. Ramsay's conflicting needs, old
Carmichael shuffles by her, and she is painfully "reminded of the
inadequacy of human relationships . . ." (62;*66*). Her thought here is
no less potent in implication than her earlier one. Carmichael, we
recall, wants nothing from her, needs nothing of her; and she feels
uncomfortable, because she interprets it as his not trusting her.
Consequently, her mind again focuses on the ugliness of *his* life: his
opium addiction, his miserable existence, his poverty, his
slovenliness. How often she went out of her way to make him like her
(here a sense of her own beauty flashes before her):

> And after all . . . she had not generally any difficulty in making people like
> her. . . . Tears had flown in her presence. Men, and women too, letting go
> the multiplicity of things, had allowed themselves with her the relief of
> simplicity. It injured her that he [Carmichael] should shrink. It hurt her.
> And yet not cleanly, not rightly (64-65;*67-68*).

She certainly is injured "not rightly," for Carmichael has frustrated her desire to give and has forced her to turn inwards, to plumb some dark recess, to suspect her own motives:

. . . all this desire of hers to give, to help, was vanity. For her own self-satisfaction was it that she wished so instinctively to help, to give, that people might say of her, "O Mrs. Ramsay! dear Mrs. Ramsay . . . Mrs. Ramsay, of course!" and need her and send for her and admire her? Was it not secretly this that she wanted, and therefore when Mr. Carmichael shrank away from her, as he did this moment, making off to some corner where he did acrostics endlessly, she did not feel merely snubbed back in her instinct, but made aware of the pettiness of some part of her, and of human relations, how flawed they are, how despicable, how self-seeking at their best (65-66;*68-69*).

Although not aware of her rationalization, Mrs. Ramsay has moved the burden of her responsibility for failure away from herself as a particular individual to general "human relations," and she thinks: "how flawed *they* are . . . how self-seeking at *their* best."[3] It is understandable, in light of her rumination, why she finds Carmichael disquieting, why "she did in her own heart infinitely prefer boobies to clever men" (85;*89*), and why "she would have liked to keep for ever [her two youngest children] just as they were, demons of wickedness, angels of delight, never to see them grow up into long-legged monsters" (89;*93*). Boobies and children can be manoeuvred, controlled, made to worship her. Carmichael can not.

Unquestionably, there is something to one woman's charge that Mrs. Ramsay was

"robbing her of her daughter's affections" . . . . Wishing to dominate, wishing to interfere, making people do what she wished . . . and she [Mrs. Ramsay] thought it most unjust: How could she help being "like that" to look at? No one could accuse her of taking pains to impress. She was often ashamed of her own shabbiness. Nor was she domineering, nor was she tyrannical. It was more true about hospitals and drains and the dairy (88-89;*92*).

Observe, in the first place, that the charge brought against Mrs. Ramsay does not mention the way she looked; in her self-defence, however, her appearance takes priority; and her sartorial deficit becomes in her mind suddenly transformed into a kind of spiritual asset. Her shabbiness, we are led to suspect, is part of the trapping

3. Throughout the chapter, unless otherwise specified, italics appearing in the quoted matter are mine.

that belongs to her deceptive self-denigrating apparatus with which she first dramatically gains sympathy and then coerces people to do what she wishes. Notice also the way in which she absolves herself of all charges by directing her attention to her charitable efforts in the community—the hospital, the drains, the dairy; these good causes contradict any accusation, however valid, levelled at her.

Despite these and other defensive measures which she unconsciously uses, Mrs. Ramsay is not without her moments of awareness, moments when she is alone and can be herself, when she need not think of others:

To be silent; to be alone. All the being and the doing, expansive, glittering, vocal, evaporated; and one shrunk, with a sense of solemnity, to being oneself, a wedge-shaped core of darkness, something invisible to others. . . . When life sank down for a moment . . . the range of experience seemed limitless. And to everybody there was this sense of unlimited resources, she supposed; one after another, she, Lily, Augustus Carmichael, must feel, our apparitions, the things you know us by, are simply childish. Beneath it is all dark, it is all spreading, it is unfathomably deep; but now and again we rise to the surface and that is what you see us by (95-96;*99-100*).

As one who practices the art of creating human relationships, she singles out Lily Briscoe and Carmichael as companions to her sensibility; for all three are joined in creating aesthetic harmony out of human experience: Carmichael creates with words; Lily, with pigments; Mrs. Ramsay, with people.

Her mechanisms of feeling, however, have their own strangely checked energies, and they lay bare those deep enclosures of the mind where contradictions flourish. For Mrs. Ramsay, despite her catalytic function in bringing people together, is herself an extremely isolated person. She is unable to express deep feelings, unable to open herself spontaneously in anger or hurt or love. Unlike her husband, she must hide her moods. Her relationship to Mr. Ramsay is, in fact, a fairly accurate measure of the aloofness and estrangement which lurk at the core of her "wedge of darkness." As she and her husband stroll before dinner, she talks of many commonplace things that have probably been said before; but her tone becomes increasingly strained, because her mind is wandering: the dahlias; the fifty pounds it would cost to fix the greenhouse; whether flower bulbs should be sent down; all the poverty and suffering in the world; would he apologize for saying "Damn you"; his inability to see the simple things around him; his tiresome phrase-making and melancholy. From his awkward habit of talking aloud to himself, her mind turns to his intellectual powers, and while examining a fresh mole hill on the bank, she reflects that

a great mind like his must be different in every way from ours. All the great men she had ever known, she thought, deciding that a rabbit must have got in, were like that, and it was good for young men (though the atmosphere of the lecture-rooms was stuffy and depressing to her beyond endurance almost) simply to hear him. But without shooting rabbits, how was one to keep them down? she wondered (108;*112*).

Virginia Woolf is here brilliantly and dramatically rendering the remoteness and isolation of a woman who does not, will not, *can not* share her husband's world. More important, she minimizes him by the demeaning juxtaposition of her thoughts: rabbits ruining her flowers are as important to her as a consideration of her husband's academic stature! Small wonder that Mrs. Ramsay finds human relationships inadequate.

If the disjointed thoughts in this passage indicate the extent of her spiritual kinship to her husband, we have legitimate cause to question Mrs. Ramsay's relations with the others around her and to question her sensitivity to the things in their lives they value most. How aware is she of Carmichael aside from the fact that she feeds and pities him? What is her interest in Lily other than a desire to see her married to Bankes, a man old enough to be Lily's father? And Tansley? To what degree is she able or willing to understand the drives which make him so obnoxiously assertive? Are all her alliances undergirded by some self-seeking motive? Does her maniacal need for match-making originate in her potential satisfaction of effecting a marriage and thereby feeling her mastery over the union?[4]

In the memorable scene of the dinner party, we discover Virginia Woolf adding several bold strokes to the constantly growing portrait

4. These questions are of singular biographic importance; for anyone who has not read Mrs. Leslie Stephen's single publication, *Notes from Sick Rooms* (London: Smith, Elder and Co., 1883), would be shocked to read on the first page of the text proper, Julia Stephen's writing: "I have often wondered why it is considered a proof of virtue in anyone to become a nurse. *The ordinary relations between the sick and the well are far easier and pleasanter than between the well and the well*" (italics mine). Aside from the morbid tone of that declaration, the influence of such a sentiment on her family must have exerted an enormous pressure. For in effect, it meant that to be of any significance to Mrs. Stephen, one had somehow to be helpless—

of Mrs. Ramsay. "But what have I done with my life?" asks Mrs. Ramsay taking her place at the head of the table. For she is confronted by a group of antagonistic personalities, all of whom are concealing their resentment by mouthing empty amenities or by remaining silent. This is the assembly, and these are her materials. Out of them she feels she must create something whole and harmonious, each part articulating smoothly with the next: "the whole of the effort of merging and flowing and creating rested on her" (126;*131*). But she is weary. She looks at her husband "all in a heap, frowning" and wonders how she had ever felt any affection for him. She glances critically at Tansley and notes that he was "thinking of himself and the impression he was making." She looks at Bankes and thinks "—poor man! who had no wife, and no children and dined alone in lodgings. . . ." She thinks of Carmichael with her characteristic mixture of fraternal commiseration and maternal protectiveness.

While she surveys these people in their most pitiable, least commendable aspect, she begins to draw them together: a comment here; a question there; a spark of interest to enliven Tansley; an appeal to Lily; a piece of beef for Bankes. When she has brought together this "house full of unrelated passions" under her aegis, she leaves them to themselves and drifts off to her own private realm where she can stand aloof and consider the success of her clever and controlling handiwork:

Now she need not listen. It could not last, she knew, but at the moment her eyes were so clear that they seemed to go round the table unveiling each of these people, and their thoughts and feelings, without effort like a light stealing under water so that it ripples. . . . So she saw them; she heard them; but whatever they said had also this quality, as if what they said had the movement of a trout when, at the same time, one could see the ripple and the gravel, something to the right, something to the left; and the whole is held together; for whereas in active life she would be netting and separating one thing from another; she would be saying she liked the

either from age (very young or very old) or from illness. Healthy, self-sufficient people could not gratify her *need to be needed.* She had to have in her orbit people who depended upon her in the extreme. Anyone who has read Noel Gilroy Annan's *Leslie Stephen, His Thought and Character in Relation to His Time* (London: Macgibbon & Kee, 1951) will realize that Leslie Stephen filled the bill to perfection; that is, like Mr. Ramsay, Stephen very much needed a wife upon whom he could depend to satisfy his many real or imaginary needs. (I want to thank Dr. Anna Battista for calling Julia Stephen's book to my attention and for making the text available to me.)

Waverley novels or had not read them; she would be urging herself forward; now she said nothing (160-61;*165-66*).

Although she says nothing, it is clear from the liveliness of her thoughts that her weariness has vanished: the energizing center of her being has become operative, as she moves these people about according to her design.

The evolution of Paul's and Minta's engagement and Mrs. Ramsay's part in it provide additional evidence of the kind of woman Mrs. Ramsay is. She has worked to make the connection between them; and when, all aglow, they arrive late for dinner, Mrs. Ramsay knows that

> It must have happened . . . they were engaged. And for a moment she felt what she had never expected to feel—jealousy. For he, her husband, felt it too—Minta's glow; he liked these girls, these golden-reddish girls, with something flying, something a little wild and harum-scarum about them. . . . There was some quality which she herself had not, some lustre, some richness, which attracted him, amused him, led him to make favourites of girls like Minta. . . . But indeed she was not jealous, only, now and then, when she made herself look in her glass a little resentful that she had grown old, perhaps, by her own fault (149;*153-54*).

Her jealousy of Minta and resentment at her youth are perplexing, not because she has these natural feelings, but because she feels them at this particular time, when she should be happy for the pair whose union she will have caused. It seems a contradiction that a woman who is so seemingly dedicated to the welfare and happiness of others should dwell at such length on herself and her own imagined losses. As Mrs. Ramsay's thoughts return again to Minta and Paul ("for her part she liked her boobies, Paul must sit by her") and the dinner that will celebrate their engagement, she thinks profoundly of a man's love for a woman. Her thoughts become a jeering reflection that "these lovers, these people entering into illusion glittering eyed, must be danced round with mockery . . ." (151;*156*). But these are words inspired by feelings heavy with bitterness and disillusionment.

Shortly after the assembly has dispersed, however, Mrs. Ramsay, alone upstairs, tries to stabilize herself. Disruptive emotions are battling within her, and she tries to smother that deeply buried conflict which aroused the jealousy and resentment at the thought of the engagement. Unaware of the real source of these emotions, she attempts to effect a moment of artificial stability by thinking: "Yes, that was done then, accomplished; and as with all things done, became solemn." However, we gain a deeper look into Mrs. Ramsay when we realize that the solemnity of the engagement is, for her, buttressed on every side by her leadership in it and their grateful memory of it. To Mrs. Ramsay, Minta and Paul would "however long they lived, come back to this night; this moon; this wind; this house: and to her too. It flattered her, where she was most susceptible to flattery, to think how wound about in their hearts, however long they lived she would be woven . . ." (170;*175*). How necessary it is for her always to be at the center of matters, to insist that a kind of spiritual immortality live on in them after she is gone, to put them and others in her debt.

What is so conspicuous here, as in her other relations with people, is not Mrs. Ramsay's concern with Paul and Minta or with anyone else, but in her preoccupation with herself. Concerned with the effect she has in directing the lives of others, she claims at the same time their approval and admiration and praise. That endless affirmation from them nurtures and sustains her own temporary sense of self-worth. Considered in this light, Mrs. Ramsay appears to reside in that depressive state where acceptance and approval become a matter of life and death for her; where ultimately nothing else will do to ease the gnawing ache of emptiness.

In the final scene of the section, we are given the last full details of her portrait. Recall that previously her reaction to her husband's weather forecast was one of unexpressed anger. For open aggression on her part, she thinks, would result in disapproval and rejection; and to Mrs. Ramsay these are intolerable. Given her husband's extreme vacillations of mood and temper, she has really no firm positive base of which she can be certain of herself in relation to him. Reconciliation, however, must occur; for that is the guarantee that her husband can at least tolerate her unwholesomely repressed anger. And throughout the section, reading sequentially only her thoughts and impressions, it becomes clear that her anger did, indeed must, remain mute. For in addition to everything else, consciously she felt herself to be an appeasing, a conciliatory person, one who placed others first, who felt subordinate to her husband—his work, his fame. Yet in this closing scene, the contradictory part of her which has repeatedly shown itself throughout rises to the surface for the last and most memorable time. She imagines Mr. Ramsay looking at her and wanting her to say that she loves him—something she can not, will not, do: "she never told him that she loved him, but it was not so—it was not so. It was only that she never could say what she felt." She then fancies his looking at her and thinking: "You are more beautiful than ever. . . . Will you not tell me just once that you love me?" (185;*190*) But for all her compliance and sympathy, she will not yield: she says nothing. She merely smiles and maintains her aloofness from his small and very natural wish. And as though by this denial she has unwittingly subordinated him, has repaid him for the hurt he had earlier inflicted, has made him feel the full force of her victory, she merely says to him, "'Yes, you were right. It's going to be wet tomorrow. You won't be able to go.'" Characteristic of her propensity to over-rate the imagination of others and to fail to recognize her own motives, she believes that she has "triumphed again. She did not say it: yet he knew." The ultimate triumph is indeed hers: whether, as she believes, in not openly expressing her love; or, as she is unable to realize, by frustrating her husband in an act of retaliatory silence.

Our introduction to Mr. Ramsay is harsh, deafening, and dissonant. He is relentless in his judgment about the trip to the Lighthouse. His intellectualism is undeviating and uncompromising. His logic will not be diverted. His opinions will not be questioned. When his wife asks him how he can be sure about the weather, nis reaction is violent almost to the point of childishness; but it tells us something about his attitude towards women in general:

The extraordinary irrationality of her remark, the folly of women's minds enraged him. He had ridden through the valley of death, been shattered and shivered; and now, she flew in the face of facts, made his children hope what was utterly out of the question, in effect, told lies. He stamped his foot on the stone step. "Damn you," he said (50;*53-54*).

That her remark should seem to shatter all structures of rationality to a mind so disciplined is not unusual; nor is it unusual that his philosophical training should cause him to interpret his wife's uncertain promises as outright lies. What is interesting, however, is his phantasy: he sees himself struggling heroically in the Light

Brigade in the valley of death at Balaclava. Part of his rage is undoubtedly from the sudden injury done to the splendid self-image he is experiencing at that moment. Although such emotional explosions are not especially conducive to human relations, one wonders why, in reality, a man of his intellectual stature should, in phantasy, entertain the idea of heroic grandeur. For his imagined heroism carries the tone of one who in the privacy of his own mind considers himself a weakling and a failure. It is the kind of full, rich dream one invents to nourish a power-starved outcast.

Somewhat later, we are given a glimpse of his metaphysic, and we feel the antiseptic disunity of an epistemological vision which sees knowledge as an alphabet which one must plod through perseveringly, letter by letter, before reaching Z, before laying claim to genius. We also learn his own secret self-estimate from this mental excursion:

In that flash of darkness he heard people saying—he was a failure—that R was beyond him. He would never reach R. . . . He had not genius; he laid no claim to that; but he had, or might have had, the power to repeat every letter of the alphabet from A to Z accurately in order. . . . Yet he would not die lying down; he would find some crag of rock, and there, his eyes fixed on the storm, trying to the end to pierce the darkness, he would die standing. He would never reach R (54-55;*57-59*).

For all his harshness and severity, then, his seeming disregard for people, and his outward sterility, we know that in his own company he is ruthlessly honest. His grandiose phantasies are compensatory measures to counter the onslaught of his terrible feelings of inadequacy. Further, the sympathy and coddling he craves are, for him, urgent and human needs, but they are the very needs which others find degrading. So that, indeed,

Who shall blame him, if, so standing for a moment, he dwells upon fame, upon search parties, upon cairns raised by grateful followers over his bones? . . . Who will not secretly rejoice when the hero puts his armour off, and halts by the window and gazes at his wife and son, who very distant at first, gradually come closer and closer, till lips and book and head are clearly before him, though still lovely and unfamiliar from the intensity of his isolation and the waste of ages and the perishing of the stars, and finally putting his pipe in his pocket and bending his magnificent head before her—who will blame him if he does homage to the beauty of the world? (57;*60-61*)

The atmosphere of his mind is lonely and brooding, but facing squarely the dark of human ignorance in a world of misery and chaos, he knows that "he was for the most part happy; he had his wife; he had his children; he had promised in six weeks' time to talk 'some nonsense' to the young men of Cardiff . . ." (70;*73*).

Neither we nor those around him can easily acknowledge how painfully sensitive he really is to others, especially to Mrs. Ramsay—that strange and aloof combination of woman, wife, mother—and Madonna. How lost and unhappy and useless he feels in noting the "sternness at the heart of her beauty. It saddened him, and her remoteness pained him, and he felt, as he passed, that he could not protect her, and, when he reached the hedge, he was sad. He could do nothing to help her. He must stand by and watch her. Indeed, the infernal truth was, he made things worse for her" (98-99;*102*).

Mr. Ramsay's deficits are many; but in his sincerest reflections, we find him habitually weighing, measuring, evaluating his worth. Sometimes he is forthright; sometimes he is drenched in self-pity; and at times he displays an almost boyish naiveté. But despite the licit charges brought by some readers against him for his sympathy-mongering, we are entitled to the suspicion that much of his self-pity is a consequence of Mrs. Ramsay's distance and solitude. Her obscure and nameless estrangement inevitably exacts from him, too, the price of being alone. He knows that she will not permit him entry into her world; he knows too that she cannot step over into his. Their walk through the garden bears eloquent testimony of her, and consequently his, enforced isolation. Even in these circumstances, however, he is acquiescent, loyal, and grateful:

The father of eight children—he reminded himself. And he would have been a beast and a cur to wish a single thing altered. Andrew would be a better man than he had been. Prue would be a beauty, her mother said. They would stem the flood a bit. That was a good bit of work on the whole—his eight children. They showed he did not damn the poor little universe entirely . . . (106;*109-110*).

If we divest Mr. Ramsay of all the judgments heaped on him by other readers and attend only to those reflections and impressions which have their provenance in him, we discover a very different man emerging. His intellectual life may be austere, uncompromising, rigorously dedicated to fact; but as a husband and father, he is not only more devoted than his wife to those who make up his world, but also more honest than she in his dealings with them. Of course he is egotistical and tyrannical and barren and cruel—indeed an "arid scimitar." But, he is also effective. He has only to say two words: "Well done!" to transform his son's world and to establish finally that precious union between father and son. So that if we read the smaller, less visible text, we see under that hand formidably raised in command, not the born leader dramatized on the novel's surface, but a man whose sense of weakness disfigures the sceptre of power into something of a holy relic. Under that barnacled carapace, then, we feel something soft, trembling, and afraid; and under the dictatorial roar, we hear the tremulous tone of an uneasy boy. This is the real Mr. Ramsay, crowded by people and shrouded in loneliness; tyrannical with certitude and tyrannized by uncertainty. At once frightening and frightened, he is the solitary figure of a man drawn in all his naked and nervous beauty.

We know from the novel's first page that James has been promised a trip to the Lighthouse. His mother's reassurance of the promise arouses in him "an extraordinary joy," but his reaction to his father's contention that the weather will not permit the expedition is astonishingly forceful: "Had there been an axe handy, or a poker, any weapon that would have gashed a hole in his father's breast and killed him, there and then, James would have seized it" (10;*12*). One may assume from James's thought that his mother "was ten thousand times better in every way than he [Mr. Ramsay] was," that the violence in his initial response was not just the violence of the moment but an emotion which has always characterized his relation to his father.

Later, his jealousy towards the Lighthouse keeper's son, for whom the stockings are being knitted, accents the possessiveness he feels for his mother. We are also made aware of the deep bases of his unwillingness to share with anyone the attentions of his mother which he feels should be exclusively his own. His jealousy is kindled again when his father interrupts the story his mother is reading him:

. . . he hated the twang and twitter of his father's emotion which, vibrating round them, disturbed the perfect simplicity and good sense of his relations with his mother. By looking fixedly at the page, he hoped to make him move on; by pointing his finger at the word, he hoped to recall his mother's attention, which, he knew angrily, wavered instantly his father stopped (58;*61*).

In a short image-laden passage, we are helped to discern how he, as a six-year-old boy, feels toward each parent: "as he stood stiff between her knees, he felt her rise in a rosy-flowered fruit tree laid with leaves and dancing boughs into which the beak of brass, the arid scimitar of his father, the egotistical man, plunged and smote, demanding sympathy" (60;*63*). These are the impressions, rendered metaphorically, of the six-year-old boy. Ten years later when he is in the boat with his father and his sister, Cam, we see no appreciable difference in his feelings towards Mr. Ramsay. The rivalry is still intense, and the jealousy is still electric. His rage is immediately mobilized when he thinks he will lose Cam to him; and he stares hatefully at his father, seeing him again as "that fierce sudden black-winged harpy, with its talons and its beak all cold and hard, that struck and struck at you . . ." (273;*283*). He searches his mind for the cause of his hatred and terror, trying to find some image which will embody his feelings. He envisions himself as a helpless child watching a wagon wheel crush someone's foot. As he circles backward in time through the coils of memory, he recalls the world of his childhood where the feelings he now harbors were first nourished:

It was in this world that the wheel went over the person's foot. Something, he remembered, stayed and darkened over him; would not move; something flourished up in the air, something arid and sharp descended even there, like a blade, a scimitar, smiting through the leaves and flowers even of that happy world and making it shrivel and fall (276;*285*).[5]

He recalls the time when he felt the urge to kill his father. He had felt helpless, and his mother "had gone stiff all over, and then, her arm slackening, so that he felt she listened to him no longer, she had risen somehow and gone away and left him there, impotent, ridiculous, sitting on the floor grasping a pair of scissors" (277-78;*287*).

Considering James in terms of his possessiveness for his mother, his jealousy of his father, his need for paternal recognition, his

5. The Hogarth edition reads: ". . . making them shrivel and fall."

impotence and rage, and the anxiety which stains his introspection, we might easily attach to him a Freudian label and summarily dismiss him as an Oedipal victim modelled after that prototype of antiquity. But to resort to that kind of verbal shorthand would be to ignore the rich and careful detail with which James was created. We would also miss the artistry with which Virginia Woolf, in three short sentences, crystallizes the response of an adolescent who has just found a father:

He was so pleased that he was not going to let anybody share a grain of his pleasure. His father had praised him. They must think that he was perfectly indifferent (306;*316*).[6]

Outside the Ramsay family are other centers of consciousness whose insights and impressions add to the complex scaffolding of the novel. William Bankes is one of them. Because he never emerges forcefully, many readers fail to see him as the deceptive character he is. The success of Mrs. Woolf's cumulative method of characterization, to a large extent, keeps the deception inconspicuous. If one suggested, for instance, that William Bankes was a selfish man who gave priority to his work because he was unable to establish deep human ties, the statement would probably be met with ardent disapprobation. If one said that Bankes disapproved of the very things in Mr. Ramsay that he himself was guilty of and, moreover, was jealous of Ramsay for having what he himself lacked; if one said that like Peer Gynt his motto in life was: "To thine own self be enough"; that human beings were an interference with his own ambitions, these statements would very likely be criticized for the irresponsibility which blemishes all rash interpretations. However, these suggestions are worth following.

We first meet William Bankes when he is observing Lily Briscoe: "Her shoes were excellent. . . . They allowed the toes their natural expansion. Lodging in the same house with her, he had noticed too, how orderly she was, up before breakfast and off to paint, he believed, alone: poor, presumably, and without the complexion or the allurement of Miss Doyle certainly, but with a good sense which

6. Here too the Hogarth volume differs: ". . . he was not going to let anybody take away a grain of his pleasure."

made her in his eyes superior to that young lady" (31;*33*). The observation is cool, critical, detached. He perceives Lily more as an intelligent and systematic schedule than as a sensitive and sensible woman.

Later he ruminates on his friendship with Mr. Ramsay and how its "pulp had gone," how "repetition had taken the place of newness." Yet "He was anxious for the sake of this friendship and perhaps too to clear himself in his own mind from the imputation of having dried and shrunk. . . .he was anxious that Lily Briscoe should not disparage Ramsay (a great man in his own way) yet should understand how things stood between them" (35;*38*). His curious thought that Lily might disparage Ramsay becomes less curious when we discover Bankes himself slurring his old friend:

. . . he weighed Ramsay's case, commiserated him, envied him, as if he had seen him divest himself of all the glories of isolation and austerity which crowned him in youth to cumber himself definitely with fluttering wings and clucking domesticities. . . . Could one help noticing that habits grew on him? eccentricities, weaknesses perhaps? It was astonishing that a man of his intellect could stoop so low as he did—but that was too harsh a phrase —could depend so much as he did upon people's praise (37-38;*39-40*).

Even his estimate of Ramsay's work takes the shape of a smoldering criticism, an insinuation that Ramsay's academic life is finished: "Times without number, he had said, 'Ramsay is one of those men who do their best work before they are forty.' He had made a definite contribution to philosophy in one little book when he was only five and twenty; what came after that was more or less amplification, repetition" (39;*41*).

When Lily admits her dislike for Mr. Ramsay's narrowness, Bankes is quick   to suggest to her that perhaps Ramsay was

"A bit of a hypocrite?" . . . for he was not thinking of his friendship, and of Cam refusing to give him a flower, and of all those boys and girls, and his own [Bankes's] house, full of comfort, but since his wife's death, quiet rather? Of course, he had his work. . . . All the same, he rather wished Lily to agree that Ramsay was, as he said, "a bit of a hypocrite" (72;*75*).

It is a strange wish in that it comes from someone who only minutes earlier was anxious that Lily should not disparage Ramsay.

At the dinner which Mrs. Ramsay has given with great effort to

please Bankes, he is bored and annoyed, yet characteristically
"preserving a demeanour of exquisite courtesy." His very presence
at the table seems to him an extraordinary sacrifice:

How trifling it all is, how boring it all is . . . compared with the other
thing—work. . . . What a waste of time it all was to be sure! Yet now, at
this moment her presence meant absolutely nothing to him: her beauty
meant nothing to him; her sitting with the little boy at the window—
nothing, nothing. He wished only to be alone and to take up that book. He
felt uncomfortable; he felt treacherous, that he could sit by her side and feel
nothing for her. The truth was that he did not enjoy family life. It was in
this sort of state that one asked oneself, What does one live for? Why, one
asked oneself, does one take all these pains for the human race to go on? Is
it so very desirable? Are we attractive as a species? Not so very, he
thought. . . . Foolish questions, vain questions, questions one never asked
oneself if one was occupied. Is human life this? Is human life that? One
never had time to think about it. . . . He was sitting beside Mrs. Ramsay
and he had nothing in the world to say to her. . . . He must make himself
talk. Unless he were very careful, she would find out this treachery of his;
that he did not care a straw for her, and that would not be at all pleasant, he
thought (134-35;*138-40*).

Here is Bankes fully decked in selfishness. The whole of his discontent originates in his feeling that he is a superior being whose
claim on success—indeed on the immortality—of his work is being
jeopardized by this distasteful, time-consuming dinner party. If we
carefully trace the play of his thoughts, we see that from thoughts of
his aversion to family life, he goes on to question the human race.
That question, however, is quickly checked with the notion that
when one was occupied, there was no time to think of such things.
The check is a revealing one, because if he were to pursue the
question, he would inevitably come face to face with the void in his
own life—a life in which everything and everyone have been
subordinated to the interest of his work and his fame. It is a life,
moreover, made chilly and remote by the emotional distance he has
had to maintain between himself and others in the interest of that
pursuit.

Charles Tansley's first appearance, like that of Mr. Ramsay, causes
us to recoil. "There'll be no landing at the Lighthouse tomorrow,"
he hammers out, nailing down his mentor's prediction and
compounding the disappointment which Mrs. Ramsay and James

already feel. He is a twitching, misguided package of rudeness; and there is little to redeem him from the hostility he arouses. Redemption, however, is not a concern, because Mrs. Woolf has not condemned him. It is true that the acid with which Mrs. Woolf describes him is often undiluted, and the laughter he inspires is often punitive and alkaline. Beneath his exterior, however, Tansley is very different in quality from those other unamiable and sometimes comic characters on the long shelf of fiction. His awkwardness is not that of a Uriah Heep; his obsequiousness is different from that of a Pastor Collins; his hostility does not have the destructiveness of a Thomas Gradgrind; his aggressiveness does not have the threatening tone of a Jason Compson. Tansley differs from these characters, because Virginia Woolf bids us not to judge him but to understand him, to see the source of his confused values. Tansley's walk to the village with Mrs. Ramsay offers sufficient evidence to guide us to an understanding of the young man. He is flattered by Mrs. Ramsay's invitation; he feels proud—even a little chivalrous—to be in her company. He feels important when she confides Carmichael's story to him. Soon he is feeling all sorts of things, but "something in particular . . . excited him and disturbed him for reasons which he could not give. He would like her to see him, gowned and hooded, walking in a procession. A fellowship, a professorship, he felt capable of anything . . ." (20;*23*).

But the circus is mentioned, and he must suspend for the moment his steaming phantasy of academic climates. Now he must make an appeal for his companion's sympathy, for he is almost overcome by the need to tell Mrs. Ramsay that he has never been to a circus, because "It was a large family, nine brothers and sisters, and his father was a working man. 'My father is a chemist, Mrs. Ramsay. He keeps a shop.' He himself had paid his own way since he was thirteen. Often he went without a greatcoat in winter. He could never 'return hospitality' (those were his parched stiff words) at college. **He had to make things last twice the time other people did; he** smoked the cheapest tobacco; shag; the same the old men did in the quays. He worked hard—seven hours a day . . ." (21-22;*24*). Preoccupied with self-sacrifice and triumph, Tansley allows his vindictiveness a moment of rest, because alone with Mrs. Ramsay, he is the center of attention.

Only at the dinner party do we realize how urgent is his need to be in the limelight. He is angry at the conversation not so much because it is flimsy table talk, but rather because it does not offer him the opportunity to flaunt his master mind, to relieve himself of his defensive vanity:

. . . he was not going to talk the sort of rot these people wanted him to talk. He was not going to be condescended to by these silly women. He had been reading in his room, and now he came down and it all seemed to him silly, superficial, flimsy. . . . They did nothing but talk, talk, talk, eat, eat, eat. It was the women's fault. Women made civilisation impossible with all their "charm," their silliness (129;*133-34*).

His anger reaches such intensity that he needs to find some outside cause to justify it and give him reason to feel exploited, to feel himself the pariah. Lily Briscoe's request that Tansley take her to the Lighthouse comes at exactly the right moment: now she can carry the burden of the blame:

She was telling lies he could see. She was laughing at him. He was in his old flannel trousers. He had no others. He felt very rough and isolated and lonely. He knew that she was trying to tease him for some reason; she didn't want to go to the Lighthouse with him; she despised him: so did Prue Ramsay; so did they all (130-31;*135*).

When we realize Tansley's Lilliputian sense of himself, we begin to understand why it is so necessary for him to perceive his image being dwarfed by others. We also begin to appreciate his thought that "if only he could be alone in his room . . . working among his books. That was where he was at his ease" (131;*135*). Nor is it difficult to understand his loneliness in view of his disturbed relations with people; his feeling himself an object of pillory, the outcast of the Hebrides; his construing what others say as attempts to humiliate him; his harboring such feral resentment for the company; and consequently his wishing to depreciate the Ramsays when the urge to assert himself is frustrated. Depreciating them conversely increases his own sense of worthiness. Consequently, the idea occurs to him that the Ramsays talked nonsense,

and he pounced on this fresh instance with joy, making a note which, one of these days, he would read aloud, to one or two friends. There, in a society where one could say what one liked he would sarcastically describe "staying with the Ramsays" and what nonsense they talked. It was worth while doing it once, he would say; but not again. The women bored one so, he would say. Of course Ramsay had dished himself by marrying a beautiful woman and having eight children (136;*140-41*).

Having thus debased the Ramsays, Tansley returns to his bruised but tender vainglory and soothes it with phantasies of hidden grandeur and power and vengeance; because "he was Charles Tansley—a fact that nobody there seemed to realise; but one of these days every single person would know it . . . . He could almost pity these mild cultivated people, who would be blown sky high, like bales of wool and barrels of apples, one of these days by the gunpowder that was in him" (138;*143*).

Lily Briscoe, the painter, is a silhouette of Virginia Woolf, the novelist. Her effort to transform her sense of the world through shape and color lays bare the aesthetic problems an artist encounters in expressing a private vision. But more than that, Lily Briscoe is the novel's unifying *persona*. Hers is the principal consciousness through which Mrs. Ramsay is kept vivid before the reader in the final section of the book. As the novel's sentient center, she is our most effective guide; for more than any other character, she is sensible to those peculiar admixtures of emotional and intellectual and moral elements which undergird human behavior.

Our initial glimpse of Lily immediately suggests how well she understands Mr. Ramsay. Standing by her easel, she hears him shouting " 'Boldly we rode and well,' " and supposes that he is in one of those imaginary flights in which he is riding off "to die gloriously . . . upon the heights of Balaclava" (29;*32*); so that she thinks, "Never was anybody at once so ridiculous and so alarming. But so long as he kept like that, waving, shouting, she was safe; he would not stand still and look at her picture" (29-30;*32*). Later when Bankes suggests that Mr. Ramsay is a "bit of a hypocrite," however, we discover her undeviating sense of honesty: "Oh, no—the most sincere of men, the truest (here he was), the best; but, looking down, she thought, he is absorbed in himself, he is tyrannical, he is unjust" (72;*76*). Yet in spite of this, she knows that Ramsay has what Bankes does not: "a fiery unworldliness; he knows nothing about trifles; he loves dogs and his children. He has eight. Mr. Bankes has none. Did he not come down in two coats the other night and let Mrs. Ramsay trim his hair into a pudding basin?" (40;*43*)[7] She recognizes,

7. The Hogarth edition reads: "He has eight. You have none."

moreover, the depth and strength of Ramsay's devotion to his wife:

For him to gaze as Lily saw him gazing at Mrs. Ramsay was a rapture, equivalent, Lily felt, to the loves of dozens of young men . . . . It was love, she thought . . . distilled and filtered; love that never attempted to clutch its object; but, like the love which mathematicians bear their symbols, or poets their phrases, was meant to spread over the world and become part of the human gain (73-74;*77*).

Lily also understands Mrs. Ramsay, her "mania for marriage," her irritating habit of "presiding with immutable calm over destinies which she completely failed to understand" (78;*81*). Alert to Mrs. Ramsay's penchant for seeing people as downtrodden and pitiable, Lily watches her looking at Bankes and wonders:

Why does she pity him? For that was the impression she gave, when she told him that his letters were in the hall. Poor William Bankes, she seemed to be saying, as if her own weariness had been partly pitying people, and the life in her, her resolve to live again, had been stirred by pity. And it was not true, Lily thought; it was one of those misjudgments of hers that seemed to be instinctive and to arise from some need of her own rather than of other people's (127-28;*132*).

Lily's image of Mrs. Ramsay sitting at the dinner table is another remarkable condensation of insight:

How childlike, how absurd she was, sitting up there with all her beauty opened again in her, talking about the skins of vegetables. There was something frightening about her . . . . Mrs. Ramsay, Lily felt, as she talked about the skins of vegetables, exalted that, worshipped that; held her hands over it to warm them, to protect it, and yet, having brought it all about, somehow laughed, led her victims, Lily felt, to the altar (152-53;*157*).

Ten years later, a little embittered and brittle from solitude, Lily recalls Mrs. Ramsay, now as someone who has

faded and gone . . . . We can over-ride her wishes, improve away her limited, old-fashioned ideas. She recedes further and further from us. Mockingly she seemed to see her there at the end of the corridor of years saying, of all incongruous things, "Marry! Marry!" . . . And one would have to say to her, It has all gone against your wishes. They're happy like that; I'm happy like this. Life has changed completely. At that all her being, even her beauty, became for a moment, dusty and out of date. For a moment Lily . . . summing up the Rayleys, triumphed over Mrs. Ramsay, who would never know how Paul went to coffee-houses and had a mistress; how he sat on the ground and Minta handed him his tools; how she stood here painting, had never married, not even William Bankes (260;*269-70*).

Having escaped Mrs. Ramsay's domination and her compulsion to manipulate people into marriage, Lily feels that "now she could stand up to Mrs. Ramsay—a tribute to the astonishing power that Mrs. Ramsay had over one. Do this, she said, and one did it. Even her shadow at the window with James was full of authority" (262;*271*).

One of the most salient features of Lily Briscoe's immensely saturated sensibility, and also one of her most sharply individualizing traits, is her ability to translate her own experience of human relations into subtle insights. She is conscious of the depth and diversity of impulses which govern behavior and cast human activity in endless enigmatic shadows. She is sensible to the imperfect vision one individual has of another; to the futility of attempting to fathom what goes on in another's "wedge-shaped core of darkness"; to the inadequacy and obliquity of human relations. Looking at Carmichael, she thinks how "they looked up at the sky and said it will be fine or it won't be fine. But this was one way of knowing people, she thought: to know the outline, not the detail . . ." (289;*299*). She recalls Tansley and is reminded of the selfish needs and pernicious self-interest which determine and shape one's notion of others:

Her own idea of him was grotesque. . . . Half one's notions of other people were, after all, grotesque. They served private purposes of one's own. He did for her instead of a whipping boy. She found herself flagellating his lean flanks when she was out of temper. If she wanted to be serious about him she had to help herself to Mrs. Ramsay's sayings, to look at him through her eyes (293;*303*).

Like Mrs. Ramsay, she questions the meaning of life and acknowledges the cause of the ugliness and emptiness and shapelessness which hover over it: the inability of human beings to communicate with one another and create harmony out of the dissonant chaos of living. Addressing herself wordlessly to Carmichael, Lily reflects that if she could put her question of life to him, "if they both got up, here, now on the lawn, and demanded an explanation, why was it so short, why was it so inexplicable, said it with violence, as two fully equipped human beings from whom nothing should be hid might speak, then, beauty would roll itself up; *the space would fill;* those empty flourishes would form into shape" (268;*277*).

Significantly, the Ramsays' landing at the Lighthouse somehow comes to mean that moment of beauty and sudden order in life which Lily seeks to express in art. So that it is only when James has "discovered" his father—their communication realized, their unity established—that she sees finally and vividly in the pattern of relationships on her canvas the fleeting harmony which constitutes her vision. It is a vision which "must be perpetually remade," just as human relations must be perpetually recomposed.

The multiple-point-of-view method of writing is an extremely complex one, because it must reflect the delicate balance of freedom of movement which the thoughts and emotions require, while simultaneously keeping that movement under the strictest intellectual control. That Mrs. Woolf utilized and modulated nine principal angles of vision in this novel should indicate how intricate the balance and the modulation had to be in order to keep experiential life suspended until her design was complete. The two most crucial aspects of the method are recording the *impressions of the moment* and at the same time rendering the subjective impressions of the multiple consciousnesses so that the entire constellation of emotional and mental processes which make up human experience is revealed to the reader.

Because human experience is conceived as a continuous and fluid thing, we need to remember that the impressions do not progress in a logical sequence; rather they are ordered according to the emotional force of one experiencing consciousness in relation to another. The meaning of life, which Lily Briscoe wants to know is, therefore, not tendered in some "great revelation"; its meaning is perceived in "little daily miracles, illuminations, matches struck unexpectedly in the dark." In consequence, the reader, always subject to the mind's vagaries, begins to see these "illuminations" as prominent beats in the rhythm of each individual's experience. From this rhythmic configuration of selected moments emerges the *shape* within which the *persona* comes to terms with the concrete world and, in dealing with it, comes to apprehend the *quality* of his experience.

"To make of the moment something permanent," reflects Lily, "—this was the nature of a revelation. In the midst of chaos there was shape" (241;*249*). Here is Lily, the artist, thinking in terms of painting, what her creator pondered in terms of the novel. The selected moments are essentially selected scenes; and the selected scenes come to life only with particular angles, or combinations of angles, of vision, the choice of which Virginia Woolf came to recognize and refine as she brought her art to perfection. Her awareness of the nature of consciousness provided her with a feeling for the *moment*—that unique stretch of time when the past filters in and saturates the present; when the inner world is projected onto and colors the outer world; when the impressions of one consciousness unite with or separate from another consciousness; when all sense and emotion and past and present and order and disorder and joy and sorrow mingle together and give shape to that ineffable experience we call "living"; and this experience is revealed largely through Mrs. Woolf's selection and arrangement of the minds she chose to mirror the mingling of those thoughts and sensations.

One important consequence of modulating the nine perspectives in the novel is its effect upon the reader. The section in which the dinner party scene (125-68;*129-73*) occurs, for example, is a *tour de force* in the multiple-viewpoint method. Here utilizing only eight angles of perspective, Mrs. Woolf not only created a sequence of astonishing and often ironic juxtapositions, but also designed a mental hall of mirrors, furnished with deep human emotions and vivid memories. Like a kaleidoscope being slowly rotated, each piece—each thought, each reverie—slips into its appropriate place to support a poised pattern of stresses and strains, a precarious balance of human relationships. *But only for the moment.* As the section ends, Mrs. Ramsay "With her foot on the threshold . . . waited a moment longer in a scene which was vanishing even as she looked, and then, as she moved and took Minta's arm and left the room, it changed, it shaped itself differently; it had become, she knew, giving one last look at it over her shoulder, already the past" (167-68;*172-73*). The rotation of this figurative kaleidoscope starts again, and a new design begins to form; it too soon vanishes to make way for another and another and still another, until the pattern is complete and the texture right.

One of the devices by which Mrs. Woolf *implies* the larger meaning behind a small event is through the juxtapositioning of her material. On the boat sailing to the Lighthouse, for example, as Cam is thinking of James and their compact, a statement within parentheses is interjected into the text omnisciently: "(and now Macalister's boy had caught a mackerel, and it lay kicking on the floor, with blood on its gills)" (252;*261*). Soon after this, Cam gazes at her father, thinking: "For no one attracted her more; his hands were beautiful, and his feet, and his voice, and his words, and his haste, and his temper, and his oddity, and his passion, and his saying straight out before every one, we perish, each alone, and his remoteness. . . . But what remained intolerable, she thought, sitting upright, and watching Macalister's boy tug the hook out of the gills of another fish, was that crass blindness and tyranny of his which had poisoned her childhood and raised bitter storms . . ." (253;*262*). Shortly following this passage is section V, narrated mainly through Lily Briscoe, which ends with her standing before her easel, crying aloud "'Mrs. Ramsay! . . . Mrs. Ramsay!' The tears ran down her face." Immediately following this is section VI, which consists of two omniscient sentences and a parenthesis enclosed within brackets: "[Macalister's boy took one of the fish and cut a square out of its side to bait his hook with. The mutilated body (it was alive still) was thrown back into the sea.]" (268;*277-78*)

Had the episode of Macalister's boy and his fish been given in any other place, it would have communicated nothing more than the senseless cruelty of adolescence. Surrounded, however, as it is by suggestions of James's antagonism towards his father, Mr. Ramsay's harshness, Cam's ambivalence, Lily's isolation, the passage, through a series of accumulated emotional clusters, assumes a density of meaning which projects the very stuff of life—the nervous irony of living directly beside irrational hatred, senseless cruelty, physical pain, unrelieved loneliness, and irretrievable loss. What is so remarkable is that nowhere does Mrs. Woolf communicate this kind of experience in grand scale or with explicit statement. Hers is the deeply-worked and difficult art of patterning.

Instead of a string of dramatic events, the form of the novel is a series of views inside the minds of human beings. By our very proximity to them, we acutely sense their experience of one another and of the outer world. We sense the pattern in which moments of awareness are arranged, so that our interest is sustained not by consequences of events (effects of what occur are scarcely to be found in the novel) but by the way one moment of consciousness enlarges and enriches another.

We are *not* "all like Scheherazade's husband"—to refute E.M. Forster's quaint and outdated phrase—"in that we want to know what happens next."[8] What we do want to know, however, is how past events or the expectations of future events have been or will be assimilated by the individual consciousness; we want to know *how* each mind feels about what has happened or what is happening or what might happen. Through a progression of interior views, this continual ebb and flow of illumination, our interest is aroused to the degree that we want to continue reading until the whole tapestry of experience is revealed and felt. We are more interested in knowing *how* James Ramsay will experience the Lighthouse when the expedition is finally made than in learning the simple fact that the expedition *is* made. Having carefully aroused our expectations throughout the novel for the moment when James encounters the Lighthouse, Mrs. Woolf gives us a vibrant picture of his consciousness feeling something for the first time in all its freshness, vitality, and truth:

The Lighthouse was then a silvery, misty-looking tower with a yellow eye, that opened suddenly, and softly in the evening. Now—

James looked at the Lighthouse. He could see the white-washed rocks; the tower, stark and straight; he could see that it was barred with black and white; he could see windows in it; he could even see washing spread on the rocks to dry. So that was the Lighthouse, was it?

No, the other was also the Lighthouse. For nothing was simply one thing. The other Lighthouse was true too (276-77;*286*).[9]

Because Virginia Woolf saw the human personality shaped by the "shower of atoms" that strike upon its consciousness, she was to create moments of heightened awareness when the mind is quickened to see order in chaos. The entire gallery of her characters, their myriad impressions shuttling between past and present, are all modulated to the service of making permanent those heightened moments in their lives.

Like E.M. Forster, Elizabeth Drew wants things to happen in the novel and criticizes *To the Lighthouse* for its "lack of any

8. *Aspects of the Novel,* New York: Harcourt, Brace and Co., A Harvest Book, 1927, p. 27.

9. The Hogarth edition reads: "The other was the Lighthouse too."

progressive action involving moral and emotional choices and decisions. . . . We see very clearly what the characters have made of them [their lives], but they are forced to remain static; it is all expansion without progression."[10] Since "expansion" implies space and "progression" time, we have only to recall the "comice agricole" scene in *Madame Bovary* to see what spatialization of form means in the novel. Flaubert's experiment comes to mind here, because Mrs. Woolf, in a more refined way than Flaubert, accomplished much the same thing in rendering the simultaneity of the moment. When a narrator embarks on a mental excursion, Mrs. Woolf brings clock time to a halt: the horizontal march of time ceases; and a vertical expansion of psychological time takes over in that limited time-area. So that the character, seemingly in cerebral isolation, not only communicates the quality of his experience but also partially reveals himself. When mechanical time ceases, then, and experiential time expands—independent of the novel's temporal progress—it becomes clear that the significance of any one moment can be understood only in that moment's reflexive relationship to the numerous other moments to which it makes reference. Speaking of *Ulysses,* Joseph Frank asserted that "these references must be connected by the reader and viewed as a whole before the book fits together in any meaningful pattern."[11] We need only re-read the third section of Mrs. Woolf's novel to see how dependent it is upon the first for its effect. Lily Briscoe's reveries, in particular, derive their integrative power by the nature of their reflexive relations to the references of all the principal angles of vision introduced in the first section of the novel.

It is important to consider how Mrs. Woolf arranges the points of view to make the structure—the formal relations of the multiple con-sciousnesses—communicate the meaning of the work. Of course no single meaning can ever be ascribed to any great work of art, because part of its enduring quality is its meaning different things to differ-ent people at different times. It is, however, possible to arrive at an

10. *The Novel: A Modern Guide to Fifteen English Masterpieces,* New York: W.W. Norton and Co., Inc., 1963, pp. 278-79.

11. "Spatial Form in Modern Literature," reprinted from *Sewanee Review* in *Criticism: The Foundations of Modern Literary Judgment,* eds. M. Schorer, J. Miles, G. McKenzie, New York: Harcourt, Brace and Co., Inc., revised edition, 1958, p. 384.

interpretation of *To the Lighthouse* by considering primarily the sequence and manipulation of its multiple perspectives. If we examine the way the angles of vision have been distributed throughout the novel, we discover that each of its three sections is dominated by a single consciousness. Almost half of the first section is transmitted through Mrs. Ramsay; more than three-quarters of the second section is given omnisciently; and more than half of the third section is filtered through Lily Briscoe. By themselves these proportions might be interesting; but they are critically worthless, unless we discern the thematic content and the emotional consistency in each section.

Critics generally agree that on the prose level the novel deals with female intuition and male intellection, permanence and change, order and chaos, the art of living and the life of art. Critical consensus vanishes, however, as soon as an attempt is made to follow through these themes. What emerges from even a cursory glance at the critical literature is the tendency to abstract the conflict into two mutually exclusive phenomena: either permanence or change, either intuition or intellection, either order or chaos, and so on. To see the disparate—the contradictory—elements and to be unaware of their reconcilability is to miss the interpretive framework which fundamentally embraces these pervasive opposites. *That Virginia Woolf should have chosen to use multiple perspectives is indication enough that no interpretation can be made which settles on one aspect at the expense of the other.*

The problem is, as Norman Friedman suggested,[12] one of relations: the relationship between one individual and another, between man and nature, and between life and art. For Mrs. Woolf the resolution to this duality was in understanding the relationship between opposites and in apprehending their essential congruity. For her, the harmonious existence of opposites in relation to one another was the nature of reality; reality existed not in "either . . . or" but in "both." James begins to mature when he realizes that "the other was also the Lighthouse. For nothing was simply one thing" (277;*286*). The novel is rife with suggestions of contradictory yet reconcilable elements; and structurally it is built along those lines.

12. "The Waters of Annihilation: Double Vision in *To the Lighthouse,*" *Journal of English Literary History,* XXII, No. 2 (1955), pp. 61-79.

"The Window" section of the novel, made up of seventeen angles of perspective, amply demonstrates the complexity of the relationship between one individual and another. The traits which define him as a recognizable entity come with repeated shifts in the multiple-consciousness design. A character is revealed not only from his interior monologues, but also from the impressions made upon others. As the section progresses it becomes clear that each individual is comprised of numerous contradictory ingredients. Mrs. Ramsay, for instance, is as maternal, generous, and loving, as she is meddling, possessive, and affection-seeking. To perceive only her flattering qualities and to ignore her unattractive traits is to miss entirely the significance of her personality and the truth of her portrayal.

Mr. Ramsay, too, with all his intellectual sternness and domestic tyranny, is an admirably unworldly man; austerely philosophical, yet immersed in home and family; grimly conscious of the dark of human ignorance, yet optimistic in the face of life's other realities; insensitive to the texture of a rose petal, yet keenly aware of his wife's subtle changes of temper.

William Bankes is dedicated to the large concerns of science, while being irritable and picayune in his dietary fads; a man of poise who respects old friends, yet frustrated in his affections and not always sincere in his friendships. Charles Tansley is an ill-mannered bundle of egocentricity, yet a pathetic human being for whom, as Mrs. Ramsay says, "success would be good." There is also Lily Briscoe, surely a complex figure of opposing tendencies: a spinster who is shy of intense human attachments, yet capable of anguished eruptions of love; a modest painter frightened of the obstacles imposed by her craft, yet brave enough to wrestle with the problems and eventually to overcome them.

In the first part of the novel, generally under Mrs. Ramsay's governance, we learn through shifting perspectives the inconsistencies in the characters and the difficulty in their relationships. It is also here that the chaos of their relations is momentarily and superficially resolved into order through Mrs. Ramsay's efforts at the dinner party which climaxes this section of the novel.

The second part, "Time Passes," is almost entirely omniscient. It is a short poetic interlude dealing metaphysically with man's relation to nature. Loss and change and longing pervade the first half of the section: Mrs. Ramsay dies; Andrew is killed in France; Prue dies in childbed; the house and everything in it are on the verge of ruin. The natural forces of the world are put into wild and destructive play. But the larger drama is seen in the human capacity to check and finally to defeat those senseless energies through a stronger force—the will to endure. As though some super-human strength were mobilized, there follows a miraculous renascence of all that has been choked and ravaged. It is significant that in this middle section, the inevitable passage of time is narrated by a ghostly presence—all-knowing, all-seeing. For in this emotional field of contrasting forces, the omniscient presence enhances our sense of the capricious whirlwinds of time and nature. That awesome voice also functions to separate Mrs. Ramsay in the first part and Lily Briscoe in the last—a separation necessary to the effect of the novel's total design.

The third part, "The Lighthouse," centers on the relationship of art to life, and Lily Briscoe is its ruling consciousness. In the boat Mr. Ramsay, James, and Cam are struggling with human relations, while on shore Lily is struggling with the formal relations in her painting. She grapples with her canvas while simultaneously reviving her old image of Mrs. Ramsay. However, it is only when she feels the need to see life "on a level with ordinary experience," to see something as it is and at the same time as a "miracle," an "ecstasy," that she begins to penetrate Mrs. Ramsay's superficial beauty and to perceive the real woman beneath it. With that new perception, Lily feels a sudden upsurge of sympathy for Mr. Ramsay—something she had been incapable of before. She begins to fathom the **Ramsays'** relationship as husband and wife, an understanding which carries with it a clearer grasp of the art of human relations—something she had not understood before.

While these moments of illumination are occurring on shore, long since disturbed relations are being smoothed on the trip to the Lighthouse. Cam's antagonism for her father vanishes; James's hatred disappears with his father's words of praise; Mr. Ramsay's anxieties are diminished. Integrity in the family is being realized at last. And running parallel with it is Lily's final understanding that in harmonious human relations there is a deep involvement in life. She realizes that for the artist such involvement is necessary before he can become objectively detached from life in order to seize its harmony and trans-figure it into the aesthetic relations of art. Only when she grasps these strange entanglements of human intercourse can she feel the full authority of being human, and complete herself as an artist. For art and life are no longer hostile to each other; and one cannot be objectively detached from art without first being subjectively involved with life. What she has come to realize enables her to feel simply that "that's a chair . . . yet, at the same time, It's a miracle. . . ." This duality of vision is essential to her understanding of the nature of reality. Lily comes to know what Mrs. Ramsay always thought she herself knew intuitively: with simultaneous involvement and detachment, art, like life, can be shaped and molded. So that now in her reaching out for Mr. Ramsay, Lily begins figuratively to see what is necessary for the achievement of that "razor edge of balance between two opposite forces; Mr. Ramsay [involvement] and the picture [detachment]" (287;*296*).

On the prose level, then, the novel is organized both in terms of its three consecutive formal divisions and its calculated distribution and modulation of the manifold consciousnesses. The fabric of the literary experience is spun between the minds of the *personae* and our understanding of what and how they feel in their relation to one another and to their experience of the larger world outside themselves.

To the Lighthouse, however, also operates on the stratum of poetry, where language heightened by poetic compression is the basic instrument informing the work's intensity, integrity, and authority. The novel does not progress on a "what-happens-next" basis, but rather moves forward through a series of scenes arranged according to a sequence of selected moments of consciousness.

If we are alert to the imagery, frequently we will see images, as simile or metaphor, gradually acquiring symbolic weight; and once a symbol is established, it is often possible to trace the novel's narrative progress through the extension and expansion of that symbol. By moving into the province of poetry, Mrs. Woolf was able to surmount many of the difficulties indigenous to prose expression. She knew how an image could grow to symbolic potential in order to carry her narrative forward; and she was sensitive to the way poetic connotations accrue to define the numerous inflections upon which the meaning of her novel would rest.

The nineteen direct references to the "hedge," for example, are illustrative of Mrs. Woolf's poetic use of imagery.[13] It is introduced for the first time with Lily Briscoe's thought: " 'I'm in love with this all,' waving her hands at the *hedge,* at the house, at the children" (32;*35*). After three additional references, it is mentioned by Mr. Ramsay as he meditates on the endurance of fame. He guesses that fame lasts perhaps two thousand years. "And what are two thousand years? (asked Mr. Ramsay ironically, staring at the *hedge*) . . . . His own little light would shine, not very brightly, for a year or two . . . . (He looked into the *hedge,* into the intricacy of the twigs.)" (56;*59*)[14] Mentioned parenthetically, the seemingly irrelevant hedge is brought up again when Mr. Ramsay stops and watches his wife reading to James the story of the Fisherman and his wife: "Mrs. Ramsay could have wished that her husband had not chosen that moment to stop . . . . But he did not speak; he looked; he nodded; he approved; he went on. He slipped, seeing before him that *hedge* which had over and over again rounded some pause, signified some conclusion, seeing his wife and child. . ." (66;*69-70*).

Somewhat later, Lily Briscoe, now the center of consciousness, takes up the image. When Bankes asks about her painting, she finds herself "becoming once more under the power of that vision which she had seen clearly once and must now grope for among *hedges* and houses and mothers and children—her picture" (82;*86*). Later still we find Mr. Ramsay looking at his wife, withdrawn into her "wedge of darkness." He is deep in thought as she watches the revolving beam of the Lighthouse: "It saddened him, and her remoteness pained him, and he felt, as he passed, that he could not protect her, and, when he reached the *hedge,* he was sad. He could do nothing to help her . . . . He looked into the *hedge,* into its intricacy, its darkness. . ." (98-99;*102-103*).

As an image, the hedge begins to enlarge in its suggestive powers as we discover its contexts becoming increasingly particularized. After "The Window" section, however, no mention is made of it again until the last section of the novel, when Lily pitches her easel precise-

13. For a similar but less detailed discussion, see Glenn Pederson, "Vision in *To the Lighthouse,*" *PMLA,* LXXIII, No. 5 (1958), pp. 585-600.

14. The Hogarth edition reads: "(He looked into the darkness, into the intricacy of the twigs.)"

ly where "she had stood ten years ago. There was the wall; the *hedge;* the tree. The question was of some relation between those masses" (221;*229*). She stands poised with brush in hand and "looked at the *hedge,* the step, the wall" and thinks ironically: "It was all Mrs. Ramsay's doing" (223;*232*). She reflects on her first attempt to paint her picture and remembered something "in the relations of those lines cutting across, slicing down, and the mass of the *hedge* with its *green* cave of *blues* and browns. . ." (234;*243*). She continues to grapple with her aesthetic problem "looking at the *hedge,* at her canvas" (237;*246*). As she ponders Mrs. Ramsay and surrenders to a fierce outburst of loneliness, she approaches part of her problem with life and art which returns her to "that problem of the *hedge*" (269;*279*). Still something evaded her, something in the apparatus of consciousness "broke down at the critical moment; heroically, one must force it on. She stared, frowning. There was the *hedge,* sure enough. But one got nothing by soliciting urgently. One got only a glare in the eye from looking at the line of the wall, or from thinking—she wore a grey hat. She was astonishingly beautiful" (287-88;*297*).

These repeated juxtapositions of the hedge and Mrs. Ramsay begin to radiate with meaning. For clearly Virginia Woolf is no longer writing about a hedge; she is using it as a poetic symbol: a barrier, a psychic blockade, an emotional wall. And as such, the "hedge" is now functioning symbolically with increasing potency.

Lily continues to wonder about Mrs. Ramsay. She wants to know "her thoughts, her imaginations, her desires. What did the *hedge* mean to her. . ." (294;*304*). Suddenly and at last, "There it was—her picture. Yes, with all its *greens* and *blues,*[15] its lines running up and across, its attempt at something" (309;*319-20*). Lily has finally understood the real Mrs. Ramsay; the barrier—the hedge—betweeen husband and wife, and the wall—the hedge—between father and son. Lily realizes that she no longer wants Mrs. Ramsay. It is Mr. Ramsay she now seeks to understand.

As the boat moves farther and farther away, Lily gets nearer to understanding and overcoming the complexity of her problem; and her vision begins to approach aesthetic unity. The instinctive need for distance—that necessary objectivity for the artist—is finally being

15. See pages 234 and *243*; the greens and blues become the hedge's equivalent.

realized; and her involvement in life begins to assume the permanence of truth: "so much depends, she thought, upon distance: whether people are near us or far from us. . ." (284;*293-94*). From that distance Lily sees Mrs. Ramsay now with that one pair of eyes among fifty "that was stone blind to her beauty." As she subdues her involvement and increases her detachment to that razor-edge of balance, she is able at last to seize the fluidity of life and strike it into the steady realm of art.

Consequently, the hedge, in the beginning generalized and seemingly unrelated to anything, begins to grow, with repetition and in varied contexts, to symbolic dimension; and **parallel** to its growth runs the narrative progression of the novel. Thus what is of central significance to the meaning of the work is handled in part through Mrs. Woolf's use of this symbol, deceptively slight though it seems.

Other isolated images might be similarly traced to some coherent terminal point of symbolic meaning: the green shawl; the pig's skull; the story of the Fisherman and his wife; Mrs. Ramsay's short-sighted eyes; the open windows and shut **doors**; the Waverley novels—these are but a few examples. However, the symbol having the most uncircumscribed power of suggestion is the Lighthouse itself. Because "the more barren and indifferent the symbol, the greater its semantic power,"[16] the Lighthouse means various things to various readers. It seems appropriate in so complex a novel that the Lighthouse be approached, in its most general terms, as a structure representing the concept of a goal—a fulfillment of some sort; something to be reached; the end of a quest involving an elaborate pattern of relations.

On the novel's poetic plane, the Lighthouse is a source of light which does not become a source of illumination until after Mrs. Ramsay's death. Accordingly, we might conceive of it as a goal of creating harmony from the dissonance of inadequate human relationships. The trip to the Lighthouse is introduced on the first page; and its mention also introduces a conflict between husband and wife, a disturbance between father and son, and later Mrs. Ramsay's domination over husband and family.

In the first section of the novel, the Lighthouse as a symbol of the goal of human harmony is ironic, because the expedition to the

---

16. Susanne K. Langer, *Philosophy in a New Key: A Study in the Symbolism of Reason, Rite, and Art,* Cambridge, Mass.: Harvard University Press, third edition, 1957, p. 75.

Lighthouse becomes a goal which is frustrated; and the harmony Mrs. Ramsay effects is superficial, flawed, and short-lived—witness the discordance in the **Rayleys'** marriage, Lily's continued spinster-hood, James's Oedipal problem. In this section, we do not see the Lighthouse but only its light—and that, only through Mrs. **Ramsay's** "short-sighted eyes" (109;*113*) when she is withdrawn from everyone around her. Her association with the Lighthouse reveals all her re-moteness and estrangement and selfhood; it also reveals the contra-dictory forces she represents in not attaining any real human attach-ments: in not going beyond her preoccupation with her self to that other-centered world of authentic human communion. Paradoxically, her involvement in life is objective: it is a means of placing herself in the center (yet without being part) of the fanfare which clutters her existence. Equally paradoxical is her detachment, because it is subjective: she withdraws to avoid seeing her own inadequacies, to reflect upon her attributes and life's cruelties and hardships, to absolve herself of real or imagined guilt. That is, her withdrawal is a gesture of self-protection.

Early in the second section, the ray from the Lighthouse appears again. This time it illuminates the indifference of nature to human effort, as seen in the destruction of the house and all of those things which once had meaning for the Ramsay family. The ray of light is a gentle and caressing one. And just before the house is to be resur-rected, the beam stares, undisturbed, at the "thistle and the swallow, the rat and the straw. Nothing now withstood them; nothing said no to them" (208;*214*). In this lyrical middle section of the novel, we begin to sense a connection between the Lighthouse and one's rela-tions to others and between the Lighthouse and the indifference of nature to human existence. The suggestiveness of the Lighthouse as an unfixed symbol increases as the novel unfolds. But more than that, as its contexts multiply and vary, the Lighthouse, symbolically extended to become an intangible goal, carries the narrative forward, because the characters have not arrived at the tangible structure itself.

In the third section, the trip is made; and as the boat approaches the Lighthouse, the problem of harmony approaches resolution. Cam comes to terms with her father; James has at last found a father; Mr. Ramsay becomes finally the acknowledged head of the family. As a father, he finds a fulfillment, which, during Mrs. Ramsay's life, was not possible.

This is by no means to insinuate that Mrs. Ramsay is to be condemned entirely or that Mr. Ramsay is to be wholly exonerated: both are seriously flawed. Nor does it suggest necessarily that James's finding a father is the proper conclusion of the book. What forcefully impresses itself upon us, however, is that in James's final emotional alignment with his father, he has grown up; and in his new maturity, James is able to view opposites simultaneously. Now he perceives the Lighthouse not only as his mother once short-sightedly saw it: "a silvery, misty-looking tower with a yellow eye. . ."; but also as his father clearly sees it: "the tower, stark and straight . . . barred with black and white. . . ." In James's acknowledging both perceptions of the Lighthouse as being true, he has ascended to that level of adulthood which sees life's antitheses in reconciliatory terms. And it is precisely because of the prerequisite self-integrating power of this double vision, that real integration among these human beings has been achieved at the Lighthouse.

On shore, Lily Briscoe is simultaneously approaching her vision of aesthetic relationships. As the distance between her and Mr. Ramsay increases, she gains a new perspective which puts Mrs. Ramsay into proper focus. Perceiving Mrs. Ramsay now the dark mass, Lily's formerly withheld sympathy for Mr. Ramsay is released. Having now experienced subjective involvement, she is able to detach herself objectively and see the integration her picture requires—an integration effected by a single line "there, in the centre" (310;*320*). That line almost certainly refers to the distant, verticle, and barely perceptible Lighthouse: the symbolic goal of human concord which is prerequisite to the achievement of aesthetic integrity.

It was Mrs. Ramsay who suggested the trip to the Lighthouse, but it is Mr. Ramsay who finally makes it. It was Mrs. Ramsay whom Lily worshipped, but it is Mr. Ramsay who now commands her vision. Implicit in this changed perspective is the idea that real harmony, whether human or aesthetic, could not have been achieved until Mrs. Ramsay's death. So that on both the literal and the symbolic—the prose and the poetic—levels, the novel's most general meaning organizes around the need for both human involvement in and artistic detachment from life, which is the one and only source of art.

Then only, when those mysterious powers of polarities effect a proper balance, will the complex nature of reality be revealed and at the same time force into artistic poise the chaotic reality of nature.

It may not seem strange to us now that in May 1925 Virginia Woolf, at the age of forty-three and at the height of her powers, would begin a novel in which "the centre is father's character. . . ." We know from her *Dairy* that she was "obsessed by them both [father and mother], unhealthily; and writing of them was a necessary act." Mrs. Woolf made this entry on 28 November 1928, on "Father's birthday. He would have been 96, 96, yes, today; and could have been 96 . . . but mercifully he was not. His life would have entirely ended mine. What would have happened? No writing; no books;—inconceivable."

No writing; no books—indeed inconceivable! Like some creative people, Virginia Woolf saw her work not so much as being an extension of, but more alarmingly, as being a *substitute* for her *self*. So that, as one eminent British psycho-therapist has written, "the work, rather than the person, becomes the focus of self-esteem. Many people of this [depressive] temperament, during the course of childhood and adolescence, give up the hope of being loved for themselves . . . . But the hope raises itself again when they start to create; and so they become intensely sensitive about what they produce, more sensitive than they are about their own defended personalities in ordinary social life. To mind more about one's book . . . than one does about oneself will seem strange to those who are sure enough of themselves to *be* themselves in social relations. But if a book . . . contains more of a real person than is ever shown in ordinary life, it is not surprising that the producer of it is hypersensitive. A good example is Virginia Woolf, who went through agonies every time she produced a new book, and was desperately vulnerable to what the critics said, in spite of the fact that most of them were her intellectual inferiors. Her depressive temperament manifested itself in recurrent attacks of depression and finally in her suicide."[17]

His life would have entirely ended mine. Had Leslie Stephen lived, his daughter would have been reft of a self, robbed of work, denied the only kind of existence she might ever know. In a world without a **self, where all is disordered and unpredictable, there can be no vital**

17. Anthony Storr, *The Dynamics of Creation,* New York: Atheneum, 1972, pp. 79-80.

anchorage, no stability on those potentially destructive shores of possibility. Biographically, this small residuum of evidence is sufficient safely to say that just as Mr. Ramsay represented tyranny to the young Cam and James, so Leslie Stephen meant chaos and insecurity to the child Virginia Stephen; that just as through the *distance of space* could the artist Lily Briscoe strike a balance in her composition, so too only through the *distance of time* could Virginia Woolf, the novelist, with intellectual detachment, smooth the deep wrinkles in her emotional attachment to her father. Only by "writing him out" on paper, by adjusting her perspective to create order and proportion, could she feel the solipsistic power of *re-creating on her own terms* a childhood world in which she had once felt so powerless. Only by giving voice and design to that menacing past could she bridge the wide gap between feeling and reason, and experience the triumph of having exhumed from those unlighted vaults of her private history the *tableaux vivants* which the outside world might be persuaded to accept as a work of art.

It need hardly be said that to love a father so enduringly and to hate so passionately what he represented evoked exceptionally strong and exceptionally inconsistent emotions. Against those feelings, equally strong restraints had to be erected in order to check that vexatious creative spirit from expressing itself inappropriately, malignantly—too personally. Emotional inconsistency toward a human being very close to one activates those yeasty tensions which ultimately cause the ferment of ambivalence. And it is difficult to suppress the opinion that Virginia Woolf—with one hand straying over the dark and distant ledgers of the past and the other holding firmly the pale and unscripted notebooks of fiction—managed to resolve the tensions and to quiet those warring opposites struggling for utterance, by casting into a poetic mold the prosaic angers and scars of earlier years. In doing so, Leslie Stephen's life, by some curious fold in the continuum of time and space, became not so much realized as *poeticized.* Now under the controlling power of his daughter's pen, his being became very beautiful, just as his death, during the act of creating the novel, must have become a little unreal. And the surest proof that Sir Leslie had not been finally put to rest can be found in *The Years* where we can still hear him rapping out orders, scolding, demanding—through the voice of Abel Pargiter. Only in this later novel, the daughter would not be complete mistress of her subject, and the battle of opposites would not settle with such finality in those calm dusts where emotions are enshrined.

The Waves

To claim anything more than a partial and imperfect understanding of *The Waves* is inevitably to run the risk of ridicule, for it is an enigmatic book. Personal and at the same time universal, it is a work at once deeply patterned but hostile to rational comprehension. The writing is without shadow, without flurry, and at times it strikes the mind's ear as being almost without sound. It is prose written for a new kind of novel, a novel yet "unchristened" which Virginia Woolf described in an article published just two months after the idea of *The Waves* [*The Moths*, a "play-poem"] came to her (*Diary*: 18 June 1927). "It [the unnamed variety of novel] will be written in prose, but in prose which has many of the characteristics of poetry. It will have something of the exaltation of poetry, but much of the ordinariness of prose. It will be dramatic, and yet not a play. It will be read, not acted. By what name we are to call it is not a matter of very great importance. What is important is that this book which we see on the horizon may serve to express some of those feelings which seem at the moment to be balked by poetry pure and simple and to find the drama equally inhospitable to them. Let us try, then, to come to closer terms with it and to imagine what may be its scope and nature.

"In the first place, one may guess that it will differ from the novel as we know it now chiefly in that it will stand further back from life. It will give, as poetry does, the outline rather than the detail. It will make little use of the marvellous fact-recording power, which is one of the attributes of fiction. It will tell us very little about the houses, incomes, occupations of its characters; it will have little kinship with the sociological novel or the novel of environment. With these limitations it will express the feeling and ideas of the characters closely and vividly, but from a different angle. It will resemble poetry in this that it will give not only or mainly people's relations to each other and their activities together, as the novel has hitherto done, but it will give the relation of the mind to general ideas and its soliloquy in solitude. For under the dominion of the novel we have scrutinized one part of the mind closely and left another unexplored. We have come to forget that a large and important part of life consists in our emotions toward such things as roses and nightingales, the dawn, the sunset, life, death, and fate; we forget that we spend much time sleeping, dreaming, thinking, reading, alone; we are not entirely occupied in personal relations; all our energies are not absorbed in making our livings. The psychological novelist has been too prone to limit psychology to the psychology of personal intercourse; we long sometimes to escape from the incessant, the remorseless analysis of falling into love and falling out of love, of what Tom feels for Judith and Judith does or does not altogether feel for Tom. We long for some more impersonal relationship. We long for ideas, for dreams, for imaginations, for poetry.''[1]

Were *we* really full of such longing? Or did Mrs. Woolf need to let something circling inside her wing its way to the external world? Was this interior something which, after the novel's publication, Mrs. Woolf herself could not explain or comprehend intellectually? For in a sense, *The Waves* is a novelist's novel. It is a poet's "play-poem." If we happen not to be novelists or poets, however, then what do we say about this exquisitely written, supremely complex, almost incomprehensible text?

Its author was aware that she had offered the public a rare piece of work, an "unintelligible book," as she herself called it. "And it sells—how unexpected, how odd that people can read that difficult grinding stuff!" she wrote in her *Diary* on 9 October 1931. Readers were attracted to the book, and E.M. Forster, whom Mrs. Woolf considered to be one of her most penetrating, wrote to her that " 'It's difficult to express oneself about a work which one feels to be so important, but I've the sort of excitement over it which comes from believing that one's encountered a classic' " (*Diary*: 16 November 1931).

The italicized overture begins with a sun *"not yet risen,"* a *"sea . . . indistinguishable from the sky"*; a wave pauses and then draws *"out again, sighing like a sleeper whose breath comes and goes unconsciously."* As the sun rises, *"a broad flame became visible; an arc of fire burnt on the rim of the horizon . . ."* (179;5).[2] In the

1. "The Narrow Bridge of Art," *New York Herald Tribune,* 14 August 1927; reprinted in *Granite and Rainbow,* New York and London: Harcourt Brace Jovanovich, A Harvest Book, 1975, pp. 18-19.
2. The unitalicized page number in parentheses following each quotation refers to the first

garden, a bird chirps, and then another. A house appears, *"but all within was dim and unsubstantial. The birds sang their blank melody outside"* (180;6).

This is the opening. It might be the dawn of time. It might be the beginning of the world. It might be merely the beginning of a day. But in that house is the awakening of six children whose lives are also "dim and unsubstantial." Outside the house and within it, everything is pure light, pure sound. Mrs. Woolf's lyrical rendering of a barely differentiated world outside the house connects with the barely differentiated lives of the children within it. In the stichomythic sequence of the children's first words, we are given the uncensored perceptions of what they see and hear. As the book unfolds these perceptions will become emblematic and gradually distinguish each child from the other.

Bernard sees a ring quivering and hanging in a drop of light. It is, we later discover, the brass handle of a cupboard. Bernard possesses the creative sensibility which sees without naming, and it is he who in the end comes full *circle*. Susan sees pale yellow, but she sees this pastel in a *slab;* and all the coarseness and thickness of her rustic life laid beside the fragile tenderness of future maternity are implicit in her perception. Neville sees a globe "hanging down in a drop against the enormous flanks of some hill." But since half of the globe is always *hidden*, wholeness in Neville's life will only exist when his body is physically—and preferably sexually—flanked by the body of another. Jinny's "crimson tassel . . . twisted with threads of gold" suggests the flamboyance, glitter, and sensuality which she champions and which will sustain her throughout life. The chained foot of the great beast which Louis hears stamping and stamping has about it something primordial, but more fundamentally it represents the chain which tethers Louis to his personal history of inferiority caused by his Australian accent and his father, a banker in Brisbane. Rhoda's "cheep, chirp; cheep, chirp" is, in this early scene in the book, least susceptible to translation. Her imitating the sound of birds, however, might be looked upon as her attempt to be something other than what she is—something non-human. But certainly her identification with birds anticipates her momentary airborne flight

---

American paperback edition published by Harcourt, Brace and World, 1960; the italicized number refers to The Hogarth Press edition (Tenth Impression), 1963.

when she, a grown woman crazed with self-contempt, leaps to her death.

We move quickly from the children's uncatalogued perceptions indoors to the outside world where we now get a glimpse of their emotions. Louis, all loneliness and fear, seeks refuge behind a hedge where he conjures up images of people, who in their remote corner of the earth, are safe for him: people "in a desert by the Nile" where he sees "women passing with red pitchers to the river" and "camels swaying and men in turbans" (182;*8*). It is this need of the young boy to escape from the present which will one day allow Louis to lace the globe with steamship lines and make him secretly read history and the classics; for distance of ancient time and place momentarily weakens some link in the chain which binds him to his immediate past.

The impulsive Jinny sees Louis and goes to kiss and comfort the lonely boy in hiding. Her impulse for physical intimacy will accompany her through a life which only ignites when she is with a man, any man, and "Our hands touch, our bodies burst into fire" (272;*100*).

Seeing the kiss, Susan feels jealousy and pain. For her passions are elemental, and she cannot be apart or divided from others. These primitive feelings, elliptically expressed in childhood, will become fully realized later when she is surrounded by sleeping children and a farmer husband in a "kitchen where they bring the ailing lambs to warm in baskets, where the hams are hung and the onions glisten" (243;*71*).

Bernard is the consoler, the maker of phrases, the storyteller. More than that, because he alone experiences life as a thesaurus of sensations and impressions, he alone, even in the dimness of childhood, senses the shifting moods and divers feelings of other people. It is fitting that he should say to Susan:

When I heard you cry I followed you, and saw you put down your handkerchief, screwed up, with rage, with its hate, knotted in it. But soon that will cease. Our bodies are close now. You hear me breathe. You see the beetle too carrying off a leaf on its back. It runs this way, then that way, so that even your desire while you watch the beetle, to possess one single thing . . . must waver, like the light in and out of the beech leaves; and then words, moving darkly, in the depths of your mind will break up this knot of hardness, screwed up in your pocket-handkerchief (184-85;*11*).

Neville, who hates "wandering and mixing things together," (187; *14*) is the child who knows that "There is an order in this world; there are distinctions, there are differences in this world, upon whose verge I step" (188;*15*). His insistence upon order and distinctions, however, will keep him forever on the *verge* of life. A rigidity is implicit in his need for order which will divide and restrict him to "either" this "or" that. However, just as order and precision refine the intellect, they diminish and delude the emotions, making it impossible for Neville to establish enduring ties with other human beings. Although he will achieve fame, he will never feel the supporting steadiness of emotional contentment, because the men in his life will "always [be] changing, though not the desire. . ." (265;*95*). With the dawn of each new day, he will never know whose body will flank his own at dusk.

Rhoda, the most markedly different from the other children, is a curious combination of obsessions. In her fear of others, she escapes to solitude where she can live in phantasy, imagining herself not only safe but strangely unvanquishable. "And I will now rock the brown basin from side to side so that my ships may ride the waves. Some will founder. Some will dash themselves against the cliffs. One sails alone. That is my ship . . . . They have scattered, they have foundered, all except my ship which mounts the wave and sweeps before the gale and reaches the islands. . ." (187;*13*). This imaginary flight to power is understandable when we realize how inadequate in actuality she feels to the others. Her phantasy world, however, also cuts her off from others, and we see the extremity of her isolation in her thought that "The world is entire, and I am outside of it, crying, 'Oh, save me, from being blown for ever outside the loop of time!' " (189;*15*) Rhoda's isolation is thus no ordinary kind of aloneness which children are often capable of feeling: it is a kind of self-severance from reality which verges on madness, a severance so complete that when energy dwindles and illusion fails, the world threatens to blast one to perdition. To the end of the section, Rhoda's childhood phantasy continues to sustain itself: "Out of me now my mind can pour. I can think of my Armadas sailing on the high waves. I am relieved of hard contacts and collisions. I sail on alone . . . . Oh, but I sink, I fall! . . . Let me pull myself out of these waters. But they heap themselves on me. . . . I am turned; I am tumbled; I am stretched, among these long lights, these long waves, these endless paths, with people pursuing, pursuing" (193;*19-20*).[3]

In the second section *"the sun rose higher,"* and the birds which *"now sang a strain or two together . . . were suddenly silent, breaking asunder"* (194;*20*). So too does the mixed social organization of the children in the first section break asunder to form a new pattern: Bernard, Louis, and Neville are sent to a boys' school; Susan, Rhoda, and Jinny go to a girls' school. But here another kind of separation begins: each child begins to perceive the other incorrectly; each begins to differ from the other in the process of individuation; and each begins to assume a posture.

On the boys' side, Bernard at his departure thinks: "Everybody knows I am . . . going to school for the first time . . . . I must not cry. I must behold them indifferently . . . . I must make phrases and phrases and so interpose something hard between myself and the stare of the housemaids . . . . There is Louis; there is Neville . . . . They are composed." Simultaneously, Louis looks at Bernard and thinks: "He is composed; he is easy. He swings his bag as he walks. I will follow Bernard because he is not afraid" (195;*21-22*). For Neville, however, arriving at the new school "is indeed a solemn moment," for here he will "explore the exactitude of the Latin language, and step firmly upon the well-laid sentences, and pronounce the explicit, the sonorous hexameters of Virgil; of Lucretius. . ." (196;*22*).

Percival, the novel's invisible center, is introduced in this section of the novel. At the chapel meeting, the responses of the boys begin to underscore their individual identities. Bernard records his impressions of the guttural sermon in a notebook for future reference. Louis finds security in the dimness of the ceremony, because "We put off distinctions as we enter . . . . I become a figure in a procession, a spoke in the huge wheel that turning, at last erects me, here and now" (198;*24-25*). He also rejoices in the authority of the school's master. For Neville, however, "The brute menaces my liberty . . . when he prays. . . . The words of authority are corrupted by those who speak them" (198;*25*).

---

3. It is interesting to note the similarity between Rhoda's exclamations and Shelley's "I die! I faint! I fail!" from *The Indian Serenade* (III, 18) and "I pant, I sink, I tremble, I expire!" from *Epipsychidion* (l. 591).

On the playing field, the differences among them continue to increase. Louis, the most industrious scholar, becomes an outsider to their games and watches the boys with envy: "If I could follow, if I could be with them, I would sacrifice all I know" (206;*34*). Neville, because of his physical weakness, finds it necessary to adopt a superior stance, to ridicule the cricketers and take refuge in the fact that he knows "already how to rhyme, how to imitate Pope, Dryden, even Shakespeare" (207;*34*). And Bernard, not caring very much whether he joins in the game, is satisfied to amuse his companions with a story, but it is just another story he will not be able to finish.

By the end of their school years, the separateness of each boy is considerable. Louis, revering his newly gained knowledge and blessing the traditions of culture and learning, continues to hear the sound of the "sullen thud of the waves"; and still "the chained beast stamps on the beach" (215;*42*). His education has not enabled him to overcome the sense of inferiority which chokes him with bitterness and envy. His will be the quest for power which wealth can bestow. Thus "I go vaguely, to make money vaguely" (220;*47*).

Bernard departs with the instinctive innocence of a sponge about to soak up every available impression. He wants to add to his "collection of valuable observations upon the true nature of human life. My book will certainly run to many volumes embracing every known variety of man and woman" (221;*49*). But even this early we have the vague feeling that no volume will ever be written, because alive and active people are Bernard's daily concern, not the solitude required by a writer.

Neville leaves, pining for Percival, sending him poems which will never be acknowledged, proposing meetings which will never be kept. And for this unresponsiveness, he will love Percival all the more. Neville's devotion to intellectual sovereignty and his pursuit of fame have already such priority that in real affairs of the heart, he will always seek out those least accessible people who will cause him the greatest torment. For he is convinced that in the torture others inflict upon him, he has his most cherished alibi and most unquestioned justification for shrieking "aloud at the smug self-satisfaction, at the mediocrity of this world. . ." (223;*51*). With his naked sense of vulnerability and insignificance, he will desperately satisfy himself emotionally with a steady stream of homosexual companions—that nightly "one friend"—to flank his side and momentarily relieve him of himself.

At the girls' school, Susan longs to be with her father, away from the falseness of imposed regulation. Vindictively she counts the days that separate her from her animals and summer breezes and farm wagons. Rhoda too hates school, because here more than ever she feels "I am nobody. I have no face. This great company . . . has robbed me of my identity" (197;*24*). Feeling alone and unfriended, she drifts further into her imaginary world in search of some phantasmal comfort. Jinny, who can neither remember the past nor anticipate the future, is happy enough at school where only the present moment is important. In her exaggerated, even triumphant, sensuality, she feeds on the moment; for even at this early age, she begins "to feel the wish to be singled out; to be summoned, to be called away by one person who comes to find me, who is attracted towards me, who cannot keep himself from me. . ." (206;*33*).

As the months pass and school is about to end, Susan already envisions her freedom unfurling with her "father in his old hat and gaiters. I shall tremble. I shall burst into tears" (211;*38*). Jinny, increasingly vibrant with the sense of her physical self, knows that there will be parties "and one man will single me out and tell me what he has told no other person. . . . But I shall not let myself be attached to one person only. I do not want to be fixed, to be pinioned" (212;*40*).

Rhoda, realizing that there is neither salvation nor satisfaction in her phantasy of being an Empress, wants to give herself to someone in the real world; but "Oh! to whom?" (213;*41*) Rhoda's refrain has a particular poignancy, because she is just beginning to feel the first blossoming of young womanhood: "Now my body thaws; I am unsealed, I am incandescent. Now the stream pours in a deep tide fertilising, opening the shut, forcing the tight-folded, flooding free. To whom shall I give all that now flows through me, from my warm, my porous body?" (214;*41*) And to Rhoda, "this is pain, this is anguish!" because in some deep chasm of her being something blocks the flow, resists the desire.[4] Rhoda echoes her prototype,

4. Rhoda's question "Oh! to whom?" is a *verbatim* borrowing from Shelley's poem *The Question* which concludes with: "I hastened to the spot whence I had come,/ That I might there present it!—Oh! to whom?" (V, 39-40). Peter and Margaret Havard-Williams ("Bateau

Rachel Vinrace, in that both are "wafted down tunnels," trapped in their female bodies. And Rhoda begins to realize very early that "This is the life then to which I am committed" (219;*46*).

The interlude of the third section bristles with fear and combat and death. The birds which had sung erratically at dawn now had *"Fear . . . in their song, and apprehension of pain. . . . singing together as they chased each other, escaping, pursuing, pecking each other as they turned high in the air"* (225;*53*). Now they also have a savage innocence and quizzical relentlessness to destroy; *"one of them, beautifully darting, accurately alighting, spiked the soft, monstrous body of the defenceless worm, pecked again and yet again, and left it to fester. . . . Yellow excretions were exuded by slugs and now and again an amorphous body . . . swayed from side to side. . . . Now and again they plunged the tips of their beaks savagely into the sticky mixture"* (226;*53-54*). Against this backdrop of life and decay, beauty and ugliness, the six *personae* are again regrouped, each experiencing more intensely and more relentlessly what living feels like.

Bernard, now at Cambridge, discovers that he is "not one and simple but complex and many. Bernard in public bubbles; in private, is secretive"; and with the high-seriousness of an undergraduate, he anticipates his future biographer's saying that " 'joined to the sensibility of a woman . . . Bernard possessed the logical sobriety of a man' " (227;*55*). The complexity and confusion increase when we are told that "when I am most disparate, I am also most integrated"; that unlike others, he has "the double capacity to feel, to reason" (228:*55*); that despite his active imagination, "I need the stimulus of other people." Even as a young man, he sees himself as "disillusioned but not embittered. A man of no particular age or calling" (230;*58*).

Neville, also at Cambridge and still under the influence of Percival, begins to feel within him the lash and frenzy of poetry

---

Ivre: The Symbol of the Sea in Virginia Woolf's *The Waves,"* *English Studies,* XXXIV [February 1953], pp. 9-17) make the point that inspiration fails in Rhoda, because "She has no contact with humanity"(12). In connection with the Shelley allusion, they indicate further that Rhoda's inability to express herself formally has its parallel in the poet's struggle to find some lyric shape to embody the disordered ideas and images which litter his unconscious mind.

struggling for utterance, but "There is some flaw in me—some fatal hesitancy, which . . . turns to foam and falsity. . . . I do not know myself sometimes, or how to measure and name and count out the grains that make me what I am" (232;*60*). Admitting his fragmentation, he wonders who he is. Is he mixed with Bernard? At the moment when he needs the intimacy of friendship, Neville goes to Bernard to explore the question of his identity. But the chameleon-like Bernard, sensing Neville's disapproval of his untidiness and envying the remorselessness of Neville's intellect, throttles the intimacy so urgently sought, by inventing amusing stories. More to the point, Bernard is trying to escape Neville's searing scrutiny which threatens to expose his own strange mixture of selves: his need to identify himself with Byron, Tolstoi, Meredith. So that in this intensely personal scene between the two young men, we are given the unspoken torment of two human beings—Neville begging to know "Whether I am doomed always to cause repulsion in those I love?" (235;*65*) and Bernard feeling devastated and humiliated by Neville's "'You are not Byron; you are your self'" (236;*64*).

Louis, who has become a clerk in London, remains the male outsider of the group. Having become the school's best scholar so that he might assert himself and "knock at the grained oak door," he sits now in a steamy eating-house, thinking of Bernard and Neville "who saunter under yew trees" (241;*69*). Filled with bitterness and hatred, he is determined to sweep up worthlessness and degradation and reduce it all to order.

Susan, not yet twenty, has returned to the country she loves. So immersed is she in the fertility and tumescence of the elemental life that she loses her sense of self and becomes merged with "the seasons . . . the mud, the mist, the dawn" (243;*71*). For her, "All the world is breeding. . . . The flowers are thick with pollen" (244;*72*). Filled with the desire for children, roaring fires, pots of jam, fresh bread, her life begins to verge on a mania for possession. Running through her soliloquy like an obstinate bass, however, is a guttural note that Susan will never be satisfied with the life she has chosen.

Jinny is at last in the world of her dreams, a world of coiffed hair, powdered noses, rouged lips; the life of night when bodies touch. Jinny's pale young man with dark hair comes to her as she bids him to approach her; and in their dance, rendered in highly erotic language, is a hint of what bodily touch feels like to Jinny:

We go in and out of this hesitating music. Rocks break the current of the dance; it jars, it shivers. In and out, we are swept now into this large figure; it holds us together; we cannot step outside its sinuous, its hesitating, its abrupt, its perfectly encircling walls. Our bodies, his hard, mine flowing, are pressed together within its body; it holds us together; and then lengthening out, in smooth, in sinuous folds, rolls us between it, on and on (246;74).

But with the music over, more wine, moonlight, and the flight of ecstasy flown, the moment, for Jinny, has ended: "Now slackness and indifference invade us. . . . We have lost consciousness of our bodies uniting under the table. I also like fair-haired men with blue eyes" (247;75). We may guess that this young hedonist, for whom each opening of the door lets in the possibility of new sexual adventure, will have countless spasms of pleasure but few moments of enduring contentment.

For Rhoda, however, each time the door opens, "terror rushes in"; people come in "Throwing faint smiles to mask their cruelty, their indifference. . ." (247-48;75-76). In the presence of a man ("I must take his hand"), her physical self-contempt attains a new height as she stands "burning in this clumsy, this ill-fitting body, to receive the shafts of his indifference, and his scorn. . . ." She also feels "an immense pressure . . . on me. A million arrows pierce me. Scorn and ridicule pierce me. I . . . am pinned down here; am exposed. . . . Tongues with their whips are upon me. Mobile, incessant, they flicker over me." That such thoughts are triggered by the presence of a man is symptomatic of Rhoda's immense fear of physical contact which for her carries the weight of bestial sexuality, something her "ill-fitting body" cannot bear. Her fear is so overwhelming that she feels "broken into separate pieces" (248;76) and cries inwardly for help. But no one can hear her.

In the fourth section, with the sun risen, the birds sang; but now *"each alone. . . . Each sang stridently, with passion, with vehemence, as if to let the song burst out of it, no matter if it shattered the song of another bird with harsh discord. . . . They spied a snail and tapped the shell against the stone. They tapped methodically until the shell broke and something slimy oozed from the crack"* (250-51;78).

Like the birds in their methodical fury and solitary song, the six *personae* emerge in this section as distinct individuals in the scorching light of adulthood. Life has separated them, but the six re-unite for the first time since childhood to celebrate Percival's departure for India. Each arrives alone at the appointed place, and a harsh discordance permeates the scene until Percival's arrival.

The section begins with Bernard's long soliloquy in which he relates the most strangely paradoxical feelings he has so far experienced. The soliloquy begins with his "great happiness (being engaged to be married)" placed beside his being "numbed to tolerance and acquiescence" (252;*80*). Since his engagement, he has been "charged in every nerve with a sense of identity. . ." and yet "I have no aim. I have no ambition" (253;*80*). He continues: "I do not remember my special gifts. . . . I am not, at this moment, myself" (254;*82*). "To be myself (I note) I need the illumination of other people's eyes, and therefore cannot be entirely sure what is my self. . . . I have been traversing the sunless territory of non-identity" (255;*83*).

A somber note is sounded here, because in some curious way, Bernard's engagement arouses in him a string of contradictory thoughts and ambivalent feelings. These are further complicated when we reread the passage and pursue an interwoven thread which hints at how marriage will figure into the complex tapestry of Bernard's identity. The thread appears with Bernard's aimless willingness to "be carried on by the general impulse. . . . Only in moments of emergency . . . the wish to preserve my body springs out and seizes me. . . . We insist, it seems, on living. Then again, indifference descends" (253;*81*). "But I am aware of our ephemeral passage." Yet "I cannot deny a sense that life for me is mysteriously prolonged. Is it that I may have children, may cast a fling of seed wider, beyond this generation, this doom-encircled population. . . . Hence we are not raindrops, soon dried by the wind. . . . This then serves to explain my confidence, my central stability" (254;*82*).

In these thoughts, Bernard's most antithetic, if not fatalistic, urges begin to constellate into something meaningful: marriage means children; children mean the indirect prolongation of life; with that assurance of extended life comes stability; and with stability one's identity begins to emerge: *"I am not part of the street—no, I observe the street.*"⁵ This stability, however, is very temporary. For with the return of identity comes the freedom to observe, and observation leads him directly to invent stories. But because he is a young man, he can still only see himself in the reflected light of others. His stories must be told to others, because those fictions are both his offering and his plea for approval. When Bernard says, "I need an audience. That is my downfall" (255;*83*), he speaks better than he knows. For it suggests that all his phrase-making and story invention really have no intrinsic value in themselves; they are, rather, a kind of social passport enabling him to sigh, "Thank Heaven, I need not be alone" (256;*83*). Consequently, without the capacity for self-estimation and at the mercy of "the illumination of other people's eyes," Bernard still needs to learn that his "downfall" is not so much his inability to bear solitude, as it is a *hypersensitivity to the feeling of being unwanted.* Until he becomes aware of that feeling, he will continue to hide behind his avalanche of words and his phrase-choked note-books; these are mere *substitutes* for himself. And as long as that substitution persists, he "cannot be entirely sure what is my self."

Arriving at the restaurant first, Neville anticipates Percival's entrance with "morbid pleasure" and begins to feel the "hostility, the indifference of other people dining here. . . ." Louis enters, and Neville sees him as "acrid, suspicious, domineering, difficult (I am comparing him with Percival)" (257;*85*). When Bernard arrives, Neville notes that "His hair is untidy. . . . He has no perception that we differ. . . . He half knows everybody; he knows nobody (I compare him with Percival)." Nailed to his chair, Neville remains tortured by his impossible love for Percival "without [whom] there is no stability" (259;*87*).

Louis sees Susan approaching and observes that to be loved by her "would be to be impaled by a bird's sharp beak. . . . Yet there are moments when I could wish to be speared . . . once and for all." Watching Rhoda enter, he senses dread, knowing that she has come only because something always "lights her pavement and makes it possible for her to replenish her dreams."

Susan sees Jinny come through the door, bringing everything to a halt, "bringing in new tides of sensation" (258;*86*). Susan, watching

---

5. Except for the italics in the interludes, those used throughout this chapter are mine, unless otherwise noted.

Louis adjust his tie, Neville straighten a fork, and Rhoda's shock of surprise, feels a flush of embarrassment at her own "shabby dress, my square-tipped fingernails, which I at once hide under the table-cloth" (259;*87*).

Rhoda sits watching the swing-door and observes that, although she senses her own insignificance, she too flutters with anticipation: "It is because of Neville and his misery. The sharp breath of his misery scatters my being" (259-60;*87-88*).

Percival finally appears. He is their hero in his simplicity, conventionality, stability. He brings with him that central illumination around which their individual differences continue to smolder. As Bernard says, "We who have been separated by our youth (the oldest is not yet twenty-five), who have sung like eager birds each his own song and tapped with the remorseless and savage egotism of the young our own snail shell till it cracked . . . or perched solitary outside some bedroom window and sang of love, of fame and other single experiences so dear to the callow bird . . . now come nearer . . . sitting together now we love each other and believe in our endurance" (260;*88*). Bernard's speech is simply another of his consoling public utterances. Although Percival has provided the illumination, no real communion has been achieved and will not be achieved until each individual member submits to a kind of ritual confession. Each thus proceeds to account for himself. What we are given, however, is an account of each *as he sees himself,* with all the force of vanity—and the distortions of self-perception.

From Louis: "I am very vain, very confident. . . . But while I admire Susan and Percival, I hate the others, because it is for them that I do these antics, smoothing my hair, concealing my accent" (263;*91*). From Jinny: "But I hide nothing. I am prepared. . . . I can imagine nothing beyond the circle cast by my body. . . . I dazzle you; I make you believe that this is all" (264;*92*). From Neville: "I shall have fame. But I shall never have what I want. . . . I excite pity in the crises of life not love. Therefore I suffer horribly. . . . I see everything—except one thing—with complete clarity. That is my saving. That is what gives my suffering unceasing excitement" (264-65;*92-93*). From Rhoda: "I am afraid of you all. I am afraid of the shock of sensation that leaps upon me. . . . To me [moments] are all violent, all separate; and if I fall . . . you will be on me, tearing me to pieces. . . . And I have no face. . . . I wait for you to speak and then speak like you" (265-66;*93-94*). From Susan: "I like to be with people who twist herbs, and spit in the fire and shuffle down long passages in slippers like my father. The only sayings I understand are the cries of love, hate, rage and pain. . . . I shall never have anything but natural happiness. . . . My children will carry me on. . . . I shall be debased and hide-bound by the bestial and beautiful passion of maternity. . . . Also, I am torn with jealousy. . . . I love with such ferocity that it kills me when the object of my love shows me by a phrase that he can escape" (266-67;*94-95*). And finally, from Bernard: "I cannot bear the pressure of solitude. . . . I am made and remade continually. Different people draw different words from me. . . . I shall never succeed, even in talk, in making a perfect phrase. But I shall have contributed more to the passing moment than any of you. . . . But because there is something that comes from outside and not from within I shall be forgotten; when my voice is silent you will not remember me. . ." (267-68;*95-96*).

Having laid themselves bare—despite the evasions, the alterations, the insistence on individual differences—the six of them experience with Percival a wholeness, a genuine coming-together, and a fleeting moment of calm.

In section five, when *"The sun had risen to its full height,"* Percival is dead. *"Now the sun burnt uncompromising, undeniable"* (278;*105*). With the source of light directly overhead at Percival's death, all shadows vanish, and all design is obliterated. The harshness of life and the starkness of fact are seen now only through Neville, Bernard, and Rhoda.

For Neville, Percival's death means a deeper loneliness than he has ever felt. His only expression is that of physical suffering, a kind which has the full character of self-indulgence: "Come pain, feed on me. Bury your fangs in my flesh. Tear me asunder. I sob, I sob" (281;*109*).

For Bernard, the news of Percival carries with it a cloud of darkness and confusion: his son is born and Percival is dead: "which is sorrow, which is joy?" He is too dazed, too numb to enunciate the myriad sensations of loss. "Yet something is added to my interpretation. Something lies deeply buried. For one moment I thought to grasp it. But bury it, bury it; let it breed, hidden in the depths of my mind some day to fructify. After a long lifetime, loosely, in a moment of revelation, I may lay hands on it. . . ." For the moment, however, Bernard is not ready to suffer his private dirge. He wants instead to be surrounded by life: he wants "someone with whom to laugh, with whom to yawn, with whom to remember how he [Percival] scratched his head. . ." (285-86;*112*). Bernard's moment of anguish is still on the horizon.

Percival's death sounds its deepest note for Rhoda. For her it means a kind of liberation. Rhoda, for whom the world is hostile, for whom living has always meant turbulence and death a seduction, sees Percival's death as an offering: he "has made me this present, has revealed this terror, has left me to undergo this humiliation. . ." (286;*113-14*). By some curious and profound mechanism, Percival's violent death has ripped away the gauze of terror and has now made dying for her an unadorned and palpable fact, something which now she too is able to face.

As a child blossoming into young womanhood, Rhoda had felt the desire to offer herself to someone, but "To whom shall I give all that flows through me, from my warm, my porous body? I will gather my flowers and present them—Oh! to whom?" (214;*41*) Now, however, that "Percival, by his death, has made me this gift, let me see the thing. . . . I throw my violets, my offering to Percival."

What this "thing" is that Percival has shown her, at first ambiguous, becomes clear when we follow the image which ends Rhoda's soliloquy: "There is a square; there is an oblong. The players take the square and place it upon the oblong . . . . they make a perfect dwelling place . . . . The structure is now visible . . . . we are not so various or so mean; we have made oblongs and stood them upon squares. The oblong has been set upon the square[6] . . . . The structure is visible. We have made a dwelling place." For Rhoda, "This is our triumph; this is our consolation . . . . Wander no more, I say; this is the end" (288-89;*116-17*).

6. In the excitement of Rhoda's revelation, the figures have become reversed. E.M. Forster has written rather dubiously that "Intellectually, no one can do more; and since she [Virginia Woolf] was a poet, not a philosopher or a historian or a prophetess, she had not to consider whether wisdom will prevail and whether the square upon the oblong, which Rhoda built out of the music of Mozart, will ever stand firm upon this distracted earth. The square upon the oblong. Order. Justice. Truth." Joan R. Noble, ed., *Recollections of Virginia Woolf,* New York: William Morrow & Co., 1972, p. 195.

Whether the square and the oblong represent, in the most abstract sense, the sturdiness of geometric construction, or whether they visually represent tombstone and coffin, it is not possible to determine. But it is certain that to Rhoda's highly altered consciousness, the square and the oblong are somehow connected with death, the "thing" that Percival has shown her. In the liberating effect of knowing that "the structure is visible. . . . Now I will relinquish; now I will let loose. Now I will at last free the checked, the jerked back desire to be spent, to be consumed" (289;*117*). And knowing now that death is always just around the corner, Rhoda, soon after Percival's death, becomes Louis's lover.[7]

In the sixth interlude, the sun's rays are slanted, and *"The birds sat still. . . . now they paused in their song as if glutted with sound, as if the fullness of midday had gorged them"* (290;*118*). Like the glutted birds, Louis, Susan, Jinny, and Neville have each reached that point beyond which there is no added satisfaction, but only repetition.

Louis, now a successful business man, has gained "a vast inheritance of experience" and is "half in love with the typewriter and the telephone" (291;*118-19*) by which he has laced the world together with his ships and brought order where once there was chaos. Louis's chained beast, however, continues to stamp, because his aggressive drive for achievement has been prompted by his need "to expunge certain stains, and erase old defilements . . . my accent; beatings and other tortures; the boasting boys; my father, a banker in Brisbane" (292;*120*). He knows that he will have all the symbols of status and

---

7. We learn that Rhoda and Louis are lovers in section six, the only part of the novel in which neither Bernard nor Rhoda appears. Their absence has an elliptical eloquence which suggests that a union deeper than love has been effected by Percival's death through which each of them has had a revelation of some kind.

In a review of *A Writer's Diary,* entitled "A Consciousness of Reality," published in *The New Yorker* on 6 March 1954 (reprinted in *Forewords and Afterwords,* New York: Random House, A Vintage Book, 1974, pp. 417-18), W.H. Auden wrote: "If I had to choose an epitaph for her [Virginia Woolf], I would take a passage from *The Waves,* which is the best description of the creative process that I know: 'There is a square: there is an oblong. The players take the square and place it upon the oblong. They place it very accurately; they make a perfect dwelling place. Very little is left outside. The structure is now visible; what is inchoate is here stated; we are not so various or so mean; we have made oblongs and stood them upon squares. This is our triumph; this is our consolation.' " That Auden should have chosen this description as an *epitaph* for Mrs. Woolf is perhaps one of the most uncanny instances in literary criticism where two poetic minds appear to be in almost direct communion. (I am indebted to Dr. Lola Szladits for bringing this Auden article to my attention.)

success, because "the weight of the world is on my shoulders" (294;*121*). Yet he still keeps his attic room, and it is there that we see his strange mixture of self-depreciation and megalomania. We can only wonder how much real satisfaction this glutted bird feels, now past the midday of his life, with Rhoda as his partner.

Susan, now flooded with a fierce, almost frightening, maternity, has at last her "wicker cradle, laden with soft limbs . . . [and] would fell down with one blow any intruder, any snatcher, who would break into this room and wake the sleeper" (294;*122*). Her life is filled with boiling kettles, milk cans, and potato beds. She is "glutted with natural happiness; and wish[es] that the fullness would pass. . ." (295;*123*), but she knows that only more of the same will visit her house, so thick it is with life and sleep. How enduring, one wonders, is this ferocious domesticity and motherhood, this "natural happiness" as Susan calls it?

Jinny, past thirty, continues to live the breathless life of physical adventure; still sending out her signals to men with a movement of the arm or a twist of the scarf; still unwilling to attach herself to any one person; still living under the delusion that "beauty must be broken daily to remain beautiful." Although there is something heroic in her promiscuity, there is also something damp and discontinuous in her knowing that "People are so soon gone" (296;*124*).

Neville, already grown old too soon, is rendered with the greatest intensity. So battered is his self-esteem—"I am ugly, I am weak" —that his life has no meaning unless some man is nearby to sit beside. Rankled with insecurity and a sense of worthlessness, Neville's dependency upon male sexuality is as morbid as his suspicious possessiveness is destructive. Worst of all is the knowledge that his life will be a mawkish procession of transient pleasures; for as he says, "if one day you do not come after breakfast, if one day I see you in the looking-glass perhaps looking after another, if the telephone buzzes and buzzes in your empty room, I shall then, after unspeakable anguish, I shall then . . . seek another, find another, you. Meanwhile, let us abolish the ticking of time's clock . . . . Come closer" (301;*129*).

"The sun had sunk lower in the sky . . . . one bird taking its way alone made for the marsh and sat solitary on a white stake. . . . All

for a moment wavered and bent in uncertainty and ambiguity. . ." (302-303;*129-30*). In this wavering uncertain atmosphere, Bernard, in section seven, sits alone and detached in Rome, thinking of all the stories he has invented, the countless notebooks he has filled with phrases "to be used when I have found the true story, the one story to which all these phrases refer. But I have never yet found that story" (305-306;*133*). Suddenly the question occurs to him: "But why impose my arbitrary design?" With it comes another brief illumination: for with the question now having been asked, Bernard is drawn back into life, "involved in the general sequence when one thing follows another. . . . And as I move, surrounded, included and taking part, the usual phrases begin to bubble up" (306;*134*)—phrases which must be told to someone. For though he continues to need an audience, continues to collect notes "for some final statement," what Bernard does not yet know is that in order to shape his impressions and phrases into "the true story," he will have to learn prolonged detachment in the act of creation. That detachment requires solitude which, now in his middle years, is still his undoing.

Susan, surrounded now by grown children, has reached the saturation point of "natural happiness"; she is sated with homely ritual and the slow mastication of rustic life. The swollen fruits of her existence sicken her "of the body . . . of the unscrupulous ways of the mother who protects, who collects under her jealous eyes at one long table her own children, always her own" (308-309;*136*), and she begins to feel buried under.

Shrunk and aged, Jinny, still with her powdered nose and pencilled eyebrows, wonders, "But who will come if I signal? . . . I shall look into faces, and I shall see them seek some other face" (310;*137-38*). Yet in her hardened determination, she will succumb neither to fear nor to hopelessness. As long as a "somebody new, somebody unknown, somebody I passed on the staircase" (311;*139*) may appear, she will march forward, crusading, in her little patent-leather shoes.

Having lost the firm tissue of youth, Neville thinks he has conquered his desire for firelit rooms and intimacy, believes that life can be lived with the pleasures of poetry and in the company of familiar faces, and nourishes the idea that "one must beat one's wings against the storm in the belief that beyond this welter the sun shines" (313;*141*). Beneath his self-reassuring thoughts, however, remains his insatiable longing. He waits still for the footstep on the stair, for the hesitation at the door, for the man who will sit by his side.

Louis, at the acme of his success, continues to return to his attic room and has, after Rhoda left him, acquired a vulgar little mistress whose cockney accent he thought would put him at ease. His opulence and his immense respectability, however, offer him little comfort. For despite his labor and achievement, he is more alone than ever and wonders if even death will give him the continuity and permanence he has so long sought.

Now in Spain, Rhoda, who felt liberated through Percival's death, has increasingly parted company with the real world and has drifted into the dream-filled regions where she need no longer suffer the concussion of other people—or the pressure of Louis's embraces. In these regions, death reigns supreme, and the salves of oblivion have their sanctuary. Percival, of whom Rhoda now seldom thinks, has shown her death, and "There is only a thin sheet between me now and the infinite depths" (319;*146*).

In the eighth section, the sun is sinking in the sky, with a wild plover *"crying further off in loneliness"* and solitary trees marking *"distant hills like obelisks"* (320-21;*148*). In a similar atmosphere of immense isolation and imminent decline, the second and final reunion of the *personae* takes place at Hampton Court. During the reunion, the life of each is going to be measured against the choices made in youth, choices which each of the six must justify.

Neville, a poet of fame, needs to carry his credentials to prove his worth; but he realizes that "the sound of clapping has failed" (323;*150*), that fame in itself has not been enough for him. Perpetually immersed in that pursuit, Neville has sacrificed and profaned much that might have been more personally enduring. Although his intimacies have been many and varied and dangerous, love (as he calls it) has left him bruised, knotted, and torn asunder. Saddest of all, he knows that "Change is no longer possible" (324;*151*).

Susan, who has seen "life in blocks, substantial, huge" (325;*152*), still gapes "like a young bird, unsatisfied, for something that has escaped me" (338;*165*).

Rhoda, more severed from the present than ever before, feels increasingly tyrannized and tortured, but walks straight toward the assembled group, no longer having to hide behind trees to "avoid the shock of sensation. . ." (330;*157*). However, it is only in her moment of peace alone with Louis that we realize the source of her courage to confront directly those whom she fears, hates, loves, envies, and despises: for in her illusory world, the recurrent image has become lurid with significance—"A square is stood upon the oblong and we say, 'This is our dwelling-place. The structure is now visible' " (335;*162*). And in that vision of death so near at hand, Rhoda has the courage to stray among the others in spite of feeling assaulted and scattered by their temporary closeness.

Louis, with all his material gain, remains apprehensive, unsure, and ambivalent. All the canes and waistcoats and mahogany desks in the world cannot outweigh his almost congenital sense of insignificance. His life-long search for glory has, by middle age, done little to bolster an authentic sense of himself. It is not surprising then that the humiliations he suffers inwardly force him to become outwardly "ruthless, marmoreal." He needs a protective shell to survive in his outcast state. We also see why, in his persistent fear of ridicule, that he is "happiest alone," and still cloistered in his attic room. Nor is there any question why Louis feels the reunion to be "black with the shadows of dungeons and the tortures and infamies practiced by man upon man" (328;*155-56*). But these shadows are really his own private demons. In making private agony a universal misery, he can feel less tyrannized by the dark powers of loneliness.

Jinny, to the very end, remains courageously defiant. At whatever cost, she has fought the same torments that the others have suffered and has daily sought renewal "sometimes only by the touch of a finger under the tablecloth as we sat dining . . ." (329;*157*). So unappeasing is her physical appetite that she consumes everything and leaves nothing behind, "no relics, no unburnt bones, no wisps of hair to be kept in lockets. . . ." Grizzled and haggard as she now is, she cannot avoid the "looking-glass in broad daylight, and note precisely my nose, my chin, my lips. . . . But I am not afraid" (330;*157*).

It is finally through Bernard that we learn the extent to which life has divided all of them. "How many telephone calls, how many post cards are now needed to cut this hole through which we come together. . . ." Yet it is he who has made the calls, sent the post cards. And it is Bernard who feels most resigned to his inability to do anything with his phrases; for as he says "what are phrases? They have left me very little to lay on the table beside Susan's hand; to take from my pocket, with Neville's credentials. I am not an authority on law, or medicine, or finance. I am wrapped round with phrases, like damp straw . . ." (326;*153-54*). His resignation, however, has in it a sustaining quality which makes the act of living something positive, despite his anxiety, loneliness, division, and inner chaos. He realizes that living is a continual effort against a common, overwhelming futility; that life is an inevitable series of "musts": Must go, must sleep, must wake, must get up—sober, merciful word which we pretend to revile, which we press tight to our hearts, without which we should be undone" (339;*166*). He senses a larger dimension to life than mere flux: there is also its continuity, but it is of a kind which consists of a continual breaking down and building up again.

In the ninth and final section, the sun has set, and *"Sky and sea were indistinguishable."* Darkness prevails, and *"there was no sound save the cry of a bird seeking some lonelier tree"* (340;*167-68*). Bernard, in final soliloquy, sums up his life and that of the others. Addressing himself to an unidentified dinner companion—possibly to the reader directly—Bernard speaks of their suffering as children to become separate human beings, their youthful remorseless egotism, his own ever-changing roles and identities, the naive belief that life is orderly and that stories have a logical sequence, and the misguided yearnings which life manages to frustrate.

After Percival's senseless death came a turning point. Bernard began to realize that nature is irrational, life, intractable, and death, inescapable. It is against the mindlessness of nature that one must fight: "It is the effort and the struggle, it is the shattering and piecing together—this is the daily battle, defeat or victory, the absorbing pursuit" (363-64;*191*).

But Bernard did give all the shattered pieces some shape, "with a sudden phrase. . . .retrieved them from formlessness with words" (364;*191*). In superimposing his artificial design on life's fortuities, however, he created only the *illusion* of order. His need to force order where it had no place, moreover, drained his energy in the futile attempt of creating an illusory world where the self and others can never be known. Bernard is consequently unknown to himself: "I am not one person; I am many people; I do not altogether know who I am—" (368;*196*). It is small wonder that he feels so acutely *what he might have been* and discontented with what he is. For in his illusions, the human ideal—not the human potential—is so exaggerated that the real man has been sacrificed to a glorified phantom. With his emotional lenses thus focused on something other than the real Bernard, he understandably becomes impoverished, "A man without a self. . . . A heavy body leaning on a gate. A dead man. With dispassionate despair, with entire disillusionment. . . . How can I proceed now, I said, without a self. . . . without illusion?" (374-75;*202-203*)

During this eclipsing of the self, Bernard has not, as some readers have claimed, undergone a transformation. Rather, he has had a fleeting vision of the real world without the distortion of personal perception. During that momentary vision, however, *the world of illusion has been displaced by a world of delusion.* For clearly Bernard has not overcome his protean sense of himself. He has only become momentarily detached from his illusory world to see in himself the incomprehensible repository of all the conflicting opposites which have made him what he is. It is a vision of depth, enabling him to see the "brute, too, the savage, the hairy man who dabbles his fingers in ropes of entrails; and gobbles and belches; whose speech is guttural, visceral" (378;*205*).

Having reached and discovered that unsavory depth, Bernard has a sudden change of mood. It is as though his story has got out of control, a door has opened too wide and has revealed more than he intended to his companion. For he turns to a delusory kind of self-aggrandizing, self-worshipping—implying a belief in his own immunity. He has only to catch the eye of his auditor, however, to see his imagined vastness and freedom and power dashed to smithereens: "That is the blow you have dealt me. . . . Lord, how unutterably disgusting life is! . . . What dirty tricks it plays us, one moment free; the next this. . . I who had thought myself immune . . . find that a wave has tumbled me over, head over heels, scattering my possessions, leaving me to collect, to assemble, to heap together, summon my forces, rise and confront the enemy" (379-80;*207-208*).

This fragmentation and chaos in Bernard confirm the delusion under which he has labored in thinking himself free from illusion, free from the illusory idealized man he would like to be. It is only when Bernard is at last alone that the one significant change to have taken place in him becomes apparent; and that is in his having learned that he desires to be alone where he can be himself, where he is no longer life's pawn blown from here to there, seeking reassurance, and soliciting approval. Earlier in the novel, he could not "bear the pressure of solitude" (267;*95*). But at last he can admit that "Now no one sees me and I change no more. Heaven be praised for solitude that has removed the pressure of the eye, the solicitation of the body, and all the need of lies and phrases" (381;*209*).

If the capricious senselessness of life was once inimical to Bernard, his acceptance of solitude has nullified its senselessness and has made death now the enemy. It is the renewed memory of Percival's death and the permanence of its isolation which mobilizes in Bernard—divided and scattered though he is—the staying power and the courage to endure his own solitude; to make the continual effort required of life; to fling himself, now in old age, defiantly against death, "unvanquished and unyielding . . ." (383;*211*). And in his heroic defiance, Bernard in a sense becomes that courageous *"bird seeking some lonelier tree."*

So much for the novel in its sequential parts. What *The Waves* means as a whole is a question of considerable difficulty. Even Mrs. Woolf seems to have had no answer. If we consider, for example, the integrating function of Percival in the novel, the tendency is immediately to see him as some version of the knight in the Grail legends. If we explore that association we are very apt to find ourselves overwhelmed with the multiplicity of sources covering hundreds of years dating from the *Perceval, ou le conte du graal* (c. 1175) of Chrétien de Troyes and the *Parzival* (early 13th Century) of **Wolfram von Eschenbach through Thomas Malory's** *Le morte d'Arthur* (c. 1469) to Tennyson's *Idylls of the King* (1859-1885) and Richard Wagner's *Parsifal* (1882). One has only to read an account of the evolution of Percival through the centuries to see how many variations there are to his story and therefore how immune to analysis is Mrs. Woolf's choice of name for her symbolic hero. Although *The Waves,* from beginning to end, reverberates with allusive images and interlocking references related to the legendary Percival, there is just enough inconsistency among the historical versions to discourage any interpretation of that heroic role except of the most tentative and provisional kind.

In her *Diary* (22 September 1931), Mrs. Woolf wrote: "What I want is to be told that this [*The Waves*] is solid and means something. What it means I myself shan't know till I write another book." That the novel is "solid" and "means something" is unquestionable. For on the most abstract and universal plane, *The Waves* suggests, first, that every human being is a distinct living unit while being simultaneously a part of every other unit of human life; that is, one is distinct from others because of the identity one has created for oneself by conscious or unconscious choices in life—choices determined by each individual's scale of values; and at the same time, one is a part of those people who have shared emotions and experiences in life. Second, the novel suggests that it is fatal to surrender completely to the unity of the moment in an effort to create the illusion of order. For there is no order except in the solitary, random moments which in memory constitute one's *conscious* progression through life. Third, that one must grasp the relationship between the polarities which co-exist in each human being and understand his daily battle with them. And finally, the novel seems to urge that one must continue to order each new day with its perpetual cycles of building up and tearing down, and yet remain unyielding in one's struggle against death. For death is the ultimate destroyer, and the effort of the living should be to defy it and to dominate it.

Approaching the novel in terms of its structure, one critic wrote that "It is finally the abstract patterns, the contrasts between interlude and soliloquy, artist and character, that hold the central meaning of the book. Virginia Woolf is showing us, simultaneously, through the patterned art of these soliloquies and interludes, how very naturally our lives must develop and how very artificially we must perceive that development in order to feel that we can understand and accept it."[8]

---

8. Elizabeth Heine, "The Evolution of the Interludes in *The Waves*," *Virginia Woolf Quarterly*, I, No. 1 (Fall 1972), p. 78.

The intensity with which Virginia Woolf conceived her six *personae* and the unhurried deliberation with which she explored their destinies insinuate another level of meaning to the novel. That meaning is connected with the private history, the apparent values, and the real choices—whether intellectual, moral, or emotional; whether conscious or unconscious—each character has *had* to make in order to survive. They are choices which have endowed each of them with their own particular cadence and determined their ultimate fates. Louis, for example, ashamed of his father, trammelled by the lowly roots of his past, and unable to crush those dark demons of inferiority which have pursued him through life, is obsessed with building a commercial empire. He not only wants the world to see his "superiority," but also, and more important, wants "to expunge certain stains." In the end, however, Louis still roams his attic room, contracted with shame and self-mockery.

Neville the neat, Neville the fragmented, is a portrait etched with the acid of a life soured and corroded by warped pleasures and derelict emotions. In his wallowing in ugliness, weakness, and suffering, Neville is a man menaced by the begrudging world from which he can escape only temporarily in the fame-encrusted poets of the past. His only way of surviving in the hostile present is to translate his fears into feelings of worthlessness, which subsequently become his cherished excuse for morbid dependency on others. That his liaisons are homosexual is important to his portrait, because the transitoriness of such relationships leaves him repeatedly in a state of loss and suffering. However, if we consider Neville's rage against the world in combination with the hopeless homosexual affairs he engineers to fill his life with suffering, we begin to realize that Neville is the kind of person *who experiences his suffering as punishment.* For the punishment then serves as an alibi to present himself to a hostile world as someone exalted and superior—someone who has been purified through pain. In this light, it is understandable that Neville's grief at Percival's death should take on that sacrificial character in his cry: "Come, pain, feed on me. Bury your fangs in my flesh. Tear me asunder." Percival's death does not become Neville's pain: it becomes Neville's punishment.

Jinny, the tousled symbol of sexuality, becomes a travesty of womanhood. For however courageous her promiscuity, in her indiscriminate greed for every man, she really wants no man at all. In her breathless bed-ridden life, her inability—which she classifies as her "unwillingness"—to establish an adult bond with any man leaves her both physically impoverished and emotionally naive. Seen from this angle, she appears as ignorant of a genuine heterosexual relationship as either a virgin or a Sapphist might be.

Susan's total immersion in the biological roles of mother and wife is rendered with disquieting ferocity. In epitomizing the fruition of womanhood, she is possessive and unscrupulous as a mother, jealous and graspingly passionate as a wife. But she is doomed to a heritage so rich in earth and element that life becomes a thick accumulation of time and a silent decay of matter.

The fatherless Rhoda, trapped in the integument of her female body and tortured by the fear of physicality, is unable to live either in the present or in the future. She is "for ever outside the loop of time." In words of a demented woman, she enunciates a horror of living so overwhelming that escape through phantasy eventually yields to escape by suicide, that departure whose guarantee is eternal.[9]

9. In section five, after having heard of Percival's death, Rhoda thinks: "Here is a hall where one pays money and goes in, where one hears music. . . . Then the beetle-shaped men come with their violins; wait; count; nod; down come their bows. . . . and Percival, by his death, has made me this gift, let me see the thing. There is a square; there is an oblong. The players take the square and place it upon the oblong" (287-88;*115-116*). It was earlier suggested that the square and the oblong had, for Rhoda, something about them peculiarly linked with death—a link hinting that the players' square and oblong conjured up for her an image of tombstone and coffin. But there also appears to be a connection between music and death—a connection, we may guess, as vivid for Rhoda as for Virginia Woolf. Just how the music of the stringed instruments is linked with death only becomes clear when we consider simultaneously four sources outside the novel itself. The first two are from Mrs. Woolf's *Diary*. In the entry of 18 June 1927, we discover: "Now the Moths [the original title of *The Waves*] will, I think, fill out the skeleton which I dashed in here; the play-poem idea. . . . I do a little work on it in the evening when the gramophone is playing late Beethoven sonatas." In another entry, on 28 November 1928, "*The Moths* still haunts me, coming, as they do, unbidden, between tea and dinner, while L. plays the gramophone. I shape a page or two; and make myself stop." Third, from Quentin Bell's *Virginia Woolf: A Biography* (New York: Harcourt Brace Jovanovich, Inc., Vol. II, p. 130): "Another important addition to Virginia's life was the gramophone. . . . Virginia, who had a fairly catholic taste, developed a particular interest in Beethoven's late quartets, and they assisted those meditations which finally resulted in *The Waves.*" And finally, in the fifth volume of his autobiography, *The Journey Not the Arrival Matters* (New York: Harcourt Brace Jovanovich, Inc., p. 95), Leonard Woolf, discussing his wife's death wrote: "I had once said to her [Virginia] that, if there was to be music at one's cremation, it ought to be the cavatina from the B flat quartet, op. 130, of Beethoven. There is a moment at cremations when the doors of the crematorium open and the coffin slides slowly in, and there is a moment in the middle of the cavatina when for a few bars

The figures of Rhoda and Bernard are the most difficult to align in the novel's organic patterning, because in some obscure way they seem at once paradoxically connected to and opposite one another. More precisely, they are connected *because* they are opposite. In his summing up, Bernard says that he "went into the Strand and evoked to serve as *opposite to myself the figure of Rhoda . . ."* (371;*199*). Just how Mrs. Woolf attempted to conjoin their opposing natures is necessarily a matter of conjecture. However, if we turn to that section of the novel in which Rhoda, repeating the words of Shelley, asks "Oh! to whom?", we come upon another utterance of hers not readily susceptible to interpretation: "I came to a puddle. I could not cross it. Identity failed me" (219;*46*). In her *Diary,* 30 September 1926, Mrs. Woolf wrote: "Life is . . . the oddest affair; . . . I used to feel this as a child—couldn't step across a puddle once, I remember, for thinking how strange—what am I? etc. *But by writing, I don't reach anything.* " In the novel's almost *verbatim* transcription of an actual life episode, Virginia Woolf has, in a sense, become the spectator of her own terrifying experience; the transcription is imagination unprotected and undisguised. From it, we may infer that not only did Mrs. Woolf siphon a significant part of herself into the character of Rhoda, but like Rhoda, Virginia Stephen herself at some stage of her childhood felt that she was without identity.

Thus, for the dreaming, phantasy-ridden Rhoda, who *substitutes* her inner world for the real world, identity has failed, because no circuits are open through which the raw imprints and tangled impulses of her vaulted life can find their way to coherent expression in the larger reality outside herself. Mrs. Woolf's avowal, then, that "by writing I don't reach anything" can be read obliquely as Rhoda's Shelleyan longing to give aesthetic embodiment to those deep waters of feeling which have remained subterranean throughout her life. For it was well-known to Virginia Woolf that in the active exercise of the creative imagination, one communicates with the deeper, richer, and darker levels of one's consciousness; and in so

---

the music . . . seems to hesitate with a gentle forward pulsing motion—if played at that moment it might seem to be gently propelling the dead into the eternity of oblivion. Virginia agreed with me." The association now of music, square [crematorium door] and oblong [coffin], and death becomes rather more insistent. And it might be of biographic interest to note that in Rhoda's madness and suicide, we see Virginia Woolf in phantasy writing out a fictitious version of her own death which would occur just a little more than a decade later.

doing, one is building an ever-enlarging sense of self—that unending process of self-discovery which yields cumulatively partial answers to the question: What am I? Who am I? Rhoda, however, does not know what she is or who she is, because she cannot establish that vital link between her inner and outer worlds which makes such communication possible. And that creative block to Rhoda, as to her creator, meant death, meant suicide.

In this very narrow sense only is Rhoda Bernard's opposite. So that if Rhoda must die, then Bernard must live. However, narrowly defining these characters as opposites raises perhaps the most difficult of all questions. For Bernard, except in his phrase-inflated notebooks, has created nothing. To the very end, he remains the novelist *manqué*. Why then has Mrs. Woolf selected him to carry so much of the novel's weight? Why has she allotted almost half of the book to his utterance? It would be easy to conclude that in having lived through all the corruptions and shocks and disappointments of life, Bernard alone has the power of integration to unite the inner and outer worlds. One might assume that ultimately he alone can bear "the burden of individual life," without seeking refuge in the many substitutes for living as have the others in their various pursuits. But to sum Bernard up so neatly does not seem altogether convincing.

For Bernard, in some curious way, is reminiscent of Camus's hero, Sisyphus, who "*is* as much through his passions as through his torture. . . . his hatred of death, and his passion for life won him that unspeakable penalty in which the whole being is exerted toward accomplishing nothing."[10]

The whole being is exerted toward accomplishing nothing may have been part of the larger—and for Virginia Woolf—more personal meaning of the novel. For while *The Waves* was crowding in imagination, she made several *Diary* entries which give this speculation some credence. On 28 March 1929, she wrote: "I am going to face certain things. It is going to be a time of adventure and attack, rather lonely and painful, I think. But solitude will be good for the new book." On 23 June of the same year: "Directly I stop working I feel that I am sinking down, down. And as usual I feel that if I sink further I shall reach the truth. That is the only mitigation; a

---

10. Albert Camus, "The Myth of Sisyphus," trans. Justin O'Brien, in *Existentialism from Dostoevsky to Sartre,* New York and Cleveland: Meridian Books, 1956, p. 313.

kind of nobility. Solemnity. I shall make myself face the fact that there is nothing—nothing for any of us. Work, reading, writing are all disguises; and relations with people. Yes, even having children would be useless."

Then we turn to Bernard who does not have Neville's fame, Jinny's relations, Susan's possessions, Louis's fortune. At the same time, he has not retreated from or acquiesced to the substitutes for responsible life through homosexuality, promiscuity, "natural happiness," or empire-building. Nor has he surrendered, like Rhoda, to suicide. Bernard, the *potential artist,* in having achieved nothing, has in a quite real sense exerted his whole being toward accomplishing nothing.

When we look at him in the frame of Mrs. Woolf's feeling that so much of what we do is mere dissemblance, that in the end really "there is nothing," then Bernard's will to persist, his determination to confront death in solitude—despite the loneliness of old age and the ache of loss—may not endow him with heroic stature; but he does acquire a kind of faded solemnity, even a faint nobility. For he is committed to life and to living; he is engaged in the struggle of life which daily renews itself—stripped of the meretricious veils of fame, fortune, and pleasure. His is the struggle which, in the existential sense, makes human destiny a human matter. So that if all work and reading and writing are disguises, then Bernard, with nothing in the end to fight against except death, becomes a lonely but luminous monument to keep alive the memory of the once life-affirming Percival.[11]

11. More than two decades ago, Aileen Pippett, Virginia Woolf's first biographer suggested that "Bernard . . . is perhaps Desmond MacCarthy . . ." (*The Moth and the Star,* Boston and Toronto: Little, Brown and Company, 1955, p. 291). Recently, Quentin Bell quoted a portion of the unpublished *Diary,* dated 18 February 1919, in which Mrs. Woolf wrote of MacCarthy: "I'm not sure he hasn't the nicest nature of any of us—the nature one would have soonest have chosen for one's own. I don't think that he possesses any faults as a friend, save that his friendship is so often sunk under a cloud of vagueness. . . . Perhaps such indolence implies a slackness of fibre in his affections too—but I scarcely feel that. It arises from the consciousness which I find imaginative and attractive that things don't altogether *matter.* . . . His 'great work' . . . only takes shape, I believe, in that hour between tea and dinner, when so many things appear not only possible but achieved. Comes the daylight, and Desmond is contented to begin his article; and plies his pen with a half humorous half melancholy recognition that such is his appointed life. Yet it is true, and no one can deny it, that he has the floating elements of something brilliant, beautiful—some book of stories, reflections, studies, scattered about in him, for they show themselves indisputably in his talk. . . . I can see myself, however, going through his desk one of these days, shaking out unfinished pages from between

sheets of blotting paper, and deposits of old bills, and making up a small book of table talk, which shall appear as a proof to the younger generation that Desmond was the most gifted of us all. But why did he never do anything? they will ask" (Bell, Vol. II, pp. 81-82).

From the content of this entry, one might easily conclude that Bernard is modelled entirely after Desmond MacCarthy, but such a conclusion is untenable. If one reads closely the published *Diary* from 18 June 1927, when the "play-poem" is first mentioned, through 7 February 1931, the day on which the completion of *The Waves* is recorded, one discovers too many similarities between Mrs. Woolf herself and Bernard to cling to the notion of MacCarthy's being the sole life model for Bernard. However, there seems little doubt that MacCarthy was very much on Mrs. Woolf's mind during the writing of *The Waves*. It seems as if Virginia Woolf, the actual, the accomplished novelist, saw a deeply hidden part of herself in MacCarthy, the would-be novelist, who could not endure—what she so often painfully did—the absolute aloneness required in creating a sustained literary work. And she seems to have felt a radiant sympathy for him in his inability to write that "great work." One senses that she recognized in him a courage, even greater than her own, in *not* bringing to fruition his artistic potential and at the same time in accepting the melancholy fact "that such is his appointed life."

An entry in the *Diary* made on 1 November 1934—long after *The Waves* was published—suggests how persistent Virginia Woolf was in her feelings toward MacCarthy. In that entry, she was considering the biography of Roger Fry and wrote "that it should be written by different people to illustrate different stages.

Youth . . .
Cambridge . . .
Early London life . . .
Bloomsbury . . .
Later life . . . and so on.

all to be combined say by Desmond and me together." The "stages" she lists are of course similar to those of *The Waves*. What is most impressive, however, is the idea of the collaboration—"all to be combined say by Desmond and me together." For her choice of writing "partner" underscores a great artistic empathy as well as a profound emotional alliance with a man who, in Virginia Woolf's mind, "was the most gifted of us all."

The Years

The Years was the last novel Virginia Woolf was ever to see published, and it is the only novel about which one feels—to use the phrasing of Charles Lamb[1]—that this writer of enormous power was so possessed by her material that she no longer had dominion over it. The ink began to flow too quickly on page after page, month after month, until the stream of words grew into a fictional flood. Exactly what went wrong during the novel's growth, no one can tell with certainty. Since the publication of *A Writer's Diary* in 1953, however, we have had the opportunity to watch this artist reflect upon her work and to trace its development at close range.

From the *Diary,* 2 November 1932, we learn that the book was not only to be an "Essay-Novel" but also that its first title was *The Pargiters.* Not perhaps an unusual title—not unusual, that is, until one's eye is caught by a rather long, earlier entry of 13 July of that same year in which Mrs. Woolf wrote about "sleeping over a promising novel" and a few lines later continues: "Old Joseph Wright and old Lizzie Wright are people I respect . . . . He was a maker of dialect dictionaries: he was a workhouse boy—his mother went charring. And he married Miss Lea a Clergyman's daughter. And I've read their love letters with respect. And he said: 'Always please yourself—then one person's happy at any rate.' And she said make details part of a whole—get proportions right—contemplating marriage with Joe. Odd how rare it is to meet people who say things that we ourselves could have said. Their attitude to life much our own." Considering Mrs. Woolf's fondness for Joseph Wright—and her fondness for playing with the sounds of words and with people's names—one locates a volume of Wright's *Dictionary* to see if the word "pargiter" appears. It is not to be found, but the word "parget" is there, which according to Wright is a verb meaning "to plaster with cement or mortar, esp. to plaster the inside of a chimney with cement made of cow-dung and lime."[2]

1. "Sanity of True Genius" (1826).

2. Vol. IV, M-Q, *English Dialect Dictionary,* 6 Volumes, Joseph Wright, ed., London:

With curiosity aroused, one turns to the *Oxford English Dictionary* and again finds no "pargiter," but one does discover "pargeter," which is defined as "a plasterer; a whitewasher"; and by figurative extension refers to "one who glosses and smoothes over." The question then arises: Is there any connection between "pargeter" and Mrs. Woolf's "promising novel" mentioned earlier? For if there is, then we are induced to trace the strange evolution of this "Essay-Novel, called *The Pargiters*" which Mrs. Woolf began in a state of exhilaration and completed four years later—in despair. The record of the book's growth suggests that its author gradually realized that all the factual matter which would constitute the essay portions was weighty emotional substance which was somehow alien to the artistic design she originally envisioned. That is to say, the truth of fact and the truth of fiction could not meet in felicitous alliance: "For though both truths are genuine, they are antagonistic; let them meet and they destroy each other . . . . Let it be fact . . . or let it be fiction; the imagination will not serve under two masters simultaneously."[3] So that in one sense *The Years* as a finished product is a remarkable specimen in fiction where fact and feeling are in deadly conflict. Consequently, throughout the book's course, the recurrent question to its author was: How would she "smooth over" those deep chasms which separate historic fact from immediate feeling.

Although it is difficult to pinpoint the moment when some long-buried seed suddenly germinates in a writer's mind, Virginia Woolf records that moment for us. In her *Diary* on Tuesday, 20 January 1931, she wrote: "I have this moment, while having my bath, conceived an entire new book—a sequel to *A Room of One's Own*—about the sexual life of women: to be called Professions for Women perhaps—Lord how exciting! This sprang out of my paper to

Henry Frowde, 1903, p. 423.

    In a letter dated 10 January 1976, Professor Quentin Bell informed me that Leonard and Virginia Woolf knew and liked a man named Pargiter, a signalman at Southease Station who stood as Labour Candidate in 1918. Credit for this information goes to Miss Michele Barrett of the University of Hull.

    3. Virginia Woolf, "The New Biography," *New York Herald Tribune,* 30 October 1927; reprinted in *Granite and Rainbow,* New York and London: Harcourt Brace Jovanovich, A Harvest Book, 1975, p. 154.

be read on Wednesday [21 January 1931] to Pippa's [Pippa Strachey's] society." What is of special interest, however, is a marginal note Mrs. Woolf made more than three years later in May 1934 when she was re-reading the 20 January 1931 entry: "(This ["the entire new book"] is *Here and Now,* I think. . . .)" The note is important, because "the entire new book" based on the speech was *not Three Guineas,* as Leonard Woolf noted in his edition of *A Writer's Diary,* but *The Years,* whose second title (of nine altogether) was *Here and Now.*[4] It also confirms our suspicion that the "promising novel" of the 13 July 1932 entry, was indeed reference to *The Pargiters,* the same entry in which Wright is given so much space. And although some risk is attached to it, if we place these slim threads of evidence side by side, it becomes possible to hazard the guess that Joseph Wright, the word "parget" in his *Dictionary,* and the novel's first title were all somehow intimately connected in Mrs. Woolf's mind—and that she was apparently fully conscious of the implications of calling her fictional family the Pargiters.

Approximately twenty months following the delivery of her speech at "Pippa's society," the curious history of *The Years* began. On 11 October 1932, Virginia Woolf, with an almost fresh manuscript notebook before her, dipped her pen and wrote: "THE PARGITERS: An Essay based upon a paper read to the London/National Society for Women's Service."[5] Sometime between 11 October and 2 November 1932, she returned to the title page, deleted the "An" and revised the subtitle to read "A Novel-Essay." This insertion of "A Novel-" tells us a good deal about the author's original plan. *The Pargiters* was indeed intended as a sequel to *A Room of One's Own,* but the design of the book was to be a new experiment in form. She would create an imaginary audience as she had done in the earlier book; only now after her First Essay on the professions for women, she would narrow her range specifically to the restrictions imposed upon a woman who chooses writing as a pro-

---

4. *The Pargiters, Here and Now, Music, Dawn, Sons and Daughters, Daughters and Sons, Ordinary People, The Caravan, The Years.*

5. The paper she is referring to is the Holograph entitled "Speech" and dated "21st Jan. 1931" ("Articles, Essays, Fiction, and Reviews" Vol. IV, 1930-31, in the Berg Collection).

Between January 1931 and the middle of October 1932, *The Waves, A Letter to a Young Poet,* and *The Common Reader: Second Series* were published as well as about a dozen periodical and newspaper articles.

fession. Having done that she would provide her reader with "short extracts from a [non-existent] novel that will run into many volumes"—each "extract" being a set of ideas ranging from sex and feminism to politics and education; and this fictional illustration would be followed by an essay explaining how the woman novelist deals with certain principal controlling ideas from factual life and transforms them into fiction. That is to say, Mrs. Woolf intended to invent as she went along; and it suited her plan to write a fictional "extract" to be followed by an Essay, then to write a second "extract" followed by another Essay, and so on to the end. By 19 December 1932, according to her own calculation, she had written 60,320 words. On that day, Mrs. Woolf had written what she considered to be the complete first draft of "Chapter One," consisting of six Essays and five fictional "extracts"—that is, the complete first draft of what was to become the 1880 section of *The Years.*

She returned to her manuscript notebook on 31 January 1933, and wrote on a fresh page: *"The Pargiters (additions to Chapter One)."* Two days later, 2 February: "Today I finished—rather more completely than usual—revising the first chapter. I am leaving out the interchapters [the Essays]—compacting them in the text: and project an appendix of dates." We know from the finished product that the projected appendix of dates did not appear. One can also safely assume, for reasons to be given later, that the "compacting" of the interchapters, although surely intended, was aesthetically—and affectively—impossible for Mrs. Woolf. The truth of fact and the truth of the imagination simply would not unite in that queer "marriage of granite and rainbow."[6] Essentially, this means that the whole idea of the essay-novel, this "novel of fact," was abandoned by 2 February 1933; and from that date on, the novel form would govern the design.

By March 1936, Mrs. Woolf was so certain that her novel was a failure that she took the unusual step of having it printed before Leonard Woolf was allowed to read it; and we know from the number of galley-proof pages (about 600) and the length of the first

---

6. See Mitchell A. Leaska, ed., *The Pargiters* by Virginia Woolf; The Novel-Essay Portion of *The Years,* New York: New York Public Library and Readex Books; London: The Hogarth Press, 1977.

published edition (472 pages) how much of the original text was deleted from the finished novel. With such drastic cutting, if the novel's semantic integrity was to be preserved, Mrs. Woolf was forced once more to render with the high compression of poetry many of the sections which were originally written with the broader explicitness of prose. As a result, many parts of the novel are highly ambiguous. Throughout the published text, we come across splinters of memory, fragments of speech, titles of quoted passages left unnamed or forgotten, lines of poetry or remnants of nursery rhymes left dangling in mid-air, communication between characters incomplete, and utterances misfired and misunderstood. In one sense, the novel eloquently communicates the *failure* of communication.

We know that Mrs. Woolf rarely, if ever, included anything in her books as pure decoration; everything was put to some service, was functional in some way. So that with the disappearance of the explanatory Essays, and with the novel itself so severely cut and glossed over, we as readers must depend perhaps too much upon the fertility of our own imaginations to fathom some meaning from the book's seemingly endless ambiguities. It therefore seems necessary to rely upon some parts of the original holograph version to show the degree to which Mrs. Woolf did indeed succeed in conveying the lives of the Pargiters, a family who because of the sexual premises of the age and their accompanying economic circumstances were themselves pargeters, and taught their children to be. But more important, we will discover in example after example the extent to which Virginia Woolf herself as novelist was also forced into becoming a pargeter— and ultimately one of great artistic fluency and moral courage.

In view of the novel's origin in a speech on professions for women, one might easily be tempted to devote the remainder of this chapter to a discussion of women's rights, educational privilege, feminism, sexual politics, and so on. Such a discussion, however, would be superfluous; for we have from Virginia Woolf's own pen the persuasive and lyrical *A Room of One's Own* and the harsher, more contentious *Three Guineas.* The more essential question is why the Essays of the 1880 section came to a halt, with only their barest threads remaining as thinly veiled autobiography parading in the vestment of fiction. It is safe to assume that the change in the book's design was not from want of skill. Mrs. Woolf had demonstrated over and over again that she was always in command of her complicated creative equipment. Repeatedly she showed her genius for re-modelling the novel, for re-casting it in this way and then in that way to suit her aesthetic purpose. Why should the mechanism of her imagination begin to falter for the first time with this book?[7]

For it is astonishing to discover how much Virginia Woolf was conscious of her own mind at work. She wrote in *A Room of One's Own,* for example, that "the mind is always altering its focus, and bringing the world into different perspectives. But some of these states of mind seem, even if adopted spontaneously, to be less comfortable than others. In order to keep oneself continuing in them one is unconsciously holding something back, and gradually the repression becomes an effort. But there may be some state of mind in which one could continue without effort because nothing is required to be held back."[8] We know from the *Diary* that the seed of *The Years* began to grow on 20 January 1931; and if the course of the book's development were traced from that date through to its completion on 30 November 1936, one would discover that for its author it became with time an increasingly excruciating effort. Does it not logically follow, then, if we are to take Mrs. Woolf's words to heart, that the effort increased in proportion to the amount of material being repressed?

The extent to which she was "unconsciously holding something back," it is not possible for anyone—even Mrs. Woolf herself, for that matter—to determine; but there is in the same section just quoted a very strange sentence worth noting: "It [the mind] can think back through its fathers or through its mothers, as I have said that a woman writing thinks back through her mothers."[9] We know

7. One wonders too why in the Holograph Essays there is so much emphasis (sexual matters aside for the moment) on money, on privacy, on education—all of these deprived the woman. If anyone in the year 1932 was in need, it was not Virginia Woolf. She had from childhood an education, private though it was of necessity, that the great Colleges of Oxford and Cambridge would be hard pressed to match in terms of intellectual freedom and moral diversity; she had from her marriage to Leonard Woolf the kind of privacy that any professional writer would guard jealously; and she had from the year 1925, with the publication of *Mrs. Dalloway,* and later of *To the Lighthouse* and *Orlando,* both money and fame—regardless of the private financial schedule she and her husband set for themselves.

8. New York and Burlingame: Harcourt, Brace and World, Inc., A Harbinger Book, 1957, p. 101; London: The Hogarth Press (Fourteenth Impression), 1967, pp. 146-47.

9. New York and Burlingame, p. 101; London, p. 146.

from personal experience that when we recall our past, we tend to think through accumulated summers, first days of school, High Holy Days, Christmases. But to think back through *fathers* and *mothers*? How is that possible? For how many different biological fathers and mothers can one have in real life? An attempt to answer may provide the reason why *The Pargiters,* an essay-novel requiring both the creative and the analytical faculties, could not continue very much beyond the point it did; why the novel form was forced into governance so that the truth or fact—or whatever one wishes to call it—could be rendered fictionally and treated poetically.

What then was it that prevented her from completing the essay-novel as it was originally planned? What nerve was she pressing in the early Holograph Volumes which sparked something stronger than conscious thought and fired the creative mind to gain control over the analytical? Part of the answer may be, as Mrs. Woolf wrote earlier in *A Room of One's Own,* that "Fiction . . . is likely to contain more truth than fact"; or as she said in the First Essay of *The Pargiters*: "I prefer, where truth is important, to write fiction." However, two passages, written some time later, in a very curious way collide with these pronouncements about the truth of fiction. The first is in the *Diary* entry of 11 June 1936, long after the "Essay" idea had been abandoned and *The Years* was in its final stages: "I can only, after two months, make this brief note, to say at last after two months' dismal and worse, almost catastrophic illness—*never been so near the precipice to my own feeling since 1913*—I'm on top again." The words with emphasis added might be read as Mrs. Woolf's way of signalling that she was digging too much into her novel and getting too close to the truth, too close to some "dangerous" memory or feeling—hence the collapse. This entry, however, is quite extraordinary in the biographic sense; for if we turn to the 1913 section of *The Years,* we find that it is one of the shortest sections of the novel, and more importantly, that it deals with the servant Crosby and the dog Rover. Crosby and Rover now point us directly to *Three Guineas* where we find Mrs. Woolf, in a cantankerous mood, writing about strong subconscious feelings in men, a discussion which leads her directly to an assault on the adult male's "infantile fixation"; and it is no surprise that her examples are of domineering fathers and submissive daughters. In her own words:

. . .but we [the daughters of educated men] . . . become aware at once of some "strong emotion" on your side "arising from some motive below the level of conscious thought" by the ringing of an alarm bell within us; a confused but tumultuous clamour: You shall not, shall not, shall not . . . . The physical symptoms are unmistakable . . . . Intellectually, there is a strong desire to be silent; or to change the conversation; *to drag in, for example, some old family servant, called Crosby, whose dog Rover has died . . . and so evade the issue. . . .*[10]

The year 1913 was a very important one in Virginia Woolf's life; and yet in that year of *The Years,* the author, by dragging in an old family servant called Crosby, has evaded some "strong emotion"; *pargeted* some deep well of feeling.

If we read the fictional extracts of *The Pargiters* text simultaneously with the 1880 section of the published version of *The Years,* we would find numerous changes of date, name, place, viewpoint, and emphasis. Some of the changes are important to the meaning, others technically necessary, still others aesthetically required; and some are there by sheer accident of memory. The most conspicuous change, however, seems to be the character of Abel Pargiter—the generalized Abel Pargiter of the original draft and the particularized Abel Pargiter of the published novel. More specifically, in *The Pargiters,* it appears that *all fathers* together with all their faults have been consolidated and embodied in the person of Abel Pargiter, the Victorian prototype which called forth from Mrs. Woolf a flood of abuse and accusation; whereas the Abel Pargiter of *The Years* appears more a particular man whom Virginia Woolf knew especially well and was especially close to and fascinated by, a particular father she loved for himself and hated for what he represented: an unremitting nineteenth-century patriarch. So that the damaging effects of Abel Pargiter's world on each of his sons and daughters somehow got translated into the accumulated injuries and their effects on Virginia Woolf herself as a result of obedience to the world of Sir Leslie Stephen. Needless to say, subtleties of characterization get lost in so heavily populated a work of fiction. But if one is correct in supposing that a change took place in the person of Colonel Pargiter, then we may suspect that as the book grew, Mrs. Woolf became increasingly

10. *Three Guineas,* New York: Harcourt, Brace and Company, Inc., 1938, pp. 196-97; London: The Hogarth Press (Fifth Impression), 1968, pp. 233-34. The italics are mine, here and throughout the chapter, unless otherwise noted.

aware that she was writing into her novel more about the Stephen family than about "one of those typical English families" she described in her First Essay. The more aware she became that her unconscious mind was exhuming material of a seriously confessional kind, the more she had consciously to be on guard in order to prevent Leslie Stephen from becoming a loathsome ghost upon whom too much blame was being heaped for the wrongs she herself had suffered from childhood. For in writing this novel of fact, she had to deal with long "forgotten" memories which forced her to plumb the subterranean world of emotion; to grope and stumble through darkened nurseries; to re-visit heavy-scented deathrooms; to re-live ancient facts of childhood and adolescence; to re-awaken states of feeling, sometimes benign, more often morbid—and somehow to catch them all in the intricate web of her art. It was the shaping and molding of all these antique and mildewed relics that most ravaged the author; for if the facts in the finished novel were to be stated—all of them verifiable, according to Mrs. Woolf—then the *truth* of those facts had to be phrased poetically, adorned, made eloquent through ellipsis, or eclipsed through synecdoche. However one chooses to state it, those recognizable facts which finally appeared in print had to be pargeted; had in some way to be smoothed over and glossed if they were to be made acceptable.

The episode of Rose Pargiter, aged ten, is as good an example as any to begin with. Nearly molested on her way to Lamley's shop, and on her way back exposed to the genitals of a sexual deviant, the little girl has suffered a trauma which she cannot talk about to anyone, not even to Eleanor; for to mention such a thing in the Victorian Pargiter household is unthinkable. The childhood shock is therefore quietly left to do its pernicious work. To leave the matter at that, however, would be to commit a gross over-simplification; for in the Holograph, Mrs. Woolf has developed the episode, and its effect upon the child, to the extent that the reader is bound to suspect some deeper, more complex intention. It becomes abundantly clear to us that Rose's adoration of her father, her fascination with the "shiny knobs" of his shrivelled right hand, her standing "erect" in imitation of him, her trying to conceal from him the stain on her pinafore—all of this points to a very strong sexual component in her attachment to her father, whose approval as a grown man, she, as a budding female, wants so much. The sexual aspect of Rose's attachment is so powerful that it is totally unacceptable to the child's mind to the extent that under no circumstances can it be admitted to any one else. Rose's thought that "Papa . . . would be very angry with her if he knew what she had seen" is the clearest attestation to the erotic nature of that thought. For she attributes feelings to her father which she alone imagines; and those feelings, were she able to articulate them, would read something like this: "Papa would be very angry if he knew that I'd seen another man's private parts—and not his own. I haven't been loyal to the man who calls me 'grubby little ruffian,' who pinches me by the ear, and who loves me in the way I love him." Thus her exposure to the man's genitals at the pillar box is traumatic for Rose, *not* because of what she has seen, but because that exposure suddenly becomes a *substitute* reality, a shocking actualization of a profoundly forbidden and dimly perceived phantasy; and the guilt generated by its actualization is so great that the episode in which Rose is really an innocent victim becomes transformed and magnified in her ten-year-old mind as *her* crime, a crime so horrible as to be totally choked off from speech.

In this episode, one seemingly insignificant detail has undergone several changes from Holograph to published text: namely, what Rose has stolen out of the house to buy: "There was still time to buy the [*red*][11] squirt upon which she had set her heart. . . . She must have the squirt that night in her bath." Given the sexual nature of Rose's encounter, it is understandable that Mrs. Woolf should delete the "red squirt" and substitute a "fleet of ducks and swans to swim in her bath tonight." In the published text, however, the swans have been eliminated and only the ducks remain. Ducks. Now a box of ducks is certainly not an unusual thing for a child to want. But why have the swans vanished? What possible difference could they make? Any seasoned Woolf reader knows that the author was very adept at performing notorious stunts with the names of people and things. In *The Voyage Out,* for example, aboard the *Euphrosyne* which is carrying Rachel Vinrace to her fatal destination, a conversation is reported in which a certain Captain Richards admitted that the most dreaded of all navigational perils was *Sedgius aquatici,* which (said

11. Italicized words within brackets indicate that the matter was deleted in Holograph.

Richard Dalloway) "'I take to be a kind of duck-weed'." In *Jacob's Room,* Seabrook's ambiguous death is connected with his having "gone out duck-shooting." In "Lives of the Obscure," the essay ends with Laetitia Pilkington enjoying "her duck with death at her heart. . . ." And in *Between the Acts,* Isa imagines herself and old Haines whom she loves "like two swans. . . . But his snow-white breast is circled with a tangle of dirty duckweed."

In the first three instances, the word "duck" is associated with death; and in the fourth, with dirt and dislocated marital affection. If we add to this what we now know from Quentin Bell's account[12] of young Virginia Stephen's sexual confrontations with her much older half-brother, George Duckworth, then young Rose Pargiter's terrifying experience connects with her purchase of ducks in an especially fitting biographic way; for that experience has filled Rose with so much sexual guilt and fear that her emotional life, we later discover, has been consequently stunted. Does it not follow then that, in the fiction, if the man at the pillar-box became the substitute reality for Rose's phantasy of Abel Pargiter, then, in real life, George Duckworth's sexual advances became a substitute reality for young Virginia Stephen's confused and forbidden erotic phantasy of her father, Leslie Stephen?

An important revision associated with Rose's episode on that night of 1880 supports this biographical reading. In the Holograph, Rose, alone in the nursery, has awakened from a bad dream[13] and imagines the "leering face" of the man by the pillar-box. She is terrified. In an effort to get back to sleep, she follows her mother's advice: "Rose counted [*twenty*] ten sheep. Then she opened her eyes. There was the bubbling grey face again. How horrible it was! She shut her eyes & determined that she would count twenty sheep before she would let herself look again. But the sixth sheep wouldn't jump. It stood perfectly still. And the face turned into the mans. . . ." A moment

12. *Virginia Woolf: A Biography,* New York: Harcourt Brace Jovanovich, Inc., 1972, Vol. I, pp. 42-44.

13. There are two sentences in Mrs. Woolf's two-page essay on Lewis Carroll written in 1939 which read almost as though she were recalling Rose's terrifying night in 1880: "Wisps of childhood persist when the boy or girl is a grown man or woman. Childhood returns sometimes by day, *more often by night.*" (*The Moment and Other Essays,* New York and London: Harcourt Brace Jovanovich, A Harvest Book, 1974, pp. 81-82; London: The Hogarth Press [Uniform Edition], 1952, p. 70.)

later, "She thought she heard the man in the passage. He was . . .
snuffing at the door."[14] In the published text, however, there is no
specified number of sheep to count; but for some reason, now it was
"the fifth sheep that would not jump. It turned around and looked at
her. Its long narrow face was grey; its lips moved; it was the face of
the man at the pillar-box, and she was alone with it." The face of the
sheep turning into the face of the man implies, as clearly as in
Virginia Woolf's first novel, a link between bestiality and sexuality.
But why has the author changed the *sixth* sheep which would not
jump to the *fifth* in the finished text? The revision seems entirely
inconsequential. Here, however, some delicate connections may be
inferred—and far from easy to describe. If Mrs. Woolf changed
twenty sheep to ten in the Holograph, she has made the number of
animals correspond to Rose's chronological age. And if the sixth
sheep would not jump, then is it not possible that some kind of
paralysis has set in with that particular sheep—and by analogy at
the age of six? An experience not necessarily in Rose's life, but from
the author's? Again we turn to the Bell *Biography* and find in a letter
to Ethyl Smyth, dated 12 January 1941: "I still shiver with shame at
the memory of my half-brother [George Duckworth, then aged
twenty], standing me on a ledge, aged about 6 or so, exploring my
private parts."[15] That memory must have remained a vivid one for
Mrs. Woolf to have written about it some fifty-three years later. If
there is any truth to these biographic connections, then we may
conjecture that by changing the reluctant sheep from sixth to fifth,
Mrs. Woolf was conscious of what she was doing and therefore
revised the detail in order to cover up her tracks—to obscure some
painful memory of fact.[16]

But however much the author swept the path behind her, we find
footprints of George Duckworth and sexuality in still another place
in the Holograph. This time we have a young man in his twenties
physically entangled with a girl of not six but of sixteen. It is the

14. The transformation of animal to man and its association with sexuality is reminiscent of
Rachel Vinrace's sexual-bestial dream and her later imagining that "barbarian men . . .
stopped to snuffle at her door."

15. Bell, Vol. I, p. 44.

16. If names of people have the significance I am trying to suggest here, it might be useful to
recall a passage in a story called "A Society" (*Monday or Tuesday,* New York: Harcourt,

scene in which Kitty Malone recalls a time "when she was about
sixteen, [*Georgie*] . . . the [*boy*] farmers son, a splendid young man
of twenty-six, had rolled her over in the hay & kissed her & kissed
her." The full name of this "splendid young man" is George Carter,
and the name George—together with the references to ducks in the
earlier section—apparently seemed too obvious to Mrs. Woolf; and
aware that a link might be established between George and ducks,
associated as they are with sex, she changed the name in the published
text to "Alf, the farm hand up at Carter's" and romanticized the
scene merely to a kiss "under the shadow of a haystack when she
was fifteen. . . ."

The name Carter, however, crops up again and assumes a very
oblique function. In the Holograph, we learn that Morris Pargiter is
working on the Evans case; but because his sister Eleanor muddled
up legal matters, "he avoided the Evans case." The issue has no
bearing whatever on anything before it or after it; and one wonders
why Mrs. Woolf has introduced the Evans case to begin with. In *The
Years,* however, the citation of the case is revised to "Evans *v.*
Carter"; and suddenly a new chord is dimly sounded. For the
eroticism associated with George Carter gives the name Evans, to
which Carter is now directly juxtaposed, a new tonality. If we recall
in *Mrs. Dalloway* that Septimus Warren Smith loved the young
officer named Evans whose death in war caused Septimus such
overwhelming homosexual guilt that madness and suicide followed,
then we may guess to what degree in Mrs. Woolf's mind, socially
(and legally) forbidden sexuality was connected with guilt, insanity,
and suicide.

Mrs. Woolf added in the published novel a new character, who
does not appear in the Holograph: she is Mira, by name, Colonel

Brace and Co., 1921, p. 14): "Never have I laughed so much as I did when Rose read her notes
upon 'Honour' and described how she dressed herself as an Ethiopian Prince and gone aboard
one of His Majesty's ships. Discovering the hoax, the Captain visited her. . . ." This of course
is a reference to the "Dreadnought Hoax"; and Rose, the Ethiopian Prince, is none other than
Virginia Stephen disguised as an Abyssinian dignitary. As Quentin Bell says of the idea behind
"A Society": "The wholly ludicrous manner in which first the Navy and then Rose receive
their respective satisfactions occupies no more than five hundred words; but the theme of
masculine honour, of masculine violence and stupidity, of gold-laced masculine pomposity
remained with her [Virginia Woolf] for the rest of her life. She had entered the Abyssinian
adventure for the fun of the thing; but she came out of it with a new sense of the brutality and
silliness of men" (Vol. I, pp. 160-61).

Pargiter's mistress. In *The Years,* we find the "fluffy-looking" Mira in full bloom; she was the Colonel's distraction: "He drew her to him; he kissed her on the nape of the neck; and then the hand that had lost two fingers began to fumble rather lower down where the neck joins the shoulders." (In a later section, it is hinted that the Colonel also had a love affair with his sister-in-law, Eugénie Pargiter.) In the Holograph, "Abel Pargiter had lost three fingers of the right hand in an affray off [*Cos*] [*with*] off the Coromandel Coast which had . . . such momentous results. The muscles [*of the*] had shrunk; & his right hand resembled nothing so much as the [*claw*] shrivelled claw of an aged bird—[*a strange*] an appearance [*that contrasted*] strangely out of keeping with the robust & well developed appearance of his other limbs."

The curious feature of this detail is not so much that Mrs. Woolf has generously restored one of the missing fingers in the published text, but that she has drawn so much attention to this "shrivelled claw." For by the time we have finished reading the novel, we discover that another image has impressed itself upon the mind by sheer sound association and repetition: it is the image of the crimson chair with the gilt claws which appears for the first time in the 1891 section of *The Years.* The chair appears in the scene where the Colonel is visiting Eugénie, and we are reminded of their insinuated adultery and his wish to tell her of Mira. On the evening of the dance in 1907, again there is the "chair with the gilt paws. The chair standing empty, as if waiting for someone, had a look of ceremony. . . ." Later the same evening Eugénie promises one day to tell her daughters the "true story." With Eugénie and Digby dead, the "crimson-and-gilt chair" reappears in the shabby rooms of Sara and Maggie on a day in 1910 when Rose is visiting them. The chair is in view again in 1917 in the flat of Maggie and Renny on the night of the air raid. In the Present Day section, North, looking about Sara's room, sees "a chair—a chair with gilt claws"; and that gilt-clawed chair makes its final appearance when Maggie and Renny are ready to leave with Sara and North for Delia's party. Maggie switched off the light and saw in the "phantom evanescent light only the outlines . . . [of] ghostly apples, ghostly bananas, and the spectre of a chair." A moment earlier, with the light still on, in Maggie's line of vision, "the heavy sensual apples lay side by side with the yellow spotted bananas" on the yellow-stained table-cloth.

Why, we may legitimately ask, has the crimson chair with gilt claws appeared at least seven times in the course of the novel? Is it in any way thematically or structurally functional? And one might legitimately argue that it works as an emblematic reminder of pomp and ceremony; that it represents the masculine, patriarchal world of Victorian England. Virginia Woolf has, however, implied another association. With Colonel Pargiter's right hand resembling a shrivelled claw forced upon our memory, the chair's footing becomes endowed with a double meaning. These claws, the author seems to be saying, are not only the gilt claws of a masculine world of abstract ritual: they are also the *guilty claws* of a particular and a collective father—the guilty claws of a crippling paternalistic world in which human values are subordinated to solemn and sterile abstractions. We have only to review the various contexts in which the chair appears to see that those "gilt claws" are connected with adultery (Eugénie), with marital deception (Mira), with perverted lust and childhood trauma (Rose's masculinity), with war (the air-raid scene), and with diseased and sullied sensuality (spotted bananas on a stained table-cloth). Finally, that chair reaches its terminal resting place in the cheap lodging-house rooms of the physically and emotionally crippled Sara, where the shrivelled claws can do no further harm.[17]

To some readers the connections between the pillar-box episode and ducks, and between the shrivelled claw and the crimson chair may be obvious. However, in a book which has so much of the original text deleted, the importance of pursuing individual images cannot be emphasized enough. For Mrs. Woolf's method has always been very close and very complex; but when she saw the necessity of drastically cutting the novel down in size, she realized too how urgently she had to rely upon the resources of poetry to make her material interlock structurally and interrelate semantically. So that if the reader is to gain access to her meaning, he must discover carefully embedded and deeply enmeshed images and assemble them in a way which reveals something only faintly hinted at on the printed page.

And if, as Virginia Woolf wrote, "The writer's task is to take one

17. The crimson chair is a very good example of Mrs. Woolf's statement that "The writer's task is to take one thing and let it stand for twenty: a task of danger and difficulty; . . ." ("Life and the Novelist," *New York Herald Tribune,* 7 November 1926; reprinted in *Granite and Rainbow,* p. 45.)

thing and let it stand for twenty," then it is extremely difficult for the Woolf critic to be convincing—and extremely easy (if he dares to take great risks) for his reader to accuse him either of critical lunacy or of possessing an overheated imagination. This is said from the unshakable conviction that the published text of *The Years* has poured into it material so complicated, so edited, and so glossed, that whichever way the novel is read—whether as pure fiction or as pargeted autobiography—its wholeness is not easily perceived, and its potential meaning never wholly underdstood. Nevertheless, it was possible to proceed on the assumption that the published version of the novel would still throw into sharpest relief those trials and errors which one inevitably finds in Holograph volumes where the writer's first attempts to concretize a private vision are unabashedly revealed.

In an effort to avoid "great risks," an attempt has been made to approach the novel by tracing four names introduced in the 1880 portion of the Holograph. They are Herrick and Campion, Antigone, and Charles Stewart Parnell. Of the many names in the text there were to choose from, these seemed to illustrate best the way Virginia Woolf utilized them to erect the complex scaffolding of the novel's visible structure as fiction, as well as to support its barely discernible sub-structure as autobiography.

Tracing these names will allow us to see how Herrick and Campion are linked with Catullus, and hence to Peggy and her relationship to her father Morris; how Antigone connects Eleanor to both Sara and Delia; and how Parnell aligns himself with Colonel Pargiter while he obliquely and simultaneously functions as a figure against whom the feelings of Eleanor and Delia toward their father may be compared. Because of the novel's intricate design, it will not be possible to deal with these "threads" independently or consecutively: they will weave in and out of the discussion until they converge in the Present Day section, the novel's grand and complexly orchestrated finale.

The Years, read as fiction, conveys an oppressive picture of life in general and of the Pargiter family in particular. In the opening of the 1880 section, Colonel Pargiter is at his club while at home his wife is "dying; but she would not die. She was better today; would be worse tomorrow . . . and so it went on" (*5;4*).[18] We learn also that he keeps

---

18. The unitalicized page number in parentheses following each quotation refers to the

a mistress called Mira. At Abercorn Terrace, the Pargiter family are at tea—all are severe, irritable, and restless. Delia in particular is impatient for her mother to die. Life inside the house is filled with discordance; and outside, with Rose's terrifying episode, life reeks with lust and perversion. Late that evening, Mrs. Pargiter finally dies. With time suspended at Abercorn Terrace, we are moved to Oxford where Edward Pargiter is reading *The Antigone,* sipping wine, flattering his vanity with Gibbs, and provoking jealousy in his homosexual friend, Ashley. At Oxford we also meet Edward's cousin, Kitty Malone, with whom he *thinks* he is in love. However, the big, shy Kitty who is constrained by her managerial mother loves and is loved in return by her teacher, Miss Lucy Craddock. The section ends with Mrs. Pargiter's funeral. (In Holograph, the 1880 section ["Chapter One"] ends with the name of Charles Stewart Parnell, mentioned for the first time.)

In the 1891 section, Edward is an Oxford don; Morris is married and a barrister; and Delia, who idolized Parnell, has left her family to work for some political cause. Now, with Eleanor and the Colonel dominating the scene, new emotional intensities are marshalled in. Eleanor, who has remained at home, lives with her father with whom she "got on extremely well; they were almost like brother and sister" (92;97). But the brother-and-sister relationship becomes highly questionable a page or two later when Eleanor is at Lamley's to buy a birthday gift for her cousin, Maggie Pargiter; for in the rush of the moment, Eleanor makes a very significant slip about whom the gift is for: "'For my niece—I mean cousin. Sir Digby's little girl,' Eleanor brought out." Here is Mrs. Woolf's way of telling us that Eleanor now thinks of herself not as *Miss* but as *Mrs.* Pargiter.[19] And no time is lost in reinforcing that idea; for when Eleanor returns home with

American hardbound edition published by Harcourt, Brace and Co. Inc., 1937; the italicized number refers to The Hogarth Press edition (Fifth Impression), 1965.

Because *The Years* is a heavily populated "domestic" novel, it may be useful to list the principal characters of the Pargiter family. The first generation is comprised of Abel and Rose Pargiter and Digby (Abel's brother) and Eugénie Pargiter. In the second generation are Morris, Eleanor, Edward, Milly, Delia, Martin (Robert in Holograph), and Rose—the children of Rose and Abel Pargiter; Maggie and Sara (Elvira in Holograph) are the daughters of Eugénie and Digby Pargiter. The third generation is comprised of Peggy and North Pargiter—the children of Morris (and Celia) Pargiter.

Structurally, the novel is composed of eleven sections: "1880," "1891," "1907," "1908," "1910," "1911," "1913," "1914," "1917," "1918," and "Present Day."

19. It is important to notice how this single brief scene has been endowed with multiple

the gift, her father, who has been considering telling her about Mira, thinks:

No, no. . . . For some reason when he saw her he realised that he could not tell her. And after all . . . she has her own life to live. A spasm of jealousy passed through him (104;*110*).

The "spasm of jealousy" gives us ample cause to wonder if we have between Eleanor and the Colonel another instance of *emotional incest* as was hinted at between Rachel Vinrace and her father, boldly insinuated between Katherine Hilbery and her father, and given a fictional twist in the relationship between Betty Flanders and her Captain Barfoot, who, like the Colonel, was missing two fingers.

But Eleanor, who at twenty-two, "had her dreams, her plans" (31;*32*), is now about thirty-three, a spinster committed to charity work. The sunflower on her terra-cotta plaque, a "symbol of her girlish sentiment," now "amused her grimly" (101;*107*). With that symbol of youthful sentiment "now . . . cracked," we understand why she felt that "She did not exist; she was not anybody at all" (95;*101*). (Nor is it a coincidence that in 1911, when Eleanor is visiting Morris's house, one of the three books left on her bedside table is *The Diary of a Nobody*.)[20]

In the 1907 section, Maggie has gone to a dance. Sara, who was crippled as a baby, must remain at home and lie still in bed. In this scene, which according to Mrs. Woolf was to be the turning point of the book, two important pieces of information are recorded. The first is Sara's reading Edward Pargiter's translation of *The Antigone*,

---

significance. By mentioning Lamley's shop again, Mrs. Woolf has pulled into memory the entire grim evening of 1880 with Rose's pillar-box episode outside, as well as the dusky atmosphere inside the Pargiter household, with everyone expecting, hoping for, the last death rattles from Mrs. Pargiter's sickroom.

20. In the Holograph (Vol. IV, dated 3 August 1933) we find ". . . a novel, a poem, & a Biography if she shd wish to read." These are later changed to *Lamb's Tales from Shakespeare, Queen Victoria's Journal of her Life in the Highlands,* and *Diary of a Nobody.* Still later, "Mansfield Park fell to the floor. She [Eleanor] blew out her candle & fell asleep." Although it is perfectly possible that Mrs. Woolf's choice of George Grossmith's satiric *The Diary of a Nobody* was deliberate, the context in which it appears in the 1911 section suggests that on a different level of meaning, Mrs. Woolf had in mind Jules Romains's *The Death of a Nobody* (translated *in 1911* by Desmond MacCarthy and Sydney Waterlow) whose central character, Jacques Godard was—as Eleanor was to become—a *collective* being. (The emotional suppressions of Fanny Price and her eventual marriage make Jane Austen's *Mansfield Park* a significant choice of novel for Eleanor to be reading in this earlier version of the book.)

the Antigone who "was buried alive. The tomb was a brick mound. There was just room for her to lie straight out. Straight out in a brick tomb . . ." (136;*146*).[21] The second takes place after the dance with Eugénie Pargiter in the bedroom with her two daughters:

"And the flower's on the floor, and everything so untidy," she said. She picked up the flower that Maggie had dropped and put it to her lips (140;*150*).

Recall that in the 1891 section, when Abel Pargiter paid a visit to give Maggie a necklace for her birthday, he brought a flower to Eugénie.

"How very good of you!" she said, and. . .then did what he had so often seen her do with a flower—put the stalk between her lips. The movements charmed him as usual (119;*127*).

Shortly after this scene, when Digby half-jokingly rebukes Maggie for playing in her best clothes, "Maggie made no answer. Her eyes were riveted on the camellia that her mother wore in the front of her dress. She went up and stood looking at her" (216;*135*).[22] Returning to the 1907 section, we hear Sara asking her mother for a story. Eugénie's reply is: "I'll tell you the true story one of these days. . ." (143;*153*).

"Yes, yes, yes," said Eugénie. "I'll tell you the true story another time. . . . She kissed them both quickly and went out of the room.

"She won't tell us," said Maggie. . . .She spoke with some bitterness (144;*154*).

If we move ahead to the 1914 section, we hear Martin, at the Round Pond, in a hushed conversation with Maggie:

"My father," he said suddenly, but softly, "had a lady. . . .She called him 'Bogy.'" And he told her the story [of Mira]. . . .
    "Was he in love," Martin asked, "with your mother?"
    She was looking at the gulls. . . .His question seemed to sink through what she was seeing; then suddenly it reached her.
    "Are we brother and sister?" she asked; and laughed out loud (246-47;*265-66*).

One wonders why the question of an adulterous relationship between

---

21. This passage has been singled out because it is again reminiscent of the confining tunnel in *The Voyage Out* which appears in Rachel's dream and later in the delirium just prior to her death.

22. In the Holograph (Vol. IV, which ends on 22 November 1933), we find Bobby (who becomes Martin in *The Years*) telling Maggie about his father's mistress, with Maggie's reply: "[*So*] I guessed that when he gave me a necklace once."

the Colonel and Eugénie was ever introduced at all; for it continues from the 1907 section into the 1908 when (with Eugénie and Digby now both dead) Martin comes to visit Abercorn Terrace and looks at his mother's portrait:

In the course of the past few years it had ceased to be his mother; it had become a work of art. *But it was dirty.*

There used to be a *flower* in the grass, he thought, peering into a *dark corner*: but now there was nothing but dirty brown paint (149;*160*).[23]

Moments later when Martin is talking to Eleanor, the subject of Eugénie is brought up:

"What a pleasure, Martin! what a pleasure!" she would say. What had her private life been, he wondered—her love affairs? She must have had them—obviously, obviously.

"Wasn't there some story," he began, "about a letter?"
He wanted to say, Didn't she have an affair with somebody?. . .
"Yes," she said, "there was a story—"
[. . . .]
"Papa," she said (153;*164-65*).[24]

In this section, Rose also makes an appearance. "She had been holding meetings in the North"; but she did not come to Abercorn Terrace for tea: "'I want a bath,' Rose repeated, 'I'm dirty'" (156;*168*). We learn for the first time that as a child, in a fit of rage and frustration, Rose had "locked herself into the bathroom with a knife and cut her wrist" (158;*170*). The section ends with:

"What awful lives children live!" he [Martin] said, waving his hand at her. . . . "Don't they Rose?"
"Yes," said Rose "And they can't tell anybody," she added (159;*171*).

The thread of what children "can't tell anybody" is woven into the next section—the spring of 1910 with Rose at luncheon with Sara and Maggie. During the meal, Rose remembers when she asked if she could

23. It is possible that Mrs. Woolf wanted the reader to see the death of Eugénie and the disappearance of the "flower" from the picture as that "dark corner"—the affair between Eugénie and Abel Pargiter—which sullied his marriage to Rose.

24. The brackets are mine; and the two sentences they contain are: "But here the electric bell rang sharply. She stopped." Here is another illustration of Mrs. Woolf's technique of camouflaging a highly revealing sequence of utterances. For if the intervening sentences were removed in the actual text, we would have Eleanor saying in effect: "Yes, there was a story; and the affair Eugénie had was with Papa."

go to Lamley's in 1880. "And for some reason she [Rose] wanted to talk about her past; to tell them something about herself that she had never told anybody—something hidden" (166-67;*179*).[25] We know that that "something hidden" is the sexual shock of Rose's childhood which she could not tell anyone about, which filled her with guilt, made men threatening, and made her "more like a man than a woman" (170;*183*). The section ends with shouts in the street that "The King's dead!" (191;*245)*

And in 1911, Colonel Abel Pargiter is also dead. So for Eleanor, now past a half-century in age, "This year everything was different" (195;*209*). Having spent her life attending her father, she now is left with no attachment to anyone and with nothing to do. Her visit to the Morris Pargiter family governs the section; and Mrs. Woolf, through innuendo, provides us with additional information about Eleanor and her place in the novel.

One of the guests is Sir William Whatney, whom Eleanor knew thirty years earlier when she used to call him Dubbin. "Somebody had once praised her eyes" (198;*213*), Eleanor thinks, looking in the mirror; and at dinner, she looked at Sir William and thought: "There were relics of the old Dubbin if one half-shut one's eyes. She half-shut her eyes. Suddenly she remembered—it was *he* who had praised her eyes" (201;*215-16*).[26] Later, on the terrace, Peggy secretly asks her mother: "'Did father say Sir William was in love with her?'. . .'Oh, I don't know about that,' said Celia. 'But I wish they could have married. I wish she had children of her own'" (203;*218*).

The most significant scene in the section, however, is that of Eleanor alone that night in her room. In it some crucial points subtly converge. Eleanor, now a fatherless spinster of fifty-five, hears Sir William in the adjoining room; he is the man she might have married, the man to whom she owed "—that moment which had been more than pleasure. . ." (212;*227*). On the bedside table, three books have been left for her. The first is *The Diary of a Nobody,* and the title recalls her thought of 1891, when "She did not exist; she was not any

---

25. "The impressions of childhood," wrote Virginia Woolf, "are those that last longest and cut deepest." (*The Common Reader: First Series,* New York: Harcourt, Brace and World, Inc., A Harvest Book, 1955, p. 89; London: The Hogarth Press [Tenth Impression], 1962, p. 121.)

26. The emphasis is Virginia Woolf's.

body at all." The second volume is *Ruff's Tour of Northumberland,* and we think of Rose, her "rough" sister, who was last touring Northumberland to hold meetings, who was apprehended by the police for throwing a brick. But Rose also brings to mind the terrible experience which Eleanor somehow "absorbed" on that night in 1880:

"I saw. . ." Rose began. She made a great effort to tell her the truth; to tell her about the man at the pillar-box. "I saw. . ." she repeated. . . .

"I saw," Eleanor repeated, as she shut the nursery door. "I saw. . . ." What had she seen? Something horrible, something hidden. But what? There it was, hidden behind her strained eyes. . . .A blankness came over her. Where am I?. . .She seemed to be alone in the midst of nothingness; yet must descend, must carry her burden—(42-43;*43-44*).

It is the third book Eleanor picks up—a volume of Dante—and in it she reads the lines:

For by so many more there are who say 'ours'
So much the more of good doth each possess.

And here the novel begins to take a strangely paradoxical turn. For Eleanor who has so often said "ours"—who once had her dreams, who refused marriage for the Colonel—feels that although Sir William's "life was over; hers was beginning" (213;*229*). Her thought strikes a sombre note, however. For now free of her father, she only begins her life in her life's decline.

A grey cloud of gloom lours on the horizon all through the 1913 section; and the brilliant May day of the 1914 section is full of ugliness, hypocrisy, and contempt. In the winter of 1917, Nicholas, the last major character we meet, is a dinner guest of Maggie and Renny. Eleanor and Sara are also at the gathering. During dinner, for Eleanor,

Things seemed to have lost their skins;. . .even the chair with the gilt claws, at which she was looking, seemed porous; it seemed to radiate out some warmth, some glamour, as she looked at it.

"I remember that chair," she said to Maggie. "And your mother. . ." she added (287;*310*).

But suddenly a siren wails. An air-raid interrupts. Death above their heads is rampant. The civilized world is being destroyed. And the crimson chair "lost its radiance. . ." (288;*311*).[27] All five of them

27. In the Holograph (Vol. V, ending on 27 February 1934) the crimson chair is not mentioned at all. In its place, we have Eleanor saying something which was edited out of the

retreat to the cellar where they finish the meal in silence. With the air-raid over, Mrs. Woolf adds to an already charged scene two grim strokes of irony: the first is Sara, physically and emotionally maimed, raising her glass with a flourish: " 'So let's drink a health—Here's to the New World!' " (292;*315*); the second is Nicholas " 'who ought to be in prison' " (297;*321*) because he is homosexual, wishing to improve " 'The soul—the whole being'. . . . 'It wishes to expand; to adventure; to form—new combinations?' " (296;*319*)

The Present Day section is the longest and most intricate of the novel. It is divided roughly into four parts: the scenes prior to Delia's party, the party upstairs, the supper downstairs, and the dawn of the new day. With its full cast of characters, the section reverberates with ancient echoes, heard now in the present, giving everything in the past new and enlarged meanings. It is virtually a fictional palimpsest. It is also Virginia Woolf at her most difficult. The reader is challenged to hold in memory fragments of talk, slivers of thought, half-forgotten images—and through them to connect effects in the present with causes in a very distant past. If we are successful in making these nexus, difficult and tenuous as they are, we begin to sense the ghost of Colonel Pargiter haunting every page of the novel's massive conclusion.

In one part of London, North Pargiter is dining with Sara; and in another part, Eleanor and Peggy, now a doctor, are on their way to Delia's party. Peggy prompts Eleanor to talk about her past; and as they pass various parts of the city, doors of memory are flung open, and we are allowed to see just enough to re-create those points in

---

published text: " 'I was wondering if it was the house [Maggie's and Renny's] my father used to come to' she said. 'It was this street; it may have been this very house; where Mira lived.' " The fact that in the published novel the crimson chair *replaces* this speech seems to me an indisputable confirmation of the symbolic function I attributed to the chair in my earlier discussion of it. Even if the reader misses the significance of the chair in its present setting, Mrs. Woolf insists on making it clear that Maggie's and Renny's house is indeed the very one where Mira once lived. In the 1880 section: "But when he [Abel Pargiter] came to Westminster he stopped. He did not like this part of the business at all. Every time he approached the little street under the huge bulk of the Abbey . . . he paused . . . and then walked very sharply to Number Thirty and rang the bell" (6;*4-5*). In the 1917 section: ". . .'Westminster must be there' [thought Eleanor]. . . . She was dining with Renny and Maggie, who lived in one of the obscure little streets under the shadow of the Abbey. . . . At last the number thirty, the number she was looking for, shone out. She knocked and rang at the same moment. . ." (279;*301*).

Eleanor's past which have made her the person she is. They pass
Abercorn Terrace, for example, and Eleanor murmurs " '. . .the
pillar box'. . ." (332;*357*); and again we are in 1880 recalling Rose's
horrifying experience which Eleanor has somehow assimilated. Then
another mnemonic door of the past opens with Delia "standing in
the middle of the room; Oh, my God! Oh, my God! she was saying. . ." (335;*361*); but Eleanor is reluctant to pursue this memory,
and we realize why when we turn back to the original scene:

"Look here, Delia," said Eleanor. . ."you've only got to wait. . ." She
meant but she could not say it, "until Mama dies" (19;*19*).

This memory brings us to the relationship between Delia and
Eleanor; and the threads which join them are the most difficult to
assemble, because they also link Colonel Pargiter to Parnell in such a
way as to suggest those very similarities between the two men which
point up emotional differences between the two sisters, differences
which have mattered greatly in the choice of life each has made.

From the previous passage, there is no doubt that Eleanor, like
Delia, wants her mother to die. Nor is there any doubt that she is
prepared—perhaps unwholesomely willing—to assume the role of
mistress of the household; to assume possession of her mother's
things, even the writing table, which will "be my table now, she
thought. . ." (34;*35*); and there is certainly no question of the deep
attachment between father and daughter.

Delia's attachment to her father is also made clear in the 1880
section: "She was his favourite daughter" (13;*13*) we are told; and
she has also a strong tendency to identify herself with him. However,
Delia is vigorously allied to another man whose name is mentioned
only once—at the end of "Chapter One" of the Holograph. That
man is Charles Stewart Parnell, the Irish nationalist leader. And Mrs.
Woolf, by juxtaposing her material in two instances, insinuates a
certain congruence between Parnell and Pargiter. The first has to do
with public freedom:

Somewhere there's beauty, Delia thought, somewhere there's freedom, and
somewhere, she thought, *he* [Parnell] is —wearing his white flower. . . .But
a stick [Pargiter] grated in the hall (12;*11*).[28]

The second has to do with private freedom:

28. The emphasis is Virginia Woolf's.

But I will not think of him [Parnell], she thought, seeing a tall man who stood beside her on a platform and raised his hat, until it's over. She fixed her eyes upon her father (86;*91*).

In 1891, with the placards announcing Parnell's death, Eleanor "must go tell Delia. . . .Delia had cared passionately. What was it she used to say—flinging out of the house, leaving them all for the Cause, for this man? Justice, Liberty?" (114;*121*) She goes to the deteriorated square where Delia lives and finds not Delia, but only "Jugs of milk with bills under them. . ." (114;*122*).

At that same moment in 1891, Colonel Pargiter is on his way to Eugénie's. Passing "a certain street [Mira's] where he used to stop and look about him. . . .But a man in public life can't afford to do those things. . . ." Pargiter hears of Parnell's death and thinks:

—that unscrupulous adventurer—that agitator who had done all the mischief. . . .Some feeling connected with his own daughter [Delia] here formed in him; he could not say exactly what, but it made him frown. Anyway, he's dead now. . . (116;*123-24*).

Later, when Eugénie asks the Colonel about Delia, he "at once lost his affability. He looked glum and formidable, like an old bull with his head down. . ." (123;*132*).

These threads begin to merge during the cab ride to Delia's party. Eleanor and Peggy are talking about North, of whom Peggy is very critical: "He says we talk of nothing but money and politics. . . ."

"Does he?" she [Eleanor] said. "But then. . ." A newspaper placard [her memory of the placard announcing Parnell's death], with large black letters, seemed to finish her sentence for her.[29] They were approaching the square in which Delia lived. . . .She looked at the metre which had mounted rather high. The man was going the long way round (337;*363*)

just as the "cab was going the long way round. . ." (117;*124*)—the cab carrying Pargiter to Eugénie in 1891 on the day of Parnell's death.

Add to this a passage from the final scene of the novel in which Delia's Irish husband, Patrick, recalls their younger days; and

Delia smiled as if some romance, her own or another's, had been recalled to her.

29. In the 1891 section, Eleanor "looked at the placard. . . .'Death' was written in very large black letters" (113;*120*).

"And I. . ." Eleanor began. She stopped. She saw an empty milk jug and leaves falling (433;*468*).

Here finally is Delia's dream of Parnell—and freedom—linked to Eleanor's finding only an empty milk jug at Delia's door on the day of his death.

Considered together, these passages encourage us to draw certain inferences. Reflect that Eleanor in 1891, about thirty-three years old, has had to refuse Whatney's love, has abandoned her dreams and sacrificed personal freedom—all to stay with a father who still had "spasms of jealousy" when he thought that "She's got her own affairs to think about. . . ." But what affairs has she had to think about while chained to the adulterous old gentleman? We may well imagine the Colonel's becoming "glum and formidable" at the mention of Delia, who escaped the male tyranny of Abercorn Terrace to seek liberty and justice in Parnell's cause; to renounce the proprieties of a patriarchal society in search of personal freedom. In this male-dominated world, Eleanor, remaining the lady, is forced to bend to its yoke; whereas Delia, tearing off the label of lady, keeps alive the woman by refusing the well-fed but suffocating life well-to-do fathers can provide their daughters.

The choice of Parnell as Delia's hero prompts a second inference. Historical accounts of one of Ireland's most influential and revolutionary leaders tell us that one of the contributing factors to Parnell's downfall was the discovery of his illicit love affair with the wife of a certain Captain O'Shea, a liaison which began in 1881, and created a scandal which was to end only at his death on 6 October 1891. Thus the link between Pargiter and Parnell is the link of adultery of which both men were guilty; and of special interest is the fact that the years of Pargiter's affair with Mira very nearly coincide with those of Parnell and Kitty O'Shea.

Once at the party, we wonder why Mrs. Woolf chose Delia as hostess, and why Peggy suddenly occupies so conspicuous a role in the final section. Here we must follow carefully the party's complicated development. Shortly after arriving, Peggy sees her father Morris come in: "And what's this?. . ."

for the sight of her father in his worn shoes had given her a direct spontaneous feeling. This sudden warm spurt? she asked, examining it. She watched him cross the room. His shoes always affected her strangely. Part sex; part pity. . . .can one call this "Love"? (351;*378*)

Minutes later, in a brief exchange with her uncle, Martin:

"But you," he said. . . "your generation I mean—you miss a great deal
. .you miss a great deal," he repeated. She waited.
"Loving only your own sex" he added (356;*384*).

Still later, one of Peggy's former teachers has praised her to Delia,
who tells Morris of it. "There, said Peggy, that's pleasure. The nerve
down her spine seemed to tingle as the praise reached her father . . .
pleasure thrilled the spine. . . . Her father brushed her shoulder as he
dropped his hand; but neither of them spoke" (362;*390-91*).

But Peggy, a professional woman, a doctor, is also a lonely, bitter,
and disillusioned human being. When the dancing begins, she
retreats to a bookcase and randomly reads from a volume the words
which express her feelings precisely: *"La médiocrité de l'univers
m'étonne et me révolte. . .la petitesse de toutes choses m'emplit de
dégoût. . .la pauvreté des êtres humains m'anéantit"* (383;*413*). In
this spirit, Peggy attacks her brother for the pettiness of marrying,
having children, writing little books to make money " 'instead of
living. . .living differently, differently' " (391;*421*). With these
words, she sinks back and thinks of the evening in 1911 on the terrace
when she asked her mother about Eleanor's sacrificing Whatney
because of her father; and there is a suggestion that that memory is
somehow connected with her present dissatisfaction and her
insistence upon "living differently." For shortly after, Peggy looks
at her brother and thinks: "He'll tie himself up with a red-lipped girl,
and become a drudge. He must, and I can't. . . .No, I've a sense of
guilt always. . . .I shall pay for it, I shall pay for it. . . .She would
have no children. . ." (396;*427*).

This passage, at first glance straightforward, upon second glance,
becomes highly ambiguous. Does Peggy mean that because of her
guilt she cannot tie herself up with some "red-lipped girl"? Or does
she mean that she cannot marry and have children, because she has
broken from the traditional world to make a career for herself? The
Holograph (Vol. VII, dated 5 August 1934) gives a sharper picture of
Mrs. Woolf's original conception of Peggy:

Her father had come in. Now that was odd she added; making another entry
in her [mental] notebook; . . .love of father & daughter. Spontaneous.
Rather suspect, all the same. Of mixed origin. Do I love my father sexually?
She looked at Morris. No: there was a great deal of pity in it. Why does one
always notice one's father's shoes? she asked.

Later in the same Holograph Volume, Peggy is described as a woman "who had never been in love; for whom the usual relation between men & women was such a boring fact." In the published text, however, Virginia Woolf, by omitting so much of the holograph material, forces us to deduce Peggy from very minute clues. So that to understand what Mrs. Woolf is hinting at, we must leave Peggy for a moment and turn to her brother North, who despised the idea of marriage, who, still smarting from Peggy's attack, goes to a bookcase and reads from a little volume:

nox est perpetua una dormienda.

The line comes from Poem V by Catullus, the great admirer and sometimes imitator of Sappho; and if we look at the five lines preceding this one, we will find a larger allusive insinuation:

> Vivamus, mea Lesbia, atque amemus,
> Rumoresque senum severiorum
> Omnes unius aestimemus assis.
> Soles occidere et redire possunt:
> Nobis cum semel occidit brevis lux,
> Nox est perpetua una dormienda.
>
> My Lesbia, let us live and love,
> And forget the gossip of censorious old men.
> Suns may set and rise again,
> But when our own brief light descends
> We must sleep one endless night.[30]

This allusion to Catullus is noteworthy, because in the Fourth Essay (Holograph, Vol. I), Mrs. Woolf wrote that Edward Pargiter "imitated Sappho or Theocritus; not Herrick or Campion" and left it at that. In the published text, they are not mentioned at all. But the very fact that Herrick and Campion are named in Holograph suggests that Mrs. Woolf had something in mind which was far more important than the poets Edward should imitate. For if we turn to Herrick, we immediately come upon his poem "To Sappho" based on Catullus V:

30. Translation is mine.

> Let us now take time and play,
> Love, and live here while we may;
> Drink rich wine; and make good cheere,
> While we have our being here:
> For, once dead, and laid i'th grave,
> No return from thence we have.

And in Campion, we find the first verse of a song, also based on Catullus V:

> My sweetest Lesbia, let us live and love,
> And, though the sager sort our deedes reprove,
> Let us not way them: heav'ns great lamps doe dive
> Into their west, and strait again revive,
> But, soone as once set is our little light,
> Then must we sleepe one ever-during night.

That Catullus was frequently translated and imitated among seventeenth-century poets comes as no news to anyone. But that Mrs. Woolf should mention Herrick and Campion in the Holograph and delete them from the published text, leaving the reader with only the last line of Catullus's poem, indicates the extent to which she deliberately withheld overt meaning; deliberately made it inaccessible except through fragmentation and innuendo. For the allusion to Catullus (and indirectly to Sappho) strongly implies that Peggy's "living differently" is to be interpreted as living the Sapphist life—or any other life which involves loving another—because, finally, "We must sleep one endless night." (There is of course the homosexual Nicholas on the scene; and his presence together with his love for the asexual Sara might be taken as a testament of what "living differently" means.) However, introducing Catullus and his love for Clodia, whom he called Lesbia, does lead us, through Peggy, back to Eleanor. And here begins the most complex criss-crossing of half-memory, literary allusion, litotic reference, and anacoluthic statement.

Now it is Sara who asks Eleanor to talk about her past. But "I haven't got one, she thought. . . .I've only the present moment. . ." (366;*395*); and a long train of memories begins: the cracked sunflower, the meeting-room blotting paper with the hole radiating spokes from it—"My life's been other people's lives, Eleanor thought

—my father's; Morris's . . .'' (367;*396*). North then looks at her and thinks back to 1911:

She had never married. Why not? he wondered. Sacrificed to the family, he supposed—old Grandpapa without any fingers. Then some memory came back to him of a terrace, a cigar and William Whatney. Was that not her tragedy, that she had loved him? . . . (372;*401*)

All of these joined memories—the cracked sunflower; the hole radiating spokes; 1911, the year of Abel Pargiter's death; William Whatney, who admired Eleanor's eyes—taken together, echo lines from Thomas Moore (1779-1852):

> Lesbia hath a beaming eye,
>> But no one knows for whom it beameth.

And

> No, the heart that has truly lov'd never forgets,
>> But as truly loves on to the close,
> As the sun-flower turns on her god, when he sets,
> The same look which she turn'd when he rose.[31]

But Eleanor falls into a deep slumber, and "this sleep, this momentary trance, in which the candles had lolled and lengthened themselves, had left her with nothing but a feeling ["a feeling of happiness"]; a feeling, not a dream" (381;*411*). In its present context, the candle in some strange way seems to connect not only with the candle she carried from Rose's room on the night of Mrs. Pargiter's death, but also with the candle in her room at Morris's in 1911, the room adjoining Whatney's. It was on that night in 1911 that Eleanor had read from Dante's *Purgatorio*. So that by enacting Dante's lines, but saying "ours" instead of "mine," Eleanor has been made the scapegoat of the Pargiter family, the repository of all its burdens since her mother's death in 1880; and since her father's death, she has become the solitary traveller who cannot speak of parched deserts or of the parchments of memory which have made up her life, the life "I can't tell anybody" (367;*396*).

---

31. To my knowledge, Mrs. Woolf never published anything about Thomas Moore; but there can be no doubt that she had read his work, if for no other reason than for his association with Byron. See especially: *Prose and Verse, Humorous, Satirical and Sentimental, by Thomas Moore, with suppressed passages from the Memoirs of Lord Byron* (1878). Also, there are numerous lines in "The Fire-Worshippers" section of *Lalla Rookh* which sound remarkably like Eleanor's "girlish sentiment" over the cracked sunflower plaque.

North Pargiter—true to the pargeter's spirit—looks at Eleanor and wonders: *"Why do we hide all the things that matter?"* And here Virginia Woolf, again as pargeting novelist, introduces through classical allusion an aspect of Eleanor we have not seen before. Now in her seventies, Eleanor is reading *The Antigone;* and Edward recites in Greek one of Antigone's lines which in translation reads:

"It is not in your hate, that I share, but in your love."

But Edward stops here: *he does not recite Creon's reply:*

"Go, then, to the shades of the dead; and if you love, love there. As long as I am alive, no woman will domi-nate me."³²

Taken together, these lines are eloquent; for they imply that throughout her life, Eleanor has lived in a world where a woman shall not master a man: Abel Pargiter's world. In that world mastered by the patriarch—composed now only of fractured and faded memory—Eleanor experienced the only real love which has survived over the years—her love for her father. In this light, we can interpret a later waking scene, when again she is filled with happiness:

She shut her hands on the coins she was holding, and again she was suffused with a feeling of happiness. Was it because *this* had survived—this keen sensation. . .and the other thing, the solid object—she saw an ink-corroded walrus—had vanished? (426;*460*)

"This," the feeling of happiness, placed side by side the coins she is clasping takes us back to 1891 when Eleanor, watching her father fumbling for coins, "felt the old childish feeling that his pockets were bottomless silver mines from which half-crowns could be dug eternally" (106;*112*). And the "vanished" walrus points not only to her "vanished" mother (and her mother's possession which became Eleanor's on the night of Mrs. Pargiter's death) but also obliquely to "That old white walrus" (395;*426*), William Whatney, whom Eleanor deserted for a deeper and stronger love, a love very much like that of Antigone for Oedipus in his last years. And Virginia Woolf adds one master stroke in Eleanor's thought that "For her too there would be the endless night. . . .a very long dark tunnel" (427-28;*461-62*). For we see, finally, in Eleanor the "endless night" of

32. Unpublished translation by Flora Ginalis.

Catullus's Lesbia *in union with* the "long dark tunnel" of Sophocles's Antigone.

"Your choice was to live," says Antigone to her sister Ismene, "mine was to die." And this, curiously (and paradoxically, because Ismene chose to obey Creon's edict) brings us to Delia who also chose to live. Her choice, however, meant abandoning the law-ridden Pargiter household; and like Ismene, who appears nowhere else in ancient literature, Delia has been locked out of the novel until its end. But it was Delia in 1880 who openly wished for her mother's death; who loved her father, but loved freedom and justice more; who courageously broke the laws of that brutal male-dominated society and escaped its tyranny. Delia thus represents all that Eleanor would not or could not be. Her filial love has been properly modified and adjusted. So that even now, herself in old age, Delia has the life-blood to gather together her family and friends, to serve them soup in mugs, to decorate office rooms with cheap roses, to pour her claret from a jug into cheap glasses. She has banished rigid decorum from her life and lives as she chooses. And so, just as Delia has buried her past, Eleanor is buried by it.[33] That Delia should be the hostess in the Present Day then seems appropriate—for she is *alive* in every sense of the word.

But why Peggy plays so prominent a role in the Present Day can only be answered in part, because too much of the material in Holograph has been eclipsed. If we look at Peggy against the figures of Eleanor and Delia, however, she becomes a partial amalgam of the two sisters. *Like* Eleanor, Peggy's attachment to her father is abnormally strong; but *like* Delia, she has left her family to make an independent life for herself. Here similarities end, however. For *unlike* Eleanor who has diminished her life for the sake of others, Peggy has aggrandized hers in the labor of *sustaining* life; and *unlike* Delia who is the mother of three, Peggy (who would have no children) cannot *create* new life. Consequently, she seems to be an unfinished product of the present; that is, she is neither wholly free from the past, nor entirely free for the future. Figuratively, she is a

33. It is no coincidence that Peggy, after asking Eleanor if she was "suppressed," returns to a childhood memory of "her grandfather . . . and a *long dark drawing-room*" (335;*361*); while Eleanor later thinks of death as "a very *long dark tunnel*." For the description equates the Pargiter household with Antigone's tomb.

variorum of yesterday, with variations for tomorrow. As such, Peggy represents the one thematic utterance which Mrs. Woolf expresses through Eleanor: "Does everything then come over again a little differently? . . .If so, is there a pattern; a theme, recurring. . .half remembered, half foreseen?" (369;*398*)

But something has gone wrong. We have spent the night in a mausoleum filled with half-remembered ghosts and recurring memories. We have, in image after image, re-visited the Hell of the past. The dawn of a new day is approaching, and the author relegates to Nicholas the proposal of a toast " 'to the human race. The human race. . .which now in its infancy, may it grow to maturity!' " (426;*459-60*). Is Nicholas, whose homosexuality condemns him socially, the likeliest person to usher in the new day? If the past was Hell and the present uncertain, can Nicholas be a marshal of the future? And the children who sing their unintelligible song[34]—are they the celebrants of that future? The questions are left unanswered.

The published novel is filled with muted despair and longing. But it ends, not so much on a note of futility as with a sense of resignation and acceptance, in the person of Eleanor. If we attend closely to the final two pages, we discover that Virginia Woolf has provided a sequence of moments which have accumulated in such a way as to suggest that pattern of repetition of which Eleanor has had only a momentary glimpse.

Let us move back to 6 October 1891 when Eleanor stood at the door of Delia's empty flat. The memory of that day is recalled by Eleanor in the Present Day; and with that memory, she looks out to see "the sky. . .a faint blue. . . .An air of ethereal calm and simplicity lay over everything" (433-34;*468*). She has begun to move toward a submerged feeling of peace. A moment later, "Eleanor was standing with her back to them. She was watching a taxi. . .gliding slowly round the square. It stopped in front of a house two doors down" (434;*469*). Now we are drawn farther back in time to 1880, on the night of Mrs. Pargiter's death, with Delia looking out of the

---

34. For some reason, it is *only* Eleanor who recognizes the song, but typically, Mrs. Woolf refuses to let her tell us what it is. In the Holograph (Vol. VIII), Eleanor says: " 'I thought it extraordinarily beautiful.' It was true. The tears had come to her eyes. Why she did not know."

window, thinking: "Was it going to stop at their door or not? . . .But then to her regret. . .the horse stumbled on; the cab stopped two doors lower down" (18;*18*). We have been given two almost identical "snapshots" widely separated in time. The cab's stopping "two doors down," once in 1880 (with their mother's death) and now again in the present (with Eleanor spinstered and Delia married), has a very subtle connection with Eleanor's earlier recalling Delia's empty milk jug on the day of Parnell's death. When read side by side, these passages imply a powerful contrast between the sisters: Eleanor's role as mistress of the Pargiter household after her mother's death, her servile observance of convention, and her *unordinary* attachment to her father have made her life one long solitary journey; whereas Delia's break with the family and her unconventional alliance with Parnell have gained her the freedom which she still preserves now in her old age.

It is significant that Eleanor murmurs "There" as she watches the young man two doors down "as he opened the door and they stood for a moment on the threshold. 'There!' she repeated as the door shut. . .behind them" (434;*469*); for immediately Eleanor turns to Morris and asks: "And now?". . ."And now?" For Morris, whom Eleanor loved best (but thought a failure) is the only male member of the Pargiter family to marry and sire children. So that in looking at her brother with the question, " 'And now?' ", it is as though Eleanor were asking Morris, with the "rather worn shoes": "And now" that you have supported tradition, now that you have observed the proprieties of society—now how do you feel? How do you feel about North who despises marriage but *must* marry? What do you feel for Peggy who *will not* have children?

But the question is a kindly one, asked by the aged woman whose sunflower of youth has long since been fissured. Having lived through the Hell and Purgatory of the years, Eleanor alone has, finally, that brief but kindled vision of paradise; for "The sun had risen, and the sky. . .wore an air of extraordinary beauty, simplicity and peace."

So much for this "novel of fact" on the level of fiction; and so much for Herrick, Campion, and Parnell. The novel may also be read as fictionalized autobiography. Indeed we are encouraged to read it as such; and despite Virginia Woolf's engrossing *Diary* and

Quentin Bell's illuminating *Biography,* the business of establishing connections between an artist's private life and his creative products is a risky one, largely dependent upon calculated conjecture. The writer of fiction is always free to disguise, exaggerate, minimize, even reverse the roles of those who populate his imaginary world; he may isolate his own most salient characteristics and habits of mind and scatter them among his principal *personae;* and he may do all of this without in the least being aware of it. It is for this reason that however well we may think we know the author's life, and however much convinced we may be of our reading of the fiction, the material, when assessed together, often presents a confusing ledger of half-hearted erasures and blatant contradictions; and those darker precincts of the writer's mind, where life becomes transformed into art, remain unlighted. So that to venture into biographical criticism is to venture upon very hazardous ground.

It may be of interest to quote a passage from *The Pargiters* Holograph (Vol. VII), in which Virginia Woolf wrote: "Probably people who have been bullied when they are young, find ways of protecting themselves. Is that the origin of art. . . : making yourself immune by making an image!" The biographer of Henry James reminds us that "Art springs usually from tension and passion, from a state of disequilibrium in the artist's being."[35] It is from a recognition of that attempt at "immunity" which generated the tension, the "disequilibrium," that an effort has been made to tread the biographic sphere of *The Years* to show that underneath its very uneven external organization, there is an overpowering emotional substructure, a cohesive organic integration, the origin of which can be discovered in the psychological tissues which bound Virginia Woolf to her father, Leslie Stephen.

On 28 November 1928, Mrs. Woolf wrote in her *Diary:* "Father's birthday. He would have been 96. . . .His life would have entirely ended mine. What would have happened? No writing, no books—inconceivable." There is no doubt that Virginia Woolf loved her father very much. But there is also no doubt that she hated fiercely the bullying world he represented. It was a world which made the woman subordinate, which dwarfed her intellectually,

---

35. Leon Edel, "The Biographer and Psycho-Analysis," *Biography as an Art,* ed. James L. Clifford, New York: Oxford University Press, A Galaxy Book, 1962, p. 238.

emotionally, and morally; and these opposing tugs of love and hate toward Leslie Stephen were ravaging to her during the long and painful growth of *The Years.* She could not make the "image" to her satisfaction. She could not create the art that would make her "immune." Without immunity, the original tension which prompted the novel not only persisted but increased. The dilemma was both circular and self-intensifying.

In her *Diary,* 15 January 1933, we read: "How odd the mind's functions are! About a week ago, I began the making up of scenes—unconsciously; saying phrases to myself; and so, for a week, I've sat here, staring at the typewriter and speaking aloud phrases of *The Pargiters.* . . .this scene-making increases the rate of my heart with uncomfortable rapidity." On 29 October 1933, she wrote: ". . .how tremendously important unconsciousness is when one writes." With so much emphasis on the unconscious, Mrs. Woolf was understandably troubled when she wrote on 25 April 1933: "The figure of Elvira [who becomes Sara in *The Years*] is the difficulty. She may become too dominant." "The difficulty," it appears, has its genesis in the fact that too much of the author was being siphoned into the figure of Elvira: "I hardly know which I am, or where: Virginia or Elvira. . ." (25 March 1933).[36]

The "unconscious," however, can play many subtle tricks on its owner, and Mrs. Woolf's unconscious was tricking her by *confusing Elvira with Eleanor.* (It would be more accurate to say that probably without being aware of it, Mrs. Woolf saw Elvira and Eleanor as two parts of the same person—herself!) The first real clue to this confusion appears in the *Diary* when Mrs. Woolf wrote of her plan "to end with Elvira going out of the house and saying, What did I make this knot in my handkerchief for? and all the coppers rolling

36. During the composition of *The Pargiters,* Mrs. Woolf wrote an essay on Turgenev in which the following observation is made: "His birth, his race, the impressions of his childhood, pervade everything that he wrote. But, though temperament is fated and inevitable, the writer has a choice, and a very important one, in the use he makes of it. 'I' he must be; *but there are many different 'I's' in the same person.* Shall he be the 'I' who has suffered this slight, that injury, who desires to impose his own personality, to win popularity and power for himself and his views; or shall he suppress that 'I' in favour of the one who sees as far as he can impartially and honestly, without wishing to plead a cause or to justify himself?" ("The Novels of Turgenev," written in November 1933 for *The Yale Review*; reprinted in *The Captain's Death Bed and Other Essays,* New York: Hartcourt Brace Jovanovich, Inc., A Harvest Book, 1950, p. 61.)

about—'' (17 August 1934); and later: ''. . .another lapse making up Elvira's speech. . .'D'you know what I've been clasping in my hand all the evening? Coppers.' '' (30 August 1934). In the published text, however, it is Eleanor who ''clenched her hands and felt the hard little coins she was holding'' (367;*395*); it was Eleanor who could ''not remember why she had made a knot in her handkerchief'' (407;*439*); who ''untied the knot in her handkerchief'' (410;*443*); and Eleanor who ''shut her hands on the coins she was holding'' (426;*460*) all evening long.

This mix-up, in itself, would not be so significant were it not for an earlier *Diary* entry about the scene with Elvira in bed, ''the scene I've had in my mind ever so many months. . . . It's the turn of the book'' (6 April 1933). For there is another ''turn of the book'' which passed unrecorded; and that is the scene, in the 1911 section, in which Eleanor, visiting with Morris, is also in bed. Both scenes, although discussed earlier as fiction, are biographically important because of one *almost* minor detail: namely, the book each has in her hand. Sara [Elvira], in 1907, is reading of Antigone's being buried alive; and Eleanor, in 1911, is reading from Dante's *Purgatorio*: ''For by so many more there are who say 'ours'/ So much the more of good doth each possess.''[37]

---

37. On 2 October 1934, with the first draft of the entire novel completed, the familiar headache began: ''. . .the old rays of light set in; and then the sharp, the very sharp, pain over my eyes; so that I sat and lay about till tea; had no walk, had not a single idea of triumph or relief.'' The *Diary* entry ends with ''Books read or in reading.

Shakespeare: *Troilus*
             Pericles
             Taming of Shrew
             Cymbeline

Maupassant ⎫
de Vigny ⎬   only
St. Simon ⎭   scraps
Gide

Library books: Powys
              Wells
              Lady Brooke
              Prose. Dobree
              Alice James

Many MSS.
              none worth keeping''

The strange thing is that Dante is not listed among the books, because we know that she was reading him at the time. It is as though Mrs. Woolf's mental censor had erased from memory one of the most important thematic threads of her novel.

Although these scenes may be interpreted in a number of different ways to establish parallels between the two characters, the question remains: How are these *past* allusions to Sophocles and Dante operating in the Present Day section to connect Eleanor (who *loved* her father) and Sara (who *hated* her father [Holograph, Vol. V])? What does the handsome, robust, aged Eleanor have in common with the untidy, crippled, middle-aged Sara? To answer that is difficult because there is so little evidence to go on in the finished novel; and the few clues we do have are extremely slight. But if we recall that it was Eleanor who mentions *The Antigone* in the novel's closing pages, then we hear again the line of Antigone which Edward recites: "It is not in your hate, that I share, but in your love" as well as the echo of Creon's reply: "Go, then to the shades of the dead; and if you love, love there. As long as I am alive, no woman will dominate me."

Some faint connections here begin to emerge, linking Antigone's love, her being buried alive, and male domination. If we look at these links closely, we are led to the conclusion that to exist in a male-dominated world, the female must somehow be subordinated—or crushed. And so Mrs. Woolf physically crippled Sara and stunted her emotional growth. This is the Elvira (in Holograph) who called herself "the hunchback," who admitted to hating her father. Eleanor, however, has been dealt a fate worse than Sara's: for with Mrs. Woolf's "I've killed Mrs. P[argiter] . . ." she has left Eleanor alone with an indulgent and possessive father; and by casting her in that role, the author has in effect buried Eleanor—like Antigone—alive.

Because so much of the original manuscript has been deleted from the published novel, many readers are apt to overlook the few hints we are given of Eleanor's aloneness. If we read the final pages of the Holograph (Vol. VIII), however, we would discover Mrs. Woolf's earliest conception of Eleanor who

. . . must have been young, almost a girl; and that girl was dead; had vanished. The sleeping street seemed for a moment the grave; and the pigeons were crooning a requiem, for her past; for one of the selves that had been hers; for one of the many million human beings who had walked, who had suffered, who had thought so intensely.

In the Sophoclean sense, then, the debilitated Sara is above ground—

and doomed; and Eleanor, in robust health, has long since been entombed. In the Dantean sense, both Sara and Eleanor Pargiter live in Purgatory. And in the biographic sense, we recognize the physically healthy but emotionally diminished part of Virginia Woolf in the person of Eleanor, and we see the neurologically impaired part of Virginia Woolf transfigured to an ugly "hunchback" in the person of Sara.

I hardly know which I am or where: Virginia or Elvira. If Mrs. Woolf admitted to this identification with Elvira, then she was also identifying another part of herself with Eleanor. So that according to the logic governing those subterranean enclosures of the creative sensibility, Leslie Stephen becomes the fictionalized Abel Pargiter. Thus, we have in essence a biographic transcription of a very *ambivalent* relationship between "the daughter of an educated man" and that "educated man" himself. But the correspondence between Leslie Stephen and Abel Pargiter is not a simple one to estimate, because there are no consistent points of identification which relate the "fictional" man to the actual. Why, for example, has Virginia Woolf lopped off Pargiter's fingers? Why has she written a revolting love scene of shiny knobs fumbling round the neck-bones of a mistress? Insinuated an adulterous affair with a sister-in-law? Immobilized the Colonel with a stroke?

We can only speculate that on the *surface* of her creative mind, the author was inflicting punishment on a man she loved by maiming him physically and morally for corrupting, so she felt, society in general and women in particular. Far more important, however, in her deepest phantasies, it appears that Sir Leslie was being punished for three other very distinct reasons: first, for Mrs. Woolf's belief "that she and Adrian [her brother] had been crushed and cramped in the womb by those important volumes"—those volumes being the *Dictionary of National Biography* which came to birth under Leslie Stephen's editorship just a few months before she herself was born;[38] second, for begetting a daughter named Adeline Virginia Stephen, who from the age of thirteen, the time of her first mental breakdown, knew that for the rest of her life she would have to live with a nervous affliction which might descend upon her at any time—a condition

38. Bell, Vol. I, pp. 38-39.

which altered the whole course of her life and robbed her of the many things which normal healthy children enjoy; and third, for being so wrapped up in his egocentric urgencies and so immersed in the moralistic ritual of proper behavior, that he failed to see, indeed was blind to, the terror and guilt of a little daughter who was forced somehow to deal with George Duckworth's sexual advances—those improper and degrading scenes which were going on practically under Leslie Stephen's puritanical nose.

One could argue that the earliest version of the novel was to the author a way of discharging all kinds of unspecified emotions. Even in the embryonic stages of the novel, we detect the author applying a mental brake to the flow of her material. Note the *Diary* entry of 5 January 1933: ". . . I am on the flood of creativeness in *The Pargiters*—what a liberation that gives one. . . ." However, Mrs. Woolf remarks in that same entry that she visualized the book "as a curiously uneven time sequence . . ."; and one wonders why the "uneven time sequence" should be *curious* to its author. For this brings us back not only to the question of how much and what parts of the novel depended upon the free play of her unconscious, but also to a later very interesting *Diary* entry concerning that slippery subject. On 12 August 1933, Mrs. Woolf notes: "I've been reading Faber on Newman; compared his account of a nervous breakdown; the refusal of some part of the mechanism; is that what happens to me? Not quite. Because I'm not evading anything. I long to write *The Pargiters.*"

I'm not evading anything. That is the crucial sentence. We would all agree that the ordinary mind (let alone the mind of genius) can do strange things; and one of the things Mrs. Woolf's mind apparently did was blot out from memory *The Divine Comedy* at a critical point in the novel's development. We know from the *Diary* that Mrs. Woolf was reading Dante sporadically throughout the novel's composition; and "Isn't it odd?" she writes on 2 December 1934, "Some days I can't read Dante at all after revising *the Ps.*: other days I find it very sublime and helpful." However, in the list of books she said she was reading (2 October 1934), Dante's name does not appear.[39] But there may be a good subconscious reason for its

39. The same is true of Marvell, whose lines from "The Garden" are cited in the scene

omission. If we look again at the volume of Dante which Eleanor is reading, we discover that the lines she turns to come from Canto XV of *Purgatorio,* the Part in which the "seven P's" (Canto IX) first appear: the seven P's being the seven deadly sins—*peccata.* But given Mrs. Woolf's technical virtuosity, might not the seven P's metaphorically refer to the seven Pargiter children? as well as biographically to the three Duckworth and four Stephen children?[40] And with Eleanor's absorbing the burdens of the family, might not there be the insinuation that Eleanor's—and by extension Virginia Woolf's—life has been one long series of purgations for the sins of the father? one long sojourn through Purgatory?

In the Holograph of *The Pargiters* (Vol. VI), we come across the provocative statement that there exists ". . . the possibility of unravelling a whole play or poem from *one word.*" And this brings us back once again to the word *pargeter,* because it forces us to reconsider the "curiously uneven time sequence" as well as the author's avowal that she "was not evading anything." For the uneven time sequence must be taken into account if we are to see how much Virginia Woolf edited out, *glossed,* and *smoothed over* in this "novel of fact." Of course a novelist is free to choose any year or time sequence which will best suit his aesthetic purpose. With the Crosby-Rover reference in *Three Guineas* in mind, however, it is possible to argue that the *year* choices in *The Years* appear to serve emotional as well as artistic ends. What is being suggested here is that the uneven time sequence only really becomes significant when we realize that Mrs. Woolf moved from one year to another, *consciously* leaving out blocks of time which were of great importance to her life and later to her work. It is as though she were leaping from one crest to another in a sea of feeling, leaving the years of misery unstated— and glossed—in the troughs.

The leap from the spring of 1880 to October 1891, for example, eliminates in Virginia Woolf's factual life not only her own birth in January 1882 (as well as her brothers'—Thoby, September 1880; and

---

between Sara and North (339; *365*). See the *Diary* entry of 16 January 1934.

40. It is surely no accident that Mrs. Swithin in *Between the Acts* remembers her mother's saying, "Never play . . . on people's names." For we need only recall in *Mrs. Dalloway* Septimus's reading the *Inferno* and consider the inhabitants of Dante's Seventh (Septimus) Circle of the Inferno to be certain that Mrs. Woolf did indeed *consciously* "play . . . on people's names."

Adrian, October 1883), but also her father's beginning to work on the *Dictionary of National Biography,* an undertaking so consuming that it might have seemed to Mrs. Woolf tantamount to keeping a demanding mistress. It was also between the years 1880 and 1891— approximately 1888, when she was about six years old—that George Duckworth's sexual "fondlings" and "fumblings" began.[41]

Between October 1891 and the midsummer of 1907, Virginia Stephen's mother died on 5 May 1895. And during the summer of 1895, she had her first mental breakdown at the age of thirteen. On 19 July 1897, her half-sister, Stella Duckworth, died. On 22 February 1904, after a lingering illness, her father died; and in the May of 1904, during her second serious breakdown, she tried to commit suicide by throwing herself from a window.[42] On 20 November 1906, Thoby Stephen, the brother she loved most, died of typhoid fever.

Between March 1908 and the spring of 1910, Virginia Stephen was writing her first full-length novel, eventually to be called *The Voyage Out.* In November of 1909, *The Cornhill Magazine* (her father was its editor from 1871-1882) rejected her manuscript of *Memoirs of a Novelist.* By March 1910, her headaches began and continued to such intensity that she was forced to abandon her novel and leave for a rest cure.

Between the summer of 1911 and January 1913—before and after the time Virginia Stephen became Virginia Woolf (10 August 1912)—with *The Voyage Out* in various stages of completion, there were more periods of headache and illness. And between January 1913 and May 1914, with *The Voyage Out* accepted for publication on 12 April 1913, Mrs. Woolf became increasingly unwell and once again slipped over the line into madness during that summer, and on 9 September 1913 she attempted for the second time to kill herself. The remainder of the year was spent under constant medical surveillance.

Between May 1914 and the winter of 1917, another breakdown occurred with "the most violent and raving months of her madness" during April and May of 1915.[43] And from the winter of 1917 to 11

41. Bell, Vol. I, pp. 43-44.

42. *The Letters of Virginia Woolf, Volume One: 1888-1912,* eds. Nigel Nicolson and Joanne Trautmann, New York and London: Harcourt Brace Jovanovich, 1975, p. 141.

43. Bell, Vol. II, p. 229.

November 1918, Mrs. Woolf was at work on *Night and Day,* while overhead the London she loved was being ravaged by the bombs and guns of World War I.

The span of time between the armistice of 1918 and the Present Day has already been documented elsewhere; and anyone who has read her *Diaries* and the Bell *Biography* will discover that there were many moments of great happiness in Virginia Woolf's life, and realize that the gaps *between* the "years" have been filled with the blackest ink imaginable. But not without good reason.

If Mrs. Woolf was *pargeting* in the fictional "curiously uneven time sequence" of the Pargiter family history, the emotional substructure of the novel nevertheless remains indelible and unadorned. We have only to look at the endings of some of the sections to sense the mute resignation to the diminution of life which permeates the novel, that pervasive feeling which somehow could not be "glossed and smoothed over." The 1880 section, for example, ends with: "The ceremony was over; rain was falling"; in 1891: "leaves were falling"; in 1907: "then the lights went out"; in 1908: " 'She's been dead these twenty years!' "; in 1910: " 'The King's dead!' " in 1911: "Darkness reigned"; in 1913: "He saw the snow falling on her black bonnet as she disappeared. He turned away"; in 1914: "Time had ceased."

During the writing and revising of the novel, Mrs. Woolf's life was being depleted by an ever-increasing scroll of obituaries: Lytton Strachey died on 21 January 1932; Dora Carrington, on 11 March 1932; G. Lowes Dickinson, in August 1932; John Galsworthy, early in 1933; Stella Benson, in December 1933; Roger Fry, on 9 September 1934; Francis Birrell, on 2 January 1935. With all these actual deaths piling up around her, it is as though door after door were being closed, shutting her off, and forcing her to re-live the past with all its fading memories, in all their faded variations.

But deaths were not the only doors closing at this time. During the revisions of the novel, two very profound friendships also came to an end.

On 10 March [1935] the Woolfs drove in a snowstorm from Rodmell to Sissinghurst to see Vita [Sackville-West; Mrs. Harold Nicolson]. As they took their leave Virginia realised that their passionate friendship was over. There had been no quarrel, no outward sign of coldness, no bitterness, but the love affair—or whatever we are to call it—had for some time been quietly evaporating, and that particular excitement had gone out of her life, leaving a blankness, a dullness.[44]

The second friend to slip away was Violet Dickinson, who as early as 1902 had assumed a very prominent place in Mrs. Woolf's life. She was probably the first person to encourage the twenty-year-old Virginia Stephen to write. In an undated letter to Miss Dickinson, written sometime between November 1919 and March 1920, we read:

I suppose nothing I could say would give you an idea of what your praise was one night—I can see it—sitting in a long room at Fritham, after a walk on the common: O how excited I was and what a difference you made to me! But I don't suppose you realise how often I think of it, or how grateful I am.[45]

Much later, in a letter sent between April 1935 and October 1936:

I hope one day we shall meet again. How are you?
V.
Leonard wishes to be reminded to you.

Sometime in November of 1936, Violet Dickinson returned all the letters Virginia Woolf had written to her. They were all in typewritten form, and bound. She returned also the only gift Mrs. Woolf said she ever gave her—a copy of Thomas Peacock. Upon receiving these, Mrs. Woolf wrote (so far as one can discover) her last letter to Miss Dickinson. It is dated 2 December 1936:

I'm not sure I do like that girl [being Virginia Woolf] but she had a lot of spirit in her and certainly was rather ground down harshly by fate. . . .how very good you were to me. . . .[46]

The end of one of her oldest friendships left another blank space and greater dullness. With the circle of emptiness ever widening, it is small wonder that the drabness and futility of life should permeate *The Years*.

44. Bell, Vol. II, p. 183.

45. Letters of Virginia Woolf to Violet Dickinson, in the Berg Collection, Folder 76.

46. Letters . . .to Violet Dickinson, Berg Collection, Folders 83-84. Early in this chapter, I called attention to Mrs. Woolf's thinking "back through fathers and mothers" and questioned her use of plurals. But if one read her letters to these two women, one would sense that whatever the exact nature of her love, there was unquestionably a very powerful ingredient of maternalism in Violet Dickinson and Vita Sackville-West which must have made them extreme-

But the published novel is a self-contained universe; and as such, with all its omissions and evasions—details of the author's life which until recently were not available to us and could not have been known to her contemporaries—readers, unfortunately, have tended to remember rather too vividly only the ring of grease and the hair in the bathtub, the bloody piece of mutton, the oozing green liquid of cabbage, the blob of spittle, the noseless face of the flower vendor. But above and below these ugly and sordid details, what seems not to have been given full recognition was the gigantic creative energy capturing in the delicate integument of language the fierce, hopeless, unrelenting sense of life diminishing.

Eleanor in the end sees the dawn of a new day as "beauty, simplicity, and peace," because Eleanor Pargiter alone is somehow purged; has risen above the years of turmoil, hatred, and loss. Her life, in Dante's terms, has been "ours." More precisely, it has been her father's, during his lifetime and after his death. If she alone resignedly accepts the metaphoric new day she will not live to see, then her "peace" in the words of Cornelius Nepos, "is born of war" ("*Paritur pax bello*" *Epaminondas,* V). But Colonel Pargiter has at least been put to rest, calmly and with some dignity; and the coiling arms of tyranny have ceased to struggle up from his burial ground.

For Virginia Woolf, however, the writing of *The Years* began in a flood of creative turbulence and ended in a desert of despair. Throughout the revisions, it eventually became clear to this acutely conscious novelist that the "image" could not be created. Artistic immunity could not be achieved. The troughs of emotion refused to be covered with plaster; resisted the gloss. Fact and feeling were increasingly in mortal contest. Sir Leslie Stephen, unlike Colonel Abel Pargiter, could not be sung to rest. His ghost and all the others in Virginia Woolf's life continued to moan and groan; persisted in haunting every page of the Present Day. It is as though she were caught in the tempest of her imagination and condemned for disturbing the memory of her past. So that when we read in the *Diary*

---

ly attractive to Virginia Woolf. If I am correct in that supposition, then they were consequently not only persons who were loved as women, but also loved as mothers. We must remind ourselves that such an attraction might well be expected of a woman who had lost her real mother at the age of thirteen. (It would be tempting to analyze in detail Mrs. Woolf's fictional treatment of the love between Lucy Craddock and Kitty Malone whose relationship to her real mother is conspicuously defective.)

what she said of *The Years* on 7 March 1937, eight days before its publication: "that I myself know why it's a failure, and that its failure was deliberate," we hear roaring beneath those words an overwhelming need to be punished—and an overwhelming need to be purged. It is as if, through this deliberately elliptical novel, this aesthetic confession, all her suffering loomed up before her in the Present and became transformed in her mind as punishment for the Past. And what greater torment could this woman endure than to *feel* purged of her creative powers: for ". . . I have reached my point of view, as writer, as being." But despite the fact that she was wrong—that she would indeed write again—we know that Virginia Woolf would not be alive to see the publication of the last of her novels.

Afterword

Professor Mitchell Leaska is a most distinguished critic, particularly in the matter of Virginia Woolf studies, as this book once more testifies. He has scruples which do him honour and which I deeply respect, in light of which he explains his decision to close his study of Mrs. Woolf's fiction with *The Years,* and not to consider her posthumous novel *Between the Acts.*

He bases this decision on a letter she sent to me, only a day or two before her suicide, in which she said that the text I had seen, and about which I had sent her an enthusiastic message of approval, was 'too silly and trivial' to be published as it stood, and that she was determined to 'revise it and see if I can pull it together', so that the Hogarth Press could publish it in the Autumn season of 1941.

How serious she was, in making this statement about wishing to re-write it, can never be known. A few days later she killed herself. Leonard, her husband and mentor, had been emphatic in assuring her, in my presence, that some of the passages in this new novel were even more profoundly poetic and disturbing than anything she had written before. This opinion he repeated to me in a letter I received after her death. 'I had expected from what she said', he wrote, 'and feared to find a loss of vigour. I may be wrong, but it seemed to me the opposite, to be more vigorous and pulled together than most of her other books, to have more depth and to be very moving. I also thought that the strange symbolism gave it an almost terrifying profundity and beauty'.

He therefore decided that the final text, so very different from the previous texts* should be given to the world forthwith. I have personally verified that what went to the printer is exactly what Mrs. Woolf sent me when she asked me to give a casting vote. All that Leonard Woolf did was to correct occasional mis-spellings and confusions in his wife's typewriting, and add the usual instructions for the printer.

I do not, however, entirely share his conviction, expressed in his Note to the original published edition, that Virginia Woolf would not

---

*These texts still exist in a form sorted by Dr. Lola L. Szladits, Curator, in the Berg Collection of The New York Public Library, after receiving them in 1963.

have made 'any large or material alterations in it, though she would probably have made a good many small corrections or revisions before passing the final proofs'. It is a large assumption, because we know from her work on the various versions of previous novels—as Professor Leaska has pointed out in his Preface—that when she revised she always did a great deal more than make 'small corrections or revisions', even cutting out whole paragraphs and adding vital new material right down to the final proofs.

At the same time we have to remember that when she wrote me the letter I have mentioned above, she was already seriously ill. Leonard Woolf revealed this to me in his extremely alarming letter which he enclosed with Virginia's. It is clear that her mind was already so shaken by the symptoms of approaching madness that she could not possibly have made a balanced judgement about the value of what she had written. If she had lived, if she had completely recovered, one can conceive that she would not have found it anything like so 'silly and trivial'. What one cannot conceive is that she would have left the text in all but unimportant details as we have it today.

It is therefore entirely understandable that Professor Leaska should feel he could not with clear conscience subject this novel to the close critical examination he has given to her other novels. One quite definitely cannot do that to an incompletely revised work. So far, I am entirely in agreement with Professor Leaska, and as I have already said I admire the delicacy of his scruples.

Nevertheless Professor Leaska himself admits that *Between the Acts* is a 'beautiful and profound novel', and I am quite certain myself that one cannot achieve a true overall view of the meaning and significance of Virginia Woolf's work without including this novel in one's consideration—in the total spectrum. Above all *Between the Acts* shows, even in our unrevised version, that the author had recovered her sense of form, which, if we had nothing to go on after *The Years,* one might well feel had foundered. And not only her sense of form, but also her capacity to irradiate a story from beginning to end with her visionary sense: with that mystical illumination which, combined with the supreme distinction of her style, her gift for making the English language express the subtlest movements of her mind and imagination, is her essential claim to greatness.

In her letter to me, Virginia maintained that *Between the Acts* was feeble because it was written 'in intervals of doing Roger with my brain half-asleep'. It was certainly begun while she was working on her biography of Roger Fry, but her diary does not confirm in any way her suggestion that the writing dragged or that her mind was exhausted or functioning only at half-pressure. On the contrary, *Roger Fry* is described again and again as a tiresome 'grind' and *Poyntz Hall* (as she originally called the novel) as an enjoyable diversion. In October 1938 she writes 'I'm taking a frisk at P.H.', and adds 'I enjoy it intensely: head screwed up over Roger'. And just before Christmas 'I rush to it for relief after a long pressure of Fry, facts'. This mood continues through 1939 and 1940. 'A holiday from Roger. And one day's happiness with *P.H.*' (February 28th 1939) 'Scraps, orts and fragments, as I said in *P.H.,* which is now bubbling'. (May 31st 1940). And finally, on November 23rd of that year, noting that she had just finished *Poyntz Hall,* she writes: 'I am a little triumphant about the book. I think it's an interesting attempt in a new method. I think it's more quintessential than the others. More milk skimmed off. A richer pat, certainly a fresher than that misery *The Years.* I've enjoyed writing almost every page'.

The mood of *To the Lighthouse* had returned. And not only the mood in which she wrote that masterpiece, but the speed and lightness. Her method in that book is of an extreme impressionism, almost *pointillisme,* covering her canvas with stabs of brilliant paint, 'scraps, orts and fragments' which are assembled into what one sees as a profoundly meaningful design as one stands back from it in the concluding sequences.

At the very beginning, in May 1938, she talks of 'the airy world of *Poyntz Hall'.* But that freshness and ease, with which the narrative flows, conceals a depth of symbol and poetic allusiveness, like the great carp itself at the bottom of the Poyntz Hall lily pool, for the understanding of which one must pause until one can see more clearly into his lurking place, beyond the fantail and the golden orfe. How skilfully the themes of the book are indicated, like motifs in a musical work, in the opening pages. The contrast of the summer night and the cesspool, the nightingale and the greedy daylight bird; lust and love, Byron's sublime lyrics and the 'snow-white breast circled with a tangle of dirty duckweed'; time stretching far back into pre-history when there were rhododendrons in Piccadilly; the successive peaks of

civilization indicated by the Roman road, the Elizabethan manor
house, the eighteenth century coming to its close with the Napoleonic
Wars, each achievement falling, destroyed from outside or under its
own internal pressures, to give place to a new one. And as the narrative develops these themes are developed and further illustrated; the
cross-currents of love between Giles and Isa, Mrs. Manresa and Giles,
Isa and Rupert Haines, William Dodge and Giles, as in Swinburne's
neglected masterpiece (it is Swinburne that old Mr. Oliver is continually repeating to himself in the intervals of the pageant). The
horror and ugliness of crude violence is illustrated again and again,
that obverse of love and harmony that Virginia had shown herself
increasingly aware of from *Flush* onwards: the troopers raping the
girl in their barracks in the 'horse with a green tail' episode, the exe-
cutions going on under Hitler across the Channel, Giles stamping on
the snake that cannot swallow the toad (and that again is the 'inver-
sion' that he is repelled and at the same time, in spite of himself,
fascinated by in William Dodge's unspoken desire for him), and the
menace of the aeroplanes that interrupt the Pageant and could smash
Bolney Minster to smithereens.

There is much, much more in the symbolism than I have touched
on here. I would only like to mention that we now know that the
wonderful moment of illumination the little boy George has before
the flower at the roots of the tree came from an actual 'moment of
being' in Virginia's own childhood. This is not, however, the place
to plunge into the deep waters of literary evaluation—and perhaps I
have already gone too far in that direction, swayed by the incredible
richness of the visionary insight in the 200 pages or so of *Between
the Acts;* but what I wanted to emphasize was the firm control and
grandeur of the *overall* design in this final testament, the supreme
effort of which without doubt cost the author her life.

It is possible to envisage, at the same time, places where—for instance in the pastiche of Restoration comedy—she might have altered
the emphasis and balance in relation to the rest of the book. Now
that *Freshwater* has been published, we know with what enjoyment
Virginia Woolf gave herself to such pastiches, and it is not impossible
to suppose that her pen ran away with her on the historical scenes of
the Pageant.

Nevertheless the basic message of *Between the Acts* is, to me at least, clear, and would not, I am certain, have been altered in any final revision. Virginia Woolf, though she called herself a Socialist mainly, I think, because Leonard was a Socialist and because she believed passionately in the emancipation of women, was not fundamentally a believer in progress; only in the successive attempts by mankind to build a more perfect model of order and civilization, an impulse continually in the course of history defeated, but as continually renewed. Giles and Isa, in that last confrontation (which still makes *frissons* run through me), have become prototypes of humanity in its unending struggle through illimitable wastes of time, and will fight, will quarrel, will destroy, but in that process will give new life to a new manifestation of creative renewal, 'not with a bang but a whimper'.

John Lehmann
May 1977

Bibliography

Books by Virginia Woolf

The titles chronologically listed below refer specifically to those editions used in this study. The Hogarth Press entries are of the Uniform Edition, with the exception of *The Pargiters*. For the most comprehensive record of her published work up to 1967, see B.J. Kirkpatrick's *A Bibliography of Virginia Woolf* (London: Rupert Hart-Davis, 1957; revised in 1967).

The Voyage Out. New York: Harcourt, Brace and World, 1969. A Harvest Book; London: The Hogarth Press (Eighth Impression), 1965.

Night and Day. New York: Harcourt Brace Jovanovich, 1973. A Harvest Book; London: The Hogarth Press (Eighth Impression), 1966.

Monday or Tuesday. Harcourt, Brace and Company, 1921.

Jacob's Room. New York: Harcourt, Brace and World, 1960. A Harvest Book; London: The Hogarth Press (Tenth Impression), 1965.

The Common Reader: First Series. New York: Harcourt, Brace and World, 1955. A Harvest Book; London: The Hogarth Press (Tenth Impression), 1962.

Mrs. Dalloway. New York: Harcourt, Brace and World, 1964. A Harvest Book; London: The Hogarth Press (Twelfth Impression), 1968.

Mrs. Dalloway. "Introduction" by Virginia Woolf. New York: Modern Library, 1928.

To the Lighthouse. New York: Harcourt, Brace and World, 1964. A Harvest Book; London: The Hogarth Press (Fourteenth Impression), 1967.

Orlando: A Biography. New York: Harcourt, Brace and Company, 1928.

A Room of One's Own. New York and Burlingame: Harcourt, Brace and World, 1957. A Harbinger Book; London: The Hogarth Press (Fourteenth Impression), 1967.

The Waves. New York: Harcourt, Brace and World, 1960. A Harvest Book; London: The Hogarth Press (Tenth Impression), 1963.

The Common Reader: Second Series. New York: Harcourt, Brace and Company, 1956. A Harvest Book; London: The Hogarth Press (Eighth Impression), 1965.

The Pargiters, The Novel-Essay Portion of *The Years,* ed. Mitchell A. Leaska. New York: The New York Public Library, Readex Books, and Harcourt Brace Jovanovich; London: The Hogarth Press, 1977.

The Years. New York: Harcourt, Brace and Company, 1937; London: The Hogarth Press (Fifth Impression), 1965.

Three Guineas. New York: Harcourt, Brace and Company, 1938; London: The Hogarth Press (Fifth Impression), 1968.

Between the Acts. New York: Harcourt Brace Jovanovich, 1970. A Harvest Book; London: The Hogarth Press (Seventh Impression), 1965.

The Death of the Moth and Other Essays. New York and London: Harcourt Brace Jovanovich, 1974. A Harvest Book.

The Moment and Other Essays. New York and London: Harcourt Brace Jovanovich, 1974; London: The Hogarth Press (First Impression in Uniform Edition), 1952.

The Captain's Death Bed and Other Essays. New York: Harcourt Brace Jovanovich, 1950. A Harvest Book.

A Writer's Diary, Being Extracts from the Diary of Virginia Woolf, ed. Leonard Woolf. New York: Harcourt, Brace and Company, 1954.

Granite and Rainbow: Essays. New York and London: Harcourt Brace Jovanovich, 1975. A Harvest Book.

The Letters of Virginia Woolf, Volume One: 1888-1912, eds. Nigel Nicolson and Joanne Trautmann. New York and London: Harcourt Brace Jovanovich, 1975.

Studies on Virginia Woolf

Books

Bazin, Nancy Topping. *Virginia Woolf and the Androgynous Vision.* New Brunswick, N.J.: Rutgers University Press, 1973.

Bell, Quentin. *Virginia Woolf: A Biography.* 2 vols. New York: Harcourt Brace Jovanovich; London: The Hogarth Press, 1972.

Bennett, Joan. *Virginia Woolf: Her Art as a Novelist.* 2nd edn. Cambridge, England: Cambridge University Press, 1964.

Blackstone, Bernard. *Virginia Woolf: A Commentary.* New York: Harcourt, Brace and Company, 1949.

Brewster, Dorothy. *Virginia Woolf.* New York: New York University Press, 1962.

Chambers, R.L. *The Novels of Virginia Woolf.* London and Edinburgh: Oliver and Boyd, 1947.

Chastaing, Maxime. *La Philosophie de Virginia Woolf.* Paris: Presses Universitaires de France, 1951.

Daiches, David. *Virginia Woolf.* Norfolk, Conn.: New Directions, 1942.

Delattre, Floris. *Le Roman Psychologique de Virginia Woolf.* Paris: J. Vrin, 1932.

Fleishman, Avrom. *Virginia Woolf: A Critical Reading.* Baltimore: Johns Hopkins University Press, 1975.

Forster, E.M. *Virginia Woolf* [The Rede Lecture, 1941]. Cambridge, England: Cambridge University Press, 1942.

Gruber, Ruth. *Virginia Woolf: A Study.* Leipzig: Verlag von Bernhard Tauchnitz, 1935.

Guiguet, Jean. *Virginia Woolf and Her Works,* trans. Jean Stewart. New York: Harcourt, Brace and World, 1965.

Hafley, James. *The Glass Roof: Virginia Woolf as Novelist.* New York: Russell and Russell, 1963.

Holtby, Winifred. *Virginia Woolf.* London: Wishart and Company, 1932.

Kelly, Alice van Buren. *The Novels of Virginia Woolf: Fact and Vision.* Chicago: University of Chicago Press, 1973.

Latham, Jacqueline E.M., ed. *Critics on Virginia Woolf.* London: Allen and Unwin, 1970.

Leaska, Mitchell A. *Virginia Woolf's Lighthouse: A Study in Critical Method.* London: The Hogarth Press; New York: Columbia University Press, 1970.

Lehmann, John. *Virginia Woolf and Her World.* New York and London: Harcourt Brace Jovanovich, 1975.

Lewis, Thomas S.W., ed. *Virginia Woolf: A Collection of Criticism.* New York: McGraw-Hill, 1975.

Love, Jean O. *Worlds of Consciousness: Mythopoetic Thought in the Novels of Virginia Woolf.* Berkeley: University of California Press, 1970.

McLaurin, Allen. *Virginia Woolf: The Echoes Enslaved.* Cambridge, England: Cambridge University Press, 1973.

Marder, Herbert. *Feminism and Art: A Study of Virginia Woolf.* Chicago and London: University of Chicago Press, 1968.

Moody, A.D. *Virginia Woolf.* New York: Grove Press, 1963.

Naremore, James. *The World Without a Self: Virginia Woolf and the Novel.* New Haven and London: Yale University Press, 1973.

Nathan, Monique. *Virginia Woolf,* trans. Herma Briffault. New York: Evergreen Books, 1961.

Newton, Deborah. *Virginia Woolf.* Melbourne: Melbourne University Press, 1946.

Noble, Joan Russell, ed. *Recollections of Virginia Woolf by Her Contemporaries.* New York: William Morrow and Company, 1972.

Novak, Jane. *The Razor Edge of Balance: A Study of Virginia Woolf.* Coral Gables: University of Miami Press, 1975.

Pippett, Aileen. *The Moth and the Star: A Biography of Virginia Woolf.* Boston and Toronto: Little, Brown and Company, 1955.

Rantavaara, Irma. *Virginia Woolf and Bloomsbury.* Helsinki: Annales Academiae Scientiarum Fennicae, 1953.

Rantavaara, Irma. *Virginia Woolf's "The Waves."* Port Washington, New York: Kennikat Press, 1969.

Richter, Harvena. *Virginia Woolf: The Inward Voyage.* Princeton: Princeton University Press, 1970.

Schaefer, Josephine O'Brien. *The Three-Fold Nature of Reality in the Novels of Virginia Woolf.* The Hague: Mouton and Company, 1965.

Sprague, Claire, ed. *Virginia Woolf: A Collection of Critical Essays.* Englewood Cliffs, N.J.: Prentice-Hall, 1971.

Thakur, N.C. *The Symbolism of Virginia Woolf.* New York and London: Oxford University Press, 1965.

Trautmann, Joanne. *The Jessamy Brides: The Friendship of Virginia Woolf and V. Sackville West.* University Park, Pa.: Pennsylvania State University Press, 1973.

Woodring, Carl. *Virginia Woolf.* New York: Columbia University Press, 1966.

Articles and Parts of Books

Allen, Walter. *The English Novel: A Short Critical History.* London: Phoenix House, 1954.

Allen, Walter. *The Modern Novel in Britain and the United States.* New York: E.P. Dutton and Company, 1964.

Annan, Noel Gilroy. *Leslie Stephen: His Thought and Character in Relation to His Time.* London: MacGibbon and Kee, 1951.

Auden, W.H. *Forewords and Afterwords.* New York: Random House, 1974. Vintage Books.

Auerbach, Erich. *Mimesis: The Representation of Reality in Western Literature,* trans. Willard R. Trask. Princeton: Princeton University Press, 1953.

Baldanza, Frank. "Clarissa Dalloway's 'Party Consciousness'," *Modern Fiction Studies,* 2 (February 1956), 24-30.

Beach, Joseph Warren. "The Novel from James to Joyce," *Nation,* 132 (June 10, 1931), 634-36.

Beach, Joseph Warren. *The Twentieth Centurey Novel: Studies in Technique.* New York and London: D. Appleton-Century Company, 1932.

Beach Joseph Warren. "Virginia Woolf," *The English Journal,* XXVI (October 1937), 603-12.

Beck, Warren. "For Virginia Woolf." In *Forms of Modern Fiction,* ed. William Van O'Connor. Minneapolis: University of Minnesota Press, 1948.

Beja, Morris. *Epiphany in the Modern Novel.* Seattle: University of Washington Press, 1971.

Benjamin, Anna. "Towards an Understanding of the Meaning of Virginia Woolf's *Mrs. Dalloway,*" *Wisconsin Studies in Contemporary Literature,* 6 (Summer 1965), 214-23.

Bennett, Joan. "Le Journal inédit de Virginia Woolf," *Roman* (janvier 1951), 6-8.

Bevis, Dorothy. *"The Waves*: A Fusion of Symbol, Style and Thought in Virginia Woolf," *Twentieth Century Literature*, 2 (1956), 5-20.

Bodkin, Maud. *Archetypal Patterns in Poetry: Psychological Studies of Imagination.* London: Oxford University Press, 1934.

Booth, Wayne C. *The Rhetoric of Fiction.* Chicago: University of Chicago Press, 1961.

Bradbrook, M.C. "Notes on the Style of Mrs. Woolf," *Scrutiny,* I (May 1932), 33-38.

Brooks, B.G. "Virginia Woolf," *Nineteenth Century and After,* 130 (December 1941), 334-40.

Brower, Reuben Arthur. *The Fields of Light: An Experiment in Critical Reading.* New York: Oxford University Press, 1962.

Brown, E.K. *Rhythm in the Novel.* Toronto: University of Toronto Press, 1950.

Burra, Peter. "Virginia Woolf," *Nineteenth Century and After,* 115 (January 1934), 512-25.

Chapman, R.T. *"The Lady in the Looking-Glass*: Modes of Perception in a Short Story by Virginia Woolf," *Modern Fiction Studies,* 18 (Autumn 1972), 331-37.

Chevalley, Abel. *Le Roman Anglais de notre Temps.* London: Oxford University Press, 1921.

Church, Margaret. *Time and Reality: Studies in Contemporary Fiction.* Chapel Hill: University of North Carolina Press, 1963.

Collins, Joseph. *The Doctor Looks at Literature: Psychological Studies of Life and Letters.* London: Allen and Unwin, 1923.

Comfort, Alex. *The Novel and our Time.* London: Phoenix House, 1948.

Connolly, Cyril. *Enemies of Promise.* London: Routledge and Kegan Paul, 1938.

Cornwell, Ethel F. *The Still Point: Themes and Variations in the Writings of T.S. Eliot, Coleridge, Yeats, Henry James, Virginia Woolf and D.H. Lawrence.* New Brunswick, N.J.: Rutgers University Press, 1962.

Cox, C.B. *The Free Spirit: A Study of Liberal Humanism in the Novels of George Eliot, E.M. Forster, Virginia Woolf, Angus Wilson.* London: Oxford University Press, 1963.

Crawford, John W. "One Day in London the Subject of Mrs. Woolf's New Novel," *The New York Times Book Review* (May 10, 1925), 10-11.

Cummings, Melinda Feldt. *"Night and Day*: Virginia Woolf's Visionary Synthesis of Reality," *Modern Fiction Studies,* 18 (Autumn 1972), 339-49.

D.R. "Three English Novels," *The Independent* (June 20, 1925), 703.

Daiches, David. *The Novel and the Modern World.* Rev. edn. Chicago: University of Chicago Press, 1960.

Delattre, Floris. "La Durée Bergsonienne dans le Roman de Virginia Woolf," *Revue Anglo-Américaine* (déc. 1931), 97-108.

Delattre, Floris. "Le nouveau Roman de Virginia Woolf" [*The Years*], *Etudes Anglaises* (juillet 1937), 289-96.

Derbyshire, S.H. "An Analysis of Mrs. Woolf's *To the Lighthouse,*" *College English,* III (January 1942), 353-60.

Dobrée, Bonomy. *The Lamp and the Lute: Studies in Six Modern Authors.* Oxford, England: Clarendon Press, 1929.

Doner, Dean. "Virginia Woolf: The Service of Style," *Modern Fiction Studies,* 2 (1956), 1-12.

Drew, Elizabeth. *The Modern Novel: Some Aspects of Contemporary Fiction.* London: Jonathan Cape, 1926.

Drew, Elizabeth. *The Novel: A Modern Guide to Fifteen English Masterpieces.* New York: W.W. Norton and Company, 1963.

Dujardin, Edouard. *Le Monologue Intérieur, son apparition, ses origines, sa place dans l'oeuvre de James Joyce et dans le roman contemporain.* Paris: Albert Messein, 1931.

Edel, Leon. *Literary Biography.* Toronto: University of Toronto Press, 1957.

Edel, Leon. *The Modern Psychological Novel.* Rev. edn. New York: Grosset and Dunlap, 1964.

Eliot, T.S. "Virginia Woolf," *Horizon,* III (May 1941), 313-16.

Forster, E.M. *Abinger Harvest.* New York: Harcourt, Brace and Company, 1936.

Forster, E.M. "The Art of Virginia Woolf," *Atlantic,* 170 (September 1942), 82-90.

Forster, E.M. "The Novels of Virginia Woolf," *New Criterion,* 4 (April 1926), 277-86.

Fox, Stephen D. "The Fish Pond as Symbolic Center in *Between the Acts,*" *Modern Fiction Studies,* 18 (Autumn 1927), 467-73.

Frank, Joseph. "Spatial Form in Modern Fiction." In *Criticism: The Foundations of Modern Literary Judgment,* eds. M. Schorer, J. Miles, and G. McKenzie. Rev. edn. New York: Harcourt, Brace and Company, 1958.

Freedman, Ralph. *The Lyrical Novel: Studies in Hermann Hesse, André Gide, and Virginia Woolf.* Princeton: Princeton University Press, 1963.

Friedman, Melvin. *Stream of Consciousness: A Study in Literary Method.* New Haven: Yale University Press, 1955.

Friedman, Norman. "Point of View in Fiction: The Development of a Critical Concept," *PMLA,* 70 (December 1955), 1160-84.

Friedman, Norman. "The Waters of Annihilation: Double Vision in *To the Lighthouse*," *Journal of English Literary History*, XXII (1955), 61-79.

Frierson, W.C. *The English Novel in Transition: 1885-1940*. Norman: University of Oklahoma Press, 1942.

Frye, Northrop. *Anatomy of Criticism*. Princeton: Princeton University Press, 1957.

Gamble, Isabel. "The Secret Sharer in *Mrs. Dalloway*," *Accent*, 16 (Autumn 1956), 235-51.

Garnett, David. *The Flowers of the Forest*. London: Chatto and Windus, 1955.

Gelfant, Blanche. "Love and Conversion in *Mrs. Dalloway*," *Criticism*, 8 (Summer 1966), 229-45.

German, Howard and Sharon Kaehele. "The Dialectic of Time in *Orlando*," *College English*, XXIV (1962), 35-41.

Gorsky, Susan. " 'The Central Shadow': Characterization in *The Waves*," *Modern Fiction Studies*, 18 (Autumn 1972), 449-66.

Graham, John W. " 'The Caricature Value' of Parody and Fantasy in *Orlando*," *University of Toronto Quarterly*, 30 (July 1961), 345-66.

Graham, John W. "Time in the Novels of Virginia Woolf," *University of Toronto Quarterly* 18 (January 1949), 186-201.

Grant, Duncan. "Virginia Woolf," *Horizon*, III (June 1941), 402-406.

Hartman, G.H. "Virginia's Web," *Chicago Review*, XIII (1960), 20-32.

Havard-Williams, Peter and Margaret. "Bateau Ivre: The Symbol of the Sea in Virginia Woolf's *The Waves*," *English Studies*, XXXIV (February 1953), 9-17.

Heilbrun, Carolyn G. *Toward a Recognition of Androgyny*. New York: Alfred A. Knopf, 1973.

Heine, Elizabeth. "The Evolution of the Interludes in *The Waves*," *Virginia Woolf Quarterly*, I (Fall 1972), 60-80.

Hoare, Dorothy. *Some Studies in the Modern Novel*. London: Chatto and Windus, 1938.

Hoffman, Charles G. "The Real Mrs. Dalloway," *University of Kansas City Review*, 22 (Spring 1956), 204-208.

Hoffman, Charles G. "Virginia Woolf's Manuscript Revisions of *The Years*," *PMLA*, 84 (January 1969), 79-89.

Hollingworth, Keith. "Freud and the Riddle of *Mrs. Dalloway*." In *Studies in Honor of John Wilcox*, eds. A. Dayle Wallace and Woodburn O. Ross. Detroit: Wayne State University Press, 1958.

Humphrey, Robert. *Stream of Consciousness in the Modern Novel*. Berkeley: University of California Press, 1954.

Hungerford, Edward A. " 'My Tunnelling Process': The Method of *Mrs.*

Dalloway," *Modern Fiction Studies,* 3 (Summer 1957), 164-67.

Isaacs, J. *An Assessment of Twentieth Century Literature.* London: Secker and Warburg, 1951.

Isherwood, Christopher. "Virginia Woolf," *Decision,* I (May 1941), 36-38.

Johnstone, J.K. *The Bloomsbury Group: A Study of E.M. Forster, Lytton Strachey, Virginia Woolf, and their Circle.* London: Secker and Warburg, 1954.

Josephson, Matthew. "Virginia Woolf and the Modern Novel," *New Republic,* 66 (April 15, 1931), 239-41.

Kettle, Arnold. *An Introduction to the English Novel* (vol. 2). London: Hutchinson's University Library, 1953.

Kris, Ernst. *Psychoanalytic Explorations in Art.* London: Allen and Unwin, 1953.

Kronenberger, Louis. "Virginia Woolf as Critic," *Nation,* 155 (October 17, 1942), 382-85.

Krutch, Joseph Wood. "The Stream of Consciousness," *Nation,* 120 (June 3, 1925), 631-32.

Leaska, Mitchell A. "Virginia Woolf's *The Voyage Out*: Character Deduction and the Function of Ambiguity," *Virginia Woolf Quarterly,* I (Winter 1973), 18-41.

Leavis, Q.D. *Fiction and the Reading Public.* London: Chatto and Windus, 1932.

Lehmann, John. *In My Own Time: Memoirs of a Literary Life.* Boston and Toronto: Little, Brown and Company, 1969.

Lewis, A.J. "From 'The Hours' to *Mrs. Dalloway,*" *British Museum Quarterly,* 28 (Summer 1964), 15-18.

MacCarthy, Desmond. *Memories.* London: MacGibbon and Kee, 1953.

MacCarthy, Desmond. "Le Roman Anglais d'Après Guerre," *Revue de Paris,* III (1932), 129-52.

Maitland, Frederic William. *The Life and Letters of Leslie Stephen.* London: Duckworth and Company, 1906. [On pages 474-76, the impressions by "one of his daughters" are those of Virginia Stephen.]

Mansfield, Katherine. *Novels and Novelists.* London: Constable and Company, 1930.

Marder, Herbert. "Beyond the Lighthouse: *The Years,*" *Bucknell Review,* 15 (March 1967), 61-70.

May, Keith M. "The Symbol of Painting in Virginia Woolf's *To the Lighthouse,*" *Review of English Literature,* 8 (April 1967), 91-98.

Mayoux, Jean-Jacques. *Vivants Piliers: le roman anglo-saxon et les symboles.* Paris: Julliard, 1960.

Miller, J. Hillis. "Virginia Woolf's All Soul's Day: The Omniscient Narrator in *Mrs. Dalloway.*" In *The Shaken Realist: Essays in Modern*

Literature in Honor of Frederick J. Hoffman, eds. Melvin J. Friedman and John B. Vickery. Baton Rouge: Louisiana State University Press, 1970.

Monroe, N. Elizabeth. *The Novel and Society: A Critical Study of the Modern Novel.* Chapel Hill: University of North Carolina Press, 1941.

Morgenstern, Barry. "The Self-Conscious Narrator in *Jacob's Room,*" *Modern Fiction Studies,* 18 (Autumn 1972), 351-61.

Muir, Edwin. *Transition: Essays on Contemporary Literature.* London: The Hogarth Press, 1926.

Muir, Edwin. *The Structure of the Novel.* London: The Hogarth Press, 1928.

Muller, Herbert J. "Virginia Woolf and Feminine Fiction," *Saturday Review of Literature* (February 6, 1937), 3-4, 14, 16.

Murry, John Middleton. *Countries of the Mind.* London: Oxford University Press, 1931.

O'Brien, Justin M. "La Mémoire involontaire avant Proust," *Revue de Littérature Comparée,* XIX (1939), 19-36.

O'Connor, William Van, ed. *Forms of Modern Fiction.* Minneapolis: University of Minnesota Press, 1948.

O'Faolain, Sean. *The Vanishing Hero: Studies in the Novelists of the Twenties.* Boston: Little, Brown and Company, 1957.

Payne, Michael. "The Eclipse of Order: The Ironic Structure of *The Waves,*" *Modern Fiction Studies,* 15 (Summer 1969), 209-18.

Pederson, Glenn. "Vision in *To the Lighthouse,*" *PMLA,* 78 (December 1958), 585-600.

Peel, Robert. "Virginia Woolf." *New Criterion,* XIII (October 1933), 78-96.

Pritchett, V.S. *The Living Novel.* London: Chatto and Windus, 1946.

Proudfit, Sharon Wood. "Lily Briscoe's Painting: A Key to Personal Relations in *To the Lighthouse,*" *Criticism,* 13 (Winter 1971), 26-39.

Rahv, Philip. *Image and Idea.* London: Weidenfeld and Nicolson, 1957.

Roberts, John Hawley. "Towards Virginia Woolf," *Virginia Quarterly Review,* 10 (October 1934), 587-602.

Roberts, John Hawley. " 'Vision and Design' in Virginia Woolf," *PMLA,* 61 (September 1946), 835-47.

Rosenbaum, S.P., ed. *English Literature and British Philosophy: A Collection of Essays.* Chicago and London: University of Chicago Press, 1971.

Rosenbaum, S.P., ed. *The Bloomsbury Group: A Collection of Memoirs, Commentary and Criticism.* Toronto and Buffalo: University of Toronto Press, 1975.

Samuelson, Ralph. "Virginia Woolf: *Orlando* and the Feminist Spirit," *Western Humanities Review,* XV (Winter 1961), 51-58.

Savage, D.S. "The Mind of Virginia Woolf," *South Atlantic Quarterly,* 46 (October 1947), 556-73.

Savage, D.S. *The Withered Branch: Six Studies in the Modern Novel.* London: Eyre and Spottiswoode, 1950.

Schorer, Mark. "The Chronicle of Doubt," *Virginia Quarterly Review,* 18 (Spring 1942), 200-15.

Schorer, Mark. "Fiction and the 'Analogical Matrix'." In *Critiques and Essays in Modern Fiction,* ed. John W. Aldridge. New York: The Ronald Press Company, 1952.

Simon, Irene. "Some Aspects of Virginia Woolf's Imagery," *English Studies* (Holland) XLI (June 1960), 180-96.

Smart, J.A. "Virginia Woolf," *Dalhousie Review,* XXI (1921), 37-50.

Spencer, Theodore. "Mrs. Woolf's Novels," *New Republic,* 113 (December 3, 1945), 758.

Steinberg, Erwin. "Freudian Symbolism and Communication," *Literature and Psychology,* III (April 1953), 2-5.

Storr, Anthony. *The Dynamics of Creation.* New York: Atheneum, 1972.

Szladits, Lola L. " 'The Life, Character and Opinions of Flush the Spaniel'," *Bulletin of The New York Public Library,* 74 (April 1970), 211-18.

Tindall, William York. *Forces in Modern British Literature: 1885-1946.* New York: Alfred A. Knopf, 1947.

Tindall, William York. *The Literary Symbol.* Bloomington: Indiana University Press, 1955.

Tindall, William York. "Many-Leveled Fiction: Virginia Woolf to Ross Lockridge," *College English,* X (November 1948), 65-71.

Toynbee, Philip. "Virginia Woolf: A Study of Three Experimental Novels," *Horizon,* XIV (November 1946), 290-304.

Trilling, Lionel. *The Liberal Imagination.* London: Secker and Warburg, 1951.

Troy, William. "Virginia Woolf: The Poetic Method," *Symposium,* III (January 1932), 53-63.

Troy, William. "Virginia Woolf: The Poetic Style," *Symposium,* III (April 1932), 153-66.

Verschoyle, Derek, ed. *The English Novelists.* London: Chatto and Windus, 1936.

Wilkinson, Ann Y. "A Principle of Unity in *Between the Acts,*" *Criticism,* 8 (Winter 1966), 53-63.

Wilson, Edmund. *Axel's Castle: A Study of the Imaginative Literature of 1870-1930.* New York: Charles Scribner's Sons, 1931.

Wilson, James Southall. "Time and Virginia Woolf," *Virginia Quarterly Review,* XVIII (Spring 1942), 267-76.

Woolf, Leonard. *Beginning Again: An Autobiography of the Years 1911 to 1918.* New York: Harcourt, Brace and World, 1964.

Woolf, Leonard. *Downhill All the Way: An Autobiography of the Years 1919 to 1939.* New York: Harcourt, Brace and World, 1967.

Woolf, Leonard. *The Journey Not the Arrival Matters: An Autogiography of the Years 1939 to 1969.* New York: Harcourt, Brace and World, 1970.

Wright, Nathalie. "*Mrs. Dalloway*: A Study in Composition," *College English,* V (April 1944), 351-58.

Zorn, Marilyn. "The Pageant in *Between the Acts*," *Modern Fiction Studies,* 2 (February 1956), 31-35.

Additional References

Allport, Floyd H. *Theories of Perception and the Concept of Structure.* New York: John Wiley and Sons, 1955.

Barfield, Owen. *Poetic Diction: A Study in Meaning.* 2nd edn. London: Faber and Faber, 1952.

Bergson, Henri. *Creative Evolution,* ed. Irwin Erdman, trans. Arthur Mitchell. New York: Modern Library, 1944.

Bertine, Eleanor. *Human Relationships.* New York: David McKay Company, 1958.

Burke, Kenneth. *The Philosophy of Literary Form: Studies in Symbolic Action.* Rev. edn. New York: Random House, 1957. Vintage Books.

Camus, Albert. "The Myth of Sisyphus," trans. Justin O'Brien. In *Existentialism from Dostoevsky to Sartre,* ed. Walter Kaufman. Cleveland and New York: World Publishing Company, 1956. Meridian Books.

Cassirer, Ernst. *Language and Myth,* trans. Susanne K. Langer. New York: Harper and Brothers, 1946.

Cassirer, Ernst. *The Philosophy of Symbolic Forms,* ed. Charles W. Hendel, trans. Ralph Manheim. 3 vols. New Haven: Yale University Press, 1953-1957.

Cullen, Patrick. *Spenser, Marvell, and Renaissance Pastoral.* Cambridge, Mass.: Harvard University Press, 1970.

Edel, Leon. "The Biographer and Psycho-Analysis." In *Biography as an Art,* ed. James L. Clifford. New York: Oxford University Press, 1962. A Galaxy Book.

Edel, Leon. "The Madness of Art," *American Journal of Psychiatry,* 132 (October 1975), 1005-1012.

Ehrenzweig, Anton. *The Psychoanalysis of Artistic Vision and Hearing.* London: Routledge and Kegan Paul, 1953.

Flügel, J.C. *The Psycho-Analytic Study of the Family.* London: The Hogarth Press, 1921.

Forster, E.M. *Aspects of the Novel.* New York: Harcourt, Brace and Company, 1927.

Frazer, James G. *The Golden Bough: A Study in Magic and Religion.* 1 vol. abr. edn. New York: Macmillan Company, 1927.

Freud, Anna. *Psychoanalysis for Teachers and Parents,* trans. Barbara Low. Boston: Beacon Press, 1935.

Fry, Roger. *The Artist and Psycho-Analysis.* London: The Hogarth Press, 1924.

Goldenveizer, A.B. *Talks with Tolstoi,* trans. S.S. Koteliansky and Virginia Woolf. London: The Hogarth Press, 1923.

Greenacre, Phyllis. *Trauma, Growth, and Personality.* New York: International Universities Press, 1969.

Harding, M. Esther. *The Way of All Women.* New York: G.P. Putnam's Sons, 1970.

Historia Regum Britanniae of Geoffrey of Monmouth, with Contributions to the Study of Its Place in Early British History, The, trans. Acton Griscom. London, New York, and Toronto: Longmans, Green and Company, 1929.

Horney, Karen. *Neurosis and Human Growth: The Struggle Toward Self-Realization.* W.W. Norton and Company, 1950.

Husserl, Edmund. *The Phenomenology of Internal Time-Consciousness,* ed. Martin Heidegger, trans. James S. Churchill. Bloomington: Indiana University Press, 1964.

James, Henry. *The Art of Fiction and Other Essays,* ed. Morris Roberts. New York: Oxford University Press, 1948.

James, Henry. *The Art of the Novel: Critical Prefaces,* ed. R.P. Blackmur. New York: Charles Scribner's Sons, 1934.

Jones, Ernest. *On the Nightmare.* London: The Hogarth Press, 1949.

Jung, C.G. *Symbols of Transformation: An Analysis of the Prelude to a Case of Schizophrenia,* trans. R.F.C. Hull. *The Collected Works of C.G. Jung.* Vol. 5, Bollingen Series XX. 2nd edn. Princeton: Princeton University Press, 1967.

Kasanin, J.S., ed. *Language and Thought in Schizophrenia.* New York: W.W. Norton and Company, 1964.

Koestler, Arthur. *The Act of Creation.* New York: Macmillan Company, 1964.

Laffal, Julius. *Pathological and Normal Language.* New York: Atherton Press, 1965.

Langer, Susanne K. *Feeling and Form: A Theory of Art.* New York: Charles Scribner's Sons, 1953.

Langer, Susanne K. *Philosophy in a New Key: A Study in the Symbolism of Reason, Rite, and Art.* 3rd edn. Cambridge, Mass.: Harvard University Press, 1957.

Lesser, Simon. *Fiction and the Unconscious.* Boston: Beacon Press, 1957.

Lever, Katherine. *The Novel and the Reader.* London: Methuen and Company, 1961.

Lodge, David. *Language of Fiction: Essays in Criticism and Verbal Analysis of the English Novel.* London: Routledge and Kegan Paul; New York: Columbia University Press, 1966.

Lubbock, Percy. *The Craft of Fiction.* New York: Charles Scribner's Sons, 1921.

Mendilow, A.A. *Time and the Novel.* London: Peter Nevill, 1952.

Olney, James. *Metaphors of Self: The Meaning of Autobiography.* Princeton: Princton University Press, 1972.

Piaget, Jean. *The Language and Thought of the Child,* trans. Marjorie Gabain. Cleveland and New York: World Publishing Company, 1955. Meridian Books.

Rader, Melvin. *A Modern Book of Aesthetics.* New York: Holt, Rinehart and Winston, 1952.

Richards, I.A. *The Philosphy of Rhetoric.* New York: Oxford University Press, 1936.

Rock, Irwin. *The Nature of Perceptual Adaptation.* New York and London: Basic Books, 1966.

Rommetveit, Ragnar. *Words, Meanings, and Messages.* New York and London: Academic Press, 1968.

Rosenblatt, Louise M. *Literature as Exploration.* 3rd edn. New York: Noble and Noble, 1976.

Rosenblatt, Louise M. "Towards a Transactional Theory of Reading," *Journal of Reading Behavior,* 1 (Winter 1969), 31-47.

Scholes, Robert and Robert Kellogg. *The Nature of Narrative.* New York: Oxford University Press, 1966.

Shneidman, Edwin S. *Deaths of Man.* Baltimore: Penguin Books Inc., 1974.

Stengel, Erwin. *Suicide and Attempted Suicide.* Middlesex, England: Penguin Books Ltd., 1964.

Stephen, Julia Prinsep Jackson. *Notes from Sick Rooms.* London: Smith, Elder and Company, 1883.

Stephen, Leslie. *Hours in a Library.* 4 vols. New York: G.P. Putnam's Sons, 1904.

Storr, Anthony. *Human Aggression.* New York: Atheneum, 1968.

Storr, Anthony. *The Integrity of Personality.* Baltimore: Penguin Books Inc., 1960.

Von Franz, Marie-Louise. *Problems of the Feminine in Fairytales.* New York: Spring Publications, 1972.

Weston, Jessie L. *From Ritual to Romance.* Garden City, New York:

Doubleday and Company, 1957. Anchor Books.

Whitehead, Alfred North. *Symbolism: Its Meaning and Effect.* New York: Macmillan Company, 1927.

Whorf, Benjamin Lee. *Language, Thought, and Reality: Selected Writings,* ed. John B. Carroll. Cambridge, Mass.: M.I.T. Press, 1956.

Wickes, Frances G. *The Inner World of Childhood: A Study in Analytical Psychology.* New York and London: D. Appleton and Company, 1927.

Index

Abinger Harvest (E.M. Forster), 60n, 81n

Alardyce, Richard (*Night and Day*), 40

Allan, Miss (*The Voyage Out*), 19

Ambrose, Helen (*The Voyage Out*), 13-22, 26, 29, 30-33, 35-38

Ambrose, Ridley (*The Voyage Out*), 13, 18, 26

Anna Karenina (Tolstoi), 117

Annan, Noel Gilroy, 126n

Antigone, 205, 208, 220, 220n, 221, 226, 227

Antigone, The (Sophocles), 206, 207, 220, 227

Aristotle, the waiter (*Jacob's Room*), 79

"Art of Biography, The" (*Death of the Moth and Other Essays*), 9

As You Like It (Shakespeare), 59n

Ashley, Tony (*The Years*), 206

Aspects of the Novel (E.M. Forster), 13, 13n, 145n

Auden, W.H., 175n

Austen, Jane, 11, 137, 207n

Balaclava, battle of, 130, 139

Baldanza, Frank, 88n

Bankes, William (*To the Lighthouse*), 125, 126, 134-136, 139, 140, 148, 151

Barfoot, Captain (*Jacob's Room*), 65, 68, 69, 83, 207

Barfoot, Ellen (*Jacob's Room*), 83

Barrett, Michele, 191n

Battista, Anna, 126n

Beethoven, Ludwig von, 185n

Bell, Quentin, 185n, 188n, 189n, 191n, 200, 201, 202n, 224, 228n, 231n, 232, 233n

Benson, Stella, 232

Bernard (*The Waves*), 161, 162, 164, 165, 167, 168, 170-174, 175n, 177, 179-182, 186-188, 189n

Between the Acts, xii, 200, 230n, 237, 238, 240

Bexborough, Lady (*Mrs. Dalloway*), 88

Birrell, Francis, 232

Blackstone, Bernard, 33n

Bloomsbury, 189n

Bonamy, Dick (*Jacob's Room*), 4, 64n, 77-79, 82-84

Bradshaw, Sir William (*Mrs. Dalloway*), 109, 110, 112, 114

Briscoe, Lily (*To the Lighthouse*), 124, 125, 134, 135, 138-142, 144, 146-155, 157

British Museum, 64n, 79

Brown, Nicholas (*The Years*), 211, 212, 218, 222

Browne, Sir Thomas, 48

Brute (Milton's *Comus*), 31, 36

Burgess, Mrs. (*Mrs. Dalloway*), 101

Byron, George Gordon, Lord, 61, 84, 168, 219n, 239

Campion, Thomas, 205, 217, 218, 223

Camus, Albert, 187n

Caravan, The (*The Years*), 192n

Captain's Death Bed and Other Essays, The, 7, 225n

Carmichael, Augustus (*To the Lighthouse*), 120-126, 137, 141

Carrington, Dora, 232

Carroll, Lewis, 200n

Carter, George (*The Pargiters*), 202

"Castaway, The" (Cowper), 144

Catullus, 205, 217, 218, 221

Chambers, R.L., 63n

"Charge of the Light Brigade, The" (Tennyson), 129

Chrétien de Troyes, 182

Clodia, 218

Cole, Reverend William ("The Rev. William Cole," *The Death of the Moth and Other Essays*), 8, 9

Collins, Pastor (*Pride and Prejudice*, Austen), 137

Common Reader: First Series, The,

6n, 87n, 110n, 200, 210n

Common Reader: Second Series, The,
6n, 192n

Compson, Jason (*The Sound and the
Fury,* Faulkner), 137

Comus (Milton), 27, 31, 36-37

Cornhill Magazine, The, 231

Cowper, William, 38, 144

Craddock, Miss Lucy (*The Years*),
206, 234n

"Craftsmanship" (*The Death of the
Moth and Other Essays*), 7

Crawford, John W., 86n

Creon, 220, 221, 227

Crosby (*The Years*), 196, 197

Cymbeline (Shakespeare), 113, 226n

Dalloway, Clarissa (*Mrs. Dalloway*),
10, 85-98, 99n, 100-104, 109,
112-117

Dalloway, Clarissa (*The Voyage Out*),
15, 26

Dalloway, Elizabeth (*Mrs. Dalloway*),
91

Dalloway, Richard (*Mrs. Dalloway*),
88, 91, 97, 98, 113, 114n, 117

Dalloway, Richard (*The Voyage Out*),
27, 32, 200

Dante (Durante Alighieri), 111n, 211,
219, 226n, 227, 228, 229, 230, 230n,
234

Datchet, Mary (*Night and Day*), 41,
47-50, 57

Daughters and Sons (*The Years*), 192n

Dawn (*The Years*), 192n

*Death of the Moth and Other Essays,
The,* 7n, 8n, 9n, 10n, 87n

Death of a Nobody, The (Romains),
207n

Defoe, Daniel, 6, 11, 87

"Defoe" (*The Common Reader: First
Series*), 6, 11, 210n

Delattre, Floris, 3

Denham, Ralph (*Night and Day*), 40,
41, 45-61

Diary of a Nobody, The (Grossmith),
207, 207n, 210

Dickens, Charles, 6, 137

Dickinson, G. Lowes, 232

Dickinson, Violet, 233

Dictionary of National Biography,
228, 231

Divine Comedy, The (Dante), 229

Dobrée, Bonomy, 226n

Dodge, William (*Between the Acts*),
240

Donne, John, 74

Doyle, Minta (*To the Lighthouse*),
127, 128, 134, 140, 143

"Dreadnought Hoax," 202n

Drew, Elizabeth, 145

Dryden, John, 165

Duckworth, George, 200, 201, 229,
231

Duckworth, Stella, 231

Durrant, Clara (*Jacob's Room*), 70-72,
75, 77-78

Durrant, Mrs. (*Jacob's Room*), 76, 77

Durrant, Timmy (*Jacob's Room*), 64n,
75-77, 82

Dynamics of Creation, The (Storr),
9-10, 156n

"Early Novels of Virginia Woolf,
The" (E.M. Forster), 60

Earnshaw, Catherine (*Wuthering
Heights*), 38

Edel, Leon, 10, 224n

Eliot, Miss Julia (*Jacob's Room*), 77

Elmer, Fanny (*Jacob's Room*), 64n,
67n, 73, 75, 79

English Dialect Dictionary (Joseph
Wright, ed.), 190, 192

Epaminondas (Nepos), 234

"Epipsychidion" (Shelley), 164n

Eros, 114

essyllt (Estrildis), 31

Estrildis, 31, 32n

Euphrosyne (*The Voyage Out*), 13, 199

Evans (*Mrs. Dalloway*), 106-110, 111n,
112, 114, 202

Evans v. Carter (*The Years*), 202

*Existentialism from Dostoevsky to
Sartre,* 187n

Faerie Queen, The (Spenser), 31n, 32n

Faulkner, William, 137

Filmer, Mrs. (*Mrs. Dalloway*), 107n

"Fire Worshippers, The" (Moore),
219n

Flanders, Archer (*Jacob's Room*), 65
Flanders, Betty (*Jacob's Room*), 64-70, 72-75, 82-84, 207
Flanders, Jacob (*Jacob's Room*), 4, 10, 63-68, 70-79, 81-84, 92n
Flanders, Seabrook (*Jacob's Room*), 65, 68, 69, 83, 84
Flaubert, Gustave, 146
Florinda (*Jacob's Room*), 64n, 71, 72, 75, 79
Floyd, Mr. (*Jacob's Room*), 69, 84
Flush: A Biography, 240
Flushing, Mr. (*The Voyage Out*), 35
Forewords and Afterwords (Auden), 175n
Forster, E.M., 8, 13, 33, 60, 81, 145, 160, 174n
Frank, Joseph, 146
Freshwater: A Comedy, 240
Freud, Anna, 17
Friedman, Norman, 147
Fry, Roger, 189n, 232

Galsworthy, John, 85, 232
"Garden, The" (Marvell), 229n
Geoffrey of Monmouth, 31
Gibbs, Hugh (*The Years*), 206
Gide, André, 226n
Ginalis, Flora, 220n
Godard, Jacques (*The Death of a Nobody*), 207n
Goldenveizer, A.B., 115n
Gradgrind, Thomas (*Hard Times*, Dickens), 137
Grail legends, the, 182
Granite and Rainbow, 3n, 119n, 160n, 191n, 204n
Griscom, Acton, 31n
Grossmith, George, 207n
guendoloena, 31
Guiguet, Jean, 34
Gwendolyn, 31, 32n, 33

hafren (Sabrina), 31
Haines, Rupert (*Between the Acts*), 200, 240
Hardy, Thomas, 6
Havard-Williams, Peter and Margaret, 166n

Heathcliff (*Wuthering Heights*), 38
Heep, Uriah (*David Copperfield*, Dickens), 137
Heine, Elizabeth, 183n
"Henry James" (*The Death of the Moth and Other Essays*), 10
Here and Now (*The Years*), 192n
Herrick, Robert, 205, 217, 218, 223
Hewet, Terence (*The Voyage Out*), 13, 17-25, 28-32, 35-37
Hilbery, Katherine (*Night and Day*), 4, 10, 39-46, 48-61, 92n, 207
Hilbery, Mr. (*Night and Day*), 46, 55-58, 207
Hilbery, Mrs. (*Night and Day*), 40, 46, 55, 56, 58
Hirst, St. John (*The Voyage Out*), 16, 19-23, 28
Historia Regum Britanniae, 31, 31n
Hitler, Adolf, 240
Hogarth Press, The, xii, 115n, 237
Hollingworth, Keith, 86
Holmes, Dr. (*Mrs. Dalloway*), 109, 112
Holograph Essays (*The Pargiters*), 195n
Holtby, Winifred, 3, 34, 60
Hours of Idleness (Byron), 61
Hours, The (*Mrs. Dalloway*), 86
Hungerford, Edward A., 86n

Ibsen, Henrik, 121, 134
Idylls of the King (Tennyson), 182
In My Own Time: Memoirs of a Literary Life (Lehmann), xii
Independent, The, 85n
"Indian Serenade, The" (Shelley), 164n
Inferno (Dante), 111n, 230n
Ismene (*The Antigone*), 221

Jacob's Room, xii, 62-84, 200; holograph, 69n, 71n
James, Alice, 226n
James, Henry, 10, 224
"Jane Austen" (*The Common Reader: First Series*), 11
Jarvis, Mrs. (*Jacob's Room*), 65
Jinny (*The Waves*), 161-162, 164, 166, 168, 169, 171, 172, 175-177, 179,

184, 188
Journey Not the Arrival Matters, The
    (Leonard Woolf), 25n, 185n
Joyce, James, 146

"Kew Gardens," 80
Kilman, Doris (*Mrs. Dalloway*), 89
Koteliansky, S.S., 155n
Krutch, Joseph Wood, 85

Lady, The (Milton's *Comus*), 31, 37
Lalla Rookh (Moore), 219n
Lamb, Charles, 190
Lamb's Tales from Shakespeare, 207n
*Lamentable Tragedie of Locrine, the
    eldest sonne of Kinge Brutus, The*
    (anonymous), 32n
Langer, Susanne K., 153n
Laurette (*Jacob's Room*), 72
"Leaning Tower, The" (*The Moment
    and Other Essays*), 7-8
Leaska, Mitchell A., 13, 193n, 237, 238
Lehmann, John, xii, 192n, 237-241
Lesbia, 217, 218, 221
*Leslie Stephen, His Thought and
    Character in Relation to His Time*
    (Annan), 126n
Letter to a Young Poet (to John
    Lehmann), 192n
*Letters of Virginia Woolf, Volume
    One: 1888-1912, The*, 231n
Levin, Konstantin (*Anna Karenina*),
    117
"Life and the Novelist" (*Granite and
    Rainbow*), 204n
"Lighthouse, The" (*To the Light-
    house*), 149, 154
"Lives of the Obscure" (*The Common
    Reader: First Series*), 200
Locrine (Milton's *Comus*), 31, 36
Locrine (Swinburne), 32n
Louis (*The Waves*), 161, 162, 164, 165,
    168, 171, 172, 175, 178, 179, 184
Lubbock, Percy, 87
Lucretius, 164

MacCarthy, Desmond, 188n, 189n,
    207n
McInnis, Nurse (*The Voyage Out*), 32

Macalister's boy (*To the Lighthouse*),
    144
Madame Bovary (Flaubert), 146
Malone, Kitty (*The Years*), 202, 206,
    234n
Malory, Thomas, 182
Manresa, Mrs. (*Between the Acts*), 240
Mansfield Park (Austen), 207n
Marbot, General Marcelin, de, 92, 93,
    113
"Mark on the Wall, The," 80
Marvell, Andrew, 229n
Maupassant, Guy de, 226n
Memoirs (Baron Marbot), 92-93
Memoirs of a Novelist (Woolf), 231
Meredith, George, 168
Milton, John, 27, 31, 37
Mira (*The Years*), 202-204, 206-208,
    212n, 214, 215
Moment and Other Essays, The, 8n,
    117n, 200n
Monday or Tuesday, 201n, 202n
"Montaigne" (*The Common Reader:
    First Series*), 110n
Moore, Thomas, 219, 219n
Morte d'Arthur, Le (Malory), 182
*Moth and the Star: A Biography of
    Virginia Woolf, The* (Pippett), 83n,
    188n
Moths, The (*The Waves*), 159, 185n
Mozart, Wolfgang Amadeus, 174n
Mrs. Dalloway, 85-117, 195n, 202,
    230n; "Introduction" (Modern
    Library, 1928), 86n
Murgatroyd, Evelyn (*The Voyage
    Out*), 31n
Music (*The Years*), 192n
"Myth of Sisyphus, The" (Camus),
    187n

"Narrow Bridge of Art, The" (*Granite
    and Rainbow*), 160n
Nation, The, 85n
National Society for Women's Service,
    192
Nepos, Cornelius, 234
Neville (*The Waves*), 119, 161,
    163-165, 167, 168, 171-173, 175-178,
    180, 184, 188

"New Biography, The" (*Granite and Rainbow*), 119n, 191n
New Republic, 12
Newman, John Henry, 229
Nicolson, Nigel, 231n
Night and Day, 39-61, 62, 232
Noble, Joan Russell, 174n
Notes from Sick Rooms (Mrs. Leslie Stephen), 125n
Novel: A Modern Guide to Fifteen English Masterpieces, The (Drew), 146n
"Novels of Thomas Hardy, The" (*The Common Reader: Second Series*), 6
"Novels of Turgenev, The" (*The Captain's Death Bed and Other Essays*), 7, 225n
Novels of Virginia Woolf, The (Chambers), 63

O'Brien, Justin, 187n
O'Shea, Kitty, 215
Oedipus, 65, 134, 220
Oliver, Bartholomew (*Between the Acts*), 240
Oliver, Giles (*Between the Acts*), 240-241
Oliver, Isa (*Between the Acts*), 200, 240-241
"On Re-Reading Novels" (*The Moment and Other Essays*), 8
Ordinary People (*The Years*), 192n
Orlando: A Biography, xii, 76n
Orlando (*As You Like It*), 59n, 195n
Othello (Shakespeare), 94, 95
Otway, Cassandra (*Night and Day*), 42-45, 56, 59n

Pargeter, 191, 194, 230
Pargiter, Colonel Abel (*The Years*), 157, 197, 203-215, 219, 220, 228, 234
Pargiter, Celia (Mrs. Morris Pargiter, *The Years*) 210
Pargiter, Delia (*The Years*), 203, 205, 206, 212-216, 221-223
Pargiter, Sir Digby (*The Years*), 203, 206, 208-209
Pargiter, Edward (*The Years*), 206, 207, 217, 220, 227

Pargiter, Eleanor (*The Years*), 4, 198, 202, 205-207, 209, 210-216, 218-223, 225-228, 230, 234
Pargiter, Eugénie (Mrs. Digby Pargiter, *The Years*), 202, 204, 208, 209, 214
Pargiter, Maggie (*The Years*), 203, 206-209, 211, 212n
Pargiter, Martin (*The Years*; Bobby in *The Pargiters*), 208, 208n, 209, 216
Pargiter, Milly (*The Years*), 206n
Pargiter, Morris (*The Years*), 202, 205-207, 210, 215, 216, 219, 223, 226
Pargiter, North (*The Years*), 203, 212, 214, 217, 219, 220, 223, 230n
Pargiter, Peggy (*The Years*), 205, 210, 212, 214-218, 220n, 221, 222
Pargiter, Rose (*The Years*), 204, 206, 207n, 209, 210, 211, 213, 219
Pargiter, Rose (Mrs. Abel Pargiter, *The Years*), 198-200, 201, 206, 207n, 209n, 213, 219, 220, 222, 227
Pargiter, Sara (*The Years;* Elvira in *The Pargiters*), 203-205, 207-209, 211, 212, 218, 225-228, 230n
Pargiters, The (Holograph version of *The Years*), 190, 192, 192n, 196-202, 205, 207n, 208n, 211n, 216, 217, 222, 224, 225, 227, 229, 230
Parnell, Charles Stewart, 205, 206, 213-215, 223
Parsifal (Wagner), 182
Parzival (Wolfram von Eschenbach), 182
Peacock, Thomas, 233
Pederson, Glenn, 151n
Peer Gynt, 134
Perceval, ou le conte du Graal (Chrétien de Troyes), 182
Percival (*The Waves*), 164, 165, 167, 170-175, 178, 180, 182-184, 185n
Pericles, Prince of Tyre (Shakespeare), 226n
Phaedrus (Plato), 79.
"Phases of Fiction" (*Granite and Rainbow*), 3
Philosophy in a New Key: A Study in the Symbolism of Reason, Rite, and Art (Langer), 153n

"Pictures" (*The Moment and Other Essays*), 117n
Pilkington, Laetitia ("Lives of the Obscure"), 200
Pippett, Aileen, 83n, 188n
Plato, 79
Pope, Alexander, 165
Powys, Theodore Francis, 226n
Poyntz Hall (*Between the Acts*), 239
Price, Fanny (*Mansfield Park*), 207n
Professions for Women, 191
"Professions for Women" (*The Death of the Moth and Other Essays*), 6-7
Prose and Verse, Humorous, Satirical and Sentimental, by Thomas Moore, with suppressed passages from the Memoirs of Lord Byron, 219n
Psychoanalysis for Teachers and Parents (Anna Freud), 17
Purgatorio (Dante), 219, 226, 230

Queen Victoria's Journal of her Life in the Highlands, 207n
"Question, The" (Shelley), 166n

Ramsay, Andrew (*To the Lighthouse*), 131, 149
Ramsay, Cam (*To the Lighthouse*), 133, 143-144, 149, 154, 157
Ramsay, James (*To the Lighthouse*), 132-134, 136, 141-142, 147, 149, 154-155, 157
Ramsay, Mr. (*To the Lighthouse*), 4, 120, 122, 124, 126n, 129-136, 139, 140, 144, 148-152, 154, 155, 157
Ramsay, Mrs. (*To the Lighthouse*), 4, 119-128, 131-133, 135-137, 139-141, 143, 144, 147-155
Ramsay, Prue (*To the Lighthouse*), 131, 138, 149
Rayley, Paul (*To the Lighthouse*), 127-128, 140
Rebecca (*Jacob's Room*), 67
Recollections of Virginia Woolf (Noble), 174n
Renny (*The Years*), 203, 211, 212n
Restoration Comedy, 240
Rhoda (*The Waves*), 4, 161, 163-164, 166, 169, 171-176, 178-179, 185,

186, 186n, 187, 188
Richards, Captain (*The Voyage Out*), 199
Rodney, William (*Night and Day*), 41-45, 47, 48, 56, 57
Roger Fry: A Biography, 239
Romains, Jules, 207n
Roman Psychologique de Virginia Woolf, Le (Delattre), 3
Rorschach test, 62
Room of One's Own, A, 191, 192, 194, 195, 196
Rosiland (*As You Like It*), 59n
Rourke, Constance M., 12
Rover (*The Years*), 196, 197
Ruff's Tour of Northumberland, 211

Sabrina (Milton's *Comus*), 31, 32, 32n, 33, 36, 37
Sackville-West, Vita (Mrs. Harold Nicolson), 232, 233
Saint-Simon, 226n
"Sanity of True Genius" (Lamb), 190
Sappho, 217, 218
Schaefer, Josephine O'Brien, 34n
Scheherazade, 145
Sedgius aquatici, 199
Seton, Sally (*Mrs. Dalloway*), 94, 95, 113-117
Seventh Circle (Dante's *Inferno*), 111n, 230n
Severn, the, 32, 36
Sewanee Review, 146n
Shakespeare, William, 59n, 79, 95, 109, 165, 226n
Shelley, Percy Bysshe, 164n, 166n, 167n, 186
Simmons, Daisy (*Mrs. Dalloway*), 96, 98, 101-103
Simmons, Major (*Mrs. Dalloway*), 101
Sisyphus, 187
Smith, Lucrezia (Rezia), (*Mrs. Dalloway*), 105-113, 117
Smith, Septimus Warren (*Mrs. Dalloway*), 4, 10, 86, 89, 95, 104-117, 202, 230n
Smyth, Dame Ethyl, 201
"Society, A" (*Monday or Tuesday*), 201n, 202n

Sons and Daughters (*The Years*), 192n
Sophocles, 221, 227
"Speech" Holograph ("21st Jan. 1931"), 192n
Spenser, Edmund, 31-32n
Steele, the painter (*Jacob's Room*), 66
Steinberg, Erwin, 104
Stephen, Adeline Virginia (Mrs. Leonard Woolf), 157, 186, 200, 228, 231, 233
Stephen, Adrian, 228, 231
Stephen, Julia Prinsep Jackson (Mrs. Leslie Stephen), 125n
Stephen, Thoby, 230, 231
Stephen, Sir Leslie, 126n, 156, 157, 197, 198, 200, 224, 225, 228, 229, 234
Storr, Anthony, 9-10, 156n
Strachey, Lytton, 232
Strachey, Philippa (Pippa), 192
Susan (*The Waves*), 161, 162, 164, 166, 168, 171-173, 175-178, 180, 185, 188
Swinburne, Algernon Charles, 32n, 240
Swithin, Mrs. Lucy (*Between the Acts*), 230n
Szladits, Lola L. 175n, 237n

Talks with Tolstoi (Goldenveizer), 115n
Taming of the Shrew, The (Shakespeare), 226n
Tansley, Charles (*To the Lighthouse*), 120, 121, 125, 126, 136-139, 142, 148
Tennyson, Alfred, Lord, 129, 182
Theocritus, 217
Three-Fold Nature of Reality in the Novels of Virginia Woolf (Schaefer), 34n
Three Guineas, 192, 194, 196, 197n, 230
"Time Passes" (*To the Lighthouse*), 118, 148, 154
To the Lighthouse, 118-158, 195n, 239
"To Sappho" (Herrick), 217
Tolstoi, Leo, 115, 117, 168
Topaz (*Jacob's Room*), 70
Trautmann, Joanne, 231n
Troilus and Cressida (Shakespeare), 226n
Trollope, Anthony, 6

Trotter, Miss (*Night and Day*), 47
Turgenev, Ivan Sergeyevich, 7, 225n

Ulysses (Joyce), 146
"Unwritten Novel, An," 80

Venning, Arthur (*The Voyage Out*), 20, 21
Vigny, Alfred Victor de, 226n
Vinrace, Rachel (*The Voyage Out*), 4, 10, 13-19, 21-38, 55, 83, 92n, 167, 199, 201n, 207
Vinrace, Willoughby (*The Voyage Out*), 14, 15, 207
Virgil, 164
Virginia Woolf (Holtby), 3, 34, 60
Virginia Woolf: A Biography (Bell), 185n, 189n, 200n, 201, 224, 228n, 231n, 232, 233n
Virginia Woolf: A Commentary (Blackstone), 33n
Virginia Woolf and Her Works (Guiguet), 34
Virginia Woolf's Lighthouse: A Study in Critical Method (Leaska), xi
Voyage Out, The, xiii, 12-38, 39, 62, 83, 199, 208n, 231; Earlier Typescript, 36-37; holograph, 37; Later Typescript, 37
Vronsky (*Anna Karenina*), 117

Wagner, Richard, 182
Walsh, Peter (*Mrs. Dalloway*), 88, 90-92, 95-100, 102-104, 107, 113, 117
Warrington, Susan (*The Voyage Out*), 20, 21
Waterlow, Sydney, 207n
Waverley Novels, The (Scott), 127, 253
Waves, The, 119, 159-189, 192n
Wells, H.G., 226n
Whatney, Sir William, (Dubbin), (*The Years*), 210, 211, 215, 216, 219, 220
Whitbread, Hugh (*Mrs. Dalloway*), 98
Williams, Mrs. Sandra Wentworth (*Jacob's Room*), 64n, 73-75
"Window, The" (*To the Lighthouse*), 118, 148, 151, 153
Wolfram von Eschenbach, 182
Women's Service League, The, 6
Woolf, Leonard, xi, 25, 185n, 192n,

193, 195n, 233, 237, 238
Wordsworth, William, 7
Workers' Educational Association, 7
Wright, Elizabeth Mary, 190
Wright, Joseph, 190, 190n, 192
Writer's Diary, A, 33, 80, 86, 118, 156,
   159, 160, 175n, 183, 185n, 186, 187,
   188n, 189n, 190-192, 195-196,
   223-226, 229, 230n, 232, 234
Wuthering Heights (Brontë), 38

Years, The, xi, xiii, 157, 190-235,
   237-239